THE SEER'S DAUGHTER

PRAISE FOR ATHENA DANIELS

The Seer's Daughter

"…the perfect culmination of paranormal mystery with steamy and sensual romance and just enough suspense and intrigue to guarantee a chilling, goose bump-invoking, story line… *The Seer's Daughter* would be a brilliant option for adaption to screen—there's a television series/movie in here for absolute certain."
—*AusRom Today*

"…as chilling as it is sexy… This is much more than a romance. The paranormal aspects along with the secondary characters really make the story. The descriptions, language, emotions, dialogue… are all cleverly written to keep you engaged and the pages turning, while the suspense will make sure you read this story with all the lights on."
—5-star Top Pick, *The Romance Reviews*

"If you are looking for a book to give you goose bumps and keep you watching over your shoulder, then I can recommend this one! … I got dragged away from this book late in the evening by my husband, as I had an exceedingly early start the next day. This didn't stop me from thinking about the book and what I had read for well over an hour after the lights went out, as well as dreaming about it!"
—Archaeolibrarian, 5 stars, Amazon review

"I love paranormal books, especially when there's romance thrown in, and this… will send a chill up your spine, raise the hairs on your neck, and make you tremble with emotions. What a rush! One of my most favorite reads this year! … It's almost like Stephen King meets Christina Dodd… I loved it; can't wait for book two!"—5 stars, Amazon review

"…a perfect blend of paranormal fiction and romantic suspense that had me completely captivated to the very last page… flawlessly delivered."
—Faridah, 5 stars, *Readers Favorite*

"One of the best ghost/demon stories I have read in a while! It had romance, witches, demons, AND ghosts! Absolutely loved it!"—5 stars, Amazon review

The Alchemist's Son

"…go the hell out and buy both of these books now because they are freaking FANTASTIC. I am not exaggerating when I say this is some of the

best romantic suspense I have ever read, paranormal or otherwise; I literally couldn't put down *The Alchemist's Son* until I got to the final, thrilling climax."
—5 stars, Amazon review

"I could not put the book down. It has so many twists and turns that keep you turning one page after another."—5 stars, Amazon review

"This book is as good as the first, with twists and turns! You get the good ol' creepy feels! You may be wanting to look behind you, or not go in your attic or basement anytime soon! I wish this author could write as fast as I can read; I would never put her books down!"—5 stars, Amazon review

"Kept me on the edge of my seat. Several scenes I was holding my breath reading what was happening next...."—5 stars, Amazon review

"If you love paranormal, romance, suspense and spine-tingling books, you'll love this!"—5 stars, Amazon review

"This book had my hair standing on end and gave me chills from start to finish. Once again I could not put it down, and loved how, no matter how hard I tried, I just couldn't guess ahead what was going to happen next."
—5 stars, Amazon review

Desperate

"What can I say other than I absolutely loved this book from the start, and the prologue really set the pace for a fast-paced plot with lots of suspense and the right touch of romance. The plot was strong and progressed well and I loved the flirty banter between Eric and Ivy, which added to the growing relationship between the pair and provided a few good sex scenes illustrating their intense chemistry... the author has done an amazing job of penning this novel and I can't wait to read more of their work in the future."
—*The Romance Studio* (TRS), 4 stars

"Suspense and steamy romance line the pages of this fast-paced thriller, with action and drama from start to finish.... If Athena Daniels keeps it up with writing like this, I have no doubts that she will establish her place amongst the most well-known authors of erotic literature.... If you're a fan of romantic thrillers, I would definitely recommend giving this one a read."
—Official Review, *Online Book Club*, 4 out of 4 stars

ALSO BY ATHENA DANIELS

Novels

The Scream Behind Her Smile

Desperate

Beyond the Grave Series

The Seer's Daughter (Book One)

The Alchemist's Son (Book Two)

Girl Unseen (Book Three)

When Darkness Follows (Book Four)

THE SEER'S DAUGHTER

BEYOND THE GRAVE
BOOK 1

ATHENA DANIELS

Sunset Coast Publishing

For Nanna

Miss you every day.

ACKNOWLEDGMENTS

There aren't words to describe my gratitude for my fabulous editor, Dana Delamar. Thanks for going the extra mile, pushing me to go the extra mile, and never tiring of my endless questions. I discovered a diamond the day I found you.

Heartfelt thanks to Kristine Cayne for casting an expert eye over the book, and for her technical expertise.

My love and appreciation, as always, to my sister Leah, who keeps me moving forward on those days when it's easier to lie down. Thanks for being my "everyday."

To my wonderful boys, for understanding the cave and how the time I spend in it makes me a better person. Thank you for cheering me on.

And much love to the awesome readers who have praised my books and encouraged me to write more. I deeply appreciate you all.

CHAPTER ONE

Sage Matthews hugged herself as the raging storm flung rain against the windows. Parting the fragile lace curtains of the small upstairs sitting room, she looked out at the familiar landscape. A flash of lightning illuminated the backyard with a crack. Sage jumped and pressed a hand to her throat. Taking a breath to calm her racing pulse, she stared at the strips of white paint peeling off the picket fence. The lawn needed a cut, and weeds ran amok in the once-immaculate garden.

She imagined she could still see her grandmother on her hands and knees, mindless of how the red soil stained her clothes, pruning the roses and geraniums, selecting only the most perfect stems to freshen the various vases dotting the house.

Sage looked to the tall crystal vase at the center of a round wooden coffee table. Her chest squeezed. The vase was empty. The way it would remain from now on.

Empty like Nan's bed, where her grandmother had comforted Sage after many a childhood nightmare. Or snuggled with Sage on cold mornings, sipping tea and sharing stories.

Empty.

Like Nan's favorite chair, where she'd no longer sit to sip her tea and crochet blankets for the local charity.

Empty. Just like Sage's heart.

A powerful rush of anger surged through Sage, overshadowing even the hollowness in her chest. Trembling, she gripped the windowsill for support while blinking away hot, stinging tears.

Nan had been taken before her time. Stolen from this earth by a hand neither her own, nor her maker's. At eighty-two years, Nan had radiated health and vitality. She had been an inspiration to everyone around her, Sage included.

She should still be here.

A robbery gone wrong, the police had said. What else could it be? It was inconceivable that anyone would want to hurt someone as kind and as universally loved as Celeste Matthews. But Sage didn't buy the explanation. If it had been a robbery, why had nothing been stolen?

Lightning cracked again, and the lights flickered out, plunging the house into darkness. An eruption of thunder rattled the windows in their wooden panes.

Hailstones pelted the house, the ice pinging on the tin roof and lashing at the glass like ball bearings flung by hundreds of ferocious, unseen hands. The storm was aggressive in its violence, as though Mother Nature herself were venting her rage at the injustice of what had happened to Nan.

A scraping noise behind her caught Sage's attention, and she scanned the shadows, searching for its source. Nothing looked out of place. In fact, the room appeared not to have changed at all since Sage's childhood. A crocheted blanket was still draped across the faded floral couch facing the television. The side tables, a separated nest of three, were covered in crossword books, and the pine wall-unit was crammed full of dusty memories.

Scrape. Scrape. Scraaape.

The tiny hairs on the back of Sage's neck stood on end, and she whipped her head around, peering through the gloom at the table in the far corner.

Was something on that table *moving*?

Couldn't be. The loss of electricity had spooked her; that was all. And even if something was moving, a house over one hundred years old with a rusting tin roof was bound to be draughty during a storm this violent.

The noise came again, a faint scratching.

It's just a draught, it's just a draught. And yet her eyes and ears kept telling her *something* was moving in the corner, and her heart continued to slam in her chest. She wrapped her arms around her middle.

She had that strange prickly sense that she was being… watched? She rubbed up and down her arms to warm skin that had turned to gooseflesh.

Lightning flashed again, allowing her to see that the table in the corner held a small object on a wooden board. She blinked a few times and swallowed. She could have sworn that object had been in a different place a moment ago. The lightning must be playing tricks on her vision.

Sage took a step closer. *Where did Nan keep the flashlight?* Cryton was a small town, and the power lines were still strung overhead on ancient wooden telegraph poles. Who knew how long the repairs would take?

Scrape. Scrape. Scraaape.

Another flash of lightning. The object had moved to the other side of the board! Sage's heart lodged in her throat, and she shivered; the room had gone cold as ice. It must be a draught after all, and the draught had pushed the object. That had to be it.

She moved closer, shuffling her feet so she didn't trip. On the shelf next to the table, she thought she could just make out a candle. *Yes!* She felt the space around the glass holder and found the box of matches she was hoping Nan would have kept next to it. She struck a match, then lowered the lit candle toward the table. Sage peered through the flickering golden glow at an ancient-looking board with old-world lettering.

A Ouija board.

Suddenly its glass pointer slid across the board, scraping loudly as if pressed by a heavy hand. Sage gasped and her heart hammered in her chest. *Run!*

Her mind was screaming, but her feet refused to move. Paralyzed, powerless, she leaned over the board, her eyes glued to the frenzied dance of the cursor.

Sage blinked, disbelieving. *It has to be a trick of the candlelight.* But the cursor continued on, flying across the surface of the board, stopping abruptly at the edge before careening off in a different direction. She stood, transfixed. This was no random event. The movements formed a pattern.

The closer she lowered the candle to the board, the brighter the flame grew until it was a small fire lapping at the wick, moving and behaving in a manner that was not natural. Riveted by the performance before her, Sage barely noticed the anomaly. She memorized the letters as the pointer raced between them.

Scrape, scrape, scrape, scraaaape.

The glass cursor moved faster, the scraping becoming louder, as though someone or *something*, was determined to get a message through.

LUCKYBEWARELUCKYMARK

Lucky beware?

Lucky Beware Lucky Mark?

Something fell off the shelf next to her, but she barely flinched.

"I don't understand—" Her voice was drowned out by a rumble of thunder that shook the walls and rattled the windows.

The glass pointer began to vibrate and make a buzzing sound, flying so fast it was little more than a blur.

"Beware lucky Mark? Is that it? What does that mean?" Sage whispered into the room that although empty, felt anything but.

With the next blinding flash of lightning, the pointer shattered into hundreds of splinters, as if it had somehow been hit by the bolt of electricity. The spray of glass fragments speared into the soft skin of her upper thigh, and she hissed from the sting.

With the destruction of the glass pointer, the Ouija board became eerily still.

As did the storm.

The screaming wind and the pounding hail abruptly stopped. The lights flickered a few times before staying on, filling the room with over-bright electrically produced light.

The air no longer felt cold, but that didn't take away the chill Sage still felt on the inside, didn't even begin to thaw the ice in her veins.

She was going to be here alone for at least another week, maybe more, while she packed up her grandmother's things, dealt with the police, and attended the funeral. Just what was going on here? Was her grief making her see things?

Maybe. Except how did she explain the shattered glass? She set about carefully removing the larger pieces from her leg. Her hand shook, and the blood made it hard to see the smaller ones. As she headed toward her bedroom for her tweezers, she paused at the door and glanced back at the board.

Her grandmother had believed in the power of Ouija boards, and though Sage had never dared use one herself, she'd developed a healthy respect for them. But never fear.

Until now.

CHAPTER TWO

Detective Sergeant Ethan Blade, Special Operations Unit, South Australian Police Force, stepped out from the air-conditioning of his black four-wheel drive Land Rover Discovery and stretched legs that had grown stiff during the three hours' drive from Adelaide. The Discovery's tinted windows had cut the sun's glare quite effectively, and he squinted and blinked, waiting for his eyes to adjust. Inhaling deeply, he filled his lungs with fresh country air, still damp from a recent electrical storm.

A cool gust of wind sprang up, swirling and not blending with the humidity, like oil and water. Ethan grabbed his briefcase and black leather jacket before pressing the button on the remote, locking the doors. The old gum tree he had parked under had roots so established, they had buckled the bitumen underneath the Discovery's wheels. A loud crack split the air, and with reflexes honed from many years on the force, he lunged to the side, just before a large branch slammed onto the exact spot he'd been standing the second before.

Welcome to Cryton, he thought wryly. Shading his eyes from the blinding sun, he looked up at the tangle of branches. The weight of wood towering above him was considerable, and the reason gum trees had earned their reputation as widow-makers.

The scratches the branch had made to the department's vehicle were too deep to be buffed out; it would need to be resprayed. Which meant a ton of paperwork when he filed the damage report. He cursed the offending branch and dragged it off the pavement so that no one would trip over it. The cold breeze that had sprung up moments before had died away, leaving only the steady warmth of the midday sun.

Carrying his jacket folded over one arm, Ethan headed down the main street, taking in his surroundings. Visibly, there was nothing unusual about the small country town situated about one-hundred-ten kilometers northeast of Adelaide. A tall, wooden welcome sign with Cryton's name and population. The post office. A heritage stone building with jutting verandas sitting with a line-up of shops that fanned out on either side of the highway, and farms and crops beyond that. The standard services: bakery, butcher, newsagency, supermarket, petrol station, hardware store, and two pubs, one at either end.

Cryton was a town like any other, and yet something raised the tiny hairs on the back of his neck. Finding no obvious cause for this alarm, he shrugged it off and continued walking. It didn't take long before he was standing in front of the shop he was looking for. The sign above the wooden door read "Beyond the Grave."

Ethan almost groaned aloud. He wasn't sure there was anything at all beyond the grave. It was a nonsense name for what he fully expected to be a nonsense shop. But such was the nature of his job, and it was not his business to judge, only to bring justice to those who had been wronged, which in this case was an eighty-two-year-old woman who had been murdered.

The splintered wooden steps protested under his black boots, creaking as he made his way to the entrance. On either side of a rickety door with rusty hinges were windows, framed in timber and flaking white paint. The sign hanging in the window to his right was turned to CLOSED.

Ethan knocked on the door, wincing as it shuddered in its weathered wooden frame. So much for security. It wouldn't take more than leaning on it to gain entry.

With a loud meow, a cat, charcoal black except for a white tip on its tail, looked up at him from its position on a wooden chair to his right. It was curled up on a crocheted blanket, and there was a bowl of clean water and dry biscuits off to one side.

He heard light footsteps, then the door was opened by a young woman. His mind blanked as he was momentarily struck. Years on the force being exposed to a vast array of human nature meant that not much surprised him anymore. Or so he'd thought.

The woman standing before him didn't belong in a shop like this. He'd expected to be greeted by someone wearing colorful flowing clothes, with armfuls of jangling jewelry and beaded or multi-colored hair, not by the vision that stood before him.

He could swear he knew her from somewhere, but he'd definitely never seen her before. He'd have remembered. Tall and slender, with long blonde hair pulled into a sleek ponytail, she was dressed in a business skirt, filmy silk shirt, and bare feet. She had a swipe of dust on one cheek and a cobweb stuck to the top of her head, its long tail waving in the air behind her.

She barely acknowledged him, instead turning toward the cat. "There you are, Liquorice," she purred, and the cat jumped up into her arms. She bent her head, and the cat nuzzled into her neck. Ethan was just about to introduce himself when the cat hissed, hackled up, and bolted down the street.

The woman frowned, but didn't appear surprised. She stuck a finger into her mouth, sucking on it briefly, before running the moist tip over the scratches on her arm.

She sighed and stared thoughtfully after the cat.

"Here." Ethan handed her a clean white handkerchief. The scratches looked angry and deep.

"Thank you," she murmured absently. With a delicate pink tongue, she moistened the cloth and dabbed at her arm.

"Do you have antiseptic?" he asked. "Cat scratches have a tendency to get infected."

She pierced him with the most startling green eyes he had ever seen. He almost took a step backward.

"I'm sorry. Who did you say you were?" Her voice was pleasant and warm.

"I didn't." He cleared his throat. "Detective Sergeant Ethan Blade, Homicide Squad." He introduced himself using his cover. The special operations unit he actually headed up didn't officially exist. Taipan was an elite group of detectives who specialized in undercover operations and investigations that the government considered sensitive in nature. Highly skilled, he was an expert in knife fighting, firearms, and heavy weaponry, as well as unarmed combat.

So why the hell had he been assigned this case? The collective skill set of Taipan was usually reserved for more than what on the surface appeared to be a standard serial-killer investigation.

He flashed his badge. "I'm looking for Sage Matthews."

"I'm Sage," she said, taking his outstretched hand with a slender, manicured one. Her hand was warm, soft, and delicate in his much larger one, and he had to force himself to release it.

"Problem with the cat?" he asked.

"Yes." Her brow wrinkled as she chewed her bottom lip. "It's so strange. Liquorice is… was Nan's cat. Mine before that. Once, we were inseparable, and now he won't come inside. Says he's scared." She flicked a nervous glance his way, then added, "What I meant to say is that he seems scared."

A cloud passed in front of the sun, casting them in shadow. She shivered as a cool breeze blew a strand of hair free from her ponytail and into her eyes.

"Can we talk inside?" he asked.

She caught the wayward strand and fidgeted with it, wrapping and unwrapping it around her fingers. Something about her demeanor pricked at his instincts. The detective ones this time. *Finally.* "Oh, sure."

The moment he stepped inside, the hairs on the back of his neck stood on end, and his pulse raced for no apparent reason. His hand twitched, instinctively moving toward his gun, but just like earlier, there was no obvious cause for alarm.

Through a haze of dust, he surveyed the shop. The ceiling-height shelves were cluttered with an astonishing array of crystals, some in the shapes of dragons and other mystical creatures. A massive collection of dusty artifacts.

He cracked his neck, took a deep breath and sneezed.

"Sorry. This place needs a good clean." Something in her tone sounded almost… *guilty?*

He followed her to the rear of the shop, where two chairs sat opposite a wooden table. Next to a dead potted plant sat an old-fashioned manual cash register that would look at home in a museum.

"You've probably already worked out why I'm here," he said. "I'm investigating the murder of Celeste Matthews. Can I ask you a few questions?"

Pain flashed across her face and she ran her fingers across the dried-up leaves of the dead plant. "I've already told the police what little I know." He hated this part of his job, bringing more pain to the victims, but it was necessary.

"The Homicide Squad has been called in to assist with solving this case. The local police have done a great job so far, but I need to go over certain facts of the case myself, which unfortunately means there may be an initial duplication of questions. I'll do everything I can to be as brief as possible."

"Homicide Squad," Sage repeated flatly, as though she were having difficulty accepting his presence. "Bob told me it was a burglary gone wrong." Bob was Robert Brady, a sergeant on the local Cryton police force.

"It will only take a moment of your time," he said, when she didn't say anything more.

"Of course, please have a seat." She indicated for him to take the chair on the opposite side of her desk.

As he did, Ethan's eyes swept the room, noting a stack of empty packing boxes and several rolls of tape. Was it falling on her shoulders to clean this up? She'd need a bobcat and a skip-bin.

Sage's skirt hitched up as she sat, revealing long toned legs. Standing out on the satiny skin of her upper thigh was a fresh and unusual pattern of tiny cuts.

"What happened to your leg?" he asked conversationally, as he turned to a fresh page in his notebook. He clicked out the nib of his pen, and when she still hadn't answered his question, glanced up to find that she had tugged her skirt back into place, deliberately covering the marks.

She picked at a piece of invisible lint on her leg and didn't meet his eye. "Nothing." She gave the answer most assured to raise the interest of any detective worth his salary.

He took his time retrieving the case notes from his briefcase, watching her squirm slightly in her seat out the corner of his eye. She gripped the pendant that hung from a gold chain around her neck, and began rolling it through her fingers. This case was getting more intriguing by the minute.

"Look, it was just a little gardening injury, all right?" she said impatiently, offering a further explanation without being asked. Curious. "Can we get to your questions now? I have a lot to do, and I'm anxious to make a start."

A pretty pink stain spread across her cheeks as she fidgeted with a plastic sharpener from the desk. Some people could lie well. Sage Matthews was not one of them. He wanted to press her further, but he'd hold off. Currently, she wasn't a suspect, and whatever had happened to her leg was none of his business, even though she stirred something within him that made him think it was.

Why was she lying? He'd see what unfolded during the interview.

Notebook and file ready, he fixed his gaze on the attractive young woman before him. The sticky strand of web was no longer blowing around, but had settled along her ponytail.

"You've got a cobweb on your hair."

"What?" Her forehead wrinkled in confusion.

"A web, from a spider. On your hair." Ethan pointed to the spot and her flush deepened. She didn't strike him as the blushing type; what was it about his presence that made her so uncomfortable?

She released the pendant and ran her hands along the blonde strands until she found it. She flicked the web into a nearby wastebasket, and he observed the lack of rings on her fingers. But only because he was a detective.

Sage withdrew a small compact mirror from her handbag, and began moving it around, trying to see the back of her head.

He suppressed a smile, but couldn't hide the amusement in his tone. "There are no spiders in your hair."

Closing the compact with a snap, she narrowed her eyes at him. Amused, he resisted the temptation to bait her further and dragged his attention back to where it should be, to the file in his hand. There was something very distracting about Sage Matthews, and he found that disconcerting.

Tapping the page with his pen, he cleared his throat. "Your grandmother's body was discovered in this shop by a… Mrs. Ada Slatterley."

"Yes." The flush that had looked so pretty a moment ago drained away.

"According to her statement, she discovered your grandmother lying just inside the front entrance on Monday, at approximately 9:10 a.m."

Sage's spine was ramrod straight, and she gripped the desk edge so tightly that her knuckles were white. Her lips had compressed into a thin line. Had someone been cruel enough to tell her the details of what her grandmother had suffered?

The next section of his file, the autopsy report, he did not read aloud.

"The victim was stabbed five times, four of the puncture wounds strategically placed in the shape of a cross, with the fatal blow slightly off-center to pierce directly through the heart. The eyeballs were removed from their sockets, and replaced with circular pieces of black cloth. A symbol, possibly a branding of some sort, was left in the palm of her right hand…"

The file photograph of the symbol showed the mark as being three curled lines coming out of a central circle. He was still waiting to hear back from the forensic pathologist regarding whether the branding had been done pre- or post-mortem.

The lack of blood at the scene indicated that the murder had taken place at a separate location, and then the killer had returned the victim to her home. Traces of adhesive remained around the mouth of the victim, but the duct tape itself had been removed, suggesting that the killer had needed to silence the victim for a period of time, but had later felt the need to remove it at some stage.

The killer's signature matched two other murders in the surrounding area in the last three months. With this third murder, there was no longer any doubt: they were dealing with a serial killer.

His boss, Chief Superintendent Ian Hallow, had assigned him this case under strict instructions to "step in, find the killer yesterday, and keep the media the hell away at all costs." Why was this case so damned important? He wouldn't have been sent here if there wasn't something deeper going on.

"It's critical that you keep the details about this investigation to yourself," Ethan said to Sage. "Don't discuss the case with anyone and do not speak to any reporters. If they contact you, refer them to me. I'll give you the numbers before I leave."

"The reporters had already covered the news before I arrived. No one has been back since."

Good. All he had to do was keep it that way.

The next series of questions confirmed the facts of the case. She had nothing further to add.

When Ethan asked if she had any idea who would want to hurt her grandmother, he studied Sage's response carefully. Although she appeared to tell the truth, something more was going on. It was only a matter of time before he put his finger on it.

Twice during the interview, Sage had whipped her head around as if someone were behind her. Shadows darkened the tender skin beneath her eyes, enhancing their color to vivid emerald. She obviously wasn't sleeping much. The way she sat in the chair, spine stiffened, hands clasped together in her lap, she looked brittle. And yet she seemed far from fragile. Perhaps life had seen to that. Her eyes were wary and knowing, making Sage seem older than her chronological years.

Ethan shrugged, still unable to dispel the unusual tension plaguing him. His gut knotted with the inexplicable sense that Sage was somehow in imminent danger, as though someone were at this very moment standing over her with a knife poised and ready to strike. He fought an irrational urge to grab her and get out of the shop.

Again, there was nothing to substantiate his reaction. His hands curled into fists, and he had to forcefully push the thoughts away. Concentrating on his notes, he kept the remainder of his questions brief and hoped these strange... *impulses* would go away.

Sage rubbed at her temples, trying to alleviate the pounding throb setting in behind her eyes. When was he going to be finished? She'd answered the detective's questions with what little she knew.

"Do you know anyone who'd want to hurt your grandmother?"

Detective Blade was busy taking notes, his eyes on his pad, and Sage was glad for the momentary respite. Something in his piercing gaze unsettled her. His eyes were too all-knowing, his presence too formidable. Her words were obviously but a small fraction of what he was assessing when she responded to his questions, and the scrutiny made her feel guilty even though she hadn't done anything wrong. She could just imagine how someone with something to hide would feel being interviewed by him. To see him in full detective mode would be terrifying.

He started to wind the interview up more quickly, writing down her answer while simultaneously asking the next question.

"No. Everyone loved her," Sage stated with conviction. The detective briefly glanced up from his notebook, his expression sympathetic.

"I mean, obviously someone didn't," she amended, feeling her cheeks heat. "What I mean is that it must have been someone she didn't know, because anyone who knew her, loved her. And I'm not just saying how wonderful she was because she was my grandmother. It's true."

"Mm-hmm." The detective scribbled more notes in his book. The scratching of his pen seemed louder with each word he wrote. And he had an aggravating way of tapping his pen on the page between questions.

She dug around in her handbag for her strong headache tablets and swallowed a couple with a chug from her water bottle. He eyed the packet but didn't comment. Lucky for him, as she was in no mood for judgment. She was going to do whatever she needed to, whatever it took, to get through this period in her life.

His mouth was moving, so she knew he was asking more questions, and through the painful throbbing in her head, she did her best to concentrate.

"Had she received any threats that you know of? Or had she reported seeing or hearing anything strange in the time leading up to this?"

"No and no. Nothing she told me about, anyway." Sage swallowed a stab of guilt over not visiting or calling Nan more often during the last few months. Their weekly phone conversations now seemed grossly insufficient. But how was she to have known that their conversation on Saturday, just three days ago, would be their last? Because really, it shouldn't have been. Sage had spoken to her on Saturday morning, and Nan had been murdered some time that same night. Sage still couldn't reconcile how someone so fit and full of life could be dead.

Will he ever finish these damn questions? All she wanted to do was go to bed so that the tablets could do their job and sweep her into blissful oblivion. Away from this new reality she wasn't yet ready to face.

Her fingers found the crystal angel pendant around her neck, a gift from her mother. The *last* gift she ever received from her. Oddly enough, Sage could still summon the precious memory; it had remained unusually vivid, even after all these years. It had been a cool autumn evening, the aroma of barbequed sausages still heavy in the air. The guests invited to her third birthday party had recently left, leaving only Sage and her mother on the cushioned outdoor swing. The last gift of the day was not wrapped; it was removed from her mother's own neck.

"Never take this off," her mother had said.

"I won't, Mummy." Sage eagerly tugged the pendant from her hands.

"I mean it Sage, whatever you do, leave this on. Always." Her mother's tone and expression had turned uncharacteristically serious, especially for such a festive occasion, and Sage hadn't understood why.

Her mother motioned for the pendant back, and then she fastened the gold chain around Sage's neck and placed a lingering kiss on her forehead.

"Why are you crying, Mummy?"

Her mother's answering smile was tender, gentle. "Because the love I have for you is far too great for my body to hold." She ran a trembling hand across Sage's cheek.

Her mother had died in a car accident a few days later.

The pain, the acute sense of loss she'd carried for twenty years, mixed afresh with the loss of Nan.

The detective interrupted her thoughts with another question. "Was there anyone else your grandmother was close to? Aside from Ada Slatterley? I'm looking for people who might be able to give me more information about anything unusual that might have happened recently."

Sage cleared her mind and did her best to focus on the detective's questions. Nan had several friends. "She was close to the women in her card group, but her best friends were Ada, Joyce Booth, Patricia Sands, and Mona Daly. She always used to say they were as mad as hatters and thick as thieves. Her words, not mine."

Using Nan's battered old address book, Sage gave him their contact details and then carefully placed the book next to the old-style plug-in phone. The little red light on the attached answering machine blinked furiously. She'd played the messages on the first day only. The kind words of sympathy were too painful for her to listen to just yet. Maybe later, when the pain lessened. Although it was hard to believe the promise everyone gave her that it eventually would.

"You mentioned that you don't live here. Can I assume that you used to?" the detective asked, with a sweeping glance around the room.

"Yes, five years ago. I live in the city now. I've taken a month's leave to pack up Nan's belongings and close the shop."

Mercifully, the detective appeared to be finished, and she leaned back in her chair while he pocketed his notebook and put his files in his black leather satchel.

"Thank you for your time, Sage," he said, standing. Clicking the ink back into his pen, he slid it into his top pocket and took out a card. "I'll be in contact again if I need further information or to keep you informed as to the progress of the case."

Sage tossed the card onto the desk without a second glance. The tablets had started to kick in, and the idea of wallowing in bed by herself no longer held any appeal. She had no idea how to deal with the debilitating weight of grief, other than to keep herself busy.

She looked at the boxes and the enormity of the task in front of her. *Best get to it now, or I'll be here for weeks.*

When she rose, the detective's eyes zeroed in on the marks on her legs, and she tugged her skirt down as far as it would go.

"I need to get back to packing up the shop," Sage said, hoping to dissuade him from any further questions about her injury.

"Well, you definitely have your work cut out for you. I hope you've got help. There's a lot of junk in here." He shrugged into his leather jacket.

Anger sliced through her. "My nan, Detective Blade, collected these artifacts from all over the world. She travelled extensively through Eastern countries, spent a couple years in Peru, and six months in a monastery where she studied with a Tibetan monk. She only came back to this shitty little town to take care of me when my mother died."

Looking around, Sage waved her arms in a full circle. "This *junk*, as you so eloquently referred to it, are objects that represent a life more full and fascinating than you or I could ever dream of living."

The detective turned to face her. "I didn't mean anything offensive. It was merely an observation—"

On some level, she knew he wasn't deliberately trying to offend her, but the anger and frustration, her pain, the… *unjustness* of her nan's death had not yet had an outlet, and now that she'd started, she couldn't stem the torrent.

As a child and a teenager, she'd never defended her nan against taunts from the kids at school. Didn't have the confidence to take them on when they egged Nan's shop late at night and kept them awake throwing stones onto the tin roof or called her a witch while they were shopping for groceries. Her nan never reacted to the tormenting, telling Sage that children didn't know any better, to rise above it and let it go. So she'd swallowed it down, pretended it didn't matter.

But it *did* matter. She was an adult now, and no one would criticize her nan in any way whatsoever.

"We all grow old, Detective, and Nan was a proud woman. There was a time when this shop sparkled. Even when she grew too frail to keep it as clean and dusted as she would have liked, she still spent her time helping people in the local area."

Sage had been shocked at the state of the shop when she'd returned. She hadn't known that her nan was having trouble keeping up with everyday tasks. Sage eyed the potted Draceana on the desk curiously, and ran a finger along a brittle, curled brown leaf that was once a broad, glossy dark green. The happy plant, as Nan called it, was hardy, and could survive long periods without water. This plant had suffered. In an abrupt and unusual way. What had happened in here?

"Sage, I really didn't mean…" Detective Blade spread his arms helplessly, but she plowed on.

"Oh, I know what you meant. You think she was just an old lady. Possibly someone who'd lost her mind or gone senile. You're looking around the shop, judging her and thinking she wasn't all there. Possibly weird or someone not worthy of your valuable time—"

"That is not true." His voice sliced through the air between them.

Sage crossed her arms. "It's not?"

"No. I'm a detective sergeant with fifteen years on the job. I assure you, I take every case seriously." He softened his tone. "Unfortunately, I never had the pleasure of meeting your grandmother, but if she raised a woman with such strength of character, the ability to love so deeply, to fight and protect the ones she loves so strongly, I think she must've been a special person."

His eyes were sympathetic and genuine. He wasn't patronizing her. Sage's anger drained away like water leaving a basin after the plug had been pulled. "Yes, she was special."

She'd been looking for a fight, an outlet. But he'd refused to be drawn in, and he'd managed to defuse her anger with just a few words. It seemed as though the detective was in fact, quite good at his job. She only hoped he was as good at catching murderers.

The emotion she'd been unable to release churned uneasily inside her, and she began to feel light-headed. "I'm sorry, Detective, but you need to leave now." Too much was bottled up inside her. Grief over the loss of her grandmother, anger at the unjustness of her death. Sage was tired, she hadn't eaten, and the strange encounter with the Ouija board had taken away any hope she'd had of sleeping last night. Taking those tablets on an empty stomach may not have been the best idea. The room spun, and she wobbled on her feet.

In a heartbeat, he was at her side, supporting her under the arm as he assisted her into the chair.

"Don't. I'm fine." She tried to shrug off his hand, but he held her firmly until she was seated. He filled a glass with water from her bottle and lifted it to her lips. She felt the warmth from his hands as he wrapped her fingers around the glass. Tears stung her eyes but didn't fall.

"Take another sip." Concern wrinkled his forehead as his eyes searched her face. The cool liquid moistened her mouth and slid down her dry throat.

"Thank you," she murmured, and he set the glass back on the table.

"Are you all right?" He spoke softly, the deep timbre of his voice vibrating through her.

Was she? No. Not yet. But she would be.

She hadn't broken down at all when she heard the news of her nan's death, nor at any time since then. Sure, she had shed some tears, but mostly she had switched into survival mode. She had called her boss and arranged time off work, closed up her apartment, made the necessary arrangements at the funeral home. Now she had to decide what to do with Nan's shop and belongings.

Damn it, Nan. I wasn't prepared for you to leave me so soon.

The detective's hand on her arm soothed her, and she stopped shaking, his strength and energy enveloping her in a cocoon of calm.

"I don't think we're ever really ready for someone to leave, no matter how prepared we try to be," he said gently.

Had she spoken out loud? She inhaled the strangely soothing scent of his worn leather jacket. It reminded her of comfort. Of strength and familiarity. She wanted him to pull her close so that she could wear it too.

"Sage?" He waited until she met his eyes. "Do you have anyone I can call? Someone who can come over and be with you?"

She stood up. "Thank you, but no. I'll be fine. I didn't mean to speak to you so rudely, and I apologize. This is just a stressful time for me, but I'm okay now. Really."

He straightened, his over-six-foot frame dwarfing the space. Judging by his frown, he was far from convinced.

"Really," she repeated, mustering as much bravado as she could summon. "I have so much to do. I need to get back to it."

"The packing can wait. I can arrange someone for you to talk to. A grief counselor. If there's no one local, I can set up a video link. There is—"

"Thank you, no. There really is no need. I'm fine. But you're right. I'll leave the packing for now, and instead head upstairs for a shower. Seems my headache hasn't gone after all. Please don't trouble yourself over me any further."

"You're no trouble, Sage." His voice was deeper, and her pulse skipped a beat. Their eyes met and held. "Detective..." she began.

"Ethan. Call me Ethan."

"Ethan." She liked the way it sounded on her tongue. "Thank you for being so nice, and understanding, but I assure you I'll be fine. I'd prefer you to be worrying less about me and more about finding whoever it was who did this."

Ethan picked up the card she'd carelessly tossed onto her desk and pressed it to her palm. His warm hand cradled hers as he closed her fingers around it. "My mobile number is on the back. Call if you need anything. Anything at all. No matter how small."

Sage turned the card over, afraid to look back at him. Too ashamed to let him see that his kindness was making her tear up again.

He hesitated, and for a single moment, she wondered what it would be like if he held her. Not for long. Just enough for her to once again feel that sense of calm, of peace. To allow his strength to fill her, to temporarily ease the hollow sense of loss that was eating away at her insides. He had a power that she sorely needed right now. His hand moved forward, as though he wanted to touch her. When he didn't, she was simultaneously disappointed and relieved.

"Lock the door behind me and make sure all the windows are secure." His voice was deeper and a little rough. "Until we catch who did this, you need to be extra vigilant."

He was almost at the door when she called out to him. "Ethan?" Hand on the door frame, he turned and faced her.

"Don't let him get away with this."

Ethan's eyes hardened and his jaw set into a grim line of determination. "I don't intend to."

CHAPTER THREE

A knot had formed in the center of her back, and Sage lifted her arms overhead in a yoga pose to try to loosen it. No luck. The antique clock chimed twelve times, signaling midnight, and darkness pressed in at the windows of her grandmother's tiny shop. Through the flickering fluorescent light, Sage surveyed the neat stack of boxes against the wall. An entire life packed up, into dull cardboard.

There were so many questions she would never know the answers to. Like where Nan had found the lovely marble sculpture in the corner, or what the story was behind the heavy book with the aged pages and the dragon on the cover.

Why didn't I ask when I had the chance?

The funeral was scheduled for Saturday, the day after tomorrow. It was to be held at the local cemetery, a short walk from the main street. *The dead center of town*, Nan used to joke.

Pouring herself a fortifying glass of wine, Sage wondered if the murderer would attend the funeral. She'd watched enough crime shows to know killers sometimes did. Would Detective Blade be there, looking over the mourners, searching their faces for guilt? Her thoughts had drifted to Ethan many times while she'd worked. He'd been a nice distraction from the constant barrage of memories that arose from going through Nan's things, but maybe it was more than that.

She'd spent far too long alone with her thoughts over the last day and a half, and maybe she was reading into things, but she couldn't shake the feeling that there was more to Nan's death than she was being told. First, there was the unexplained delay over releasing her body for the funeral, followed by the sudden appearance of a city detective and his not-so-casual warning not to talk to the media. Something about the way he'd said it made her think there was more behind his request than standard procedure.

Why did her thoughts keep wandering back to him? Sure, he was handsome beyond measure, with serious eyes and hard lines on his face, even when his expression was relaxed. Not to mention he looked tall, dark, and dangerous in his black leather jacket, gun belt and cuffs, like the detective Sage had a crush on in a popular television series.

His hair was long, a little unruly, and definitely not conforming to her expectation of a "cop cut." When his hair had fallen over one eye, he'd held his pen like a cigarette as he pushed it back into place. A smoker, either past or present.

Something moved out of the corner of her eye. The tiny hairs on the back of Sage's neck stood on end, and she became strangely uncomfortable.

She was being watched.

Her chest constricted, making it difficult to breathe, and her hand shook as she placed her glass in the sink. Bracing herself, she turned around, fully expecting to discover someone behind her. The murderer?

But the room was empty. And silent as death. Heart pounding, she rubbed the gooseflesh on her arms. The temperature seemed to have dropped several degrees in a single second. On the surface, everything appeared normal. A quick check confirmed that the windows were securely locked, the blinds drawn.

Sage let out a nervous laugh. *That's it.* She was calling it a night. Too much time alone was beginning to frazzle her nerves.

Opening a small tin of cat food, Sage headed out the front door, tapping the spoon on the side of the can like she always used to. Standing on the porch, she called for Liquorice, but he didn't come. She frowned. Was he getting his meals elsewhere all of a sudden?

It had broken her heart to leave behind her little companion when she'd taken the job in Adelaide, but cats weren't allowed in Sage's city apartment. She intended to ask Ada to look after Liquorice. With three cats of her own, Ada would probably welcome the idea, and Liquorice was already familiar with Ada and frequently visited her home, only two streets away.

Sadly, Liquorice might have already decided that Ada's house was a much more fun place for a cat to live. He'd brought much comfort to Sage during her childhood, at times her only friend other than Nan. He'd provided a solace she could desperately use now.

In case he eventually showed up, Sage filled his bowls with fresh food and water and called out once more. She was just about to head back in, when Liquorice sauntered around the side of the house, meowing as he approached.

"There you are." Sage bent down to pet him while he lapped at his dinner. "Are you going to stay with me tonight?" she asked, stroking his silky black fur. "I could really use the company. It's hard for me to take care of you if you won't come inside the house."

Liquorice stopped eating to briefly look into her eyes. In that moment she knew he wouldn't be coming in. He was scared.

But more disturbing, he was scared for *her*.

"Did you see what happened to Nan?" Sage asked, letting her hand still. Was Liquorice afraid because he'd seen the killer?

Could she see what he'd seen? Sometimes when she petted him, she felt that she was picking up images from him. Maybe they were things she imagined, but maybe not. It was worth a try.

"May I?" she asked, seeking his permission. He butted his head against her hand. She'd take that as a yes.

She reached out to him, then hesitated. *Can I really do this? Am I more like Nan than I realize?*

Liquorice butted her again with his head and mewed. As if he wanted her to do it.

Sage closed her eyes and reached outward with her mind.

An image formed, something strange, horrifying. She yanked her hand back as if it had been burnt. What she'd seen, what she'd felt, made no sense. The picture that had formed in her mind was not human. Not of this world. It was something dark, shadowy, malicious. A menacing essence that had existed in the past event but was also somehow able to see her now. What did it mean? Did it have something to do with the feeling she'd had of being watched?

Liquorice jumped into her arms as though seeking her comfort, and she cradled him, running her hands over his fur as she cooed reassurances.

It occurred to her then that Liquorice was giving *her* comfort. *He's worried about me.* The only reason he was coming back to the house was to make sure *she* was okay. But whatever had happened in the house had traumatized him enough to never want to go back in.

"Don't you worry about me," she said. "I'm sorry you saw all that evil. If I could take away those images, I would. Sadly, I can't, little buddy."

She shook her head, and a lump filled her throat. If only she could talk to Nan about what was happening, about seeing the images in Liquorice's mind. Apparently she did share some of Nan's gift after all. Had she suppressed her natural talents all these years for fear of being a freak?

Liquorice pawed at her hand until she looked at him. He cocked his head and gave one of his little mews that sounded like a question.

"I'm okay, you silly cat." She laughed. "I talk to you just like a human, don't I?"

He head-butted her again and she set him down by his bowl. "Go on, finish your food. I know you're hungry."

At her urging, Liquorice went back to his dinner. Sage sighed and glanced at the potted geraniums, pleased to see they were looking much healthier. She'd done little more than pluck off their dead leaves and water them, maybe giving them a good vibe or two, but Nan had always said Sage had a green thumb. Just like Nan did.

But, like the potted Dracaena on the inside desk that was now also thriving, she couldn't imagine Nan allowing her plants to suffer through neglect. Sage cast her mind back to their weekly conversations. Nan had talked about the arrival of spring on September first and her gardening plans for the upcoming season. No, something else had happened to the plants. But what?

When he finished eating, Liquorice gracefully leapt onto the chair and circled a couple times before settling into a ball. "Be safe out here." Sage kissed the top of his head, tucked the blanket around him, and smiled at his loud contented purr. That was all she could do for now, and she hoped it was enough.

Picking up his empty bowl, she took it inside and washed it at the sink. Her eyes went to the little carved wooden witch on a broomstick that had hung in the kitchen window for as long as she could remember. It had straw hair, a black cape, and a knowing smile on its face. Nan had been called a "witch" again and again behind her back, and Sage had always thought that carving had been a joke of hers, one she'd shared with Ada and her other friends. They all had one just like it in their kitchens.

But if Sage could see images in Liquorice's mind, and Nan could talk to spirits… could that little witch mean something more?

Sage stared at it, then shook her head. She really needed some sleep, didn't she?

Securing the locks on the shop door, Sage contemplated the narrow staircase that led to the living space above. The stairs hadn't looked quite so steep earlier in the day. She conjured a vision of herself soaking in the clawfoot tub, and it gave her just enough incentive to start the climb.

After the warm, bubble-filled water had soothed her aching muscles, Sage slipped into her most comfortable sleep shorts and matching cotton top. She had chosen to sleep in her nan's bedroom instead of the one she used to use. It made her feel closer to Nan. And also in some way, she felt safer in there. Being all alone in this old house, especially after the incident with the Ouija board, gave her the creeps.

A cloud of leftover steam floated into the hallway as Sage opened the bathroom door. Even though her body was still heated from the water, she shivered. The sliver of light underneath the door to Nan's room was only about six steps away. But still, she hesitated.

Even when she'd been a kid, the hallway had always seemed to be strangely cold. With its old wooden floors and faded rug running down the center, it should have been comforting, familiar. But for some reason, for as long as she could remember, Sage had always felt like she was being followed whenever she'd walked along it.

But not tonight. Tonight she didn't look back. Instead, she bolted the six steps in two, and slammed the bedroom door behind her. Blood racing in her ears, she laughed nervously. Good God, had she been reduced to a child who was scared of a monster hiding underneath her bed? She'd lived alone in the city for years, and never once had she felt unsafe by herself.

Something about the house was different now, as if its very essence had changed. Was she reacting to the fact that Nan had been murdered downstairs? Or was it just that strange incident with the Ouija board?

As unnerving as she'd always found the house to be, she'd never felt unsafe while her nan was there. Nan was a force of nature, with a kind smile, a positive attitude, and an alternative way of looking at life.

Sage remembered jumping into her nan's bed when she'd woken one night, frightened by the sound of an ambulance's sirens screaming past the shop. *Don't think of it like someone has been hurt,* Nan had told her, her hands running soothingly over Sage's hair, *think about it like help is on its way.* To this day, those words ran through her mind whenever she had to pull over to the side of the road to allow an ambulance or police car to pass.

Her chest tightened and a lump caught in her throat as she climbed into bed and looked at the side that shouldn't be empty. "I miss you so much, Nan," she said, choking on the words.

Somewhere below, a door slammed, and she bolted upright. Frowning, she tried to picture which door it could be, positive she had closed and locked all the doors and windows. She had checked twice. It could mean only one thing. She had an intruder.

Was it the murderer returning? Did he intend to kill her like he had Nan?

Swallowing an almost debilitating surge of fear, Sage crept barefooted across the room and grabbed the Stanley knife she'd been using earlier for packing. The handle felt cool, but reassuring, in her grip.

Her heart galloping wildly, Sage paused in the doorway to listen for any further sounds. Silence. Darting frequent glances over her shoulder, she made her way downstairs.

"Hello?" Sage called out, and as she reached the bottom of the stairs, she flipped the light switch. The aging fluorescent globe flickered a few times before staying on.

Blade in hand, she searched the room to find everything just the way she'd left it. Doors locked, safety chain still secured on the inside. No sign of a break-in.

Parting the blinds, she peered out the window. Perhaps someone was trying to scare her. Memories of the tricks played on her and Nan throughout her school years rushed back, but the kids she'd gone to school with were all adults now. Her age. Surely they'd outgrown childish pranks. She turned on the outside light. There was no one there.

The breath she'd been holding released in a gust, and she rolled her shoulders. Had she really heard a door slam? Looking around, she could see no indication that it had actually happened. She replayed the sound over and over, until it became white noise.

What she needed was a good night's sleep. Heading back to the bedroom, she detoured on impulse past the desk and picked up Ethan's card. She turned it over to where he'd written his mobile number. It differed from the one neatly printed on the front. His private line?

The card in hand, she headed up the stairs and contemplated calling him. But what would she say? *Sorry to call, but I think I'm losing my mind.* Yeah, right. Even the promise of his whisky-smooth voice soothing her frayed nerves was not enough to justify having him think her foolish or irrational.

Safely back in the bedroom, Sage was just about to turn off the overhead light when something in the corner of the room caught her eye.

A crystal. Large and beautiful, it felt cool in her hands. It was heavy, but fit easily in her palms and was covered in long prismatic points.

Placing the stone on the bed, Sage noticed another next to a stack of books in the opposite corner. That crystal was slightly larger, more angular and green. Setting it alongside the one on the bed, Sage looked to the corner opposite and found another. A stunning piece, with a brilliant cluster of clear points that she recognized as quartz. The one in the last corner was dark, almost black, with colored veins running through the stone.

Sage studied the crystals on the bed, a little awed by their beauty. Of all the products in Nan's shop, it was the crystals that Sage was drawn to. Why had Nan hidden such magnificent pieces rather than display them? Straight away, Sage decided she would take them to Adelaide. They'd look perfect in her hallway cabinet.

Carefully, Sage wrapped the crystals in tissue paper and placed them in an empty shoebox beside her suitcase. After securing the lid, she looked longingly at the bed. She really needed some sleep. Turning out the main light, she slipped between the sheets and started to shiver, as though someone had opened the window and let in a blizzard.

Pulling the blankets around her, she eyed the room, teeth chattering, unable to shake off a dark sense of foreboding. Something was suddenly different, and she struggled to breathe, as if a heavy weight were pressing on her chest. Her nan had always said that crystals affected the energy of a space. Had moving them disturbed something?

Sage shook her head. *What am I thinking?* Using the energies of crystals had always been Nan's thing, not hers. Crystals were pretty rocks. Nothing more. And the strange feeling in the room was only a manifestation of her fear of being alone, knowing that a murderer was on the loose. A murderer who had been in this very house. *Breathe. Relax. Get some sleep.* She sucked in another breath, but it stuck in her throat. The air felt… thicker.

A door slammed downstairs, and she grabbed her phone and Ethan's card. Sage pressed the numbers on the keypad, but the screen remained dark, even when she pounded the phone with her palm. How could the battery be flat? It had been sitting on the charger all afternoon. Her mind raced. *Calm down, Sage. Think.*

Did she really believe there was an intruder? She could go and check again, but would she find anything this time either? Doubtful.

So what then, did all this mean? If something else was going on here, what was it? Could it be something that fitted more with her Nan's beliefs? Something… supernatural?

She should have been able to scoff at the thought. But the Ouija board, the doors inexplicably slamming, her continued feelings of unease, and the shadows she'd seen out the corner of her eye—they all added up to something. Even right down to Liquorice not wanting to come inside. Could she be dealing with something out of the ordinary?

Good God, Sage. Get a grip. She rubbed at her eyes, yawned, and settled back into bed.

Another noise. A scraping. Like shoes scuffing along the floor.

Her blood turned to ice. *No, it couldn't be.* Was that the Ouija board's cursor moving in the next room? But how? The glass had shattered; she had the marks on her leg to prove it.

Scrape. Scrape. Scraaape. The sound was unmistakable. It had been burned into the cells of her memory forever.

What. The. Hell.

Her mind had to be playing tricks on her. Simple as that. But she knew how to fix that problem. She refused to be cowed by an inanimate object.

Jumping out of bed, she marched into the sitting room next door and flicked the switch, flooding the room with light. The Ouija board was there in the corner, just where it had been on Tuesday night. Not moving. No haunted cursor hovering over the surface.

Snatching it up, she threw the horrid board into the fireplace, smiling when the old, brittle wood splintered against the bricks. *Goodbye and good riddance.* Striking a match, she tossed it on the board, then watched as flames chewed across the wood and eventually reduced the cursed thing to ashes.

Wiping her hands together in satisfaction, she headed back to the bedroom and climbed into bed. She'd just begun to close her eyes when she heard something disturbing. Something that made her stomach roil, and her heart come to a shuddering halt in her chest.

The noise started soft, but as it grew louder, it seemed to be seeping from the very walls of the house.

A deep, low vibration that sounded something like… *laughter.*

Forget sleep.

She was packing her bags and heading back to the city.

CHAPTER FOUR

He sat cross-legged in the dirt and tossed another stick into the fire, the only light he had to see by, but that light didn't penetrate far into the inky darkness surrounding him. An inch-long ant crawled across his bare foot, and he studied it for a moment before flicking it into the fire, fascinated by the crackle of the flames as they consumed the tiny creature.

He drew deeply on a roll-your-own cigarette. Looking up at the half-moon in the starless sky, he blew out a stream of smoke, then released a long guttural growl. The primal cry rose up through his body and carried out across the unnaturally still night.

A smile slowly spread across his grimy, unshaven face.

His master was pleased.

With him.

The face of a pretty woman with blonde hair and green eyes danced in the flames of the fire.

"She's here." The voice of his master spoke directly into his mind.

He didn't need to ask if she was to be the next one.

He already knew that she was.

The image of her face tempted and tormented him as he patiently awaited further instructions.

CHAPTER FIVE

Ethan didn't need to go back and talk to Sage Matthews. He'd fought it ever since their brief meeting on Wednesday, but damn it, he couldn't get her out of his mind. And he also couldn't shake the feeling that she was in imminent danger, even if he couldn't logically describe why. Finding himself driving down the main street for the fifth time, he finally gave in and pulled over across the road from Beyond the Grave.

His black 4WD was his mobile office and far more luxurious than his hotel room. The department paid for his accommodations while he was working a case, and as was usually the way in towns like this, the rooms were basic at best.

Cryton was not a popular tourist destination, so there was no need to cater to holiday makers. His room was sparsely furnished, dark, and smelled like its previous occupants (for the last twenty years). He could have stayed somewhere further out, perhaps at a nice resort, but when he was on a case, staying close to where the crimes had occurred was more important than creature comforts. He'd been working undercover for years and had slept in places that made his current hotel room seem like Buckingham Palace.

He opened his laptop and entered the password, then set it on the console between the seats and pulled up what information he had on the victims.

The first was a fifteen-year-old boy, Toby James. Toby had run away after being grounded by his parents for skipping school. He'd climbed out of his bedroom window and boarded a Greyhound bus headed north. During the interview, the driver of the bus had told Ethan that the boy was visibly upset and had no money to get home. The driver allowed him on board for free, believing he was helping the boy get back to his parents, not run away from them. Toby had hopped off the bus on the outskirts of Cryton at approximately three p.m.,

Thursday, July 2, and had not been seen again until his body was found two days later in bushland three kilometers off the main road.

According to his parents, running away had been out of character for the straight-A student. Ethan shook his head. Where had the boy been going, and who would have wanted to hurt him? Toby's social-media profile hadn't provided further clues.

The second victim, Roy Peterson, was a thirty-seven-year-old male hitchhiker. Recently divorced, with two young children, a boy aged seven and a girl aged nine. According to his ex-wife, Roy had left four months prior with what he could carry, to travel around Australia. He'd been on some kind of back to nature, soul-searching expedition. His ex had sounded the alarm over his welfare when Roy failed twice in a row to make his regular phone calls to his kids. His body had been found on the morning of Saturday, August 1, near an abandoned mine two kilometers from the main street of Cryton. Not far from where Ethan was. *Not far from where Sage is right now.* His gut tightened.

And finally, there was Celeste Matthews, Sage's grandmother. Discovered dead in her shop by her elderly friend Ada Slatterley, on Monday, September 7.

All three victims had been stabbed five times, in the same manner as Celeste Matthews, and their eyes had been removed and covered with black circles of cloth. And all of them had been branded in the same fashion. What message was the killer trying to send?

The brand itself was quite peculiar. A symbol, a circle with three curled lines extending from it. Ethan had played around with the markings. If you placed three sixes directly on top of each other and then rotated each six by a third, you had the symbol. Six, six, six. The Devil's number. Not exactly original, but considering the mark was on the right hand of three dead bodies, it was chilling just the same.

Why had the killer chosen those three victims? The victims had not been sexually assaulted, nor were they all the same sex or age, nor did they share the same occupation. Since the killer had left no DNA at the crime scenes, figuring out the connection between the victims would provide a valuable lead.

Hoping that this time the killer had made a mistake, Ethan had ordered the body of Celeste Matthews to be analyzed once more. This was their last chance, as she would be in the ground tomorrow.

He looked across the road at the shop and wondered how Sage was holding up. At one point during his questioning of her on Wednesday, she'd looked close to breaking down. It was obvious how close she'd been to her grandmother, but who did she have now? His report detailed that Sage's mother, Celeste's only child, had been killed in a car accident in 1992, when Sage was three. The whereabouts of the man listed as her father on her birth certificate were unknown.

Like her mother, Sage had no siblings, and no extended family other than her grandmother. Ethan's chest tightened. He remembered all too clearly what it was like to grieve alone.

But why was he spending so much time wondering about Sage in the first place? Witnessing debilitating grief from the loved ones of victims was a difficult, but familiar, part of his job. He felt for them, the ones left behind. He sympathized with their loss; his own was still all too fresh. But he'd always been able to push everything aside and focus on his job.

But Sage... somehow during that one brief meeting, she'd touched something deep inside him. Stirred his instincts, both the detective ones as well as the purely masculine ones. He felt like a miniature gas hotplate had been lit and set to a low burn inside his stomach.

A feeling niggled at his subconscious, and he didn't know how to neatly compartmentalize it. It must be the reason he'd driven past the shop more often today than he should have. Had the initial attraction he'd felt toward her affected his judgment? Affected his ability to think clearly and objectively? Or was his interest in her spurred by his instinct that there was more to her than she was letting on? Could she be hiding something related to the case?

He thought of that strange prickling sensation he'd felt when he'd entered the shop and the way she'd lied when he'd asked what had happened to her leg. Something was going on. But what?

Engine still idling, he sat in his Land Rover across the street from where he assumed she was right now, and shook his head. If he had any sense whatsoever, he would keep his distance from Sage Matthews. The most valuable thing he could do for her was catch her grandmother's killer and ensure her safety.

Forcefully, he dragged his mind back to the piece of paper in his hand. A list of the residents of Cryton, their names all crossed off, except for three. The next list contained people who lived in the surrounding area. It was standard legwork, which would have been much easier if his partner had been there to share the burden.

No doubt the local cops had already interviewed the necessary people, but Ethan would personally interview each one again himself. Despite what they said in training, this job was not about procedure. It was about instinct.

Although he was sure the local guys had done their job properly, Ethan wouldn't get the details he needed from their reports. Reading an answer to a question on paper told you what the subject had said, but it didn't tell you if their pupils had been dilated or if they'd started to sweat or fidget with their shirt collar.

This job was more about what was not said than what was. If he didn't run on pure gut instinct, he wouldn't have solved half the cases he did.

Ethan cut his engine at the same time his phone rang. Recognizing the name that flashed on the screen, he left the doors and windows up and pressed the button to answer it hands-free.

"Think of the Devil," he said in greeting.

"Ethan?" The voice of Nate Ryder, Ethan's partner and best friend, came through scratchy on the other end. "Hold on, let me walk out into the corridor... reception is bad in the room."

Ethan smiled and pictured his partner, over six foot two of muscle and attitude, standing outside his room, still managing to look formidable despite wearing the requisite hospital gown. Though Nate was an inch shorter than Ethan, he was the more solidly built of the two.

"That any better?" Nate's voice came through clearly.

"Yeah. Still giving the nurses trouble, I hear."

Nate lowered his voice. "Thank fuck I'm out of here tomorrow. Not a moment too soon."

"Ah, come on. How many sponge baths did you get?"

"What good is foreplay if there's no main course?"

Ethan chuckled. Nate was definitely on the mend. Still, Ethan's voice turned serious when he said, "How are you bud, really?"

"Take more than a bullet to stop me."

"I, uh... I'm sorry, mate."

Nate's voice lost its jocular edge. "You apologize one more time, and I'm going to kick your ass. It wasn't your fault, and nobody but you thinks it was. Shit happens."

And shit had happened. When Ethan's cover had been blown on his last assignment, all hell had broken loose.

He'd been set up, and his partner had taken a bullet to the shoulder as a result. A couple inches over, and Nate would have been killed.

All because Ethan had been given a snow job by a roughed-up young girl, and he'd followed her into the clubhouse without verifying her story or identifying the risk. Standard procedure. Procedures he often flaunted, but never before to the detriment of someone else.

But the girl had looked so scared. And so young. Perhaps ten or twelve, with signs of physical abuse, and she'd appeared drugged. Ethan shook his head in disgust. He shouldn't have put it past those scumbags to use a child as bait. It was some consolation that the members involved were now dead. But like any successful crime gang, you could take out the leaders, but it was never long before someone else rose up to take their place. It was like playing a video game with an enemy who had an inexhaustible number of new lives.

"Seriously, Nate, how's your shoulder?"

"Just a scratch. Everyone around here reacts like a bunch of girls." Nate paused, and Ethan could hear voices on the other end.

"Listen, mate, the doc's here to sort out my discharge for tomorrow. I'll see you Sunday. You can give me the low-down then. And Ian said to watch your back. Apparently things are not as they seem—whatever the hell that's supposed to mean." *When was a case ever what you expect?*

Disconnecting from the call, Ethan pocketed his phone and tapped his pen on his page. Chief Superintendent Ian Hallow was a straight-up type of guy. Cryptic messages were not his style. What did he mean by that "things are not as they seem" comment? If Ian had further information on the case, he should have supplied it.

A group of three women walked past Sage's shop, one pushing a pram. Ethan watched them absently, while going over his notes. Two of the women stopped in front of the shop and one pushed the other toward the door. They collapsed in giggles.

Ethan opened his window so he could hear what they were saying.

"I dare you to go in," the one with the pram said to the larger one with brown hair.

"She's probably in there mixing up an evil spell as we speak. Brewing it right now, in her huge black cauldron. Eye of a spider, hair of a rabbit, fingernail from a… baby!" The last was said with an exaggerated lunge at the pram, and they all laughed some more.

Ethan gripped the steering wheel, his knuckles turning white.

"I bet that's what happened to her grandmother. Crazy old bat probably drank one of her potions instead of her tea."

Ethan opened the door and stepped out. The women glanced his way, then hurried down the street. All three were approximately Sage's age. Perhaps they'd gone to school with her. His jaw clenched. The thought of Sage attending school with nasty girls like that did something unpleasant to his insides.

He was out of the car now anyway; might as well go across and check on her.

———◆———

Ethan tried the handle to test the lock and cursed when he found the door open. Hadn't he told her to keep this place locked up?

The bell jangled loudly above his head, and when the door closed, he silenced the offensive ringing with his hand. It took a moment for his eyes to adjust from the bright sunshine outside.

"Can I help you, Detective?"

His head whipped around and his eyes connected with a set of stunningly bare legs. Acres of satiny skin led from bare feet right up to a pair of cut-off denim shorts.

"What are you doing up there?" He walked over to where Sage was perched precariously on the top rung of an old, rickety, wooden ladder, taking items off a top shelf. Ethan tested the ladder's stability. It wobbled easily and she shrieked above him.

"What the hell do you think you're doing? You'll make me fall."

"Sage, come down from there." He averted his eyes as she slowly worked her way down the ladder while he held it still. Her legs were endless, and it took considerable effort to not watch her ass sway from side to side with each rung she descended.

When she was down, she stood in front of him with her hands on her hips, making her chest strain at the fabric of her thin shirt.

"That ladder is not stable," he said between gritted teeth.

"It was, until you decided to pretend you were shaking monkeys out of a tree." Her green eyes flashed, and her tongue swiped over her lips, leaving them ruby red and glistening.

What the hell was I thinking coming back here? Have I lost my mind? Can she sense what she does to me? Ethan groaned just thinking about it.

He looked up. There was still a lot of stuff to be cleared off those top shelves. Which meant she would be spending a lot more time on that decrepit old ladder. How was he going to just walk away and concentrate on his job, knowing that she could fall at any moment and end up lying there needing help? And how long would it be before someone found her?

Shutting his eyes, he searched for that cool, emotionless, trancelike state he normally slid into while working a case. He should be able to walk out the door the same way he had come in. This job wasn't personal. He was working a homicide case. There was a serial killer he urgently needed to catch and put behind bars before he attacked again. *It's not personal.*

But with Sage standing before him, he became achingly aware that he was dangerously close to crossing a line. Dangerous, not only professionally, but also personally.

Already, he was far too involved in the way he thought about her. Worried over her. Quite simply, he couldn't put her in that neat little box labeled "victim's relative." She was not just another case.

She was… well she was *Sage*. And there was no way she was getting back up on that ladder.

"Stay here. I'll be back." Resigned to his fate, he held her eyes. "Lock that goddamned door behind me, and don't even think about climbing up on that death trap before I get back."

———◆———

Sage stared at the door the detective had just exited, her mouth hanging open in astonishment. Who the hell did he think he was, telling her what she could and couldn't do?

The unexplained things going on in the house weren't going to push her around, and neither was Ethan. As scared as she'd been last night, in the light of day, Sage felt a little silly. Walls couldn't laugh. And even though she'd *thought* she'd heard the Ouija board moving, she hadn't actually *seen* it. Not last night anyway. Now that it was nothing more than a pile of ashes in the outside bin, she hoped to have put paid to the whole incident.

Bathed in the early morning sunshine that had streamed in through the window, she'd dozed off for a couple hours that morning on Nan's comfy recliner and had woken up feeling refreshed.

What had she been thinking last night? She wasn't going back to Adelaide and leaving all of Nan's belongings unattended and vulnerable to looters. She had a job to do, and she was going to do it.

Sage contemplated the ladder, a single-rung, splintered old wooden beast. Okay, it wouldn't win any occupational health and safety awards, but it was all she could find in Nan's overcrowded garden shed outside. And she hadn't been in any real danger—not until *he'd* got hold of it, that was.

And no matter what Ethan said, she had work to do, and it was taking more time than she'd anticipated.

Repositioning the ladder, Sage grabbed a fresh box and climbed back up the ladder to the top shelf. The dust was the thickest up here, as though the older Nan got, the less high she could reach to clean.

Sage could have kicked herself. While she'd been in the city living life a world away, Nan had been struggling to cope with day-to-day tasks. Sage should have come back more often. Paid more attention. Hired a cleaner. Something. Anything. Especially after Nan had given up her own life of travel and exploration to bring Sage up and care for her.

Blindly reaching forward, Sage felt for the next item to pack. Something stabbed her finger.

Ouch! She snatched back her hand and put her finger into her mouth to suck away the blood that had beaded on the tip. She scanned the dark shelf and hoped she hadn't been bitten by a spider. If everyone had an Achilles' heel, spiders were hers. At least her finger wasn't throbbing as though it had been injected with venom.

Perhaps she'd cut it on some broken glass? She rose on her tiptoes, and ignoring a brief wobble of the ladder, peered into the darkness.

There was something back there, something with two glowing eyes. Was it a mouse, a rat? A vicious top-shelf-hiding, man-eating rodent?

Her eyes finally adjusted to the darkness. It was no rodent. Rather, it was a figurine of some kind. An ugly gargoyle with two shining red eyes and a Devil's fork on the end of its tail.

That's strange. What could make its eyes glow in the darkness of the top shelf? A shelf that didn't look like anyone had touched it in well over ten years. At least. There was no light to reflect up there and a battery couldn't have lasted that long. Could it?

Icy air rushed over her arm, and a shudder ran the length of her spine.

Great, there was a draught up here too. Must be a hole in the roof. She made a mental note to see what she could do to secure the services of a structural engineer in the area. Ada would know the name of the local builder or who to contact.

How odd that Ada hadn't made any attempt to see her since she'd arrived. Nor had any of Nan's friends, for that matter. Perhaps people were leaving her alone in her grief? Or maybe they had left messages on the machine that she still hadn't checked. She made another mental note to check the machine. She was going to have to get a mental diary soon, if she kept going at this rate.

Sage grabbed the ugly figurine, and at the same time, a dark shadow flitted past her. She whipped her head around for a better look, but nothing was there. Taking a deep breath to calm her racing heart, she shook her head. The stress of this whole situation was definitely affecting her. She'd take a long holiday when this was over.

A sudden clang at the front door made her jerk. The ladder slipped, falling to the left, and she leaned to the right to rebalance it.

Too late. Sage shut her eyes and screamed as the rickety old ladder did exactly what the detective had predicted, and plummeted toward the ground.

Chapter Six

Ethan let out a string of curses as he carefully pulled the ladder out of his Land Rover, the midday sun, unseasonably warm for this time of year, making his forehead bead with sweat. On the drive back from the hardware store, somewhere between the butcher's and the second-hand shop, aptly called *Second Chance*, he wondered at what point exactly he had lost his mind. He was glad his partner wasn't here to witness this. Nate would never let him live it down.

He ought to be working, instead of making sure Sage Matthews didn't break her neck.

Ethan still had three interviews outstanding on his list, and he'd discovered there had been two additional people in town last weekend. Two visitors that had not been interviewed or mentioned in the file. Important information that he'd discovered only because of his thorough routine, and his almost obsessive need to qualify all information himself. Perhaps one of those two people was the killer?

He had fed the names through to Zach, his off-the-books wiz of a computer analyst, and was eager to see what would come back. Being special operations meant Ethan had access to information not generally available to members on the force, but Zach was his secret weapon, Ethan's own personal contact and an old friend. Zach had creative—and not always legal—ways of finding information. The two visitors would remain high priority on Ethan's list of persons of interest until they could be ruled out.

At the entrance to the shop, the potted plants on either side of the steps caught his attention. Dead yesterday, they were now alive and thriving. Although reason pointed to the fact that she'd replaced them, the way one plant, in full flower, had curled itself through and around the wooden slats of the seat, it appeared as though it'd grown over a period of time. *Clever.* Surprisingly, despite the way she dressed in smart business attire, he could easily imagine Sage barefoot in the garden, pretty hands in the soil.

Ethan set the ladder down and tested the door handle. It was unlocked. Damn that woman! Couldn't she follow a simple instruction?

The ladder clanged against the wire screen door as he carried it in. He cursed again.

He'd taken two steps into the shop when he saw Sage start to fall. Operating on instinct coupled with pure adrenaline, he only just managed to catch her.

She landed directly in his arms, like a fallen angel. He stumbled but held onto her. There was a moment of stunned silence while neither of them moved, the pounding of his heart the only thing he could hear. As he held her, her soft body molding perfectly against his, all he could think was how *right* she felt this close.

She blinked up at him, her green eyes wide and slightly dazed, her mouth open. He wondered how her lips would taste if he kissed them. How soft their pink flesh would feel between his teeth. The shock cleared from her eyes and recognition set in.

Ethan took a deep, calming breath, and his lungs filled with Sage's gentle fragrance. There was her unique scent that he recognized from Wednesday, mixed with something else… rose or geranium and lavender? It reminded him of his Grandma Lyn, and was not at all what he expected. It was enough to bring him to his senses.

Gently he set Sage down and held her shoulders until she was steady on her feet.

"Didn't I tell you to wait for me?" His voice was sharper than he'd intended.

Her eyes narrowed. "Since when do I take orders from you?"

She pointed to the ladder he had dropped when he'd seen her start to fall. "If you hadn't frightened me half to death barging in here with that monstrosity, I never would have fallen in the first place."

"You're blaming *me*?"

"Yes." She placed her hands on her hips, causing her chest to thrust forward. "I didn't ask for your help."

He inwardly cursed. He was head of an elite special operations unit of the South Australian police force, not a bloody handyman. What the hell was he doing, running around finding a ladder for her in the first place? "Sage," he said, with a patience he didn't feel. "A fall from that height could have caused you serious harm. And you're completely alone in here with no one to help you… What the devil are you holding?"

Sage glanced at her hand, as if surprised to find something in it. Slowly she uncurled her fingers, revealing a hideous gargoyle creature, its mouth open in a sinister smile, and its tongue curling out of one side.

"What is that?"

"I… I don't know," she whispered, swallowing hard. "I found it on the top shelf. Its eyes were glowing red…"

The color had drained from her face, and Ethan took the object from her shaking fingers. Its eyes were indeed red, but definitely not glowing. He glanced questioningly at her. The skin on her arms had turned to gooseflesh, and she was shaking. He guided her to a chair and urged her to sit. She must be suffering from delayed shock.

"You've had a bad scare. If I hadn't arrived when I did, you could have been seriously hurt. Sit down for a while and rest."

"I know what I saw," she said, shrugging off his hand.

He grabbed a sheet of tissue paper from the stack, wrapped the figurine, and placed it in an open packing box.

Sage's lips were devoid of color as she sucked on the tip of her finger and stared at the spot where he'd put the object. A minute ticked by. Then another. Still, she didn't move.

"Sage, before I leave, I need to know that you're okay." Ethan wanted to take her in his arms and comfort her, but held himself back. Barely. He had already crossed too many lines when it came to Sage Matthews. Something about her made him forget himself. Forget that she was the victim's granddaughter and he the detective investigating the case. He was sworn to a job he took more than just seriously. It was his life.

She sucked in a breath and raised her chin. "I'm okay."

He didn't want to leave her, almost doubted his ability to, but he needed to get back to work.

Ethan picked up Sage's dodgy death trap of a ladder and took it outside. Ignoring the infernal ringing of the bell jangling overhead, he came back in, set up the new ladder and used the attached straps to secure it to the shelving.

When he'd finished, Sage was no longer on the chair where he'd left her, but in the corner, putting a teabag into a cup. Damn it. Why hadn't he thought to make her a cup of tea? Tea was always what was needed in situations like this. Her spine was straight, her shoulders squared, but her hand shook, scattering sugar crystals off the spoon before it reached the cup.

Sage, he already sensed, was a strong woman. Only children often grew up faster, especially if they'd suffered the loss of a parent. Smart. Tough. Independent. But something had really shaken her up. More than just a scare from a near fall. More than grief, no matter how great. Something else was troubling her. Had the serial killer made contact? Threatened her in some way? His hands turned to fists at his sides.

"Sage, is something going on that you need to tell me about?"

She kept her back to him. "I'm fine. Thank you, Detective, for the ladder." The chink of the spoon against the china cup as she over-stirred her tea picked at his nerves.

Once again, he found himself fighting a powerful desire to wrap her in his arms and comfort her. Rest her head against his chest and run his fingers through that silky blonde hair while he encouraged her to talk.

He took a deep breath, then another. This was just a case. No different than any other. The only way to help her was to do his job. Catch the killer. Stick to procedure.

Ensure her safety.

But to do his job properly he needed all the information.

"You would tell me if there was anything else I should know? And anything you tell me, no matter how small, would be in strict confidence and could make a huge difference in how quickly we solve this case." *Tell me what's made your hands shake so badly.*

She said nothing, so he tried again. "Has someone threatened you? You can tell me anything, especially—"

"There's nothing else," she interrupted, her voice flat and expressionless. "You need to leave now, Detective." Raising the cup to her lips, she blew across the surface of the liquid without turning around.

"Detective" again. Damn. It felt as though she'd just shut him down, and his chest tightened with the loss. *It's for the best.*

Ethan forced himself to leave, concentrated on putting one foot in front of the other until he was at the door. Setting the handle to lock, he closed it behind him and tested that it was secure. He peered through the window, but could no longer see her. He hoped she had taken herself upstairs to rest and didn't go back up the ladder.

He let out a long string of curses on the way to the car. What the hell was wrong with him, obsessing over her so much?

His partner was arriving Sunday. There was no one like Nate to shake some sense into him. Help him put all this into perspective, because he sure as hell couldn't think objectively when it came to Sage Matthews.

And she—or someone else—might very well die if he didn't get his mind back on the job.

———◆———

Sage waited until the bell on the door stopped jangling and she could no longer hear the detective's vehicle before she emptied the remainder of her tea in the sink.

She turned to face the box.

Taking a deep, fortifying breath, she moved toward it and easily found what she was looking for. The scrunched up tissue paper stood out amongst her neat wrapping.

For a moment she considered getting a hammer and giving the bundle a good working over, but she had to know. The tissue paper floated to her feet and she was left holding the ugly figurine in the palm of her hand. It was still just as hideous, with its wicked grin, forked Devil's tail, and pointed ears. But its eyes were not glowing. They were red, but definitely not glowing.

She carried the object around the shop to see if she could recreate glowing eyes, but nothing happened. Even climbing up the newly secured ladder and setting the gargoyle in the darkness of the top shelf didn't make its eyes glow.

Was Ethan right? Was she simply so emotionally overwrought and exhausted from lack of sleep that her mind was playing tricks on her?

She climbed back down the ladder and threw the ugly thing in the box without re-wrapping it. It landed face up, its red eyes fixed on her. As though it was… *looking* at her. She shivered.

That confirms it. She was in certain danger of losing her mind.

And I still have the funeral tomorrow to get through.

CHAPTER SEVEN

Sage looked around the cemetery at the huge turnout for Nan's funeral. A warm breeze blew hair into her eyes, and she brushed the strands behind her ear. It didn't seem right that the sun was shining. Rain should be mandatory at funerals. How dare the day be so cheerful when Sage felt as though her world had been torn to pieces.

A gaping hole had opened in Sage's life now. An emptiness that would never be filled. Her throat ached with all the words she'd never get to say.

Groups of people stretched back from the gravesite as far as Sage could see. She hadn't realized there were that many people in Cryton. And they were all here for Nan. Farther away, gathered under the shade of a tall river red gum tree, were Nan's circle of friends. Once a group of seven, now only five remained. Raylene Keyton had passed away some months ago, and now Nan. Stumbling slightly, Sage made her way to Ada, who was the closest person to Nan she had left. Was it her imagination, or did they tense up as they became aware of her approach?

"Ada," Sage said, the words catching in her closed throat. What the hell did she say? *Nice day, good to see you, you're looking well, thank you for coming.* It wasn't a nice day, nobody was looking well, devastation was etched in every line of their aging faces, and of course they would come; Nan had been closer than their very own families who visited less than they ought. There was nothing to say at a ceremony dedicated to the day when the most important person in your world would be buried in the ground. So she said nothing, just rested a commiserating hand on Ada's spindly arm instead.

Behind her wire-rimmed glasses, Ada's kind blue eyes watered, as her gaze wandered affectionately across Sage's face. "You get lovelier every time I see you," she said. "But you look tired dear, and much too thin. Celeste would want you to be taking better care of yourself."

Sage's chest squeezed painfully, and she managed what she hoped was a reassuring smile. "I'll do my best."

A rush of cool wind raced over them, a striking contrast to the warm day. Joyce gasped, and her eyes darted around. A ripple of unease rolled through the group, and they clutched at black shawls and handbags.

"What is it?" Sage asked.

"Ada, unless you're going to bring her in, you'd best not talk to her at all," Joyce said, and Pat and Mona murmured their agreement. At seventy-nine, Joyce Booth was referred to as the "baby" of the circle of friends, and she had a fiery, no-nonsense demeanor. Her gray hair, dyed blue/blonde, was neatly set in old-fashioned curls. Dark red lipstick bled into the lines around the firm set of her mouth.

A bird screeched above them. As one, they looked up to find a single black crow on an overhanging branch. "He's watching," Mona whispered loudly. "Come on, let's go."

"It's just a crow," Sage said.

"Is it?" Joyce asked, turning her piercing gaze from the crow to Sage. Joyce certainly sounded as sharp as ever; it was the words she uttered that gave away her shaky grip on reality.

"Of course it's a crow," Sage said patiently. They were hardly an uncommon occurrence around here. "What else could it be?"

"I want you to reconsider, Ada. Please, bring her in," Patricia Sands said, her words tumbling out too fast. As uneasy as she appeared, Pat's face was flawlessly powdered, as always, her lipstick a flattering shade of peach. Tall, slender, and attractive, Pat easily looked a decade younger than her eighty years.

"No," Ada said firmly. "We made a promise. Celeste wanted her left out of it."

"But what about the prophecy? The grimoire?" Joyce asked. "Ada, you can't take all that responsibility on your own."

"I can, and I will," Ada replied. "We've already had this conversation. Now go wait for me by the car. I need a minute with Sage."

"Foolish is what you are," Joyce said. "I can only hope you come to your senses before it's too late."

Joyce, Pat, and Mona hurried away, leaving Ada and Sage on their own.

"What was that all about?" Sage frowned as she watched their retreat. Mona was known to be a little zany, even loopy, but perhaps they had all reached the age where they were beginning to lose their marbles. At least Nan's mind had been as sharp as ever to her very last day. She wouldn't have wanted it any other way.

"What did you promise Nan to leave me out of?" Sage asked, focusing her attention back on Ada.

"You shouldn't be here, child. You must leave." Ada's bony fingers dug into the soft flesh of Sage's upper arm. "You must leave after the funeral. I'll handle everything. Just like I promised Celeste I would. Go back to the city before it's too late."

"Too late for what?" Sage asked.

Ada didn't reply; instead she gripped the pendant around Sage's neck. "This is not just jewelry." She tugged on the pendant for emphasis. "Whatever you do, never take this off," Ada said, echoing the words Sage's mother had said twenty years ago. Surprised, Sage was about to take a step back when Ada wrapped her arms around her neck and began to tremble and shake.

"Oh, Ada," Sage murmured, returning the embrace in earnest. No doubt Ada's apparent confusion was caused by overwhelming grief. Sage had felt her own grip on reality slipping since her return. "It will be all right," Sage said as Ada pulled back.

Ada looked as though she was about to speak, but something she spotted over Sage's shoulder caused her reddened eyes to widen like saucers.

"What is it?" Sage asked, whipping her head around. All she saw was the crow sitting in the tree, peering down at them.

"I have to go," Ada said. "He's watching me with you. Look after yourself, child. And remember what I said." Ada turned and quickly shuffled off to catch up to her friends.

"Ada!" Sage called, but Ada didn't acknowledge her. Didn't turn around. Tears stung Sage's lids, and she bit her lip to prevent herself from calling out a second time. It was clear something had spooked Ada. Sage felt her loss keenly. She could have used Ada's comfort, could have offered her own back. They had both loved and lost Nan; they were both hurting. They should have been able to share sorrow, and borrow strength. Instead, Sage was left feeling utterly alone, confused, and concerned over the nonsensical ramblings of Nan's friends. Prophecies indeed!

Sage hugged her arms around her middle and glanced back up at the crow, preening its glossy black feathers. As though sensing her regard, it met her gaze directly. Its black eyes flashed vivid red, and Sage blinked in surprise, a tremor rolling down her spine. When she looked again, the eyes had returned to normal.

Had she really seen that flash, or had it been a trick of the sunlight? She'd often felt as though she had a natural affinity with animals and nature, which she attributed to her lonely childhood. Sage hadn't had imaginary friends to talk to; she'd had animals. But the energy she got from this crow was almost... menacing?

Shaking her head, she moved away and made an effort to clear her mind. She didn't have the emotional strength at the moment to worry about strange crows. Not here. Not today. She was however, worried about the toll Nan's murder seemed to be taking on Ada and the other ladies. They all seemed to be sharing some kind of delusion, with all that rambling about prophecies. And what the heck was a grimoire? She shook her head. Everyone had different ways of coping with grief, so who was she to judge? She'd visit them all over the next day or two to check on how they were doing.

As she moved closer to the graveside, an uncomfortable weight suddenly bore down on Sage. It sat heavy on her skull, like a hat made of lead.

Faces filled her vision, some familiar, some not, and Sage realized she didn't belong here. Had never belonged here. She was like a leaf that had blown in from a neighboring tree. Never quite fitting in.

Sage had always believed she'd known her grandmother well, yet as she looked around and saw so many people she didn't recognize, the fact hit home that there was so much more to her nan than she'd thought. Logically, she should have realized that. Nan had lived so much more life than Sage had, but Nan's focus on Sage had made her feel as though she were the only person in the world, as though she alone mattered.

Without Nan, Sage wasn't special to anyone. She existed. Breathed air. Ate food. But what did any of that matter? In the grand scheme of things, Sage was nothing. Insignificant.

Tears ran unchecked down her face. She'd lost the one person who'd really cared about her. She certainly hadn't mattered to Jesse, the boyfriend who'd cheated on her one of her coworkers. Even her friends back in the city wouldn't miss her that much; they had each other, and they'd done just fine without Sage before she'd come along.

Sage looked over to the group of girls she'd attended school with. They were all grown up now, and there were only three of them instead of seven. The other four had moved away like Sage had. The huddled-together girls weren't looking at her, but she imagined their whispers were the same ones she'd heard in the corridors at school. *Here comes the freak. Watch out, you'll get freak germs.*

Freak germs…

Given all the crazy things she'd been thinking during the last three days, maybe she really did have them.

Sage's lungs felt compressed, like she was being dragged down by quicksand. She shook her head. Where were all these overly negative thoughts coming from? Was she feeling this way because of the funeral? Or was it something else, something more sinister? It almost felt as though something was prying into her mind, forcing these ideas in. Ideas that weren't hers.

Sage reached the edge of the grave. She peered into the hole and let her fingers travel over the soft petals of the red rose she'd picked from Nan's garden that morning. The freshly dug soil assailed her senses, and she knelt down in its dirty softness. For a moment she fantasized about lying atop the coffin in the ground, and she leaned forward as if to do so. She caught herself. *Strange.* Another thought that was not like hers.

It was time to say her final goodbyes to the most wonderful person she had ever known. *Oh Nan, did I ever thank you for everything you did for me while you were alive to hear it?* Sage tugged at the rose, letting some petals fall onto the glossy mahogany of the coffin.

Did I ever tell you how much I appreciated that you gave up your life of freedom and travel to look after a three year old thrust into your care?

More petals fell. *You never once complained or made me feel as though I were a burden.* There was nothing but a stem in her hand now, and she tossed it in with the petals. *You were always there for me, and I'm sorry I wasn't there for you the one time it counted. Perhaps I could have stopped what happened.*

Goodbye, Nan. You were too good for this earth. Sage's tears formed droplets in the freshly dug soil. People stared, but no one approached.

The faces around her faded into the background, and a shadow fell upon her as a cloud passed across the sun. A black, mist-like form moved from behind the gum tree to her left to disappear behind another. What the hell was that?

Sage's pulse began to race. Her vision blurred, black spots appearing and disappearing like splotches of paint from an angry artist. She gasped for air that no longer contained oxygen. Heartbeat thrashing past her ears, Sage wrapped her fingers around the angel pendant and closed her eyes. She thought she cried out, but if she did, the sound didn't make it past the constriction in her throat.

All at once, a blanket of calm washed over her. As if Nan were kneeling right there beside her. Sage imagined that she could feel her nan's warm, wise hands rest on her shoulders, that she was breathing Nan's calming lavender scent one last time.

The leaden depression lifted from her and the thick blanket of fog dissipated from her mind. The day looked brighter, clearer.

Sage pulled back her shoulders. The funeral director sprinkled the first handful of dirt, saying words she couldn't hear.

Slowly, she stood and turned. She drifted away from the crowd without conscious thought of where she was going or what she was going to do when she got there. But life went on, and Sage would go on with it.

———◆———

From his place at the other side of the cemetery, Ethan watched Sage walk away. His chest compressed painfully at her obvious grief. He wanted to go to her. Wrap his arms around her and give her the comfort she desperately needed. The amount of willpower he exerted to keep himself from going to her nearly crippled him.

But he had a job to do. Quite often the murderer came to the funeral of his victim. Only when he caught the killer would Sage be safe. That was the only thought strong enough to keep his feet anchored to the ground.

Out the corner of his eye, he watched Sage drift down a dirt path and over a hill leading away from the cemetery. She'd left before the ceremony was even over. Was she all right? Where was she going? A few people looked in her direction, nodded and talked amongst themselves, but no one went after her.

Anger burned hot and thick in his chest. What the hell was wrong with these people? Wasn't anyone going to offer Sage comfort and a shoulder to cry on? She had grown up here. She knew these people. His vision clouded around the edges as he waited impatiently to see who would do the decent thing.

Nobody moved. Not one fucking person. He circulated through the groups of people. Heard murmurs of regret and sadness. *Poor Sage,* they said. But no one followed her. Made sure she was okay. Let her know she wasn't alone in her grief. He wanted to bang their heads together.

Ethan was just about to go after her when he saw a shadow move near a clump of trees along the cemetery's edge. He would have missed it had he not been watching so intently the spot where Sage had left.

The figure straightened, making it easier to see who it was. The thin man's face was pale, but weathered. His collar-length blond hair was thin and scraggly and looked like it hadn't felt the tines of a comb in years. He was of average height and leaning against a tree, smoking. Observing.

The man's gaze was focused on the path of Sage's exit, and Ethan watched him push off the tree, flick his butt in the dirt, and head off in her direction.

Son of a bitch. Could that be who they were looking for? Keeping the man in his vision, Ethan went to a nearby group of elderly ladies who were chattering amongst themselves and immediately recognized Ada Slatterley.

"Excuse me, Mrs. Slatterley," he interrupted, "do you know who that is?" He pointed in the direction of the man who in a matter of seconds would disappear out of sight.

"Who?" Ada asked, squinting through her glasses. "Oh, that would be Lucky."

"Lucky?"

"Yes, Luke Keyton. He is touched, that fellow. Not right in the head." She tut-tutted. "He's harmless, though. We hardly see him now that his mother has passed away. Dear old Raylene. He—"

"Thanks. I'll come by to see you later." Ethan hurried off. He could no longer see Lucky on the hill.

Sage was out there somewhere.

Alone.

————◆————

Luke Keyton sat on the opposite side of the cheap laminate desk in the investigation room at the local station. Average height, slim build, twenty eight years of age.

"Mind if I smoke?" Keyton asked, pulling a crumpled pack of loose tobacco from his top pocket. His greasy blond hair hung limply around his face, the collar of his light-brown polo shirt done up to the top button.

"Smoking is prohibited in public buildings," Ethan said automatically. Keyton wore no jewelry, not even a watch. He smelled of stale tobacco and strong body odor, showers plainly not a priority.

"I'll be damned," Keyton said, shaking his head. "That mean I can't smoke?"

"Got it in one," Ethan confirmed.

Keyton opened the tobacco packet and pulled out some Tally-Ho rolling papers.

"You know I just said you can't smoke, right?"

"Right."

Ethan placed his tape recorder on the center of the table and pressed record. He stated his name, rank, and the date and time for the record.

"Lucas Graham Keyton has agreed to come in for questioning of his own free will. Mr. Keyton, will you state your name, address, and date of birth for the record?"

After Keyton did as directed, Ethan eased back into his chair, stretched out his legs, and affected a casual expression to enhance the impression of an informal conversation.

"What do you do for work?" Ethan asked.

"Don't work. Who'd give me a job? Me da always said I'm useless as an ashtray on a motorbike." His expression hardened. "But he was wrong."

"Your father passed away when you were—" Ethan consulted his notes. "Fifteen. Is that correct?"

"Uh-huh." Lucky stared at a point on the wall to Ethan's left, his eyes narrowing into hard slits.

"You didn't get along?"

"Nup. You brought me in here to talk about me da?"

"No. Just making conversation. Where were you on the evening of Sunday, September sixth?" Ethan asked.

Keyton sprinkled tobacco in a line over a Tally-Ho with dirty fingernails.

"How should I remember? What day is it today?" he asked, rolling the paper into a perfect cylinder.

"Today is Saturday, September twelfth. Sunday was six days ago." Keyton's expression remained blank. "Last weekend," Ethan prompted.

"Last weekend, I was with Virgil," Keyton said, running his fingers along the cigarette, smoothing out any lumps.

"Good. Was Virgil with you at your place, or did you go somewhere else?"

Keyton licked the seam of the thin paper to seal his cigarette and eyed it critically. "We were at me place."

"Very good. Can you tell me how to contact Virgil so that I verify this?"

He twisted the end until the paper broke off. Using the table, Keyton butted the end into a perfect stump and set it aside.

"I don't contact Virgil. He contacts me."

"What do you mean by that? He calls you on the phone?"

Luke Keyton shook his head, his hair falling across his eye. It caught on his lashes, moving as he blinked, but he didn't brush it aside. "Don't have a phone. Too damned expensive. Gotta have a job to have one of them things."

"How does Virgil contact you then?"

"He visits me."

"You mean he just turns up at your place?'

"That's right." Keyton wiped his nose with the back of his hand, and pushed the hair off his face.

"Is Virgil at your place now?" Ethan asked.

"Nup."

"When did he leave?"

"Dunno." Keyton reached into his pocket and pulled out a box of matches.

"You remember you can't smoke in here, right?" Ethan said, failing to keep the annoyance out of his voice.

"Right." Keyton placed the matches next to his neatly rolled cigarette. "Haven't heard from Virgil for a couple days."

"Did he say when he was going to be back?" Ethan asked. *Christ, this is like pulling teeth.*

"Dunno. Doesn't tell me. But I think it will be soon."

"What makes you say that?"

Keyton took out a paper and began rolling another cigarette. Habit, or a nervous reaction to the line of questioning?

"'Cause we have unfinished business," Keyton finally said.

"And what business would that be, exactly?"

"Can't say."

"Can't or won't?" Ethan asked, narrowing his eyes and leaning forward.

"You pick."

Ethan changed tack. "Did you know Celeste Matthews?"

"The crazy witch lady? Sure, I knew her."

"How?"

"Can I have a drink?" he asked. Ethan nodded to the officer leaning against the wall in the corner, who filled a plastic cup with water from the cooler.

Ethan waited while Keyton drained the cup in one go. A trickle of water ran out the side of his mouth, leaving a dark patch on his shirt.

"How did you know Celeste Matthews?" Ethan asked.

"Friend of Ma's."

"When did you see her last?"

"Dunno."

Keyton crunched the plastic cup in his hand, the crackling loud in the small room.

Ethan placed his hand firmly on Keyton's and removed the cup. "Think a little deeper. Was it recently?"

"Can I have another drink?"

"No."

Keyton sighed. "Would have been a while ago. Winter, 'cause it was cold, and she was handing out all these stupid blankets she makes."

"Made," Ethan said. "You didn't have cause to go into her shop on Sunday?"

"Now why would I wanna do that?" Keyton asked with a smirk.

"You tell me."

"I got no reason to go there. She was Ma's friend. Not mine."

"Where were you on Friday night, the thirty-first July?" Ethan asked.

Keyton rolled his eyes and groaned. "How the fuck—"

"Today is Saturday September twelfth, remember? We've just been through all this. July thirty-first was a Friday. Six weeks ago."

"Dunno."

"Think. Harder." Ethan leaned forward, his hands slapping the table a little louder than he'd intended.

"Hell, man, don't go gettin' all hot and heavy. I can't remember what I did yesterday most of the time. Time is irrelevant to me. Why should I even care what day it is? Got nowhere to go, nowhere to be. "

"You would remember if you travelled anywhere recently. Is it possible you were in Cryton, or were you somewhere else?"

Keyton, having finished rolling his second cigarette, tapped it on the table. "Been travelling around. Seein' sights. Can't spend me whole life stuck in the middle of whoop whoop. Got back last week."

"How long were you travelling for?"

Keyton looked up at Ethan in exasperation. "Time again, mate. What do I care how long? I got me all the time in the world."

———— ◆ ————

Later that night back in his hotel room, Ethan typed in the series of passwords that logged him onto his laptop.

The interview with Luke Keyton had continued for two hours, circling around countless times and getting nowhere. Lucky was not the brightest crayon in the pack, but as yet, Ethan had nothing to link him to any of the murders. He'd see what he could turn up when he validated Keyton's alibi: Virgil, no last name, vague physical description, no address, and no phone number. With nothing to hold Keyton, Ethan had finally let him go. The local guys knew Keyton's family and were frank about their relief in seeing him walk free. Lucky's mother, Raylene, had run the local church group until she'd passed away six months ago. Everyone had sympathized with the kind-hearted woman who'd raised a touched son as a single mother.

Ethan fired up his email and fed the scraps of what he knew about Virgil through to Zach. On the surface, there was not much to go on, but Zach had gotten a lot more with a lot less.

Ethan's thoughts drifted to Sage. He hoped she was safely back at the shop. He also hoped that someone in this town had the decency to go to her. Too bad it couldn't be him.

Maybe when the case was over? Not that he could afford to be thinking like that at the moment.

The ping notifying him of new email sounded, and he scrolled the list, looking for one from Zach. He was in luck. Received forty minutes ago. The message contained information on every name Ethan had sent through to him: addresses past and present, dates of birth, places of work, vehicles owned, registrations, details of minor court appearances, traffic infringements, fines, and numerous other pieces of information kept in government files and other, less-legal databases that Zach had access to.

Sifting through pages and pages of information, Ethan was pleased. Zach was as thorough as usual. They'd been friends since they'd first worked together as constables. Over the years, Zach had ventured into his specialty of information technology, before branching out and forming his own company, while Ethan had become detective sergeant earlier than usual, then moved into the special operations unit, Taipan. Though he too had plans to start his own company one day. He already used his own contacts and people anyway.

Reading through the file a second time, Ethan paused at a line on the eighth page. It was a traffic infringement issued by a motorcycle cop.

1SPY817 clocked doing eighty-three in a sixty zone at 7:13 p.m. 6th Sept on the highway just outside Cryton.

The vehicle was registered to a Ted Masters and placed him in the vicinity at the time the second victim was murdered. Finally, something concrete to follow up. It was a long shot, but it wouldn't be the first time something as simple as a speeding fine brought down a case.

He shot a note back: *Thanks, Zach. Locate Ted Masters and advise on whereabouts ASAP. EB*

Ethan leaned back in his chair and sifted through the file photos of the victims. What was the link between them? These things were rarely random. What connected a fifteen-year-old runaway boy, a thirty-seven-year-old father turned hitchhiker, and an eighty-two-year-old grandmother?

What was he missing? Was Ted Masters, a forty-seven-year-old mechanic, the killer? And if so, why? Nothing out of the ordinary in his file, no criminal history. Nothing in his past to indicate he could viciously murder three people and leave such a powerful calling card.

Ethan would wait for Zach, then start the interviewing process on Masters. Friends, family, neighbors, teachers…

He needed a break in the case soon. He grabbed his keys and locked the room. There was nothing better than a drive to clear one's head. And it wouldn't hurt to check on Sage.

CHAPTER EIGHT

Sage sat on the edge of Nan's bed and bent to take off her shoes, letting the tears run unchecked down her cheeks. Lying back on the bed she used to jump into with Nan when she was young, she allowed herself to sob. Crying didn't make her less strong, especially today.

The funeral had been harder than she'd expected, and those moments when she had felt herself being dragged into a dark place, as if she'd had no control of her thoughts or emotions, had frightened her. Regardless of the hardships of her youth, she'd always managed to remain fairly positive. But today, she'd felt herself on the edge of a yawning pit of darkness, and she'd nearly fallen—or been pushed—into it.

Was that how people who had depression felt? Then again, perhaps that was a normal reaction to grief and exhaustion. She had nothing to compare Nan's funeral to.

Her mind wandered to the unsettling conversation she'd had with Nan's circle of friends. Ada had warned her that she should leave before it was too late. *Too late for what?* And what had she meant when she'd said that the pendant was more than just jewelry? Instinctively, Sage traced her fingers over the angel's wings, and across the intricately carved symbol on the back.

Clasping the pendant had immediately calmed her when she'd seen that eerie black shadow. Why? She'd always associated the pendant with her mother, whom she chose to picture as an angel watching over her. Though today, at the graveside, she'd felt Nan with her too. Strongly. She took a deep breath. Now she had two angels looking after her, not one.

Sage thought back to the black shadow she'd seen. Or thought she'd seen. She didn't know what it could have been, but she clearly remembered how it had made her *feel*. She'd been nothing short of terrified when she'd noticed it out of the corner of her eye. As if she'd known on some level that whatever it was hated her, and meant to do her harm. Of course that didn't make sense, but that had been how it felt. Was it just a manifestation of her grief, her feeling of being overwhelmed and alone?

The whole experience had been beyond strange. And Joyce, Pat, and Mona had seemed to be having some kind of debate over her. They didn't want her involved in something. Actually, they'd said *Nan* hadn't wanted her involved. What could that be? The strange conversation aside, they also hadn't acted as expected, offering no hugs or words of condolence.

Instead, their expressions had been a mix of sorrow, pity, and... something else. They hadn't met her gaze, instead talked about her in the third person as though she hadn't been standing right there. It wasn't like them to be so rude. Then they'd left without as much as a goodbye. They were all in their eighties, or close to it. Was it possible that all of them were losing it, at the same time? She definitely needed to check in on them all soon.

Sage blew her nose with a tissue from the box in the calico and lace holder on the bedside table and sat on Nan's bed for what felt like an eternity. She had cried all her tears. The longer she sat, the more restless and fidgety she became, the memories wrapping like a vise around her chest.

Reaching for her mobile phone, she dialed Rebecca's number. The comfort of her best friend's voice was exactly what Sage needed right now. The call went to voicemail, and a quick look at the clock confirmed that at this time on a Saturday night, Rebecca would be having drinks at their favorite bar. Where Sage would be had she been back home. No good trying her other friends then; the tight-knit group would all be there as well.

With no one to talk to, she might as well keep busy. She pondered her next task—emptying Nan's large wooden chest of drawers.

Anyone looking in the window would say that Sage was indeed mad, tackling something like that so soon after the funeral, but she'd done enough moping. The sooner she packed up this place, the sooner she could get back to the city and her life. Far away from this strange town and its even stranger residents.

She rifled through the drawers, checking their contents, making a mental plan of how to organize the packing. The bottom drawer was stuck, and she had to use both hands to force it. She gasped when she saw what was inside.

Diaries.

Nan's diaries. Neatly stacked with their spines facing upward, showing the year. Sage ran her fingertips over the worn covers. There must be what... twenty of them in there? Exactly twenty, since that had been how many years since Nan had moved back here to look after her.

Almost reverently, Sage selected one from the middle and opened the journal to a random page, her eyes floating over Nan's neat handwriting. Diaries were so personal; it felt as though she were holding a piece of her nan in her hands. And Sage supposed she really was. The pages were filled with her grandmother's words, her energy, her thoughts and personality.

Sage couldn't wait to get these shipped back to her apartment in the city. She intended to read each individual one, start to finish.

Were there more around somewhere—perhaps in the attic? Ones from Nan's journeys around the world and when she was young. Those would be fascinating.

Sage put the diary she'd selected back into its correct place and chose another. The year Sage had left to begin her life in the city. She flicked through the pages and smiled. Nan always started each entry with the weather.

Saturday, 11th January
36 deg, sunny

Ada stopped by the shop this morning, bringing some of her homemade jam. I didn't have the patience to talk with her, not after the events of last night.

Last night? What had happened last night? Intrigued, Sage flicked back to the previous page.

Friday, 10th January
33 deg, partly cloudy and humid

Today my heart broke as I sent her away. My life is only half complete now I have lost my sunshine, but her safety is too important. I know I risk her never coming back, but it is now too dangerous for her to stay.
The darkness is getting more active. Taking more chances. I need to know she is safe.
Old Mrs. Richards came in with complaints about her arthritis again…

Sage looked up from the page blankly. A life she recognized and yet didn't. What was Nan talking about—what darkness? Sent her away? Sage hadn't been sent away. She'd chosen to go live in the city, so that she could have a career, experience life.

A loud thump came from the hallway outside the bedroom door. She stood to investigate and stopped. Every night since she'd arrived, she had been hearing more and more strange sounds. Too many to be attributed to the settling noises an old house made. But what could be causing them? She didn't believe it was an intruder or someone in the house, because she never saw anyone, and as far as she could tell, nothing was missing.

Another sound. Sage stilled and listened. It was a low, rolling noise, like a heavy marble traveling along the floorboards and down the length of the hallway. The slam of a door downstairs made her jump. She didn't need to check this time to know she wasn't going to find anything. She never had discovered the source of the draught.

Sage crossed to the window and looked out. The almost-full moon was high in the sky, its silver glow penetrating the darkness. She could clearly see the large gum tree next to the window, illuminated by the streetlight. Its leaves were absolutely still. There wasn't even a slight breeze. *What made the door slam?*

For no apparent reason, the hairs on Sage's skin stood on end. Not just the ones on her arms, but the ones on back of her neck too. An unexplained fear, unlike anything she had ever felt before, came over her. A sense of dread, of imminent death, as if someone were standing right in front of her with a butcher's knife.

But there was no one there. She was alone.

Is this what it feels like to lose your mind?

The sensation passed as suddenly as it had arrived. Sage lowered herself onto the side of the bed. She was being paranoid. Clutching the pendant around her neck, her fingers traced the outline of the angel's wings. She hadn't had enough sleep, she hadn't been eating regularly, and she'd been doing too much.

And it *was* the day of her beloved nan's funeral, after all. She needed to start taking better care of herself. For the sake of her sanity, she wasn't going to do any more packing tonight. She changed into her sleep shorts and slid into bed, even though she wasn't the slightest bit tired. She would do without a bath or shower tonight—despite her little pep talk, no way was she crossing the hallway to the bathroom.

Pulling up the covers of her nan's bed, she didn't feel the same sense of safety she'd felt when she'd first arrived. What had changed? It didn't make sense, but she was sure the room somehow *felt* different ever since she'd packed up the crystals. But that just didn't make sense.

Then again it didn't need to make sense. If it helped her sleep, perhaps she should put them back? Could she remember which corner each one came from? Would it matter?

Stop it, Sage. Crystals were pretty stones. Rocks. *And any sane person would know that rocks can't help you sleep.*

Instead, she sprayed herself again with Nan's perfume from the bottle on the dressing table. The lavender and rose blend comforted her, as if she could close her eyes and imagine her nan right beside her.

Grabbing the mystery novel she was halfway through off the bedside table, Sage attempted to focus on the words. She loved reading and quite often used it as an escape from reality. But no matter how hard she tried to zone out, she found herself reading the same sentence over and over, unable to be drawn into the story.

A shiver rippled across her arms and down her legs, and she pulled the covers even tighter around her against the chill. It was spring, and had been an unseasonably warm day. The nights had been cool but pleasant, and she expected tonight to be no different. Maybe she was coming down with the flu? That would explain her confused mind. She checked her head for signs of a fever.

She glanced across at the floor fan, which showed the current temperature reading on its front, and blinked. That couldn't be right. The digital numbers were declining at a steady pace, from sixteen degrees Celsius to three.

A scraping noise came from the far side of the room. Her eyes widened and her mouth dried as she stared at the shelf. It was cluttered with numerous objects and statues of mythical dragons and witches. Only now they were all in a single line—*all eyes looking at her*.

The light on the bedside table went out, plunging the room into darkness. Outside the door, she heard footsteps in the hallway.

She opened her mouth and screamed.

CHAPTER NINE

The digital readout on the dashboard read 2:55 a.m., and the sound of the Land Rover's engine rumbled through the unnaturally still night. There seemed to be a curious lack of nightlife noise in this town. Very curious.

Ethan often drove in the middle of the night when life refused to give him the peace he craved. The details of this case and the lack of progress frustrated him no end. The crime scenes, despite the strategically applied signature markings on the bodies, were almost unnaturally devoid of evidence. Not a single trace of DNA had been found, which seemed unbelievable, considering the amount of time the killer must have spent preparing the bodies to be discovered the way they were.

He could only hope that Zach wouldn't take long to get back to him with the current location of Ted Masters. Was it only coincidence that Masters had been in the vicinity of both murders at the time they'd occurred? When Ethan finally interviewed Ted, he would know instinctively whether Masters had anything to hide. Communication was only ten percent verbal. The other ninety percent was made up of nonverbal cues, such as body language. Without conceit, Ethan knew his talents lay in being able to accurately read that ninety percent.

He turned onto the main street of town and headed toward Beyond the Grave. This was a murder investigation after all, and he was driving past only to make sure everything was as it should be.

Yeah right. Keep telling yourself that.

Ethan reached into the console for a packet of cigarettes and touched nothing but cold plastic. The urge to have a cigarette while he drove remained, even though he'd given up smoking years ago. Thank God the console was empty, because with his current frustration level, his willpower wouldn't stand the test.

At this late hour, he expected Beyond the Grave to be quiet and dark, but lights were on in the downstairs shop. Had Sage forgotten to turn them off? Maybe she'd left them on for security.

He pulled over a little way down the street from her shop and sat in the vehicle for a few minutes, a strange sense of unease prickling the hairs on the back of his neck. She wouldn't be awake and packing in the middle of the night, would she? In his mind, he saw her almost tumble from the top of the ladder again, and his stomach tightened.

The digital clock on the dashboard clicked over to three a.m. as he killed the engine and exited the vehicle. He turned up the collar of his leather jacket against a chilly gust and put his hands in the pockets.

A flock of birds suddenly sprang to life, flying off into the darkness. Crows, to judge by their cawing. He looked up at the large shadowy tree they'd left, its branches reaching way over the shop, and wondered what had spooked the birds. He doubted it was him. Years of training had made walking silently an integral part of his makeup. Instinctual. He was not in the habit of scaring birds out of trees. He scouted the ground for signs of a fox or other predator. Nothing. Again, there was silence. An absolute silence, not even the loud chirping of male crickets calling for mates.

As he arrived at the front door of the shop, the light behind the roller blind in the window flickered. He reached for the handle, but the door opened before his hand even touched it.

Anger instantly churned in his gut. How could Sage be so damn careless? Anyone could have walked in. Hell, he just had. What was she thinking?

"Sage?" he called, his voice clear and loud in the silence. He stepped fully inside. "Sage, are you down here?"

No response.

He locked the door and jiggled it in its frame to test it. The lock was inadequate, but at least it was secure. He would have words with Sage about her lack of security consciousness. And he'd make sure she got larger and stronger locks. It was back to the hardware store for him tomorrow.

After he took a few steps inside, a wave of nausea hit him. The hairs on his arms were standing on end, and there was a strange... *heaviness* in the air. As though each breath he took compressed his chest, instead of filling it with oxygen.

Where was Sage? Fear for her safety surged through his blood, and images of what the killer would do to her flooded his mind. Ruthlessly, he pushed them aside and shouted her name.

A noise, like dragging furniture across floorboards, came from overhead. Was the killer upstairs with her right now?

Every instinct on high alert, Ethan pulled his gun and swiftly climbed the narrow staircase. Reaching the top, he discovered a hallway with two doors on the left and two on the right. Which room was Sage in?

"Sage! Where are you?" He paused briefly, listening for a response.

Another scraping noise. Coming from the room on the right at the end.

In a blink, he was at the door, trying the handle. It was locked. "Sage, open the door."

"Ethan?" Her voice on the other side of the door was high pitched and breathless, her fear putting his instincts into overdrive. The door handle rattled and turned, but the door didn't open.

"Ethan! The door. It's stuck." He could hear her pulling frantically on the door from the other side, and it was all he could do to not break the door down to reach her.

But when he tried the knob, it turned, opening easily. Sage blinked at him for a fraction of a second before hurtling herself into his arms. Taking a step backward for balance, he caught her. Her arms wrapped around his neck almost painfully, her breathing ragged as she buried her face against his chest.

He pushed her behind him, sheltering her with his body, as gun drawn, he scanned the room.

"What happened? Is someone in here?" The window was closed, no signs of a struggle. The bed covers were rumpled as though she had been sleeping, and he could see nothing that would have caused her terror. Keeping her close, he searched the room, leaving nothing to chance. Satisfied the room was safe, he turned to her. She was pale and trembling, her eyes wide.

The son of a bitch had been in there. "Sage, take a deep breath. I need you to tell me what's going on."

She didn't answer, but her eyes kept flickering to various objects in the room. The fan, the shelves, the door. What the hell had happened? A tsunami of conflicting emotions churned inside him, desperately needing an outlet.

"Stay here, and lock the door behind me." He needed to search the house. Perhaps the intruder was still here.

He moved toward the door, and Sage gripped his arm, her nails digging into his skin.

"Don't go," she pleaded. He growled, torn between her request and his instinct to catch the intruder. Instinct won.

"Lock the door," he repeated gruffly, and waited until he was sure she had. He then searched the house from top to bottom. There was not a square inch of the place he didn't check. No signs of forced entry, no signs of an intruder. The open front door was the only anomaly.

He returned to her room and knocked. She unlocked the bedroom door and let him back in, her expression grim. Sitting down on the bed, knees underneath her chin, she looked fragile and small. His heart squeezed in his chest.

"Sage, honey. I need you to start talking." The bed dipped under his weight as he took a seat next to her. "Was someone in here?"

She burrowed into his side. He used one hand to brush the silky hair away from her cheek, and he gently tilted her chin so he could see her. Scared wide eyes blinked up at him, rousing his protective instincts all over again. He almost growled out loud.

"I… uh, intruder. No… yes… no…" She pulled away from him and glanced down. "I don't know."

"You don't know, meaning you suspect there was someone, but you didn't see who it was?" He kept his voice calm and even, even though he was almost crazy with frustration.

She gave an almost imperceptible shake of her head, and a tear squeezed out from her eyes. His chest tightened.

"Sage, you're killing me. I need details."

Staring ahead sightlessly, she didn't answer. Ethan willed some of the tension to leave his body. At least she was not in immediate danger. Something had scared her senseless, and he'd comfort her until she was able to tell him.

"Come here." He wrapped an arm around her shoulder and pulled her close. She leaned into him, her head automatically finding the perfect fit against his chest. As if being in his arms was the most natural thing in the world. His heart swelled as he breathed in her sweet scent and ran a hand over the softness of her hair. *I am crossing the line.* Fuck the line. No one else in this town seemed to give a damn about her.

Eventually she pulled away and looked up at him, her expression a little rueful.

"Sage, honey. I really need you to start talking to me. Now." He used his detective voice. The one very few people ever argued with.

"I... I can't. Don't know how...." She shook her head. Frustration had already torn his insides to shreds. He was going to have to punch something.

Lord help whoever had put that look of terror in her eyes.

———— ♦ ————

Sage gazed at the handsome detective sitting next to her on the bed and watched him run a hand through his hair. His eyes were swirling pools of intensity. Dressed in a soft, fitted white T-shirt and khaki chinos with thin black leather bands around one muscular wrist, Ethan was attired more casually than she had seen him before, but then again, it was three-thirty a.m. She'd initially been grateful for his presence, but now her mind was filled with questions. Just how had he ended up coming to her aid?

"Why are you here?" Sage asked, as she fleetingly wondered whether it was Ethan who had slammed the door downstairs. "How did you get in? I locked the front door." She sat back, putting some distance between them. What did she really know about Detective Blade, aside from what he'd told her? He hadn't even shown her a badge.

"No, you didn't." His eyes narrowed, and his voice grew crisp. "The front door was open. I just pushed on it and walked right in."

"I checked it. Twice. I know I did."

"Sage," he said slowly, "I can only tell you what I found when I got here."

So many things didn't make sense. She was no longer sure what she knew and what she didn't. But still... there had been strange noises downstairs, and now, strangely Ethan just happened to be here.

"What were you doing here in the first place?" Feeling too exposed in her sleep short set, Sage hopped off the bed, grabbed her dressing gown and wrapped it tight around her body.

Ethan stood as well, a frown creasing between his brows, making his eyes appear even darker. "I was performing a routine drive-by when I saw the shop light flickering and thought to check it out," he said evenly. "The front door was open, and I heard odd noises upstairs. I drew my gun, came up, and found you scared out of your wits. The reason for which, I might add, you have yet to explain."

Sage released her breath, the tension easing from her shoulders. She couldn't blame any of this on Ethan. Of course he wasn't responsible for the objects on the shelf or the temperature of the room plummeting. The only question now was if she were imagining it all. But there'd been too many strange incidents for her to not start believing that something else was going on in the house. But what?

Ethan sat back down on the bed and patted the spot next to him. "Come here. I know you're afraid of something, but it shouldn't be me. I can't help if I don't know what went on here."

Reluctantly, she sat beside him. Could she tell him? He'd think she was crazy for sure. But if anyone could offer a rational explanation for any of this, it would be him.

She opened her mouth and shut it again. Where did she begin? A glance at the current room temperature readout on the fan showed a stable sixteen degrees Celsius. The shelf was once again a jumble of objects, and the door handle appeared to be in working order. What had happened wasn't logical. It wasn't even possible.

Is this what it feels like to lose your grip on reality? Her hands were shaking, so she tucked them underneath her legs to keep them still.

Ethan's gaze softened. "You're safe now. Just tell me exactly what happened, and we'll work it out from there." He raised his arm in invitation, and she slid under it as if it were the most natural thing in the world. She hated appearing weak, but she craved the sense of safety he gave her like an addict craved street drugs. What had happened tonight had shaken her to the core.

But whatever had been going on was quite obviously over now. Had she really been so terrified only moments ago?

A door slammed downstairs. In an instant, Ethan was on his feet, his gun in hand. "Stay here," he ordered.

"You're wasting your time."

"What?" Jaw clenched, muscles tensed, he looked ready to fight.

"That's been happening all night."

"I'm going to check it out." He started through the door.

"You won't find anything," Sage called out, but he had already gone.

After a few minutes he returned, his eyes narrowed and his body wound up like a coil. He let out a breath, then leaned against the door frame, arms folded across his chest, his casual posture contradicting the storm clouds brewing in his eyes.

"You have thirty seconds. Start talking."

Sage sighed. "I told you you wouldn't find anything. This house… Strange things have been happening. Things I don't know how to explain."

"Try," he said with barely restrained patience.

"The door we just heard slamming? It's been doing that all night. And the nights before this. And there are other noises too. Unexplained footsteps. Weird sounds, like a marble rolling across the floor. A drastic temperature variation in a room. Tonight, the door handle wouldn't open. I was trapped in here. Couldn't get out. If you hadn't come—" She cut herself off and shuddered.

Ethan rolled his shoulders, as if to ease the tension in them, and his expression softened to one of… sympathy? Compassion? She didn't like either option, because they both meant he thought her a fool. He stepped away from the door.

"It's an old house," he said gently. "They make strange noises. The insulation is never very good, draughts are common, and sometimes those draughts are strong enough to slam a door shut. And wood can swell, causing a door handle to become stuck."

"What about the footsteps?"

He shrugged. "Could have been a mouse scuttling down the hallway."

"Don't patronize me." How easily he discarded what she told him, even though that was exactly what she'd expected him to do. And he had given her reasonable explanations. But still…

"It was more than a draught. I saw the temperature gauge on the fan drop to three degrees in a matter of seconds. The creatures on the shelf had turned, and all their eyes were looking at me…" Her voice caught and broke.

He knelt before her and tucked a strand of hair behind her ear. Tears of frustration stung her eyes, and she blinked them away furiously. *Was* she losing her mind? The way he was looking at her almost convinced her that she was. She could hardly blame him. What she was saying sounded insane even to her own ears.

"You've had a big day." His voice was soft, his tone reasonable. "Funerals are exhausting emotionally as well as physically. I don't know how long it's been since you slept, but it's late, and being overwrought and overtired can make you see things, experience things, you wouldn't otherwise."

"You think I'm losing my mind."

He smiled. "No, honey." Strangely, the endearment didn't sound overfamiliar, but perfectly right. "I just think you need to get some sleep."

It stung that he could so easily discount everything she'd told him. She was tired and confused, but she didn't want to be treated like an overemotional female. She swallowed a rush of hurt and anger. "I'm telling you I have felt things. Unexplainable things. I've seen things that reason says shouldn't happen. But I *know* they happened, Ethan. Because they happened to me. You have to believe me."

"I believe you believe it. But grief is powerful, and it affects people in different ways. You're run-down, tired, and alone. It would be quite normal for your mind to play tricks on you in such an extreme state of emotional distress."

Her heart sank. Of course he wasn't going to believe her. What had she expected? He was a man of action. Of logic and reason. But wasn't that why she'd told him in the first place? So that he could give her some much-needed perspective? As much as it rankled her that he didn't believe what she'd said, she also desperately wanted to believe his explanations. Any other alternative was simply too terrifying to contemplate.

Ethan drew back the covers of the bed and gestured for her to get in. Shrugging off the gown, Sage slid into the bed.

"I'm sorry to have wasted your time," she said. "I *am* tired. I haven't been sleeping well at all since I've been back. Do you mind showing yourself out?"

He crouched down and picked her phone up from the floor and placed it on the bedside table. He was close enough that she could feel his body heat and smell the masculine fragrance of his soap.

Whether it was because she was wearing next to nothing and in her bed, or something else, her body instantly responded, her nipples tightening and desire streaking through her. Her cheeks heated and she glanced away. *Please God, don't let him notice.*

"Get some sleep. I'll be back tomorrow."

Sudden panic gripped her. What if it happened again? *Oh, for heaven's sake, Sage. Suck it up already.*

"I'll be in my car out front if you need me."

"Thank you. I'll be fine now, and I'll feel much better after a good night's sleep." She injected as much confidence into her voice as she could find.

"Good night, Sage."

He started to rise, and she grabbed his wrist. "Ethan?" She must have surprised him because he froze in place above her, his eyes piercing as they met hers.

"Yes?" His voice was deeper and a little rough.

"Thank you."

His dark eyes intently searched her face, and a muscle along his jaw twitched as if there was something he couldn't quite say. "You're welcome," he eventually said.

She was still gripping his wrist, but she didn't let go. Couldn't.

As she stared at him, something flared in his gaze. Could it be desire?

"I have to go. I'll check on you tomorrow." His husky tone belied his words. She didn't let go, and he didn't pull away. They were trapped in the moment, the air alive and crackling between them.

"I have to go," he repeated. But there was no conviction behind it.

Without conscious thought, Sage leaned forward and kissed him. His lips were warm and full, and heat roared throughout her body. He hesitated for the barest fraction of a second before taking over. His hand, large and strong, cupped the back of her neck, and he deepened the kiss. Her body softened, her mind blanking as she surrendered to the sensual pull of his mouth. Tangling her fingers in the silky hair at the base of his neck, she tugged him even closer. His scent flooded her nose and she let out a soft sound. With a groan, he licked deeper into her mouth.

Mother of all things holy, the man knew how to kiss! Every inch of her skin was on fire and aching for his touch. She ran her hands across his shoulders and down his chest, resenting the thin layer of fabric that kept her from the warmth of his skin. Tugging at the bottom of his T-shirt, she caressed his taut abdomen, then slid her fingers up and across the rippling muscles of his chest. The contact was electric, and she reveled in the low sound it elicited from him.

He leaned into her, his weight pushing her into the mattress, and the juncture between her thighs grew hot and demanding. He pushed up her singlet top and found her breast. When his fingers brushed over her pebbled nipple, streaks of pleasure shot through her.

"Ethan," she gasped, wanting more. Wanting all of him. Now. She tugged at his shirt, undoing the top two buttons before ripping the remainder.

He pulled back. Hands on her shoulders, he held her in place. Blood thrummed through her veins as she looked into his handsome face, flushed but set into hard lines. His breathing was as ragged as hers, and he dragged in a couple breaths before trying to speak.

"We can't," he rasped, looking as though it were the hardest thing he had ever said. Appearing almost tortured, he released her. Standing, he turned his back to her while he tucked in his ripped shirt. His hands curled into fists at his sides, and he squared his shoulders before turning back to her, his face etched with pain.

"I have to go." He meant it this time, and he left before she could say another word.

Alone, the room almost unbearably silent, Sage pulled the blankets up to her chin. Her body still tingling with the remnants of unfulfilled desire, her mind grappled to come to terms with what had happened. With what would have happened had he not changed his mind. Why had he left? Was it something she'd done?

What the hell had she been thinking? Ethan was the detective on Nan's murder case, for heaven's sake. Sage closed her eyes and waited for the wave of mortification to pass. She was the one who'd kissed him first, and although he'd responded, equally, or so she'd thought, she'd apparently been wrong.

He'd just gotten up and left. Without explanation. At the height of one of the most intensely sensual experiences she'd ever had. Sage attempted to swallow past the lump constricting her throat. Images of the way he'd looked at her, of the way he'd felt beneath her hands, of how he'd tasted, replayed through her mind. How could she have read the signals so wrong?

She officially could no longer trust her confused, tired mind. With no choice other than to heap tonight in with the list of other strange and unexplained things that had occurred, she could only pray that when she saw Ethan again, he'd also pretend that tonight had never happened.

———◆———

Ethan pressed the remote and the Land Rover sprang to life, unlocking the doors and lighting the interior.

What the hell had he been thinking? Christ, he had more self-control than that. Or so he'd thought. Control in the bedroom was something he had always been able to rely on. *She's the victim's granddaughter, for fuck's sake. On an active case.*

But he'd never been so turned on by a woman in his life. Christ almighty, he wanted to fuck Sage more than he wanted to take his next breath.

Thrusting the key into the ignition, he pressed his boot on the accelerator, giving the motor a series of harsh, unnecessary revs. The tires spun before they found traction. His erection strained painfully against his pants, not softening in the slightest. He couldn't imagine it was going to either, not while the taste of her was still on his tongue and the smell of her was still on his clothes. The way she'd ripped his shirt had threatened to shred his control. She'd be a hellcat in the sack.

"Fuck. Fuck. Fuck." He thumped his hands on the steering wheel in time with the curses. He'd never acted so unprofessionally. Damn it, he knew better.

But the fear in her eyes, her vulnerability, the feel of her bra-less, full breasts against his chest, all that sweet innocence, mixed with wild, sensuous woman… The image of her staring up him, her face flushed, her breasts bare, was now burned into his mind, and he cursed again. What was it about Sage Matthews that was making him half-crazy with both lust and a powerful need to protect her?

Hitting the brakes hard, he swerved to avoid hitting a red kangaroo in the middle of the road. The Land Rover swayed, and he corrected a little too much, almost sending the vehicle careening into a large gum tree.

That fucking kangaroo must be near on two meters high. Ethan threw the vehicle into a hard U-turn, sending out a spray of red dirt and rocks from his spinning tires.

He sounded his horn at the kangaroo to get it to move off the road. Slowly, it turned its head. When its gaze locked with Ethan's, he felt it like a jolt of electricity. The hairs on his nape stood on end, and he experienced a terrifying and unjustifiable rush of fear. It was just a kangaroo. But the damn thing had eyes that appeared strangely… *human.*

And then they weren't. The kangaroo bounced off the road, disappearing into the bush. *What the fuck?*

Its eyes had appeared somehow illuminated from within. Glowing. Intelligent.

But that was impossible. The headlights had caused the kangaroo's eyes to appear altered. That's all.

Ethan pulled into the servo and topped up his tank, not because he needed to, but to give his racing heart a chance to return to normal.

Once he felt under control again, he parked in front of Sage's shop and put the windows down. He wasn't going anywhere until morning.

Sage had him tied up in knots. He'd almost imagined seeing strange things himself tonight. He needed to get a handle on this situation. On himself.

He'd crossed a dangerous line tonight, and he couldn't afford to let it happen again. Distancing himself from her was the only hope he had of thinking clearly enough to catch the serial killer.

But how the hell was he going to stay away?

CHAPTER TEN

The bell on the door jangled downstairs, and Sage sighed. She had just
sat down with a coffee and the intention of reading some more of Nan's
diaries. After the unsettling events of last night, Sage was curious as to
what Nan had thought was going on with the house and the so-called
"darkness." Was the "darkness" similar to what Sage had experienced before
Ethan had arrived?

It was going to have to wait. Marking her page, she closed the diary and
put it on top of the wooden chest and headed downstairs. Who would be here
this early on a Sunday? Her pulse raced with the thought that it might be
Ethan.

All morning, she'd been trying not to think about him and what had almost
happened between them. Ethan was the detective assigned to Nan's case.
Anything between them would complicate and potentially compromise the
investigation. She sighed. As much as it had hurt her pride last night, in the
light of day, she knew he'd done the right thing by leaving.

Heading down the stairs, she skipped the last three steps on impulse,
landing with a bounce on the bottom like she had when she was a child.

The sound of applause startled her, and she whirled around to see a
stranger.

"Can I help you?" Sage asked. The man standing there was classically
handsome, with fashionably trimmed facial hair and striking light-blue eyes.
He looked to be in his late twenties, his dark brown hair cut short at the back
but longer on top. A tight black T-shirt stretched over his muscular chest, and
artfully tattooed biceps peeked out from the sleeves.

Walking up to her, he smiled, revealing perfect white teeth, and held out
his hand.

"How did you get in?" she asked, glancing at the front door.

"It was open. You would have to be the lovely Sage Matthews."

"Yes." Ethan had locked the door last night when he'd let himself out, and she'd rechecked it herself when she'd come down to make a cup of tea earlier. How could it be open? "And you are?"

"Please excuse my manners." He grinned again. "You surprised me, that's all. I was told you were attractive, but... damn." His easy-going charm did little to relax her.

He took her hand and squeezed it. "Mark Collins, lead investigator and founder of Debunking Reality, Paranormal Research and Investigations. Pleased to meet you."

Paranormal investigations? What the hell?

"Please, have a seat." She indicated the visitor's chair and seated herself at the other side of her desk. Mark settled his large frame into the chair. He appeared to be as tall, if not taller, than Ethan, and his knees bumped against the underside of the desk before he stretched his legs out, crossing them at the ankles.

Enthusiasm flickered in his eyes, and another smile played on his lips. "I'm so excited to be here." He ran a hand through his hair and studied her. "You appear a little surprised by my presence. I thought you'd be expecting me. I left several messages on the shop number."

Sage glanced at the answering machine, its red light blinking rapidly.

"My grandmother passed away recently, and I couldn't bring myself to listen to what I assumed to be only condolences from Nan's friends. I have my own mobile phone. It never occurred to me that someone would try to reach me through the shop."

"I'm sorry. I did hear about what happened. Such a tragedy. I didn't know your number, and the shop number was the only one I had. But never mind. I'm here now." He flashed her another smile. He'd smiled more in the few minutes he'd been here than she had seen Ethan smile in the whole time she'd known him. Mark Collins reminded her of a puppy. A long-limbed, squirming puppy that couldn't quite contain itself. His excitement made her uneasy. What did he want from her?

"I don't meant to be rude, but I still don't quite understand the reason you're here, Mr. Collins."

"Please, call me Mark."

The smile froze on her face.

Beware. Lucky. Mark.

She had purposely not given much thought to the Ouija board incident until now. A chill prickled over her skin, and she rubbed her arms. Once again, he avoided answering her question.

"Mr. Collins, I did not receive your messages, and I still have no idea why you're here or why you look as though I'm about to hand over your lottery winnings."

Neither her words nor her tone dimmed the smile on his face or the sparkle in his eyes.

Mark leaned forward and placed his elbows on the desk. "Then please accept my sincere apologies and allow me to explain."

———◆———

Ethan was parked across the road from Sage's shop waiting for Nate, who was due to arrive any moment. He'd arranged to meet here so that he could introduce Nate to Sage and bring his partner up to speed with the case. He also wanted Sage to know that she could call on Nate as well as him should the need arise.

Most importantly, having Nate directly involved would keep things between Ethan and Sage impersonal and the case on track.

The events Sage had reported last night suggested her safety might be in jeopardy. He wondered if she'd managed to sleep after he'd left. He knew he hadn't. He'd watched the shop until the sun rose. After that, he'd stopped by the hotel to change, and then headed in to the police station to chat with the local guys and see if they'd turned up anything new. They were all working overtime but no closer to solving the case.

He couldn't stop thinking about how distraught Sage had been when he'd first arrived last night. He'd replayed the conversation with her a million times. She'd said she'd heard noises, seen things. She didn't strike him as a person who was flaky or prone to overreaction. And she'd seemed convinced of what she'd experienced and had appeared appropriately distressed and confused.

Maybe someone *had* been in the building, and he just hadn't noticed or perhaps had scared the intruder away. The thought made his blood run cold.

What if he hadn't turned up in time, and the intruder had gotten to her? Sage had said the front door was locked. What if the intruder had managed to pick the lock?

After he introduced Nate, he'd check the locks and increase the security of the whole place.

His phone rang, and he groaned when he saw the number on the screen. He could send it to voicemail, but avoidance wasn't his style.

"Hi, Jen. Make it quick. I'm working."

"Ethan, don't be like that. I miss you. Do you know when you're going to be back yet?"

Ethan cringed. "You know I'm unable to answer questions like that. I'll stay for however long it takes to solve the case."

A matching black Land Rover Discovery pulled in behind Ethan's, and through his rear vision mirror, he saw Nate alight from the vehicle and stretch his long legs. Raising his hands above his head, Nate craned his neck from side to side. *Guess that shoulder really wasn't bothering him that much.*

"Are you getting close to solving it yet?" Jen asked.

Ethan gritted his teeth. "No."

Nate opened Ethan's passenger-side door and slid in. They greeted each other with silent nods and a touch of knuckles.

"How long do you think? A day or two? There's a party next Saturday, and I want you to take me. All my friends are going with their boyfriends, and I don't want to be the only one going alone."

"Then take someone else." He tried to keep the edge out of his voice.

"I don't want to take someone else. I want to take you."

"Jen, I'm on a case," Ethan repeated patiently, but felt his blood pressure rise.

At the mention of Jen's name, Nate grinned and sank back in his seat, clearly amused.

Ethan shot him a glare. How was he going to get himself out of this one? He'd met Jenny one night when he was out having a drink with Nate after work. An exotic dancer with a killer body, she'd held the whole club captive with her seductive moves and lush curves. He'd taken her home that night and they'd had a few hours of fun. He continued seeing her after that on occasional weekends, for what he'd thought was a mutual arrangement of casual sex.

Somehow, and at what point he wasn't sure, she'd started to consider them to be in a relationship. Since then, he'd been trying to extract himself from her, something he'd yet to succeed in doing. He rubbed at a sudden painful throb in his temples.

"Jen. Take someone else. Even if I wasn't away working this case, I wouldn't want to go."

"You're just a commitment-phobe who's scared of getting involved. I understand, and I know why. Which is why you're just going to have to trust me," Jenny said, her voice all sweetness.

"I am not a commitment-phobe, and I am not scared of getting involved. I simply don't want to." Nate chuckled, and Ethan thumped him on the arm, which only made him grin more. "Listen, I've told you before. I'm not your boyfriend. My job—"

"You know how understanding I am about your job," she interrupted. "I don't mind you being away, but you have to learn to call me when you're gone. Let me know that you're thinking of me. That's how relationships survive in this type of situation."

Was he talking to himself? What was the right way to get out of something that the other person was trying so hard to make work?

"I'm sorry, Jen. I don't know how I'm supposed to say this to spare your feelings. I like you; you're a nice girl. But I can't be your boyfriend."

"You're having a hard time committing, that's all. It's very common. Especially after what happened with your parents. Like I said, I understand. We just need to spend more time together, so you learn to trust me. Trust *us*."

Ethan sank back in his seat and rubbed his eyes. He was going to have to be harsh. But how could he be cruel to someone who was just so… nice?

"I'll come to you then," she said. "I have a few days off before I'm due back at work. You can work when you need to, and we can be together when you're off duty."

"No." Ethan shuddered at the thought. "Don't come here. I can't be distracted during a case. I don't work like that. We'll talk when I get back. I can tell you now though, all the talking in the world won't change the way I feel. I like you, but not in the way you want me to." He softened his tone. "You're an extremely attractive, smart woman. You can have any man you choose. You deserve someone who will treat you better than me. Someone who can be there for you."

She made soft noises, like she was crying on the other end, and Ethan shifted uncomfortably in his seat. There had to be a better way of doing this type of thing, surely.

"Look, Jen? I need to go. Take care of yourself. I'll see you around." He hung up the phone before she could say anything further. He hoped she'd gotten the message this time.

Nate smirked. "Teach you for getting involved with the entertainment."

"What's that supposed to mean?" Ethan shot a withering look at his partner. "Her profession has nothing to do with this situation. Jen is a nice girl. And smart too. She's working as an exotic dancer to finance her business degree. She wants to open her own health and fitness club," he said, surprising himself by defending her. His reluctance to get involved had nothing to do with her as a person, or what she did for work. He just didn't care for her *that way*.

"Then what's the problem?"

"You've managed to piss me off quite a lot for someone who just got here," he growled.

Nate winked, obviously enjoying how uncomfortable Ethan was. "I'm just sayin'—"

"Shut the hell up. I don't feel that way about her, and never will. I'm not wired that way."

Nate's face lost its teasing expression, and his tone turned serious. "You have a life still. Don't be afraid to live it."

Ethan fell silent. Nate was referring to his parents. His mother had been murdered while cooking the family dinner, the killer hired by someone Ethan's father, Chief Superintendent Simon Blade, had put away for life. At sixteen, Ethan had walked home from school to find his mum slumped on the kitchen tiles in a pool of blood. The smell of roasting chicken always took him back to that day. His father, consumed with loss and guilt, had committed suicide some months later.

What had happened was no secret within the force, and Jen believed it was the reason he was afraid to commit. Fear that someone could take revenge on his loved ones to get back at him. Ethan supposed that sounded reasonable. However, it had nothing to do with his feelings—or lack of them—for Jen.

Jen thought she could "fix" him, make him whole. And that was why he didn't want to be a complete arsehole to her. She really did have her heart in the right place. The trouble was his heart wasn't involved at all.

"Leave it be." Ethan said in a tone that signaled he would not discuss her any further. He changed the subject. "You're looking better than when I saw you last."

Nate looked good. Strong and well-rested. With his bandaged shoulder hidden underneath his shirt, there was no outward sign of the recent ordeal that had almost cost him his life.

"Thanks. Pity I can't say the same about you. You look as though you haven't slept in a week." When Ethan didn't reply, Nate nodded to the shop across the road. "That where the third victim was found? What does the sign say?"

"Beyond the Grave," Ethan said. He glanced over at the shop and did a double-take. There was a strange car parked out in front. When had it arrived? He must have been too involved in his conversations with Jenny and Nate to notice. Which more importantly meant that he hadn't seen who was driving.

"That the granddaughter's car?"

"No." Sage drove the white Holden Astra compact parked in back.

Damn it. He was slipping. He couldn't afford to make any more mistakes on this case; Sage's life might depend on his vigilance.

"Let's go in. I'll explain everything back at the hotel later."

————◆————

The front door opened, and Sage winced at the protesting bell. She had planned to remove it, but it only seemed to be a problem when Ethan came through the door so heavy-handed. The bell wasn't quite so strident when anyone else walked in.

"Detective Blade." Sage stood, and her pulse skipped at the sight of him. He was wearing fitted cargo pants that hugged him in just the right places with an open casual black shirt over a white T-shirt. Holster, cuffs, and other accessories hanging off his belt, he oozed masculine power and strength. Even Mark Collins's movie-star good looks couldn't give Sage the physical rush that Ethan did.

"Miss Matthews, this is my partner, Detective Senior Constable Ryder."

"You can call me Nate," Ethan's partner said, stepping forward and shaking her hand. What a striking, and formidable, team the two detectives made. She could imagine girls falling at their feet and criminals shaking in their boots. The already small shop shrunk substantially in size with three tall, handsome men inside.

Sage introduced Ethan to Mark, and the men shook hands. Mark was smiling, but Ethan's eyes were narrowed. He stood with his feet slightly apart, arms crossed over his chest, the posture making his muscles bulge. She remembered all too clearly how it had felt to have those arms wrapped around her, and her cheeks heated. She turned away.

"Did you need to speak to me, Detective?" Sage asked.

"It's okay. I can wait until he's finished," Ethan said, with a nod in Mark's direction.

Mark looked between Sage, Ethan, and Nate, and when it became obvious that the detectives weren't leaving, Mark sighed and sat back down. Sage sat as well, but Ethan and Nate remained standing. "I was just about to explain to Sage that I'm here to investigate the potential paranormal phenomenon that

65

has been reported to our organization."

"What paranormal phenomenon?" Sage asked, her mind racing. "Reported by whom? I think you have the wrong place."

"The paranormal activity was reported by Mrs. Ada Slatterley, and this is definitely the right place." Mark smiled his movie-star smile again.

Sage sat upright, her spine stiffening. "I can assure you there is no paranormal activity that needs investigating here, Mr. Collins. Mrs. Slatterley is elderly, has suffered a great loss, and sadly, I think she's starting to lose her grip on reality. I'm sorry you've wasted your time."

Mark's smile didn't dim. "I think you might be in denial, Sage. Sorry, I didn't ask. May I call you Sage?"

She nodded that he could. What did he think she was in denial about?

"According to Mrs. Slatterley, there have been unexplained, shall we say, nocturnal activities occurring in this shop. She said that your grandmother experienced a lot of activity in the lead-up to her death. She mentioned an evil presence lurking in this house, a 'darkness.' Now, I was wondering, have you experienced anything unusual since you've been here?"

Sage glanced briefly at Ethan before turning to answer Mark. "Nothing that can't be explained away."

Mark nodded as if she had confirmed his suspicions. "Right. What I suggest is that we set up some equipment and see what turns up."

Ethan's features darkened, and he glared at Mark. "No."

It was Sage's turn to glare at Ethan. He didn't get to speak for her.

"Listen, Mark," Sage began, in what she hoped was her best reasonable tone, "I've just lost my grandmother. You may not know, but my nan was murdered. The only evil presence around here is the person who killed her."

Mark reached out and touched her hand across the desk, and Ethan made a low sound in the back of his throat. She'd had enough of Mark's overfamiliarity, and she sat back, folding her hands in her lap. It struck her though that his behavior was designed more to antagonize Ethan than to flirt with her. Curious.

"Mr. Collins," Sage said, her head beginning to pound. Already prone to suffering headaches, she'd had an unusually high number since she'd returned. "I really do think you have things confused. This is a murder investigation, not a paranormal whatever it was that you said. The police are handling it."

"Collins," Ethan interjected. "Miss Matthews is correct. The murder of Celeste Matthews is an active criminal investigation. You may consider this your first and final warning to stay out of the way until it's concluded."

Not appearing offended at all, Mark turned to Sage and said smoothly, "Perhaps it would be a better idea if I came back later so we can discuss this in private."

"You won't be doing that." Ethan's words sliced through the air. "I'll repeat myself so we're clear. You will stay away from Sage, and you will not do anything that will even remotely jeopardize or interfere with this investigation."

"Is that so?" Mark said, rising out of his chair. "Or what?"

Ethan stepped forward until he was eye to eye with Mark. "Or I will arrest you. For a start." The air crackled between them; all it would need was one spark to burst into flames. Sage looked to Detective Ryder, hoping he would step in and defuse the potentially volatile situation. But he merely stood, arms folded across his chest, intently watching the exchange before him, his stance clearly meant to back up his partner.

Sage rose. She'd had enough. She would not allow Mark Collins, a relative stranger, to walk into her nan's shop and create a scene. "I have to agree with Detective Blade." Although she thought her voice sounded controlled, her hands were shaking. "Mr. Collins, I'd like you to leave."

Mark glared at Ethan for another tense moment, before finally turning to Sage, his expression softening. "Yes. Yes, of course. You're grieving, and the detective is being an arrogant ass. I'll come back tomorrow."

Ethan's right fist clenched and his shoulder tightened. He looked ready to flatten Mark, but Nate stepped forward, placing a hand firmly on his partner's chest. If glares were knives, Mark would have been sliced to ribbons by Ethan's.

Mark reached for Sage's hand and placed his card in her palm, curling her fingers around it. Just before Mark's life ended prematurely, Nate stepped in, guiding Mark firmly out of the shop.

"I'll catch you back at the hotel, Blade," Nate said as he paused by the door.

"Thanks mate, I won't be long." Ethan and Nate shared a look that Sage couldn't interpret.

Alone with Ethan, Sage slowly sank back into her chair. Her emotions felt raw and too close to the surface.

Mark's words had felt too much like a truth she was not yet ready to hear. Although she'd asked him to leave, deep down, she believed there might be something to what he'd said.

Ethan knelt down beside her and placed his hand on her shoulder. Like last time, his touch calmed her, and she absorbed his strength and comfort.

"Are you all right?" he asked.

She told him she was, but she was no longer sure. Although never experiencing anything herself, she was not a complete stranger to the supernatural.

Nan had been very spiritual, and she had done "readings" on people in this very shop. She had often talked about communicating with her spirit guides or angels, but that uniqueness had just been something Sage had known and loved about her soft-hearted nan. Not once had she heard her grandmother talk about ghosts, hauntings, or evil spirits.

Except in her diary. Perhaps Nan just hadn't talked about things like that with *her*? She'd obviously discussed them with Ada, and must have expressed enough concern that Ada had decided to call in paranormal investigators. Sage needed to find out what Ada knew about what was going here. *Why hadn't Ada told me what she was doing?* She'd certainly had the opportunity at the funeral. It would have been the polite, decent thing to do. *Oh, Sage, don't be surprised when a team of paranormal investigators arrives at your doorstep.*

Did the supernatural really co-exist with us? And if so, just how much did that realm affect the natural world? Nan had certainly believed in, and claimed to communicate with, the "light," meaning angels and spirit guides, so following that logic, she'd also believed in the existence of evil spirits, or "darkness."

So, if the strange events that were occurring in the house were to be attributed to the supernatural, was it the light or the darkness causing them? Sage had a hard time believing anything good would willingly cause such fear and terror in a person. Which would then mean...

An icy chill ran the length of her spine. Just how much power did an evil spirit have? How much could it affect the natural world? Sage had been scared—okay, she'd been terrified—but she hadn't been physically hurt. Was such a thing even possible?

A heavy, unsettling sensation took residence in her gut. Sage sensed she would be finding the answer to that out personally in the very near future.

CHAPTER ELEVEN

The crackle of the fire resounded in the eerily still night air. There was not a nocturnal animal to be found within a ten-kilometer radius. Animals were instinctual beings, after all.

"I saw her, Virgil," he said into the flames. His words slurred, but he wasn't drunk. In fact, he never drank. Not anymore. His words blended together because his tongue was too big for his mouth. That's how it felt anyway. It was harder for him to get the words out than it was for other people. That's why people thought he was dumb. But he wasn't dumb. He wasn't.

Virgil was the only one who could see he was smart. That's why Virgil came to him and nobody else.

"She's pretty," he continued, speaking into the fire. "'Bout time you gave me someone pretty. The old bag wasn't anywhere near as much fun as this one will be."

Green eyes, long blonde hair, and a slim but curvaceous body moved and swayed seductively before him. He mentally undressed her, so that she was dancing naked. He reached to touch her, and withdrew his hand, cursing sharply as he sucked on his burnt fingers. He had to remember that fire was hot.

Look but not touch. Not until Virgil told him he could.

"She looks good in black, Virgil," he said, when the burning of his fingers had turned from pain to pleasure. He shifted his position because his pants had become uncomfortably tight.

"I watched her at the funeral. She looked so good wrapped in darkness. Our color. I didn't touch her though. I didn't. I won't. Not until you tell me I can."

Virgil never told him in advance what was happening, so he did his best to tamp down his excitement and wait.

But he wasn't going to have to wait much longer.

The stars faded away. A different type of darkness was descending. His moment to act would be soon.

CHAPTER TWELVE

Ethan's phone buzzed on the bedside table. He answered it, not recognizing the mobile number on his screen. "Blade."

"Ethan? Is that you?"

Sage. He was instantly alert. "Yes, honey, it's me." *Honey? Very professional, Blade.* He glanced at the digital reading on the bedside table. 3:01 a.m.

"I'm sorry if I woke you."

"You didn't. What's wrong? Are you all right?" He'd stripped down to his underwear, about to climb into bed. He'd spent the rest of the afternoon, and most of the evening, working the case. Nate had spent the day at the station doing what he did best and getting to know the local guys, learning their strengths, and getting everyone to work together as a team.

Nate had outlined the facts of the case on a large whiteboard, with circles and lines pointing to pictures of suspects and maps with pins indicating the locations of the victims. Nate was a people person. Ethan was more of a lone wolf, and maybe that was why they made such a good team. Nate could get anyone to confide in him, and he gained intel others couldn't. Ethan acted on gut instinct, and got results. They worked well together and had earned a reputation as the top team in the department before they were secretly promoted into Taipan.

Watching his partner in action tonight, he was pleased that Nate had finally got out of hospital and was here. He was exactly the right person to pull everyone together and put them all on the same page. And what this case needed was manpower. Because what they had were questions, and what they didn't have were solid leads.

By the time they'd finished, everyone was exhausted and they'd called it a night, intending to start again at first light. Nate had caught him on the way back to his car, indicating he would meet up with him in the morning. Ethan knew he wanted to say his piece about Sage. He'd let him. Not that it would do a damn bit of good.

But right now, he had more pressing issues to worry about. "Sage? Are you okay?" She'd gone silent, the only sound her erratic intake of breath.

"Yes... No... I, I don't know." He could barely make out her faint voice in his ear.

"Which is it, yes or no?" Holding the phone against his shoulder, he slid his jeans back on and looked around for a T-shirt.

"Ethan? I think someone's here." Her voice was a scared whisper.

His heart raced as if someone had injected pure adrenaline into his system. Ethan tried to quell the sense of dread that rose up within him. He was responsible for the situation she was in.

He'd had every intention of arranging surveillance on the shop tonight in addition to getting her new locks. But every time thoughts of Sage had entered his mind, he'd pushed them aside, determined not to be distracted. But in doing so, he'd missed a vitally important detail, one that could get her killed.

He took the phone away from his ear only long enough to slip on a shirt. "What room are you in?"

"Nan's bedroom."

"If the door can be locked, I want you to lock it. If not, find something heavy to put in front of it." He stepped into his boots and grabbed his cuffs and pistol.

Sage's voice came back on. "I locked the door. It's an old lock. I'm not sure it will hold."

"Stay on the line. I'm on my way." He took the stairs two at a time. He didn't have time to wait on the lift. Luckily his hotel wasn't far from her shop. He'd be there in a few minutes.

"Ethan? I hear footsteps again. There's someone in the hallway. And I heard a voice. I couldn't make out the words. Just a deep voice. And laughter. And doors were slamming. Not just once but several times. Hurry, Ethan, I'm scared."

The phone cut out. Wheels spinning, he gunned the motor, pushing the engine to its limits. Never before had he had such a powerful driving force inside him. It felt as though he were trying to control an explosion of lava with a pitcher of water. In his mind, there was a straight line from him to her door, and to hell with anyone who got in his way.

Was the murderer in there with her? If anyone so much as laid a finger on her, he would... He would what?

To hell with his job. He'd kill them with his bare hands.

———— ◆ ————

Someone was there. *Something* was in the room with her. Sage huddled up on the bed, the covers pulled tight around her. As if that was going to help.

She'd just started to fall asleep around three a.m. when the house sprang to life. Similar things to the last few nights but more of them. Was Mark right? Could there be an evil presence in the house? From what she was discovering in the diary, Nan and Ada seemed to think so. Whatever was going on in the house was getting stronger.

There was a crash followed by other odd noises downstairs. She should go and have a look, but terror, unlike anything she had ever experienced, held her trapped, paralyzed in the bed. The Stanley knife she'd been using to cut the packing tape was on the chest of drawers. She'd taken it with her Wednesday night when she'd heard noises and gone downstairs, but now... Now she just couldn't bring herself to open the door. Why? She'd done it Wednesday, and she would have done it back in Adelaide. But tonight she couldn't, not because she was afraid of what she would see, but of what she *wouldn't* see. She'd rather come face to face with Nan's killer instead of what she imagined was on the other side of the door.

The bedside table light flickered. Oh God no. Not again. Mercifully, the light stayed on. For now. She shivered as the air in the room became cooler yet thicker somehow, like something was compressing her chest, making it harder to breathe. She couldn't check the temperature on the fan because after what had happened last night, she'd unplugged and removed it. The shelves were bare now too, since she'd thrown out every single figurine that had eyes that could turn and look at her.

Ethan would be here soon. He'd check out the downstairs noises. Her phone battery had died while she was talking to him, and she had it on the charger beside her. She was waiting for his call so she could go down and let him in.

A dark smoky mist formed in the corner of the room, but when she blinked, it was gone. Wide-eyed, she let out a whimper and started to tremble. The worst part was her internal reaction to all this. Even more than the horror of unexplained noises, doors slamming, and moving objects was the cold, dreadful *feeling* inside her. The sharp claws of terror that crawled beneath the surface of her skin. Her heart pounding a staccato rhythm in her chest, her hands and forehead clammy with sweat. And on top of it all, the shivering, as if she'd never be warm again.

She took a deep breath. *Stay calm. Ethan will be here soon.*

Something she couldn't see, but could sense, was in the corner of the room. She could *feel* its eyes on her. She pulled the bedcovers more tightly around her. *Ethan, where are you?*

Something yanked at the bedspread, snatching it onto the floor. She screamed and sprang off the bed. She put a hand over her mouth and her stomach roiled, sickened with terror. Not taking her eyes off the covers on the floor, she shuffled backward until she reached the door.

And then, she heard heavy steps walking determinedly toward her, but she didn't fear those ones. She knew the difference.

Ethan was here. Her knees almost gave way with relief.

"Sage? It's Ethan. Let me in." The power and authority of his voice entered and filled the room as though there wasn't an inch of solid wood between them.

The old-fashioned key fumbled in her fingers in her rush to unlock it. The instant the latch turned, she hurled herself at him. He pushed her behind him, shielding her with his body. Gun drawn, he assessed the room.

"Where is he?" he demanded.

"Who?" she asked from behind him.

"The intruder. Did you see him?"

"Oh. Uh... no."

He searched the room, and she released her grip on his arm. Things were different now. The instant he'd stepped into the room, the energy in the air had changed. Her heart had stopped racing with the sense that someone was there intending to do her harm.

The room became simply a... *room* again. With the prickling sensation of impending doom gone, the fear slowly drained away as if had been nothing but a bad dream.

"Did you hear anything identifiable about his voice?"

"No," she said, starting to feel uncomfortable and even a little guilty. This was the second time Ethan had come to her rescue, and she still had nothing to tell him. There wasn't an intruder—at least, not a human one. But how did she tell him that, without sounding loopy and neurotic?

"I did a brief search when I arrived. This room is safe. Stay here, while I do a more thorough check on the rest of the house."

His large body was alert and tense, veins prominently displayed on his bulging muscles. Eyes intense, jaw locked, he was in full detective mode, and despite her recent fear, she found it sexy as hell. Now that he was here, and already knowing he wasn't going to find an intruder, she couldn't help but admire his exquisite male form. What did that say about her?

However, she had some explaining to do when he came back. What was she going to tell him? Perhaps she could pretend there really had been an intruder?

Sage stayed by the door and waited. Even with Ethan here, there was no way she was going near that bed.

After what felt like an eternity, Ethan returned and holstered his weapon. He ran a hand through his hair and turned his piercing gaze on her.

"There's no one here. Sage, honey, what's going on?"

"I don't know." She fidgeted with the hem of her singlet. She was going to stick to the truth. "I don't care what you try to tell me, I know I'm not imagining things."

"You think someone was in the house?"

"No. I think something else is going on here."

He released a slow breath and rolled his shoulders, the expression on his face easing. "I can't confirm signs of forced entry because you didn't lock the front door again. I told you about that last time. Anyone could have..."

"I *did* lock the door," she interrupted. She knew she had. Just like last time. She'd checked it twice, even turned the knob and tugged on it.

"No, you didn't. I just walked straight in tonight. Again."

"I locked the door, Ethan." She raised her voice. She was not a child.

"Either someone has a key, or it's a defective lock," he said, eyeing her carefully. "I'm sorry I didn't get to it today as I'd intended. I'll replace it in the morning."

A door slammed downstairs. Ethan started forward, as if to investigate it, but she held on to him. "You won't find anything."

"There might be someone—"

She tugged on his shirt, her fingers bunching the material. "Don't you listen? There's *no one* there. There wasn't when you checked earlier, and there wasn't when you checked last night."

"Sage, you'd better start talking. You call me because you think someone is here, and now you're telling me there isn't. Which one is it?"

"It's not a person," she said softly.

"Jesus, Sage." Swallowing, she kept her eyes downcast. She couldn't look at him. Didn't want to see the look of pity that would be there.

"You can go," she said flatly. "I'm sorry to have troubled you."

"Now wait a minute. I'm not going anywhere, and you didn't trouble me."

She looked over at the bed. She was exhausted, but she wasn't going to get back in there. Ever. She had nowhere else to go though. She couldn't even book herself into the motel this late. The administration office closed at eight p.m. The air left her in a rush. It would be daylight in a few hours.

"I'll walk you out," she said, grabbing her phone and bag and heading to the door. Her limbs felt heavy in defeat. "If you wanted me gone, you've got your wish," she mumbled to... no one. "I'm leaving."

"Wait," Ethan said, reaching for her arm. "You're leaving?"

Nice work, Sherlock. "I have nowhere to go. I'm going to sit on the porch until daylight." She tried to shrug off his hand.

"But... why? There's no intruder. I'll secure the building and arrange surveillance. Hell, I'll do it myself. You'll be safe."

"You still don't get it, do you?" She whirled on him. "I'm not scared of anyone getting in. I'm scared of what's already in here."

Confusion washed across his face.

"What does it matter to you, anyway? You've done your job. Thanks for coming, but you can go."

She was venting her anger in the wrong direction, but she couldn't stop. He was the only one there. She stalked off down the hallway, and he chased after her.

"Sage! Will you... will you just stop a minute?"

Turning, she met his gaze dead on. "What?"

"I'm sorry." He ran a hand through his hair. "You don't need to sit on the porch, you'll freeze," he said, gesturing to her attire. *Okay, it would probably be a good idea to get dressed first.* She stalked back to the bedroom. He followed, but she blocked him at the door.

"I don't need you to help me get dressed," she said, attempting to close the door.

"Sage. You don't need to get dressed at all. You need sleep."

"You don't get to tell me what I need." She turned away before he could see the tears that sprang to her eyes. Damn him.

He came up behind her and placed his hands on her shoulders. "Sage, I'm not leaving. So, please sit down and tell me what you think is going on."

She spun around, and his arms fell back to his sides. His hands fisted as though he was fighting not to put them back on her shoulders, and his dark, intense eyes searched her face in concern. But not just concern; there was something else there as well. It was that something else that took the wind out of her sails, her anger dying away.

"Will you believe me if I tell you?" she said.

He sighed. "I won't know until I hear it. Talk to me, Sage." Sage eyed the bed warily. *No way.* Ethan walked over, picked up the blankets and straightened the bed, fluffing the pillows. It was a strangely familiar and intimate thing to do. He sat down on the edge and patted the spot beside him. "Come here."

She eyed the bed cautiously. The intense fear she'd felt earlier had evaporated. The bed, with Ethan sitting on it, now looked comfy and inviting. Was it really anything but?

Just like last time, Ethan's presence made everything safe and normal. She began to feel a little silly trying to hold onto her side of the argument. She didn't know what was going on here anymore than he did. But whatever it was, it wasn't going on now. She straightened her spine and sat next to him.

She released a long breath, at the same time he did. They looked at each other in surprise, then laughed. The tension between them evaporated.

"I'm sorry," she said and meant it. "I was a bitch to you just now, and you didn't deserve it." He'd rushed over when she'd called him, and she had all but abused him for it.

"I'm sorry, too," he said. "Do you want to tell me what happened tonight?"

She blinked up at him. "Do you mind if I don't?" Exhaustion was taking its toll. The terror and frustration of earlier had drained away, leaving her worn out. Her body sagged.

He put an arm around her. "Relax," he said. "You're so tense." His fingers landed on the tightness in her shoulder, and he began to knead it. She couldn't help it; her eyes closed, and she moaned. His touch did the nicest things to her.

She didn't know what was going through his mind. Didn't know what he thought of her. He probably thought he was dealing with a crazed lunatic. But he could think what he wanted as long as he kept doing that to her muscles.

As much as she had desperately wanted to tell him what she'd heard and felt, she didn't because he wouldn't believe her. Why would he? He was a man whose life revolved around facts and evidence. The more she'd try to explain, the flakier he'd think her. And for whatever reason, it had now become extremely important that he didn't think badly of her.

So she said nothing and let the peace and comfort she now felt only when she was in his arms push everything else away. Eventually, she grew tired, her body heavy, and he laid her back on the bed.

The blanket tucked under her chin, she peered up at him. "Thank you."

He was only a few inches away, so close she could feel his warm breath on her cheek. The hard lines of his face had softened, and he looked at her with tenderness.

"Sleep well, Sage." Her lids became too heavy and she let them close. Exhaustion finally had its way with her. His fingers traced across her cheek, tucking a strand of hair behind her ear. She sighed.

Last night he had kissed her, and a part of her hoped he would again. But when she peeked up through her lashes at him, she knew he wouldn't.

Tonight was about something else. She wasn't sure what, but the energy was different. The low hum of feminine awareness she felt around him was there. It always was.

But now there was something else as well.

"I feel safe when you're here," she murmured sleepily.

"You are safe," he replied, and she knew it to be true. She allowed herself to drift into a soft sleep, while Ethan watched over her.

Ethan pulled the chair over from the corner and carefully removed Sage's bag and other personal items before he sat down. He wasn't sure what was going on here, but something, or someone, was scaring her witless.

Whatever it was, she wasn't making it up. She wasn't acting, and it wasn't an elaborate ruse to get him to come over; she was genuinely scared. Dark rings shadowed her eyes. She was damn near the breaking point. Someone was going to great lengths to scare her, and he intended to find out who and why.

She looked so pretty lying on the bed like that, her blonde hair fanned across the pillow, her rosebud lips slightly parted. His heart rose in his chest and lodged somewhere in his throat. Transfixed, he watched as her eyes moved under her lids and all the tiny muscles in her face relaxed into an image of peacefulness. So soft. So perfect.

He'd wanted to kiss her so desperately, but somehow he'd resisted. Pawing at her like he had the night before was the last thing she needed right now.

"Rest now, honey," he murmured. "No one can hurt you on my watch." Her lids flickered slightly, but there was no other sign she'd heard him. He didn't know what had made him say that, but the instant the words had left his mouth, he knew them to be true to his very soul.

As he leaned back in the chair, his eyes on Sage, a strange feeling bubbled up inside him. He wasn't going anywhere. The only way anyone was going to get to her was through him. Without doubt, he would kill to protect her.

Aside from the occasional door slamming downstairs, the house was quiet. As the minutes ticked by, he wondered how he was going to explain this to Nate in a few hours. Hell, he couldn't even explain it to himself.

All he knew was there was no longer a choice.

Sage was his to protect.

Stretching his long limbs, he settled into the worn fabric of the chair, and kept silent vigil over her until the sun rose in the morning sky.

Chapter Thirteen

When Sage woke the following morning, the sun was already past the roof of the garden shed, the cloudless, brilliant blue sky holding the promise of a lovely spring day. She sat up in surprise. It must be well after ten. She couldn't remember when she'd last slept so late. Hugging the blankets to her, she remembered how they had been pulled from her last night. Had that really happened?

She glanced at the chair where Ethan had sat watching over her while she'd slept, and a rush of warmth flooded her body. She'd never met anyone like him before. She didn't know what she was to him, but she clearly wasn't just another case. The physical attraction between them aside, spending the night watching over someone while they slept was not a standard part of his job.

Something deeper was definitely building between them. But what?

She reached for her dressing gown. It was early spring and the mornings were still cool. Time to rise and finish packing the last of Nan's belongings. It would soon be time for Sage to head back to Adelaide and her old life.

Strangely, that thought no longer held the same appeal it had a few days ago. It should have filled her with excitement to be getting away from here, yet it didn't.

Sage headed downstairs and made herself a coffee. Glancing at her diamante-encrusted mobile phone on the bench reminded her of the matching one her best friend Rebecca had. She remembered the fun they'd had choosing them. Of all the designs, they'd both settled on the same one.

It was Monday, and Bec would be at work. Yesterday they would have spent the better part of the day in bed, recovering from an excess of Saturday night drinks. Often the morning after, they had lain in bed talking on the phone about the guys they'd met and danced with. Picturing Bec made Sage smile. Though she could call Bec at work for a few minutes, she couldn't bring herself to dial the number.

With everything that she'd been through since her return to Cryton—Nan's murder, the evil entity she was becoming convinced was in the house, meeting dark and serious Ethan—it now felt as though there were a lifetime of difference between her and the life she used to lead back in the city. Somehow the earth had shifted. Sage felt changed somehow, like she didn't quite fit into that same carefree but empty life she'd been living.

Cupping both hands around her coffee mug, she headed back upstairs and opened to the place in the diary she had started to read when she'd been interrupted by Mark yesterday.

Mark. What was she going to do about him? She took a sip of the coffee, feeling it warm her from the inside out. The very idea of allowing a paranormal investigator in the house was bizarre and not something she would have ever imagined herself doing. Or even needing. And there was something about him that she didn't quite trust.

And yet... Last night the "activity" in the house had escalated to a new and terrifying level. And the thought of sleeping here alone again tonight? She shuddered. She couldn't call Ethan again. No matter how safe he made her feel, in this situation, he couldn't help her.

It was time for her to step up and find out exactly what was going on in this house. Was it something paranormal? Was it the murderer, as Ethan suspected? Or was she the recipient of an elaborate practical joke? Maybe Wendy and her friends hadn't grown up all that much. They could be behind this, laughing at the freak. But the quilt getting tugged off the bed last night... How would they have staged that?

No, whatever was going on in the house had also been happening to Nan for the last five years. Sure she would find the clues she was looking for in Nan's diaries, Sage located the most recent one, and took it, the diary from when she'd left for the city, and her coffee into the bedroom she'd used when she was a child.

The room looked exactly as she'd left it, all those years ago. She flicked the switch, and light radiated onto the floral-quilted single bed pushed against the far wall. The fireplace, unused, had been boarded up years prior, and was now just a decorative mantelpiece. On the white-painted bedside table sat her beloved doll lamp. Its lace-edged calico shade sheltered the beautiful golden-haired princess whose embroidered gown made up its base. Perhaps it would be better if she slept in there tonight?

The springs made their usual protestation as she sat on the edge of the bed. She still remembered the day she'd left for the city, full of hope and excitement. Even though she'd been leaving Nan, it had been one of the most thrilling days of her life. With all the naïveté of youth, she'd always assumed her home would be the same as she'd left it, unchanged from the days of her childhood.

Though this room was the same, the essence of the house, her nan, was gone.

Sage rose and opened the closet door to find her old clothes exactly the way she'd left them. She trailed her fingers over her favorite white skirt, and its beaded cords knocked together in a musical chime. These clothes represented a long-ago time. A simpler one.

She caught her reflection in the oval mirror in the corner—tailored knee-length skirt, silk blouse, hair swept back into a bun. She looked professional, smart, but was that really her? Or was it just an image, a mask she'd invented? The reflection showed the person she'd chosen to be when she'd left Cryton. Neatly packaged and presented to the world.

Did that version of herself make her happy? She couldn't say. The only times she remembered feeling truly happy and at peace were with Nan. And on a few occasions with Ethan.

Without much conscious thought, she unzipped the skirt and let it fall to the floor. She instantly felt freer. Removing her fitted shirt, she stretched her arms, loving the lack of restrictions. In only her bra and panties, she removed the pins and clip from her bun and shook out her hair, letting it fall in soft waves around her shoulders, enjoying the feel of it against her skin.

Jumping onto the middle of her bed, Sage sat back against her pillows. Setting the most recent diary aside, Sage picked up the older one and turned to an entry dated just six weeks before she'd left. Sage remembered that time clearly; she'd just graduated and had enrolled in the only university nearby to get her business degree. Until that point, Nan had agreed with her decision. The university was a reasonable drive away, but she could take most of her courses online, and thus stay at home most of the time.

Then one morning, Sage had woken to find Nan at the kitchen table, hunched over a cup of tea. Her normally steady hand had wobbled as she took a sip, and Nan had still been in her bedclothes.

"Nan, are you okay?" Sage had asked, unable to keep the concern from her tone.

"Yes, yes, dear. Have a seat." Nan had patted the chair next to her.

When Sage was seated, Nan said that it would be a better idea for her to move to Adelaide and get some real-life experience. It would be easier for Sage to get her degree there, and she could gain some work experience at the same time.

"But what about you, Nan?" Sage asked, slightly panicked at the thought of leaving.

"I'll be fine dear. I have Ada and the girls." Sage smiled. Nan always referred to her elderly friends as if they were all still schoolgirls.

"Life is too precious," Nan continued in an atypically serious manner, "and much too short to spend it treading water. Do you want to just hang around and wait for me to die before you begin to live your life?"

Sage was taken aback. Nan rarely said anything negative. Nan was the most positive person Sage knew. She took in the rest of Nan's appearance, the stray strands of gray hair sticking up and not smoothed into her usual neat curls.

"Nan, don't say things like that."

"I have lived a full life, child. Now it's time for you to live yours. You can't live it from this little town, and I cannot enjoy what remaining years I have left knowing I'm holding you back."

"Don't be silly, Nan. You're not holding me back from anything at all. Me living my life and you living yours are not mutually exclusive."

Nan leaned in close and took Sage's hand, Nan's wrinkled skin almost translucent over the old, gnarled bones of her fingers. Liver spots dotted her hands, but to Sage they were beautiful.

"You must leave this town, Sage. Imagine a dream, then go out there and live it. Anything is possible. Everything is possible. There is nothing you cannot be. There is nothing you cannot achieve. Go. Be happy. If you don't want to do it for yourself, do it for me."

Sage wiped away a tear as she remembered that morning. No amount of pleading or discussion had changed Nan's mind. Eventually, Sage had agreed, before growing excited by the thrilling yet scary step of moving away to live alone in the "big smoke."

She'd found a job working in one of the huge high-rises in the city and rented a neat one-bedroom apartment close by. She'd been so thrilled to pick up the keys for her very own apartment and start the first day at her new job.

The trouble with goals though was that they weren't always as fulfilling as you'd thought they'd be.

When had her attitude changed? The excitement and newness of that time had faded away after the first couple years. The daily routine of getting to work on time in the peak-hour rush, the moods her boss took out on her and her colleagues, had started to wear thin. The lunches and after-work drinks with the girls she enjoyed, but soon they too had become something she did, just for something to do.

Certainly she'd believed she was enjoying it all at the time, but now, so far away and looking back, Sage couldn't find any enthusiasm for going back to her old life the way it was. Same people, same stories, same disastrous dates, same unsatisfying sex, same empty apartment. Especially now that she had kicked her cheating boyfriend to the curb.

The only trouble was she didn't have any desire to stay in Cryton either. Just where did she belong? Something had changed her, in a way that felt permanent. But what that something was, she didn't know.

Sage picked up the most recent diary and held it against her chest a moment, closing her eyes and swallowing a wave of sadness. This was the last diary her nan would ever write in. Sage turned to a random page a couple months ago, and began to read.

Friday, 4ᵗʰ July
17 deg, storm forecast later

A young boy was found dead this morning, a short way down the river from here. Murdered two nights ago, on the full moon. Ran away from home. Such a shame. Much too young to die. Ada is convinced, as I am, that his death is no coincidence. I've located Mary's diary and have begun reading it. Dear God, that poor woman.

Liquorice has stopped coming inside at all now, even in the daytime… It was busy in the shop this morning and Joyce stayed to help out. I am still having trouble sleeping.

What is the boy's death connected to? Who is Mary? And what happened to her for Nan to comment, *"Dear God, that poor woman?"* That was the trouble with diary notations; they left out so much detail.

Tuesday 21ˢᵗ July
21 deg, partly cloudy

I'm beginning to feel unwell. I am cold all the time, and the lack of sleep is taking its toll. He is continuing to grow in strength and I don't feel as though the girls and I are making much difference. I'm sleeping with the heater on. Can't think of what the bill will be like this month…

Hmm… Sage had experienced the same cold draughts, and they weren't just in Nan's room. They were all over the house and at odd times… She flicked through more pages.

Friday, 24ᵗʰ July
22 deg, warm with cold patches (ha ha!)

Time is running out. I'm being watched constantly now, and am starting to really fear him. The ceremony I performed and the crystals of protection I placed in the bedroom are helpful, but are no match for his growing power.

Mary came to me again last night, and warned me to be careful with the grimoire. He is watching. Waiting. He wants me, my energy. He's feeding off the souls of the boy and the hitchhiker, but my high light-energy will boost his evil considerably. My connection with Mary, already strong since she'd led me to her diary in the attic, has strengthened. I've always been able to communicate with those who've crossed over, but now it is somehow easier. They are around me, so vivid, so strong. The souls of the people who were murdered a hundred years ago.

And this house itself seems to have come alive. I have wondered recently, if it is the doorway to the other side. But of course, the portal is over the circle, isn't it?

Pray Sage is far enough away from all of this to be safe. So hard to pretend to smile and be happy when I am so tired. And so terribly worried. I only hope I can succeed, and spare her.

Baked a carrot cake for the girls tonight…

This entry had been written approximately four weeks before Nan's death. A harsh and icy chill settled deep in Sage's bones. She scanned the remaining pages, but found few references to what had happened after that. Where was this "grimoire" Nan referred to? And what was this about a diary in the attic, and who the heck was Mary?

Sage had to speak to Ada straight away. Her warning at Nan's funeral echoed in Sage's mind. "You need to leave now, before it's too late." She too, had mentioned the grimoire. She'd also said she'd take care of "it" as a promise to Nan. According to Nan's diary, Ada had considered the boy's death connected to what was going on, so it followed that Nan's death was connected as well. Nan clearly expressed fear over her own safety. And Sage's before that, when she'd encouraged her to leave town five years ago.

The more she thought about it, the more she was convinced that Ada could answer at least some of her mounting questions.

It made sense that if Ada thought that something supernatural was going on, she wouldn't have told the police. Or perhaps she had, and they hadn't believed her? Perhaps that was why she'd called Mark?

Sage closed the diary. As unbelievable as the diary entries would sound to the average person, Sage knew with absolute certainty that her Nan's mind had been sound. If Nan had believed there were supernatural presences in the house, then there were. It was now up to Sage to discover more about who they were and why they were there. And how they were connected to Nan's death.

The key, it seemed, was to find out exactly what was going on in the house. Was it some type of doorway as Nan had suggested? Mark had offered to set up cameras and other recording devices to gather proof. The idea, the more she pondered it, became less weird, and seemed more like the next logical step. Ada had obviously called him in for a reason. He was a paranormal investigator. If there was something paranormal going on, she should let him investigate, right?

If he did gather some sort of evidence, at least it would prove to Ethan that she really had experienced the things she'd described. He would be forced to concede that something yet to be explained was going on in this house.

There it was again. Because of her childhood, Sage had stopped letting other people's thoughts and opinions concern her. But for some reason, what Ethan thought about her mattered. A lot more than it should.

He mattered. A lot more than he should.

Realizing she was still in nothing other than her bra and panties, she went to her old closet and put on what she used to regard as her favorite outfit. The cool, flowing fabric felt beautiful against her skin. She gave a little twirl, and the bottom of the skirt flared out in a wave. It was a complete contrast to the look she'd been wearing since moving to the city. She felt pretty, carefree. Wearing this outfit again transported her back to a more simple time. With Nan. A time before there'd been a "darkness" or "evil presences" in the house.

It was time for Sage to have a little chat with Ada.

Sage needed to find Mary's diary, find the "grimoire," whatever that was, and figure out what any of this had to do with Nan's death.

But first, she needed to call Mark.

CHAPTER FOURTEEN

C are to explain what happened yesterday?"

Ethan didn't pretend to misunderstand. His partner had pounded on his door a little after ten that morning. Another night of only a couple hours of sleep. He groaned and rubbed at his temples.

"You look like shit, too," Nate continued, piercing him with a look. "Where the hell were you until six this morning?"

"Sage reported the possibility of an intruder. I checked it out."

"Was there?"

"No."

"What time was that?"

"3:01 a.m."

"Again. Where the hell were you until six this morning? It doesn't take three hours to decide it's a false alarm."

"Don't question me like a fucking suspect, Nate." Lack of sleep was certainly not helping his disposition. "I wasn't sure at the time that there hadn't been an intruder. She'd heard noises, and strange things had been happening. I heard a door slam myself. I stayed until I could be sure she was safe."

"She's off-limits."

Ethan's temper flared. Running his hands through his hair, he faced his partner. "Don't you think I fucking know that?"

Even though they were the same words he'd been repeating continually to himself, hearing his partner voice them made Ethan want to hit something.

"You so much as think about her inappropriately, and Ian will have you ripped off this case quicker than you can blink. He won't let your feelings for a girl interfere in this." Ian tended to look the other way when Ethan walked that fine line between rules and resolution. Up to a point.

More and more, Ethan was beginning to feel hemmed in by rules and procedures. And having Nate question his professionalism and ability stung.

"Come on, mate. You know damn well I won't jeopardize the case." Nate was far more than his partner and best friend. They had worked closely together on many cases; their very lives depended on the trust between them.

Nate sighed. "Shit man, I know that. But don't try telling me there's nothing at all between you and the golden goddess. The tension crackling between you two was so strong it needed a sign warning against being near a naked flame."

Ethan groaned. "Golden goddess" was apt, even if it wasn't altogether helpful. "Listen, mate, I'm doing my best to keep my distance, but she could very well be the next target. If she calls me worried that there's an intruder, I'm going to respond."

"Uh-huh." Nate looked unconvinced. "Well, I've said my piece; the rest is up to you." He shrugged and changed the subject. "We know that Ted Masters has returned to his place, but we don't know how long he'll stay there. Let's hit the road. I'll drive."

Nate jangled his keys and was already out the door before Ethan had time to protest. *Choose your battles.* With the small amount of sleep he'd had, it probably wasn't a bad idea to let Nate drive anyway. But Nate needn't think he'd get away with shit like that so easily next time.

———◆———

Later that afternoon, on the way back from interviewing Ted Masters, Ethan was once again behind the wheel, and he went a little out of the way and just happened to drive past Beyond the Grave. The interview with Masters had been brief, but it allowed them to rule him out. His alibi was airtight. His wife had been in labor at the time, hence the speeding ticket he'd received for racing to the hospital. He was present throughout the full eighteen hours of his wife's labor. They were now back to the drawing board.

"Goddamn son of a bitch," Ethan muttered, screeching to a stop directly across from Sage's shop.

Nate raised a brow questioningly, sitting up in his seat. "What is it?"

"The fucking ghost buster. I told the knob to stay away from her."

Nate's shoulders relaxed and he groaned. "Oh, come on—"

But Ethan was already out of the car and storming across the road.

———◆———

"What the fuck are you doing here?" Ethan asked, glaring at Collins.

"Chill out, mate. *She* called *me*." Collins's voice couldn't have been more smug.

"You did?" Ethan turned to Sage, knowing he hadn't kept the surprise from his voice. She'd been making drinks in the kitchen at the rear of the shop, but walked over when she'd heard Ethan and Nate come through the door.

"Hi, Ethan." She gave him a look that he felt all the way to his toes.

He almost stumbled backward when he saw her. What a vision. An angel in flowing, soft material that hugged her figure in just the right places. He loved the type of clothing he'd seen her in so far—tailored and professional. But what she was wearing today somehow fit her more perfectly. Suited her better. Fit the picture he had somehow formed in his mind of her in a flourishing garden. Her hair was down, in long, silky waves that cascaded past her shoulders. The afternoon sun caught the strands and framed her face in a golden halo.

That same sunlight also penetrated the sheer fabric of her sleeveless top, turning it transparent. Goddamn, he could see the lace detailing on her bra. Which meant Collins could too.

And there was ghost-boy, moving toward her proprietarily, taking a cup from her hand, his fingers touching hers. Ethan watched the cozy little scene stunned, and admittedly more than a little hurt.

Sage smiled at his partner. "Hi, Nate."

Nate returned her smile and greeted her with his usual effortless charm.

"Any progress on the case?" She turned those striking green eyes back in Ethan's direction.

He tried to read her expression. What was Collins doing in the shop with her? "Progress, yes. Are we any closer to solving the case? No."

Her lush mouth curved into a frown. "Then… how can I help you?"

He could feel Nate's gaze on him, brows raised in amusement. Sage's question felt like a fist to the gut. What had he been thinking, barging in here like he owned her? The moment he'd seen Collins's black BMW parked out front, instinct had kicked in and emotion had taken over, disabling the rational part of his brain. His first coherent thought had been to assure himself that she was okay, and the second had been to make sure Collins wasn't anywhere near his woman.

His woman? Holy hell. At what point had he laid claim to her? Last night? No. If he was honest, it was when he'd kissed her.

It did appear, however, that he was the only one under that impression. Why had she not told the ghost hunter where to go like she'd promised?

Ethan looked from one to the other, his gut churning. "Sage, did you really call him?" His voice cracked slightly when he asked the question, and he hoped nobody noticed.

"Yes. I, uh… After what happened last night, I thought it couldn't hurt." Sage looked directly into his eyes, as though wanting him to understand.

He didn't.

"Why?" He knew he was making a spectacle of himself, standing there, demanding she answer to him, but dammit, he needed to get his head around what was going on here.

"Mark offered to set up some cameras, to see what—if anything—turns up. If it turns out, as you suggested, that my mind is playing tricks on me, then a little investigation will confirm it."

"And if he finds anything?" *Where did that come from?* He didn't believe in that supernatural shit.

"Well, I need to know that too, don't I?" She rolled her shoulders as though easing tension, and he caught a flash of perfectly toned stomach above her skirt. "I know you think you have a reasonable explanation for everything that's been happening, but while you can explain some things, you can't explain others. Plus, I can't keep calling you at all hours of the night."

"Yes, you can. I expect you to call if you feel concerned for your safety. There's a murderer still out there. If I can't get here, I'll arrange for someone else to go to you." He ignored the look Nate was giving him.

"That's the whole point. I don't know if it is the murderer, or… or something else." Collins put a hand on her shoulder as though to comfort her. Ethan ground his teeth so hard, he could feel the enamel chipping off.

"Ethan, this whole situation is getting out of hand." Sage shrugged so that Collins's hand fell off her shoulder. "I need answers, and I don't know what else to do. Mark has offered a simple solution, and I see no harm in letting his team set up some cameras. If nothing else, we might find out where the draught is coming from to stop the doors from slamming." She attempted a small laugh, but it fell flat.

"I don't fucking believe this." Ethan cursed again under his breath. What could he say to change her mind? "So what then… he's going to be here with you, alone, all night?" Something unpleasant ground away in his gut. It shouldn't bother him if she allowed Collins to go on a ghost hunt in her house.

Except it did. A lot.

"Mark *and* his team," Sage said, as if that made the situation better.

It didn't.

Sage should be turning to him, not this jackass.

"Why are you explaining yourself to him?" Collins asked, making him a marked man, pun intended.

"Detective Blade has been very kind to me." Detective again? *Kind* to her? Had she forgotten about that kiss, about the way she'd ripped his shirt? There was no way he was mistaken about the chemistry between them. Hell, it was more than simple chemistry. Just her name set off a powerful explosion inside him.

The thought of Collins being with her, there to comfort her if she got upset… Ethan identified one of the powerful emotions tearing up his insides. Jealousy. It wasn't something he was familiar with, and he didn't like it.

But what choice did he have, except to stay out of the way? Sage wasn't his. Couldn't be his right now. His mind raced, his stomach roiled, but he was forced to concede that Sage could make any decision she chose.

Ethan closed in on Collins, leaving only a couple inches between them. "Collins, she gets so much as a scratch on her, and your life won't be worth living." Christ, now he was making threats. In front of witnesses. He was a cop, for fuck's sake.

Nate was obviously thinking the same thing, because he instantly stepped forward, placed a heavy hand on Ethan's shoulder, and pulled him back.

"What my partner meant to say, Mr. Collins, is that at this point in the investigation, Sage is very much at risk until we discover who murdered her grandmother and why. Until then, there is no guarantee the murderer won't come back."

Ethan clenched and unclenched his fists at his sides, letting Nate work his people-skills magic while Ethan tried to muster up some semblance of control.

"Even though you'll be conducting your paranormal investigation on the inside tonight, my partner and I, who are undertaking a *criminal* investigation, will be keeping a close watch on everything that goes on from the outside. Detective Blade was simply trying to warn you of the danger Sage could be in and the subsequent risk to yourself," Nate said, his tone eminently reasonable. "Or, perhaps now that you have all the facts, you may feel that you don't wish to continue with the paranormal whatsit at the moment anyway. There's always the option of coming back when the police investigation is over."

Great option. When Sage was safe and no longer here. Another prime example of why Ethan would be forever indebted to his partner.

Movie-star Mark was tall, but Nate was taller. His muscular build added to his air of "don't mess with me." Nate could do a no-nonsense, get-out-of-our-way talk in a friendly, calm tone like no one else.

Except Collins didn't seem intimidated in the slightest.

"Fine. You stay outside, and I'll be inside... with Sage," Collins said, directing his comment to Ethan.

The space between them crackled, the tension shooting up Ethan's blood pressure. Nate stepped between them, effectively blocking the direct path Ethan had at Collins.

He needed to get the hell out of there before he did something he should, but wouldn't, regret.

"I mean what I said, Collins. Not so much as a fucking scratch," Ethan growled over Nate's shoulder. With a final glare at the ghost-hunting pretty-boy, Ethan turned and headed to the door. The bell jangled loudly above his head as he flung the door open. Reaching up, he closed his hands around the offending contraption and ripped it off.

As the door slammed shut behind him, he crushed the metal into an unrecognizable ball in the palm of his hand and threw it as hard as he could down the footpath.

He caught the knowing look his partner gave him on the way back to the Land Rover.

"Not a word, Nate," he warned. "Not a fucking word."

———— ◆ ————

Sage watched Ethan leave with a heavy heart. He was angry. No, he was furious.

"What crawled up his ass and died?" Mark asked, putting his large black leather bag on her desk.

Sage bristled. "He's a cop, and he's just doing his job. You antagonizing him like that doesn't make the situation any easier. He's trying to catch the person who murdered Nan."

Mark didn't have to be so smug. Sure, she'd agreed to let him set up his cameras, but Mark made it seem as though he'd won some sort of power struggle between the two men. Had she done the right thing?

The look Ethan had given her when he'd found out she'd called Mark stayed in her mind's eye. And it had confirmed what she'd suspected. He did look at her as more than just a case. Just as she thought of him as more than just a detective. She had desperately resisted the urge to explain what she'd discovered in Nan's diaries, to make him understand. But he'd want to take them as evidence. Parting with Nan's diaries would be like parting with a piece of Nan. Unbearable. And he'd likely not believe them anyway.

Sage resigned herself to doing more of the investigating herself and relying less on Ethan.

Mark pulled his laptop out of his bag. "Yeah, well, he deserved it. I'm sick of people insulting what I do just because they're too closed-minded to believe it."

"He's a man of logic and reason," Sage found herself saying. "Finding facts and getting justice is his job. He doesn't believe in anything that can't be supported by hard evidence." If she didn't need Mark to help her find out once and for all what was going on in this house, she'd send him packing.

"Just because he doesn't believe in this, doesn't make it any less true." Mark set up his laptop on her desk. He dragged a chair around and sat in front of it, making himself right at home.

Retrieving some electronic equipment from his black case, he spread it across her desk, untangling various cords. "My team are due to arrive just at dusk. Would it be all right if I take a walk around while it's still daylight to start planning the correct placement for the infrared cameras and recording equipment?"

"That would be fine."

Mark gave her a wide, genuine smile, and she felt herself relaxing slightly. Maybe this would work out after all.

"I need you to point out the areas of the house that have been experiencing the most activity," he continued. "You mentioned something happened in a bedroom last night?"

"Yes. Nan's bedroom."

"Well then, Sage, take me to the bedroom." His eyes glinted as he held out his hand to her. He was only joking with her, trying to lighten the mood, but his words made her feel uncomfortable.

"It's this way." She ignored his outstretched hand and headed up the stairs.

"Oh, come on, Sage. Most women can't wait to get me in the bedroom."

Sage whipped her head around to find him laughing at her.

"Jeez. I'm joking," he said, holding his hands up in front of him in mock defense. "Sorry. I forgot this is not an easy time for you. You're a bit highly strung for my poor sense of humor. I'll tone it down."

And like the actor, or performer, he surely was, he schooled his expression into one of morose seriousness, and despite herself, she laughed.

"There. That's better. You have a beautiful smile," he said with a grin. "Stop worrying so much, and leave what happens tonight to me. Investigating paranormal activity is something my team and I have done lots of times. It will work out fine, you'll see."

She hoped he was right, but if the notations in Nan's diaries and what had happened last night were any indication, the paranormal activity in the house wasn't your usual garden-variety type. As far as she could tell, the entities in the house were evil, menacing, and, Lord help them all, seemed to be getting stronger by the hour.

CHAPTER FIFTEEN

After Mark had left that afternoon, Sage had walked to Ada's house, determined to find out everything she knew. Only Ada hadn't been at home, so Sage had left a note taped to her front door asking her to call or come into the shop as soon as she could.

During the walk back, Sage worried about Ada, and hoped she was all right. It was so strange that Ada hadn't made more of an attempt to seek her out. Especially since Ada had almost been like a second mother to Sage while she was growing up. Not to mention that she had information about what was going on that she wasn't sharing. Why?

She kicked at a stone on the path. Perhaps Ada had gone to spend some time with her eldest son in Murraytown? If Ada didn't get back to her today, she'd see if she could locate her son's number in Nan's diary and call him tomorrow. In the meantime, she'd do what she could to locate Mary's diary and the grimoire.

The sun was setting, brilliant orange and red streaks behind dark gray clouds. Sage struggled with a strong sense of foreboding. Had she made the right decision, allowing Mark and his team to monitor the house?

As the shop came into view, Sage looked for Ethan's black Land Rover, but the space he liked to park in across the street was empty. She swallowed a stab of disappointment.

She hadn't seen Ethan since he'd stormed out of the shop earlier. She was sure she didn't have anything to feel bad about, but she still felt guilty about bringing Mark in tonight, almost as if she were being... unfaithful? She had to laugh. Did she imagine herself in a relationship with Ethan, after one unrepeated kiss? Never mind all the creepy things that were going on, that was the thought that confirmed it. She was officially certifiable.

She unlocked the front door of the shop and glanced at the time. Mark's crew would be there any minute.

As if on cue, a large black van with "Debunking Reality (Paranormal Research and Investigations)" emblazoned down one side pulled up and parked out front.

Sage walked to the front door to welcome Mark's team. Ethan might not approve, but she'd done the right thing.

Tonight, she'd finally get some answers.

———————◆———————

Ethan needed to stop thinking about Sage and that ghost-hunting idiot and focus on the case. He was kicking around his hotel room after another seemingly wasted afternoon, following up leads that had brought them no closer to discovering the serial killer. Nate was at the desk in the corner, on the phone to Ian.

With the Ted Masters lead amounting to nothing, it was time to go back to the drawing board. There had to be something he was missing. He still hadn't figured out a connection between the victims. And until he had one, he couldn't even begin to predict who would be the next victim. The only sure thing about this case was that they were dealing with a serial killer, which meant it was only a matter of time before he struck again.

The other thing he still hadn't worked out was why he and Nate had been brought in from the Taipan unit. This business belonged to the homicide squad. Special Ops were normally reserved for infiltrating major crime syndicates, terrorist organizations, high-profile kidnappings, cases like that. So why had Taipan been assigned to this case?

There must be something beneath the surface here, something that he didn't see yet. When he'd consulted Ian again, he'd received another uncharacteristically cryptic message. *I can't tell you anything more than this. Dig deeper. Think outside the box.* What was Ian hinting at? What couldn't he talk about?

Could it possibly have something to do with the strange things Sage had experienced? Ethan thumped his hand on his makeshift desk, earning him a glare from his partner across the room. Despite his resolve to put Sage out of his mind, like a magnet, his thoughts were continually pulled back to her.

Unless… maybe he *shouldn't* stop thinking about her? Perhaps she was the key? Something about Sage pricked his instincts. Something that had nothing to do with his inconvenient attraction to her. Every time he walked into that shop, the hair on the back of his neck stood on end. Why?

Instinct. It had never before let him down. The problem was, it was no longer pure. Because of his feelings toward Sage, he was now second-guessing every instinct he had regarding her situation. He was looking for proof to back up his hunches, and he never did that. He'd always operated on sheer gut instinct. But with her… With her, he kept worrying that he was being overprotective or emotional. Geez. Emotional. He didn't get emotional when he worked a case. Hell, before this, he wasn't sure he even *could* get emotional.

And then there was Collins, who was all too quick to come up with an alternative reason for the string of strange occurrences. Ethan didn't know how yet, but what was going on in the shop was related to the murders. It had to be.

He turned back to his laptop and fired an email off to Zach, requesting everything he could dig up on Mark Collins and his team. Ethan had tried yesterday to contact Ada Slatterley so he could verify Collins's claim that she'd called him in. Could Collins and his team be the source of the so-called "paranormal events" Sage had been experiencing?

Leaning back in his chair, Ethan tapped his pencil on the still-blank page of his notebook, little dots and dashes forming each time the lead connected with the paper.

"Ian is turning up the heat," Nate said, tossing his phone onto the desk. It landed loudly and skidded to a stop just before falling off the table. Even Nate was becoming frustrated with their lack of progress. "He can't keep the media away for much longer. For some reason, he doesn't want them involved."

That was strange. Media was a tool to be used when they didn't have much to go on. It was surprising the amount of information they could glean from the public. "Why not? We need more leads. Maybe someone other than the bus driver saw the boy come into town."

Nate shook his head. "He was adamant. He said to dig deeper."

"Dig deeper? Is that *all* he has to say?"

"Seems like it." Nate shrugged.

"Did he say why Taipan was assigned to this?" Ethan asked.

"No." Nate sighed and crossed his arms. "In a nutshell, Ian said we have to turn something up in the next twenty-four to forty-eight hours, or the shit is going to hit the fan."

"Mm-hmm." Ethan's pen tapped on his notebook. *Dig deeper.*

"So hit me with it. I know something's on your mind. You have that look in your eye. The one when you get one of your instinct hits."

Instinct hit. Nate had coined the term not long after they'd begun working together, all those years ago, and it had stuck. "Thoughts?" Nate prompted.

Dig deeper? Okay then. Ethan held up a hand while he shot off a second note to Zach requesting he dig up everything he could about the history of Cryton. Old newspaper stories, everything he could find as far back as he could go.

He turned to Nate. "I've asked Zach for two things: more information on this town, and whatever he can turn up on Collins and his team of kooks."

"Oh, come on, mate..." Nate slumped back in his chair and rubbed his eyes.

"Hear me out. This hasn't got anything to do with Sage."

"Yeah, right," Nate muttered. "I hoped you were onto something."

"I might be. Someone is hell-bent on terrifying Sage for some reason, and it may be the lead we're looking for."

Nate sat back up, giving him his attention again.

Perhaps Ethan might have seen this angle earlier on, had he not been constantly telling himself to stay away from her.

"Twice now, Sage has reported the possibility of an intruder, and despite her being sure she'd locked the shop door, it was open both times when I arrived. Even though I didn't find anyone on the premises, there could have an intruder as she claimed. Perhaps someone with a key? We don't know who her grandmother gave keys to."

"Did you find any evidence of an intruder while you were there?"

"Nothing other than Sage's testimony, which included hearing doors slamming, footsteps in the hall, and voices." He'd heard the doors slamming too. With every word he spoke, his concern grew. He'd so easily dismissed her claims, and maybe that had been a mistake.

"Was anything stolen?"

"Not that she reported. Maybe she's being harassed by someone from the town, maybe she has a stalker who followed her here, or maybe the killer is playing games with her."

"Fuck. Why the hell didn't you put any of this in the report we just emailed off to Ian? We would have been able to at least tell him something."

Ethan rubbed at a painful throbbing along his temples. "Well, there's a little more to it than that. Some of the things she reported didn't fit in with the usual break and enter."

"Such as?"

"She claimed the temperature in a room plummeted to three degrees and that the door to that room locked by itself. She also said that doors slammed without help of wind or draught, and..." Ethan groaned and sat back in his chair, knowing how this was going to sound. "She claimed to see glowing eyes on a gargoyle, and at one point all the figurines on a shelf had turned and were looking at her..." He let his voice trail off. Why had he even mentioned it?

"She sounds a bit touched. Or perhaps she just wants attention."

"You see, that's the rub. She seems perfectly sane, and I can tell when someone's lying. She wasn't. It's just that... well, it can't possibly be true. But something about it is bugging me."

Nate looked thoughtful for a moment. "And then, as if by pure coincidence, Collins appears on her doorstep offering his assistance."

"Precisely!" Ethan said, relieved he and his partner were back on the same page.

"You want to sit surveillance on the shop again, don't you?" Nate asked, and they both reached for their belts and strapped on their holsters.

"You got a better idea?"

Mark walked into the shop, his finely honed body encased in denim jeans, a leather belt, and a tight black T-shirt with the Debunking Reality, PRI logo blazoned across the chest. His team followed close behind, loaded down with bulky equipment. Before Sage could say anything, Mark stopped them. "Careful with your stuff, guys. The items in the boxes belonged to Sage's grandmother and have sentimental value."

The three team members mumbled their acknowledgement and drew their equipment in closer as they weaved through the path of boxes to where Sage waited.

Smiling broadly, Mark placed his camera on her desk, and grabbing her shoulders, leaned in to kiss her cheek. Something inside her softened toward him. The man had no shortage of charm, that was for sure.

"Everyone, this vision before you is the lovely Sage Matthews."

His muscles flexing underneath his tight T-shirt with every movement, Mark indicated the man next to him. Although Mark didn't give her the rush that Ethan did, she was female, and Mark had a body that was hard not to appreciate.

"Sage, this is Joe Clarke, co-founder of our paranormal research and investigation show, *Debunking Reality*. He's our technical and electronics whiz." Joe gave her a small smile and placed some equipment on her desk so he could shake her hand. He had light brown hair and was a little younger and a couple inches shorter than Mark.

"Joe has a degree in computer science and has created the very software we use to analyze the footage we capture." Mark paused while he peered at Joe like a proud father. "Paranormal investigators around the world are lining up to buy his software. The sales from it help fund our investigations."

"Nice to meet you, Joe." Sage smiled.

"You too," Joe replied, then went straight to work. Serious guy.

Mark turned to the other man on the team. "This is Ryan Donovan, our main cameraman." Ryan stepped forward to shake her hand and gave her a broad grin as he eyed her up and down, his large hand dwarfing hers. Definitely friendlier than Joe, and maybe more of a flirt than Mark, though he kept any comments to himself. Ryan was about the same height as Mark, but even more solidly built. Clearly he spent a considerable amount of time in the gym.

Once Ryan stepped away, Mark motioned the final member of the team forward. "And last but definitely not least, is Pia Williams. She's our expert on thermal imaging. That thing around her neck is a Flir thermal camera." Pia was short and petite, with strikingly beautiful features and long, straight red hair. She wore her foundation light, her lipstick dark red, and her eyeliner artfully flicked up on the edge of her eyes.

Pia stepped forward and touched Sage's hand. She didn't release it immediately; instead, she held it for a moment too long. Her quietly confident manner made her seem as though she were privy to secrets that most people weren't.

"Good to meet you Sage," she said, raising her eyes to a space just above Sage's head.

"Pia is also a psychic medium," Mark continued, "which is helpful if we come across an intelligent sprit who wishes to communicate."

"Wow," Sage said, immediately fascinated by Pia and her compellingly knowing eyes. "Nan could do that too."

"I know," Pia said, looking at Mark.

"You may get an opportunity to watch Pia in action yourself tonight," Mark said evenly, but Sage did not miss the silent exchange as they held each other's gaze a moment too long. A ripple of unease rolled through her. What weren't they mentioning?

"We don't normally let clients tag along during our investigations," Joe grumbled.

"Thank you, Joe," Mark said. "Although he might have been a little more tactful, what he said is nevertheless true. We don't normally allow clients to accompany us. Aside from the public-liability issues..." He paused for effect. "Only kidding. We mostly never lose clients to other dimensions now."

Sage forced a laugh, only because it was polite, but it came out sounding uneasy. "So why did you want me here tonight? If I remember, it was your suggestion, not mine."

Again that silent exchange between Mark and Pia.

"Pia said this case is a little... unusual. And as such your presence would be beneficial. Whatever Pia wants—" He smiled broadly, but Sage recognized it for the show-business mask it surely was. It appeared that for Mark, acting came as naturally as breathing.

"Unusual how?"

"No need to worry, Sage. It's going to be fun. Just think, you're getting a rare opportunity to see how professional paranormal researchers conduct their investigations. Think of it as a free behind-the-scenes episode of *Debunking Reality*." He paused and rubbed his hands together. "Well, that concludes the introductions. Do you have any questions?"

Sage didn't miss how he'd carefully evaded the one question she'd already asked, but she let it go for now.

"Nice to meet you all," Sage said, deliberately pushing her unease aside. The group before her, holding what appeared to be expensive equipment, looked very professional. Not that she'd really known what to expect, or that she'd even given it too much thought.

Strangely, she hadn't done any research on Mark's organization before she'd agreed to let them come. Other than knowing that Mark had a television series called *Debunking Reality*, which was developing quite a following, she didn't know much at all. An internet search to qualify their credentials should have been her first move before inviting them into her grandmother's home. She wouldn't have hired a hairdresser or booked a party without doing a little checking, and yet here she was letting these people in without a second thought. And she still hadn't heard a peep from Ada to even verify that she'd called Mark in.

Thank goodness his team weren't long-haired, drug-smoking hippies banging gongs and waving incense. To each his own and all that, but it was far more reassuring that they appeared to be folks who would look at home in any corporate organization. Sage hadn't had a chance to watch an episode of *Debunking Reality*, and before she'd come back to Cryton, a ghost-hunting show would have been near the bottom of her list of preferred viewing options.

She just had to hope these folks knew what they were doing.

"Why did you call your show *Debunking Reality*?" she asked. "Shouldn't it be *Debunking Ghosts* or the paranormal or something?"

Mark gave her an intense look. "No, Sage. I mean it exactly as it sounds. I already *know* the paranormal exists. I'm debunking reality. Reality as it is commonly perceived by the ignorant."

Again, the easy smile made its way to his face to take the sting from his words. And again, a tremor of unease rolled through her.

"Relax," Mark said, touching her on the arm. "It truly will be fun. You'll see."

He picked up the camera he'd set down on her desk. "If it's okay with you, we'd like to have a look around and start positioning our equipment and getting it ready for this evening."

"Of course. Please, make yourselves at home."

As they opened bags and took out various electronic devices and cameras, Sage dreaded what they were going to discover tonight. If there was an evil entity in the house, what danger did it pose? And could it really have had something to do with Nan's death?

Long cords attached to cameras slithered across Nan's floor like snakes. Monitors and various other pieces of equipment were being plugged in, making the shop resemble a movie set. Friendly banter between Mark and his team bounced between them and off the walls.

Her head began to pound, and finding herself unable to watch, Sage headed outside and sat on the chair. She picked up Liquorice's blanket and hugged it to her chest. She plucked a blood-red flower from Nan's now-thriving geraniums and inhaled its fragrance. Taking a series of deep breaths, she tried to slow her racing heart.

What was that expression? Oh yes: It's too late to close the stable door once the horse has bolted.

How big a mistake had she made, allowing Mark and his team here?

CHAPTER SIXTEEN

The light on the camera glowed red, indicating that it was recording. Mark was speaking into the lens, and even without looking through the viewfinder that Ryan was holding, Sage knew that the camera loved Mark. He was a natural, exuding that rare mix of star quality and charisma required to captivate an audience.

Mark raised up a piece of equipment. "What I'm holding is a POV camera, which is a full-spectrum camera. It sees in ultraviolet light and infrared. This allows us to cover the entire electromagnetic spectrum."

He glanced in her direction and gave her a wink. She smiled in return. All night he had been fun like that. Including her, and making her feel as though she was special. He'd been right by her side for the last few hours, explaining what all the equipment did and what everything was called. The sense of trepidation she'd felt earlier had completely disappeared.

A strange noise came from one of the pieces of equipment and Mark picked it up. He made a show of looking at his watch. "Time, one forty-five a.m. The EMF detector has just picked up a change in the electromagnetic field."

So far, things had been relatively quiet, and Sage had begun to relax. If she didn't think about what had happened to bring them here in the first place, she would even believe she was having fun. They had been in "lock down" since earlier this evening, turning off the lights and shutting off all unnecessary electrical devices, including mobile phones and laptops. With the easy banter between the team members, she could almost pretend she was hosting the slumber party she'd never had while growing up.

"Careful, Sage. Don't trip over these cables just here," Mark said, taking her arm and guiding her past the spot he was referring to. They were navigating their way around through the viewfinder of the night-vision camera. At one point Mark shut the camera off to show the unseen audience how dark it was. Surprisingly, they were able to see quite clearly through the green haze of the camera's night vision.

Numbers flashed on the screen of the little machine Mark was holding.

"What's the reading?" Ryan asked, coming over. "4... no, 5... no, 5.5." Ryan let out a low whistle and put his digital camera back to his face to capture the reading.

"Is there someone here with us?" Mark called out to the room. "Will you allow us to talk with you?" He then turned to Ryan's camera, explaining to an unseen audience, "An EMF meter detects the level of electromagnetic frequency. A reading within the 3-7 range could indicate the presence of paranormal energy. At 5.5, we're at the high end of that reading."

"How do you know the reading isn't coming from manmade sources of electricity?" Sage asked.

"The beautiful lady poses a very good question," Mark said theatrically. "We will indeed go through all the data captured and rule out any possible manmade causes, but during an investigation, a high EMF reading is a powerful tool to assist us to detect a paranormal presence because natural sources of electromagnetic energy behave differently than manmade ones. This particular meter has a temperature sensor as well, and when both the EMF reading and the temperature rise and fall in unusual ways, it often indicates evidence of a paranormal presence. We have means of eliminating false readings due to outside interference, such as mobile phones, which can make false hits on the meter when they call nearby towers." He turned from the camera to Sage. "You can watch us do our testing tomorrow if you wish."

Sage was fascinated. Who knew ghost-hunting was such a serious science?

"Whatever entity is here with us, make a noise to let us know you can hear us," Mark said to the room.

Sage trembled, but she didn't feel unsafe. It was hard to feel too scared when she had three large, confident, capable men and an experienced psychic medium in the same room with her.

"Joe, you getting anything on any of the static-vision cameras?" Mark asked.

Joe was sitting at Sage's desk, six monitors spread out before him.

"Not yet," Joe replied. Through night-vision goggles, Sage could see Joe hunched over, intently monitoring all the screens, making the occasional adjustment via his keyboard.

"We quite often capture things you can't see with your naked eye, but that can clearly be seen when we analyze the footage later," Mark explained to Sage over his shoulder.

"Do you see that?" Ryan spun his handheld camera to the far corner of the room.

"Yes," Mark whispered. Sage saw it too through her night-vision goggles. It was a shadow that appeared as a floating, mist-like form.

"Orbs and other light anomalies can often be inconclusive or explained away as things like dust particles on a camera lens or a distant car headlight through a crack of a blind, but dark shadows in darkness not so easily," Mark said to her, his voice hushed. "Darkness is simply a lack of light. You don't turn on a darkness switch when you enter a room, instead you turn off the light source. So when it's already dark, and we catch a shadow without a light source, it's exciting."

Sage wasn't sure how excited she was, but could understand why Mark was. Capturing anomalies like that was what he was here for.

The shadow moved up and to the left before disappearing. "Does that prove something supernatural is going on here?" Sage whispered. The hairs on the back of her neck were standing on end, and Mark reached for her hand.

"We haven't proven anything yet, but I'd stake my career on the fact you have something paranormal going on." His excitement wasn't contagious, at least not to Sage.

In the hand that wasn't holding hers, Mark held the EMF scanner, which was still fluctuating, but giving consistently high readings. A cold breeze whooshed past them. Or did it pass *through* them? More than a draught, the icy sensation running through her body set her pulse racing and her heart pounding. The sudden flood of adrenaline made her want to flee the room. She clung to Mark's hand, unable to stop her nails from digging into his skin. "Temperature's dropping," Ryan called out.

"If there is someone in the room with us, make a sound. Let us know you're here."

BANG!

They all jumped. Sage almost climbed up Mark's side. The noise sounded like it had come from upstairs. None of the team were currently up there, and because Sage had explained the issue with the doors slamming, they had all been deliberately closed tight.

"Thank you," Mark spoke into the darkness. "Can you do it again?"

Another noise. This one was different, more like a low scraping sound.

"Looks like we're dealing with an intelligent spirit," Mark said.

"Intelligent?" Sage's voice was an octave higher than normal.

"I mean that it's able to communicate with us. It can understand what we're saying and can respond. Sometimes all we find is residual energy. A sudden death, for example, can leave an energy imprint."

Could the spirit be her nan? "Can we find out who it is?"

"Pia, have you been able to tune in to this entity? Can you sense what it is? Male or female? Child or adult?"

Pia, who had joined in with the good-natured banter earlier, easily holding her own with the men, had been silent for a while now. "This is different than anything we've encountered before." Her voice was deadly serious.

"Do you think it's a negative entity?" Mark asked, still walking around the room with his meter.

"Yes. But Mark, it's bigger than that."

"How so?"

"I'm trying to get a read on it..."

Just then the shadow-detector light went on in the back room, making a short, high-pitched beeping.

"I just saw a ball of light float from left to right," Ryan whispered urgently.

"Did you get it on film?" Mark asked.

"Yes."

"We often capture electronic voice phenomena, or EVP, at the same time an orb appears as an answer to a direct question we've asked," Mark said. "We can also pick up the energy hit on the EMF detector."

"Wow." Sage was impressed. The whole thing almost seemed less frightening when explained in such a scientific way.

"Mark?" Pia called out, her voice wavering. "I don't like this. I'm not sure I want to continue." She paused. "I'm scared."

"You've been scared before, Pia," Mark said reassuringly. "Stop trying to connect, and just take five."

"No, Mark," Pia said. "I'm not just scared. My skin is crawling with a feeling of absolute dread. Like the dark angel of death has risen and is in here with us."

Oh crap. Sage didn't like the sound of that. Now that someone else had experienced it, Sage knew that it hadn't been in her head. It was real. And it was here with them.

"Mark, we just picked up an anomaly on the hallway camera," Joe said.

Sage's heart was pounding, her breath coming in ragged pants. Something really bad was going to happen, even with the team surrounding her. She *knew* it. She could feel it.

Mark gave her a reassuring squeeze. "Stay by me. You'll be fine," he said, but it didn't ease her tension.

"Can you say something? Can you tell us who you are?" Mark said to the room.

"The camera's battery just died," Ryan called out. "I'm swapping over to a fresh one."

"Thought you made sure everything was fully charged before we began?" Mark said.

"I did."

"Are you using our battery energy?" Mark called out to the room.

No one moved, waiting for a response. "Can you tell us your name?"

A voice, low and unintelligible, seemed to come from the ceiling. Sage gasped. She'd heard that voice before.

"It's okay, Sage." Ryan tried to reassure her. Wide-eyed, she clung to Mark like her life depended on it. And judging by the sinking feeling inside her, she needed a life raft.

"We can hear you," Mark said. "Can you say something again?"

Silence for a heartbeat, maybe two.

Then the voice again. It came as a low chilling vibration that seemed to float above them, rather than travel like sound normally would, making it hard to understand.

"I can't make it out. We'll have to replay it during analysis," Ryan said.

"We've engaged it. I don't want to waste this opportunity. Let's get something irrefutable on tape."

"I'm on it," Ryan said.

They slowly edged their way through the shop, the store room, the kitchen area, the outside laundry, every now and then calling out to encourage a response.

When they got no further response, Sage's pulse settled to somewhat normal. Whatever—or whoever—it was trying to communicate with them seemed to have disappeared.

"So, what do you think it was?" Sage asked when they were back in the front part of the shop again.

"Pia? Any hits on who this is yet?" Mark asked.

Pia had taken a seat at the table near Joe. She didn't respond. "Pia? Are you okay?" Mark said.

Pia looked up, then rubbed a hand across her eyes. "I've got a splitting headache. It's interfering with my ability to sense things tonight. I'm sorry."

"Do you want to stop?"

Yes, Sage wanted her to say. "No, I'm all right. Keep trying to engage it. Stir up something for Ryan to catch. I'll rest for a bit, then I'll try again to get a read on it."

"Update time." Mark signaled for Ryan to focus the camera on him. He pressed a button on his watch, which caused it to glow.

"Time is 2:10 a.m. So far, we've had EVP, electronic voice phenomena, in the form of a disembodied voice. We've also had an orb, an unexplained dark shadow, and the sounds of doors closing, all around the time we were experiencing a high reading on our EMF scanner."

Mark held up his hand, signaling Ryan to pause taping. "What do you say we set up the EM pump?" From Mark's explanation of the equipment earlier, Sage knew that an EM pump was an electromagnetic pump used to generate energy that supernatural entities could draw on to create EVPs or even to allow the spirit to manifest.

A chill ran the length of her back, and she fought a wave of nausea. She'd had a taste of what this entity was capable of, and she didn't want to give it any extra power.

"I'll get it," Ryan said, moving to the equipment set out on the desk.

"Are you sure that's wise?" Sage wrung her hands together.

Mark turned to her, reaching out to run his hand soothingly through her hair. It was too dark see him smile, but she imagined he was. "Don't worry, babe. I won't let anything happen to you."

"Can you give it just a teeny jolt of power? Not full wattage?" Sage asked, and Mark chuckled.

"Let's set it up at the base of the stairs," Mark said, "and we'll head back up to Celeste's room. Okay, Ryan. Fire it up."

The energy in the room changed the instant he flicked the switch. Sage staggered slightly, and Mark caught her hand to steady her.

"What the fuck?" Ryan whispered loudly from behind them. "Something just pushed me! I swear to God I felt a hand shove my left shoulder."

"Keep filming!" Mark said to Ryan. "Do you see?" Mark called out to the room. "You can use the energy generated from the EM pump to help speak to us. Even manifest if you can." Ryan followed Mark with the camera as he moved about the room.

Sage's skin prickled, and her chest tightened as though the oxygen in the room were being depleted somehow. She started to shake, goose bumps breaking out over her body. Mark rubbed his arms, letting her know he felt it too.

"Come on," Mark demanded. "Show yourself. You're all big and tough when you're scaring Sage all on her own. Now is your chance to come forth and show us who you are. Use me, use all of our energy, to manifest. Come forward and show the world what you are and prove what we already know. That there is life after death."

"Temperature in the room dropping," Joe called out. "Eighteen, twelve, ten, seven, five..." Sage shivered, and a foul odor, like rotting flesh, filled the room. Ryan swore and Mark coughed.

"We know you're here with us. Why don't you try talking to us? Tell us your name, or touch us. Show us you're here."

The temperature in the room had turned bitterly cold, and Sage unhooked her hand from Mark's and hugged it around her middle. She clamped her teeth together to keep them from chattering.

"Fuuuuuuuk!" Ryan said, jumping to the side. "Something just touched me on the leg. It's burning."

Mark turned his small flashlight on Ryan's lower leg. He had lifted up his jeans, and they saw three scratches appear, then darken with blood. Mark and Ryan locked gazes.

"What is that?" Sage asked through a constricted throat. "Is that a scratch? How did that happen?"

"It's a claw mark," Ryan said, his face pinched in pain.

A claw mark? Sage's pulse was skittering all over the place, and her skin was clammy despite the cold air in the room. What the hell was in there with them?

"A series of three scratches is a sign of a demonic entity, the three thought to mock the holy trinity," Mark explained, shining the torch on the angry red marks on Ryan's leg.

Sage's mouth completely dried.

"Do you want us to leave?" Mark called out again. "Make another sound if you want us to leave."

A loud bang resounded in the room.

"LEAVE. US." The words, deep and muffled, but clear enough to understand, hung in the room.

There was a collective gasp from the team.

"We would have captured that on the voice recorders," Mark said, his voice brimming with excitement. "Can you say something else?" he called out to the room. "What did you mean when you said, 'leave us'? Who do you want to leave? Me? Ryan, Joe or Pia? Or do you want us all to leave and be alone with Sage? "

They all held their breath, Sage until she almost passed out. But there was only silence. She didn't know what she'd do if the thing said it wanted to be left alone with her.

"Who are you? Tell us your name."

Ryan cursed viciously, flicking his right hand as though it had been burned.

"What is it?" Mark turned the flashlight onto Ryan, grabbing his hand to hold it still.

In the center of his right palm, there was an angry red mark.

"What did you touch?" Mark asked, grabbing the camera from him so he could continue filming.

"Nothing. It just started to burn like hell."

As Mark continued his commentary, focusing the camera to get a clear shot of Ryan's palm, a pattern began to form. It was a type of... flower? A circle, with three curling lines radiating from it in equal thirds.

"Damn, it stings like the devil," Ryan said, sucking air through gritted teeth.

"Run it under water," Sage said. "It's the best thing for burns."

"Wait," Mark said, eying it intently. "It is a symbol. A six rotated three equal times. Six, six, six."

Ryan and Mark locked gazes. "It was in response to our question."

Mark nodded. "Yes. We asked who it was. We asked it to tell us its name."

"Six, six, six. The devil's number."

"Satan," Mark confirmed.

Icy fear raked Sage's body and froze her heart even as the room temperature swiftly returned to normal.

"It feels as though whatever was here with us just left," Mark said, taking in the room.

"There isn't the same heaviness in the air now," Ryan said. "And my hand doesn't hurt anymore." He held his palm up to the flashlight again. The mark had completely faded away to nothing. The room felt normal, the smell had gone. It was almost as if the whole incident had been in their imaginations.

"Two of the static night-vision cameras upstairs have caught something. The hallway and Celeste's room," Joe called out.

"We're heading upstairs now. Is that where you want us to go? Are you trying to get us to go upstairs? Will you talk to us up there?"

Mark moved toward the stairs, while terror kept Sage's feet fixed in place. Whatever had been down here with them was now up there. *Six, six, six.* The answer to the question of who was in the room with them, who had left the claw mark on Ryan's leg.

If Mark thought she was going to waltz up to where Satan himself was likely waiting for them, he was out of his mind. She was getting the hell out of there. Tugging on Mark's arm, she halted him.

"No." Sage could barely get the word out. Her throat seemed to have clamped shut. "I don't want to do this anymore."

"Come on, Sage. We're finally getting something. This is what we're here for. This is what it's all about."

"I've got a really bad feeling."

"This is why we don't let the client stay during investigations," Joe said from his position behind the monitors. Sage tossed him a dirty look, not that he could see it.

"Joe," Mark said, then softened his voice as he spoke to Sage. "You're just scared. You can stay down here if it makes you feel better."

This whole communicating with supernatural stuff was freaking her the fuck out. It was terrifying. Plain and simple. But her need for answers outweighed her fear. "I'll come."

They'd just started up the tired wooden steps, when there was a sudden crash, as if an object made of glass had been hurled to the floor.

"What the fuck?" Mark stopped abruptly, and Sage ran into him, but it was Ryan who jumped and smacked into Sage, causing them to all fall over on the stairs. It would have been almost comical if it hadn't hurt so much. *Did Ryan get that on film?* A glance at Ryan picking his camera off the floor and turning it on told Sage he probably hadn't.

"What was that?" Mark asked, helping Sage stand up, holding her shoulders until he was sure she was steady. He was fulfilling his promise to make sure she was looked after. But she suspected it was just in his nature.

"A glass," Pia said, standing up and moving to the sink. They were the first words she had spoken for a long time.

"Don't worry about it. I'll clean it up tomorrow," Sage called out to her.

"I didn't drop it," Pia said, her voice wavering. "It exploded."

Just like the Ouija board glass.

"Jesus!" Ryan yelled, and finally his voice sounded something like what Sage was feeling. His breathing had revved up, and his voice came in harsh bursts. "I just felt the most terrifying chill. Like... like pure evil just walked right *through* me."

They were standing near the bottom of the stairs, and Sage glanced nervously up the narrow, almost pitch-black staircase. No way was she walking up there now. But it also didn't feel right downstairs anymore either. The air had become heavy again, threatening, as though the entity had the power to make it become thick enough to choke on if it chose. And there was a sinister mist above her head, as though a dark cloud of pure evil lined the ceiling.

"All right then, let's head up." Mark gave her hand a reassuring squeeze. It didn't help.

But she refused to let it beat her. As scared as she was, she had to face it, didn't she? She had to *know*.

Ryan started up the stairs in front of them, and Mark tugged on Sage's hand. Robotically, she followed, the creaking of the wood under their feet as loud as if it had been magnified through a megaphone. Adrenaline coursed through her, every sense amped up. She had to know, but she didn't want to.

"Mark?" Pia's voice was shaky.

"Yes? Pia, are you okay?"

"I'm… I'm not feeling too well."

They all backed down the stairs again, this time managing not to trip over each other.

Mark let go of Sage's hand and moved to Pia's side. Sage felt overwhelmingly vulnerable with the loss of his touch.

"I… can't… breathe… something… compressing… my chest…" Pia's voice was weak, shaky, and she took great gulps of air. Impending doom settled over Sage like a heavy fog.

"Ryan, lights! We're calling it a night." Mark left Pia's side briefly to turn the EM pump off. "Whoever is doing this, you can stop now. We're leaving."

"Mark?" Pia said. "My head… I'm so dizzy."

"I said, we're leaving. Back the fuck off and leave Pia alone." Mark's voice was an angry command to the unseen entity.

The room filled with brilliant florescent light as Ryan restored the power. The lights flickered once but fortunately stayed on.

Pia had a glazed, faraway look to her eyes. Her face was flushed and she was shaking, bent forward with her arms wrapped around her middle.

"Pia, honey, look at me," Mark said, lifting her face with both his hands.

She appeared to try to focus on him, but failed. A flash of fear washed over Mark's face, but otherwise he remained calm and in control.

Sage was petrified, her heart racing a million beats per minute. She wanted to sprint out the door and keep running. It was only the fact she had absolutely nowhere to run to that kept her rooted to the spot.

"What's wrong with her?" Sage asked, despite her deep fear of the answer. She carefully stepped around the shards of broken glass littering the floor to prepare a cool, damp cloth in the kitchen. It seemed grossly insufficient, but she wanted to help.

"I don't know." Mark put a hand on Pia's forehead to check her temperature. He moved his hand in front of her eyes, tracking her eye movements.

Ryan was at Pia's other side, handing her a glass of water.

"Uh, guys… the camera in the hallway upstairs just caught a full-bodied manifestation," Joe said, eyes glued to one of the monitors.

"Make sure the camera is recording everything that is happening," Mark said, his attention fully on Pia.

"I have to get out of here," Pia said. "It wants us all to leave." Pia's color was returning to normal, her voice once again steady. Sage wanted to kiss Pia. Leaving was the best idea she'd ever heard.

"Except Sage," Pia added, and Sage's stomach plummeted.

Pia looked directly at Sage, and her eyes filled with tears. "Oh, God, Sage…" Pia choked on a sob, her face haunted, terrified.

"What?" Sage's voice was little more than a rasp. She was trembling, and she took a breath, tried to steel herself for what Pia was about to say. But Pia compressed her lips and looked down, saying nothing.

Mark patted Pia's knees and stood up. "We'll talk somewhere away from here. You're looking a bit better. Are you feeling better now too?"

"Yes." Pia took another sip of water and dabbed at her forehead with the cloth. Sage didn't want to ask what had made Pia look at her that way, didn't want to know what was making her cry. She never wanted to be told. No way could she ever prepare herself for anything that could put that kind of expression on someone's face.

This was all a bad dream. A nightmare. It had to be.

"Ryan, Joe, start packing up down here. I'll go upstairs and grab the static cameras." Mark moved toward the stairs.

"Wait." Sage ran after him.

She didn't want to go upstairs. There was a full-bodied manifestation—whatever that was—upstairs. But she was scared that Pia might change her mind and tell her what she knew, and Sage considered an apparition the lesser of two evils. She hurried to catch up with Mark, latching onto his hand.

"Hey, ease up there, tigress, I need that hand." Mark grinned at her.

Sage only held on tighter. Mark leaned forward and pressed a chaste kiss to her forehead. "Relax, Sage. Take a deep breath. Everything is going to be just fine."

How the hell was he so calm? What did it take to rattle his nerves?

A full-bodied manifestation was waiting for them when they reached the top. Perhaps even Satan himself, if the mark on Ryan's hand was anything to go by.

They were all out of their minds. Had to be. No one in their right mind would deliberately walk into such a situation.

The air was crackling as though it had become electrically charged. The current touched her, skittering across her skin like tiny winged insects. The energy in the room was restless. Filled with… anticipation?

But no one else seemed to share her sense of dread. Sage pushed through her fear, which was not something intellectual like being at the top of a high-rise building looking down. It was something different from that. The energy was a tangible force in the room. An evil vibration that seemed directed at her. As though this were personal. It triggered her baser instincts, the primal fight-or-flight response within her. Instinctively she gripped the angel pendant around her neck.

She desperately wanted to flee. Instead, Sage swallowed the bitter taste of terror, steeled her spine, and for the third time that evening, they began the trek up the stairs.

Even though the lights were on, the stairs seemed more forbidding than ever.

CHAPTER SEVENTEEN

They didn't see any apparitions in the hallway, thank God. But the air was thicker than downstairs, making it even harder to breathe. The hairs on the back of Sage's neck and along her arms were standing on end, and she *knew* she was being watched. Observed.

The lights were all on, but it still somehow felt dark, and her vision had blurred around the edges. Her heart was racing.

Mark moved swiftly, packing up the equipment in the hallway, the bathroom, and Sage's childhood bedroom. Absently she wondered why having the light on wasn't much comfort. The light had been on during the other manifestations as well.

"Aren't spirits or ghosts or whatever, not supposed to like lights?" Sage asked as Mark disconnected a static night-vision camera.

A small smile played around the edges of his mouth. "God, you're cute, Sage."

Had her question really been that naïve? "What I mean is, you always turn out the lights during an investigation, and children who think ghosts are in their bedroom always want the lights on..."

Mark grinned at her as he wound up a cable. "Some entities are sensitive to light and will retreat, but mostly we prefer it being dark to help capture evidence such as light anomalies. Using night-vision technology, we can pick up fluctuations and changes in energy that can't be seen otherwise."

That sounded reasonable. "So the light doesn't always 'chase them away,' so to speak," Sage mused. That made sense, and explained why the entity had manifested even with the lights on.

"Sometimes, but not always," Mark said. "Depends on the entity and how powerful it is."

Sage sat down on Nan's bed and watched Mark pack up the last camera. His presence filled the room. Now that they were packing up, she was starting to feel better. As though it was a signal to the spirits that they were finished, and no longer wanted to play.

As Mark moved about the bedroom, his toned abdomen accentuated, not hidden, by his tight black T-shirt, she marveled at how different it felt having Mark in the room compared to when Ethan was in there with her. With Ethan, the attraction between them was so powerful she was unable to focus on anything else.

"Wow, look at that, it's beautiful." Mark was staring into the shoe box of crystals.

"Isn't it?" Sage smiled. "I'll show you the others. I found them in the corners of the room a few nights ago."

Setting the shoe box onto the bed, she took out the top stone and carefully unwrapped the other three crystals.

Mark's whole demeanor changed. He didn't rush to pick them up like she'd expected. She looked up at him curiously.

"You said they were in the corners of the room."

"Yes. All four. A shame, don't you think? Stones this beautiful should be on display."

Still Mark didn't move to touch them. Instead he walked to the door and called for Pia.

"Pia, if you're feeling up to it, would you mind coming up here a minute?"

"Coming," Pia called, her voice sounding normal again.

"I'm glad Pia is sounding better," Sage said.

"Pia is what is called a sensitive, which means she's more susceptible to the subtle energies around us. She will quite often be the first to feel things, and when she does, she feels them the strongest."

Pia stopped at the entrance, her hands on the door frame, and looked in. "What is it?" Her eyes lit on the stones. "Oh, fuck." Pia's face fell. "Where did you find these?"

Pia and Mark were looking at each other, having a whole conversation without a single word being exchanged.

"Why are you both looking at the crystals like that?" Sage asked.

A door slammed downstairs, and she jumped. She looked at the digital clock on the bedside table, just in time to see it click over to three a.m.

"This is about the time I started hearing things the last few nights."

"Dead time," Pia said.

"What?" Sage didn't like the sound of that.

"Three a.m. is what is known as Dead Time, Devil's Time, or the Demon's Hour. That point when the night is darkest, the energies are lowest, and the veil between the worlds is at its thinnest. It is the point of night where most people are asleep and lights and electrical devices are turned off. It is the time when it is easiest for the lower energy spirits to cross the veil separating our world from theirs."

Sage shuddered.

"The number three is also a demonic symbol, and most transition stages of a demon haunting turning into an infestation or possession happen between three to four a.m."

"A little too much detail, Pia," Mark said, giving her a pointed look. "Sage already looks as though she's about to pass out. Let's keep the explanations brief."

"No," Sage said, ignoring the little voice in her subconscious that said, be careful what you wish for. "I don't want to feel like the child in the room that everyone is too scared to talk around. This is happening to *me*. With Nan no longer here, this is *my* house. I need to know exactly what's going on here. No sugar-coating."

"Sage is right, Mark. We're going to need to tell her. And she needs to know about that other thing we discussed as well."

Mark nodded. "I know, but not here, and not now."

What other thing? Sage didn't get to ask before another door slammed. This time the sound was louder, and it didn't sound like any door in the house. There was a metallic screech before the slam, like the rusty hinges on a prison-cell door. The energy in the room went from bad to worse. The atmosphere in the room felt almost… violent.

Fear, hot and prickly-cold, flooded Sage's body. Mark appeared uneasy for the first time.

"Joe, Ryan, was that you?" Pia called out from the door to the bedroom.

"No." Two voices confirmed from downstairs. They heard Joe and Ryan come up. "I was just about to ask the same of you." Joe said, appearing at the bedroom door. He looked at the three of them, then his gaze dropped to the stones on the bed.

"Sweet Jesus. Where the hell did you find them?" Joe asked, his face falling.

Sage had had enough. "Will someone please tell me what's wrong with these crystals?"

Joe looked at Mark, who looked at Ryan, then at Pia. "You'll explain it better, Pia," Mark said.

Pia sighed. "They're stones of protection."

Sage swallowed. Protection. That wasn't so bad. And now that they mentioned it, Sage remembered Nan writing that she'd done that in her diary.

"After you removed these from their respective spots, did you notice anything? Any change?" Pia asked.

Sage swallowed hard. That was when she'd started to no longer feel safe in Nan's room. "Yes. Things started to happen in here after that." The temperature fluctuating, the figurines moving on the shelf, something snatching the covers off the bed… "Okay then. I'll put them back," Sage said, reaching into the box and removing the black stone. Easily fixed.

Pia glanced at Mark, then back at Sage. "Do you remember which corners the stones were in?"

"No. Why? Is that important?" The stone grew hot and Sage had to drop it before it burnt her palm. "Ouch!" She waved her hand to cool it. "Will someone tell me what the hell is going on?"

Again, a serious look passed between Pia and Mark. "Depending on what unfolds in the next hour, we may need to attempt to put them back to the best of your memory," Mark said, his tone ominous.

"There is a ceremony that needs performing at the same time. I don't remember it precisely so I'll need to look it up. But discovering the use of these specific crystals confirms what I've been intuiting all night," Pia said.

Mark nodded, his face as serious as Sage had ever seen it. "Pia, you'd better tell Sage what you know about these particular stones of protection."

"We worked a case about a year ago," Pia began, walking all the way into the room. She leaned against the dressing table and closed her eyes briefly as though not wanting to relive the memory.

"We were in a nursing home that had been taken over by a powerful demonic entity. The stones of protection your grandmother used are for warding off a specific type of demon. According to medieval demonology, there are particularly evil entities, devils, sometimes referred to as master demons. They serve Satan himself. Anyway, the nursing home had been infested by one of these powerful and malevolent spirits. A spiritual advisor had been called in, but one night, he'd had an 'accident.'" Pia used her fingers to make quotation marks. "He'd supposedly fallen down the stairs and broken his neck. That night, things went from bad to worse, and one of the elderly residents removed the stones, presumably because they were so beautiful... Another theory was that he became possessed, and the demonic presence instructed him to remove them. Either way, the following morning, they discovered all the doors jammed closed and every single person inside dead. Fifty-three people. The blood covered not only the floor, but also the walls and ceilings." Pia shivered. "But the most disturbing part of the story is—" She leaned forward as though about to impart a horrifying secret. Sage braced herself.

"Pia." Mark cut her off after glancing at Sage, whose expression must have reflected the turmoil she was feeling on the inside. "I think we'll leave the rest of the story for now. Why don't all of you head back to your cameras and see if we caught anything when the door slammed."

Pia straightened, and with one last glance at the stones, left the room, with Ryan and Joe following close behind.

Sage tried to swallow past the lump in her throat. "Mark? Do you think we're dealing with one of those evil master demons here? Nan must have believed so. She had a gift like Pia. She wouldn't have used them otherwise." The entity in the nursing home had killed fifty-three people. Had the one in here killed Nan? Would it kill Sage too?

Her terror must have been reflected in her eyes because he came around the bed and took her in his arms.

She felt nothing other than his desire to reassure her, but the embrace felt uncomfortable. She pulled away.

"It's too early to say what we are dealing with," Mark said, putting the last of the cameras into the black bag. "I'll be in touch when we've had a chance to analyze the footage from tonight."

"Nan must have had reason to think so," Sage said. "She wouldn't have used them otherwise."

Mark shrugged. "It may have been an accident. I mean, she may have just used the crystals for protection, not knowing their deeper use." Sage nodded, but didn't think that was likely. If Nan had chosen that specific combination, it would have been for a good reason.

The bedroom door slammed shut. Mark immediately went to the door to reopen it, but found it jammed shut. There was no wind, no logical reason why a solid wooden door would of its own accord close with such force. Ice slithered through her veins to her very core.

"Joe, Ryan, Pia?" Mark called through the wood. "Can someone come and open the door please?" To Sage, he said, "I could break it down, but I won't damage it unless it becomes necessary."

The temperature in the room plunged, turning bitterly cold. Frigid. It was happening again. Sage clutched Mark's arm. Her teeth began to chatter, and he pulled her close.

The wind howled outside the bedroom window, as if a storm had sprung up, even though no bad weather had been forecast. Something fell and broke in the next room.

"I don't think they can hear me. I'll call Joe." Mark tried to turn his mobile back on, but the phone didn't respond. "The battery's flat. Completely drained. It was fully charged when I arrived."

The door handle rattled, and they heard Joe's voice. "Mark? Sage? Are you guys in there? Something very strange is happening out here. Unlock the door and come down."

Mark went to the door and tried the knob again. "Can't. The door won't open from this side."

Pia let out a blood-curdling scream downstairs, and Joe called out to her. He hurried off, his footsteps receding.

"Mark? I'm scared." Sage whispered. Understatement of the century. She'd thought the entity had terrorized her before. This was on a whole new level.

What had it done to Pia?

Mark gave her shoulders a squeeze. "No need to be. I've got you."

She watched his eyes, bright and alert, flick around the room for signs of any other activity. He was not only calm, but... *excited*.

He turned on his voice recorder and began speaking into it, but stopped when he realized that the batteries on that too, were dead. He tapped it a few times before slipping it back in his pocket.

Heavy footsteps came down the hallway, stopping at the door. Sage grabbed Mark's shirt so tightly, she ripped part of his pocket off.

But it wasn't anything supernatural; it was Joe. And he was pounding furiously on the other side of the door.

"Mark! You have got to get out here! We need you!"

"Try again from your side," Mark shouted through the wood.

Joe struggled frantically with the door for a moment and Sage heard the hinges protest as he heaved his body into it.

"Stand back, I'm going to kick it in." Joe called out.

Not letting go of her arms, Mark positioned Sage behind him, sheltering her with his body.

The door crashed open in a splintering of wood.

"You have to come downstairs. Now!" Joe demanded then frowned. "What the fuck is going on?" He rubbed at his arms. "Why is it so cold in here?"

"What's happening downstairs?" Mark asked.

"Fuck, man. I've never seen anything like it. The equipment went berserk, there was this foul smell, like rotting meat, and then Pia fainted. You've got to help her. She's on the floor, out cold."

"Pia doesn't faint." Mark was already moving toward the door. "Do you want to stay or come with me?" he asked Sage, pausing at the threshold.

"I'm not staying here," Sage squeaked and grabbed onto Mark's arm.

Just as they were about to leave the room, the window shattered. Sage screamed, and a flock of crows crashed inside, peppering the room with glass shards, black feathers, and red splashes of blood.

CHAPTER EIGHTEEN

He rose from his favorite chair, his thoughts coming into focus, a vision forming.

Virgil was making contact.

He walked to the skull in the corner of the dank room and ran a dirty finger along one of the blood-encrusted feathers that stuck out of the eye socket. He listened intently in the silence.

Then, nodding his agreement, he grabbed his keys, and for the first time since the old woman, started the engine of his rusty white panel van.

Chapter Nineteen

It was ten past three a.m., and Ethan and Nate had been sitting surveillance on the shop for three and a half hours without incident. The whole place was locked (for once), windows included. Ethan had checked, and the place was quiet and dark. The black Paranormal Research Investigations van was parked out front and had not moved.

"What do you think they keep in there?" Ethan asked, referring to the sizeable van with tinted windows.

Nate smothered a yawn and shrugged.

"You want me to take you back to the hotel so you can get some sleep? All seems pretty quiet here. I can sit the rest of the night on my own."

"If one of us needs sleep, it's you, my friend. You look like a damn zombie," Nate said, eyeing him closely. "The ghost busters will be after you next. I can see you starring in their next show."

Ethan made a disgruntled noise.

"I can see your name in lights now," Nate continued, forming a square with his hands raised in front of him. "Ghost Hunters 'R' Us save the world from the cop-zombie apocalypse."

"Dickhead." Ethan glared at his partner without heat.

"Why did the ghost cross the road?" Nate asked, grinning. "To get to the *other side*."

Ethan groaned and leaned back in his seat.

"What did one ghost say to the other ghost?"

"What?" Ethan mumbled

"Do you believe in people?"

"Oh, Jesus," Ethan moaned. "I'm taking you back to the hotel. Lack of sleep is affecting your brain."

"You calling it a night too?"

"No. Won't be able to sleep until I know Expose-a-Ghost has left."

"All right. I won't deny I'm feeling a bit shady, but it's nothing a good strong coffee won't fix. Let's refill our travel mugs at the hotel then return and sit the rest of the night out."

Ethan started the engine. He could use a good strong coffee himself.

"The moment ghost boy leaves though, you're getting a few hours shut-eye," Nate said seriously.

"Yes, Mum."

As they made their way back to the shop, the scent of coffee from their oversized travel mugs permeated the inside of the vehicle.

"When Collins gets married and has a family, where do you think his kids will go?" Nate asked.

Ethan glanced at the time. Three thirty-one a.m. They'd been gone for sixteen minutes.

"If I ask what, will you can the lousy jokes?"

He glanced over. Nate was holding his coffee mug, grinning from ear to ear. "Okay," Ethan said, "tell me. Where will his kids go?"

"To a day-scare center."

As they neared the shop, an ambulance with the siren blaring and its lights flashing pulled up out front. Ethan's heart stopped dead in his chest. Sixteen minutes. They'd been there all night and had left for only sixteen goddamned minutes. Fuck Murphy and his screwed up Law.

"What the hell?" Nate said, reaching for his gun and strapping on his utility belt.

Dread, thick as tar, flowed through Ethan's veins. What the hell could have happened in the short amount of time they'd been away? He hadn't heard any reports called through on his radio. Nate, wondering the same thing, was checking his. "Dead," he said. "How long do the batteries last on these things? Weird that both of ours stopped working at the same time."

Ethan's knuckles were white on the steering wheel. "If that ghost buster has put one fucking scratch on her..."

With a screech of tires, they pulled up behind the emergency vehicle. Ethan leapt from the Land Rover and headed on an intercept course for the ambulance attendant, who raced to block the door.

"Detective Sergeant Ethan Blade, Homicide Squad." He flashed his badge at the guy and shouldered his way inside.

He scanned the carnage before him. His first thought was that there had been a break and enter. Overturned objects littered the floor, appearing to have been swept off shelves by a violent hand. Had the serial killer struck again?

More sirens blared in the distance, quickly becoming deafening. More flashing red and blue lights came through the window, bouncing off the walls and confusing his vision. Four uniforms entered the room, barking short reports into and out of hand-held radios.

The room was overcrowded and he struggled to breathe, couldn't seem to fill his lungs with the necessary amount of oxygen. Never had he felt so invested in what was happening during an investigation.

Two ambulance officers were kneeling over a body in the center of the room, and Ethan's heart lodged firmly in his throat. Members of the ghost-busting team stood nearby, grim looks on their faces.

No! He was uncharacteristically frozen to the spot. He had to force his feet to move, terrified of what he would see when he was close enough. There would be nothing he could do to prepare himself for seeing Sage's limp and injured body on the floor.

"It's not her," Nate called back to him. His partner's words were enough to snap him out of whatever personal hell he had been momentarily thrown into, and his feet began to move. Sure enough, though the body on the floor was a woman, she had bright red hair. *Not her.* Not his Sage.

Then where was she? He scanned the sea of faces. Time slowed as he surveyed the wreckage of the room, afraid of what he would find.

And then she appeared at the bottom of the stairs carrying what looked like a jug of water and a stack of cloths, and his knees nearly buckled with relief. Strands of her golden hair had come free from her ponytail, and her face was pale, her eyes bleak. But she appeared uninjured.

A lump formed in his throat, and he stumbled slightly, like he'd been punched in the stomach. Then came a euphoric rush of relief so great, he almost didn't care that Collins had one arm firmly around her shoulders.

Almost.

His hands involuntarily curled into fists at his sides and a low growl rose from somewhere deep inside his chest. He'd never felt such a swing of emotion in one single night before. In his life. And he wasn't sure he liked it.

She noticed him. Handing Collins the cloths and water, she pushed away and rushed straight into Ethan's waiting arms. Her nails dug into his back as she clung to him, and she buried her head into his chest. Her body shook, and he tightened his embrace, smoothing one hand over her hair.

"Are you okay?" he asked, kissing the top of her head.

He felt her nod against him.

"Will someone tell me what the fuck happened here tonight?" he growled to the room in general, but his narrowed gaze fell on Collins.

Collins spared him the briefest of glances before rushing to the side of the woman on the floor, who he now recognized from his enquiries as being Pia Williams. The attendants were lifting her onto a stretcher.

Ethan looked over to where Nate was standing, notebook in hand, getting initial reports from the other members of the ghost-busting team. Ethan left it to his partner. He'd get his opportunity to question them thoroughly when they came back to the station.

He would be even further indebted to Nate after this. Having a capable partner left Ethan free to concentrate on his main priority. Sage.

She'd wrapped herself around him like a koala, making it hard for him to satisfy himself that she was indeed unhurt, so he lifted her and carried her to a chair at the rear of the room, where there was a little less activity. He swiped a bunch of equipment to one side, clearing a space in front of her. Then he filled a glass of water in the kitchen and helped her take a sip. Sinking to his knees in front of her, he searched her face.

She was pale, her eyes glassy and bright. "Oh, Ethan, I'm so glad you're here. It was… awful. Oh God!" She buried her face in her hands, and he drew her once again into his embrace. His urgent need to understand what the fuck had gone on here was nearly driving him insane.

"Was there an intruder? Did someone break in and try to hurt you?"

Eyes bright, she looked up at him. "No."

"Did you see anyone?"

"No."

A muscle near his eye twitched. "Tell me what you remember. What you saw. No matter how small."

Her jaw firmed. His fingers dug into his palms.

"What happened to Pia?"

"I… I don't know—"

"Okay, then who caused all this damage?"

"Not who. What."

He hesitated a moment, while he let her answer sink in. "So, what are you saying? A *ghost* did this?"

She pulled away and narrowed her eyes at him. "You don't believe me."

"I believe that you believe it," he said softly, and he hoped, reasonably.

She crossed her arms across her chest. "Don't talk to me in that condescending tone. I'm not making this up! We were all here; we all saw. The doors and windows were all locked. No one broke in. Something was already in here. Something not human." She looked up at him, as if willing him to believe her.

He wanted to. Dear God, the way her bright green eyes were pleading with him, he'd give her the whole fucking world. Just… not that. What she was saying, what she wanted him to believe, it wasn't logical. Therefore it couldn't be.

Her face fell. "Even with four other witnesses, you still can't open your mind enough to believe it."

The pain in her gaze almost undid him. The last thing he wanted to do was hurt her, but damn it, this whole situation was threatening his control. Her four other witnesses just weren't that credible in his book.

"You want me to believe a *ghost* did all this damage?" He waved his arm in an arc to indicate the room. "You want me to believe a *ghost* hurt Pia?"

Anger raced like wildfire through his veins. Not at her, but himself. It was his job to put away the serial killer, and if he had, Sage wouldn't be standing there right now shaking with fear. She wouldn't have been subjected to that freak Collins and his investigation tonight. And she also wouldn't have that look of worry on her face.

She made a soft noise, a small cry like she was in pain. "Nothing. I don't want you to believe anything at all."

She sounded defeated, and his heart constricted as he surveyed the mess around him. Someone had gone to a lot of trouble to stage this. And they'd managed a good enough job that Sage had believed it. His gaze rested on Collins, who was now hovering over the stretcher as it was being carried out of the store. His face was creased in concern. On the surface, he appeared genuinely concerned for Pia, but it could all be an elaborate act, staged for his show. Ethan didn't trust the guy. Didn't trust any of them.

Sage jumped up when she heard the front door open. "Mark, wait! I want to come too."

She rushed to Collins's side, and he automatically put an arm around her shoulders.

Fuck that. Ethan crossed the room in quick strides. He reached for her, but she shook him off.

"Sage, where are you going?"

She looked at him, her eyes an ice-green shade he never wanted to see directed at him again. He'd cause serious harm to anyone who'd hurt her, and yet it was he who'd dealt her the blow this time. Frustration held him trapped. Powerless. He wanted to reach out to her, but he didn't know if he could take another rejection. His arms remained at his sides while his mind raced for the right words to fix this.

"Leave me alone, Detective. If you think I would lie to you, make all of this up, then you don't know me at all."

"I know you wouldn't lie," he said earnestly. She had to believe that. It wasn't Sage he blamed for whatever had gone on tonight. She was simply the victim in an elaborate setup he had yet to understand the reason for. But he would.

"If you think you know what's going on here, good," Sage said, her voice cracking. "Do whatever you need to, to make all of this go away. But I don't have to listen to your high-and-mighty attitude and let you make me feel like a fool."

"Sage—"

Collins gave him a smirk. "Instead of hassling us, why don't you do what my taxes are paying you for, and catch the person who killed Sage's grandmother so that she may find some peace."

Despite an overwhelming desire to pound Collins into next week, Ethan restrained himself. Ignoring the fact the man's comments had once again hit a raw nerve, it was interesting to note that Collins believed the serial killer was a separate issue to what was going on in the shop. Even more interesting that he sounded so sure about that.

Ethan thought it more logical to presume this break-in to be related to her grandmother's murder, since Celeste's body had been discovered in this shop. Wouldn't it be natural to first assume the killer had returned for some reason?

Ethan glanced around the room. It was highly possible the killer had returned and was looking for something. Something he'd dropped when he'd returned the body. Or perhaps something he'd left when he'd abducted her in the first place. Something the killer knew could tie him to the murder.

The place had been in darkness while the investigation had been conducted earlier, and Ethan could attest that from the outside it had appeared to be empty. Was it possible that during the brief period of time when he and Nate had left to get coffee, the killer had returned, been surprised by someone in Collin's team, and Pia had been caught in the confrontation when the killer panicked?

"Collins, I'd like to ask you a few questions about this evening," Ethan said, taking out his notebook.

"Fuck you." Collins face flamed red.

The stretcher carrying Pia was being loaded into the ambulance.

"Sage, do I have permission to perform a search on this building?"

"Do whatever you feel is necessary." The hollowness in her voice nearly ripped his heart out of his chest.

"Let's go." Collins urged Sage out the door. Tears slid silently down her cheeks and Ethan could do nothing but watch as Collins ushered her into his black BMW and pulled out after the ambulance. Ethan ruthlessly reined in the rage that flamed inside him. *I should be the one comforting her. Not that arrogant arsehole.*

For Sage's sake, he needed to stop this madness, this out-of-control obsession he had for her.

He had to focus his energy on things that were within his control. Like solving this case. Carefully stepping over fallen items, he moved to join his partner. The whole place needed to be searched top to bottom. He could only hope the killer hadn't managed to find whatever it was he'd come back for. It could be their first real lead in this case.

A case where the stakes had just been raised. His chest constricted with the knowledge that the danger to Sage had just skyrocketed. What if the killer had returned not to find something he'd left behind, but to find something he wanted? Was Sage his next target?

CHAPTER TWENTY

As she approached the front door of the shop, Sage took a deep breath, inhaling the fragrance of Nan's potted geraniums bordering the steps. She could almost see her grandmother, snipping off the spent flowers while keeping up a steady stream of cheerful chatter. "Do you know that rose perfume is made from geraniums, not roses?" she'd say. Sage's throat tightened. *Oh Nan.* She gently pushed the image aside. She needed to be ready for what she was going to see.

After removing the strip of crime-scene tape, Sage hesitated at the door, her stomach fluttering, her hand hovering over the knob. The police had been in there searching for God knows what. She hadn't returned the messages Ethan had left on her phone while she was in the hospital with Pia and Mark, so she had no idea what he wanted. His calls could wait; she wasn't ready to talk to him just yet. If it was that important, he'd have turned up at the hospital. It still hurt, more than it should, that he could so easily dismiss what she had to say.

She'd spoken briefly to his partner, Nate Ryder, however. He'd been even more persistent than Ethan, and a bit cleverer about it too. When Nate had been unable to get through to her on her phone, he'd reached her through Mark's. He'd told her that forensics had finished dusting the shop for fingerprints and wanted to know if she'd come into the station to file a report. She'd refused. File a report for what? She didn't believe there was a break and enter. She wasn't about to put her ghost theory in writing and be a laughingstock. And with Pia not willing to file a report either and without any obvious sign of a break-in, Nate told her the police would suspend the investigation, so she was allowed back in the shop.

Now that she was here, she found herself filled with trepidation over what she would discover inside. Was the entity that they'd encountered last night—the entity that had attacked Pia—still there? And if so, was Sage in danger?

She'd better wait for Mark, who was finishing up a call in the car. Sage glanced at the chair where Liquorice had been sleeping. Empty. His water and food bowls were full and appeared untouched.

From reading Nan's diary, she knew that Liquorice had stopped wanting to go inside several weeks ago. But Sage had felt some measure of comfort that at least he'd been eating the food she'd left out for him and was sleeping on the warm blanket she'd left on the chair. Now, it appeared that he'd abandoned the place entirely.

Was he okay? She'd loved that little fur ball from the minute Nan had first brought him home. Sage had been thirteen at the time, and had shut herself in her room after a particularly hard day at school. Nan had seen her tears, and the next thing she knew, a tiny black kitten with pure white whiskers had been placed in her hands.

Wherever Liquorice was now, she hoped he was safe. An emptiness pierced her chest. Without Nan, and without Liquorice, the house was now devoid of all life and love.

"Let me go in first," Mark said, finally catching up to her, arms full of computer equipment. They had just come from the hospital. The doctors could find nothing wrong with Pia and were unable to determine what had caused her to pass out for well over an hour. After a series of blood tests, she'd been released just after eleven that morning. The team had gone back to their hotel rooms to get some sleep, and Mark had offered to come back to the shop with Sage.

Pia had not yet spoken about what had happened, and Mark hadn't pressed her. "There'll be plenty of time to go over the results after you've had a chance to rest. In any case, I need to review the footage we took before we talk," he'd said to Pia, after they'd settled her into the hotel.

The team had chosen to stay in a hotel complex in the nearby town of Boulderton, a fifteen-minute drive from Cryton, where the accommodations weren't so luxury-challenged.

Sage followed Mark inside and while he set down his computer equipment on the table, Sage immediately began opening the blinds and windows. Carefully stepping over broken glass, her attention was drawn to small drops of blood on the faded rug. Was it Pia's?

She closed her eyes, fully aware that last night could have been much more serious. Mark put a hand on Sage's shoulder, and when she opened her eyes, he gave her a gentle, reassuring smile. "Pia will be fine," he said. "We all will. Nothing happened that we can't handle."

Mark's assurances did little to ease Sage's tension, her sense that despite what had happened last night, they'd only seen a sample of what this entity was capable of. There was an atmosphere, an energy, in the house that even in the light of day was disturbing. Like the heaviness left in the air after a violent argument.

Sage began to roll up the stained rug. "Let me help," Mark said. "What do you want to do with this?"

"I'll never get the blood out without the attempt showing. The rug was old anyway, so there's no point keeping it. Let's put it in the outside bin."

As Mark carried the rug outside, Sage picked her way to the small kitchen in the back of the shop and put the kettle on.

"Would you like a coffee?" Sage asked when Mark returned. He was examining a fallen tripod for damage.

"Yes, thanks. Strong, one sugar. I'm going to give sleep a miss. I want to analyze the footage straight away."

As Mark, headphones on, began the painstaking task of reviewing last night's footage. Sage began cleaning up the broken glass and picking up fallen objects. The mess aside, the shop otherwise seemed the way it always did. Sage had worried that when they'd turned on the EM pump last night that they may have... *manifested* the spirit. She'd half expected to walk in to find whatever they'd uncovered last night still there. But she didn't see the entity or any new disturbances beyond black fingerprint dust around doors and windows and drawers, and slightly disordered cupboards from the police search.

After a couple hours, Sage had the shop clean and tidy, with the remainder of the stuff on the shop's shelves packed neatly into boxes. Mark looked ready for a break and had taken his headphones off. Sage put a jug of water on the table and took a seat next to him.

"Did you get any of what happened last night on film?"

"Yes, it appears we did. I'll get Joe to clean up some of the audio and enhance some of the images when he wakes up, but I think we captured some damn good proof of what is going on here."

"Can you show me?"

Mark smiled. "Not yet. It's policy to go over this properly with the client in the standard format. I need go over the findings with Pia first, then we'll prepare the official report, which will be presented to you in full."

Sage frowned and Mark placed a hand on hers. "Trust me. We're a professional team, well-experienced in this field. I'd even go as far as to say we are the best team of paranormal investigators out there. You'll know everything there is to know when we have it properly collated and the parts where necessary debunked." He smiled reassuringly. "Relax, Sage. You're in good hands."

"Can you at least tell me if you've encountered activity like this before?" Sage slipped her hand out from underneath his and placed it on her lap. He was only being friendly, but his touch made her uncomfortable nevertheless. She'd have preferred to never speak about evil entities ever again, but she needed to know she wasn't alone. They'd also presumably come up with a solution to rid people of said entities. She deliberately didn't mention the nursing-home incident Pia had told her about, hoping that was an extreme case. Isolated or perhaps even exaggerated.

"Many times."

"Tell me about one," Sage said. Maybe if she heard about other occurrences, her own experience wouldn't seem so strange. So overwhelming. After all, if there were teams dedicated to investigating the paranormal, it meant things like this happened all the time.

"You did really well last night, Sage." Mark eyed her over his glass of water. "If you enjoyed that, you would have really enjoyed The Bird Cage Theatre." He grinned. His playful tone helped ease her tension.

"Dare I ask what a Bird Cage Theatre is?"

"It's a saloon and brothel in Tombstone, Arizona, that operated during the silver boom around 1881 to 1889."

"Strange name for a brothel."

"The prostitutes performed shows in cage-like boxes. We got some great footage there, some EVPs, and a partial apparition, but as it's quite a popular destination for paranormal investigators, we have nothing a whole lot of other people don't have. Still, it was a good night."

"I think I remember watching something about that. Staking out dead outlaws is not my idea of a good night, but I'm glad you had fun."

"Yeah, Ryan had a blast. Reckons he was groped by one of the ladies of the night."

"Eeew." Sage wrinkled her nose. "He's a good-looking guy. I didn't know he was that hard up for a girlfriend."

Mark laughed. "I won't let him know you think he's good-looking. He'll get a big head." His expression turned serious. "So many times, the team and I have experienced things, but weren't able to capture them on film. We might have had a terrifyingly active night, but in the end, we could be left with only our word, and a few sketchy images and sounds as proof. The public have been fooled by what have turned out to be fake pictures and images in the past, and they are, quite rightly, less trusting of what they see. But it's damn frustrating."

He leaned forward, and his eyes narrowed. "I can promise you, that before I leave this world, I will have captured irrefutable evidence to prove to the skeptics that there *is* more to our existence than this flesh-and-blood life. There *is* life after death, Sage. A world of energetic beings, negative and positive entities, that under certain conditions can interact with our world. I'm going to be the one to prove it, and put this debate to rest once and for all."

With seemingly renewed determination, he turned back to the computer screen. Sage empathized with his frustration. After what she'd seen and experienced, she too wanted proof. Something that Ethan and others couldn't dismiss as her imagination.

Ethan. Her heart skipped a beat. She shouldn't have spoken to him so harshly last night. When she'd walked out on him, the control she'd had on her emotions had been tenuous. After the terror of what she'd experienced, she could hardly be blamed.

But Ethan hadn't deserved to be the recipient of her anger. Ethan had just been… well Ethan. Her pragmatic detective with the voice of reason who was only doing his job. He felt the way he did only because he hadn't been present during the investigation, he hadn't experienced what she had. She couldn't blame him for not immediately believing her. Hell, she wouldn't have believed it either, had she not seen it with her own eyes.

Sage released a long, slow breath. As attracted to Ethan as she undeniably was, and in ways deeper than just the physical, the difference in their beliefs would be an insurmountable hurdle if they got involved any further. Ignoring the sharp stab that twisted inside her chest, she made up her mind. It would be much better if they maintained a professional distance.

Not wanting to interrupt Mark, she moved to the corner of the shop where Nan had conducted her "readings." Sage had deliberately left this to be one of the last areas to pack up. Somehow, behind the curtain-defined partition that contained a small cloth-covered table holding a lamp and a crystal ball, she could almost still feel her nan's energy.

In Nan's private space, Sage took a seat at the chair and placed her hands on the cool round crystal and drifted back to her childhood. The time spent waiting patiently in the shop, playing with statues of dragons and fairies as if they were her friends. And in a very real way they were.

The country school she'd attended was small, and there had been only a handful of girls around her age. The painful sting of their taunts had never dulled. *Freak. Witch.* They had walked on the other side of the hallway when she'd passed, and none of them had wanted to play with her. There had been two ringleaders, Wendy and Charmaine. The other girls had simply followed their lead, as if they had been scared of turning the bullying on themselves by daring to even speak to Sage.

Why were the most popular girls the nastiest? They already had it all; most often the prettiest, they could get the coolest guys. Why did they still feel the need to grind others under their heels?

Nan had been the only one who'd cared, and this shop, and their home above it, had been the only places Sage had ever felt safe. That must be why she'd developed such a deep connection with plants and animals, both tame and wild.

During her first year at school, not long after the dead plant incident, she'd been out on a school excursion when she'd come across a baby bird that had fallen from a tree. She'd cupped it in her hand, the poor little thing. A tear had rolled down her cheek and landed on its head a split-second before it took off out of her hands and flew away. She'd been so happy, so filled with joy, that she'd clapped her hands together and jumped up and down on the spot. Only to stop when she was pushed to the ground by Wendy.

Freak, freak, freak, Wendy and her friends had chanted, forming a circle around her. Later they said she'd woven some witch's spell, used wicked magic to bring the bird back to life. But she hadn't.

The bird must have been alive all the time. It had fallen from the tree and had just been in some kind of shock, hadn't it? But that hadn't mattered to the mean girls. The die had been cast.

Sage pulled Nan's crystal ball closer to her and peered into its depths. She'd never been able to see anything in it, even after she'd asked Nan how to do it.

"It's not so much that I can see things in the ball," Nan had said. "It's more that people will listen to answers when they think they are given to them from a divine source."

"So you're just making it up?" Sage had asked, incredulous.

"That wouldn't be accurate either. My time with the monks taught me how to listen to inner guidance. Our inner beings, or guides, are always communicating with us, giving us impulses to do this or say that. Go somewhere at a particular time, or not go somewhere at all. We all have one. We've all used it. Some more than others."

Nan had stroked the crystal ball and leaned forward. "We all have a gift, and when I became aware of mine, I spent time honing my ability. Like a muscle, the more you use your gift, the stronger it gets. And the messages I'm given really do help people and make a difference in their lives. I like that, Sage. It gives me a sense of purpose. Makes me feel as though I'm doing something worthwhile in life."

"But how do you know the information you get is right?" Sage had asked.

"Well dear, if what I had to say was wrong, or if people didn't find it helpful in some way, they wouldn't keep coming back, now would they? Everything I say is positive. Uplifting. My sole intention is to add something positive to someone's life and never something bad. People come back because my readings make them feel good. Give them something to look forward to. Sometimes that's all people need, a reason to believe. But if they looked inside, they would realize they didn't need me at all. That knowledge was inside them all along; they just didn't know where to look."

Nan had always understated her wisdom. She had a much greater gift than simply knowing things. She had an uncanny ability to make you see things in a different, better way. Nothing was too big of a problem after you spoke to Nan about it.

"Do I have a gift?" Sage had asked then, and she had never forgotten the look that had crossed Nan's face.

"Yes, Sage, you have a very rare and special gift. And when the time is right, when you are willing, you will be shown what it is." She'd mumbled something that sounded like a prayer under her breath and turned away.

Sage had never discovered her supposed gift, and had long since given up believing she had one. Truth be told, she didn't want it. But if it was the ability to pick things up from Liquorice's mind... well, that wasn't so bad, was it? And it wasn't much of a gift anyway. All she'd gotten was an impression that didn't make sense, other than as an expression of his emotions. So really, aside from perhaps inheriting her Nan's green thumb and affinity with animals, she just wasn't "special" in the way Nan had been. Which was more than fine with her. Her childhood had been hard enough.

Her thoughts drifted to her mother, and Sage wondered what she would have made of it all. Would she be upset that Sage had shirked—even unwittingly—her responsibility and left her grandmother to face this evil alone?

A chill raced down her back, and she fingered the angel around her neck.

She wished she could remember her mother more clearly; all she had were the memories of a three-year-old girl, faded and few. She imagined her mother around her now, like the beautiful angel she wore around her neck, lending her strength. Telling her to not let this go. To not allow Nan's killer to go unpunished. Giving her strength and protection through the angel she wore.

Could the entity they'd encountered last night be responsible for Nan's death? The entity was powerful; it could move objects, slam doors, shatter glasses. It had clawed Ryan's leg, burnt his palm. Then there was what it had done to Pia...

"Mark?" Sage said, walking back over to him. "Sorry to interrupt, but other than that incident at the nursing home, have you ever seen or heard of any ghosts or spirits that have hurt anyone? I don't mean a scratch. I mean seriously hurt."

Mark looked up sharply. "Why?"

"I was just thinking of Nan—"

On the desk, Mark's mobile phone rang, and she stopped talking so he could answer. He picked up the phone and listened for a few seconds. "I'll be right there." He disconnected the call and looked over at Sage. "That was Joe. Pia is awake and wants to talk. It's urgent. I'll be back later with the team and deliver the report. You'll get all your questions answered then." Mark packed up his laptop and his black satchel.

"Wait," Sage called. "I'm coming with you." Mark had been on his way to the door, but stopped and turned back to her.

"No. Pia needs to talk to me. Alone."

Sage slammed her bag onto the table. "Dammit, Mark, this concerns me. *All* of this relates to me. To you, this investigation is about finding proof, but in reality you're only here because *I* need answers."

Mark's features softened, and he moved to her side. "You'll get your answers, Sage. I promise you. But there are things you don't know. Things about Pia, her ability, and even what we suspect is going on here."

"Then tell me. Or even better, let me come and hear for myself. Stop shutting me out."

He placed a hand on her arm. "We *will* tell you what we think is going on here, after Pia and I have had a chance to speak privately. Then, we'll arrange to sit down and tell you everything. But not until we're ready, and not until I'm clear myself about what to do and have come up with a plan."

Sage sat down rigidly on the chair. "All right. But I expect you back as soon as you can, telling me everything you know."

Mark smiled. "Count on it. Will you be all right? Alone here, I mean?"

Sage glanced around. Most of the occurrences had happened at night, particularly between three and four in the morning. Although she wasn't completely comfortable after what had happened last night, her uneasiness wasn't intolerable. She still had a few more things to finalize before she was finished, so she'd make the most of the daylight hours.

"Absolutely. Go to Pia. I'll be fine."

"Take care of yourself. And call me if you need anything. I'll drop everything and come." He held her eyes for a moment too long, and she looked away. Taking a step toward her, he kissed her forehead and left.

Mark was such a sweet man. And so handsome.

And he knew—he *understood* what was going on here. He believed her. His mind was open to the "more" that there was in the world.

Mark would have got along well with Nan. He would have appreciated her perspective and loved her gentle, uplifting energy. And Nan would have approved of Mark. He was the exact type of man Nan would have wanted to see her with.

Ethan wasn't classically handsome in the way Mark was. Ethan's features were steely and rugged. Oh, he was handsome, no denying that, but in a rougher, more dangerous way. His chiseled jaw was often set in a hard line, and his dark eyes were hooded and serious. He put her on edge. His power and authority were borderline scary, and the challenge they presented thrilled her. What did that say about her?

If she wasn't mistaken, Mark had outwardly expressed his interest in her. When this was all over and nothing but a distant memory, Mark was the type of man she should allow herself to be seduced by. Not Ethan. Mark was sweet. Mark was the sensible choice. If only he made her stomach flutter and her pulse race like a certain detective did.

Chapter Twenty-One

"Are you ready to hear what we know so far?" Mark asked, spinning the laptop around so the screen faced Sage. It was early evening, and instead of bringing the whole team back as planned, Mark had returned with only Pia. The three of them sat around the small kitchen table in the shop. Sage had opened a bottle of wine, and they were nibbling on cheese and crackers. The white lace curtains on the windows billowed with a fresh and cool evening breeze.

Sage took a deep breath. "Yes." As much as she dreaded it, she wanted to know. She *had* to know.

Mark looked at Pia. "Before I show you the footage we captured last night, I want Pia to give you a little background."

Pia appeared tired and a little fragile. Shadows spread underneath her heavy eyeliner, making her skin deathly pale against her striking red hair. She set down her wine glass and focused her all-knowing, sky-blue eyes on Sage. "As a psychic medium, I can communicate with those who have crossed over." Pia spoke without a trace of hesitation, as though she couldn't care less whether anyone believed what she said.

"What most people don't understand is that I don't demand answers or force my ability. I can't walk around commanding the spirit world to tell me what the lotto numbers will be or how long it will take for someone to finally become pregnant. Two things I am constantly asked from disbelievers of my ability." Pia paused, as if gauging Sage's reaction, so she nodded encouragingly.

"Although I can sometimes see a child on the other side waiting to come through, that isn't something I see every time someone asks. If I'm meant to pass on a message, I will be given that information. If it is a person's destiny to learn particular life lessons first, I won't be told anything at all. This can greatly upset someone who wants answers." Pia took a sip of her wine and bit into a cracker. A few crumbs fell onto her black T-shirt and she flicked them off with jet-black fingernails. The perfect manicure Sage had admired yesterday was now ruined. Pia's nails were chipped, maybe even bitten. Apparently Pia was nowhere near as calm as she appeared.

"My gift," she continued, "if you choose to call it that, is not a constant tool that I can wield for my own purposes. It's not a secret power that gives me access to answers to someone's life destiny if the person isn't ready to hear it."

"Pia passes on the information she gets. She doesn't get to choose what the information is," Mark said.

"And sometimes the information doesn't make sense right away," Pia added, "but I've found that it always does in hindsight. That's why I've learnt to trust it. You'll get to understand what I can and can't do as you get to know me better. But getting back to last night..." Pia paused and chewed on a chipped fingernail. Then, as though conscious of what she was doing, she lowered her hand to the table and covered it with the other one.

The knot in Sage's gut tightened. She gulped the remainder of the wine in her glass and poured another round for everyone. She had a feeling at least she was going to need it.

"There were a few different spirits with us last night," Pia said. "But there is one particularly strong energy I wish to talk about right now. Her name is Mary." Sage's blood ran cold. A *few* spirits? One was bad enough. Not to mention that Pia had just mentioned the exact same name that Nan had referenced in her diary.

"Nan wrote about being visited by a Mary in her diary," Sage said. She took a swig of her wine to calm the butterflies that had taken off inside her stomach.

"Your grandmother was a very gifted psychic," Pia said. The look she gave Sage was long and penetrating.

"If you're wondering if I take after her, the answer is no," Sage said ruefully.

"No," Pia agreed. "You take after your mother."

"My mother?" Sage's hand instinctively went to the angel around her neck. Pia followed the movement with knowing eyes. She started to say something else when Mark kicked her underneath the table. Pia glared at him and he returned it with one of his own.

"What aren't you telling me?"

"Nothing," Pia said, but looked at Mark as she said it. "Mary lived in this house a long time ago. There is also the spirit of a little girl, Sandra or Sandy. She looks to be about six or eight years old. I think she's Mary's daughter."

Sage was about to tell Pia that Nan had written about having found Mary's diary, but changed her mind at the last moment. Instinct held her silent for now. She'd find the diary and read the information it contained before deciding whether to share it. Sage remembered Nan's notation, *Dear God, that poor woman.*

Although Sage believed Pia to be genuine, if Pia came to her with information that she could not have possibly known any other way, information that Sage could verify through something like Mary's diary, Pia's credibility and talent would be indisputable.

"Do you know why Mary is still here?" Sage asked instead. "In the house, I mean. Is she trapped here or something?"

"I didn't have enough time to reach out to her because another presence appeared at that time. Something evil. Demonic, we believe the energy to be."

"That was the thing that attacked Ryan." The words were barely a whisper on her tongue. "And you."

"Yes. The scratches on Ryan's leg appeared to be claw marks. A series of three scratches is often a sign of a demonic entity, the three thought to mock the holy trinity." Mark had said the same thing last night.

"Come to think of it, the knocking I heard before was often in groups of three," Sage said. Mark and Pia exchanged another glance.

"Was that entity what made you pass out?"

"Yes," Pia said, turning back to Sage. "I've never encountered an entity quite so powerful before. Usually entities, even the malevolent ones, are rather limited in their abilities. The most common thing they can do is move objects, even throw things across the room. Occasionally they can touch you, and at worst they can give you a scratch or a push, which can be life-threatening if you're somewhere vulnerable, say at the top of the stairs. But never have I been overpowered and knocked out in that manner. Because I'm more sensitive than others, I always make sure I go into every investigation fully protected."

"But obviously not protected enough," Sage said, concerned.

"No," Pia said irritably and glanced at the pendant around Sage's neck. "Seems I was significantly under-prepared. But I didn't know what I was going to encounter when we went in last night." Pia's irritation appeared to be more at herself than at anyone else.

"Are you okay now? Did you protect yourself before coming here tonight?" If the entity were still here, what was there to stop him attacking Pia again? Sage glanced around, but the room appeared the same as it always did.

"I'm fine. And yes, I have taken steps to increase my protection, but as we won't be engaging it tonight there is little reason for concern." Pia popped a square of cheese in her mouth.

"Have you had dinner? Would you like me to see what I can find for us to eat? I'm sure I don't have enough ingredients here to make anything extravagant, but I can easily whip up a Vegemite sandwich or two if you'd like?" It seemed strange to be offering to make a meal during such an unsettling conversation, but the familiarity of a mundane task would give Sage a sense of normality. She felt as though she hadn't taken a full breath since Pia and Mark had arrived.

Pia waved a hand in dismissal. "Mark and I will eat with the team when we get back to the hotel, but thank you."

"Pia's a lot stronger than she looks." Mark smiled at her affectionately.

"I am. I'll rest this evening and we'll come back tomorrow night."

"But why?" Sage stammered. "I mean why would you put yourself at risk like that?"

"I'm not at risk." Pia sounded so confident. But how could she be?

"We've engaged that entity, Sage." Excitement laced Mark's words. "Listen to this." He pressed a couple buttons on the screen, and Sage clearly heard words in the enhanced audio.

"That was my name," Sage gasped. "It knows our names."

"Yes," Mark said. "We're dealing with an intelligent spirit, not just residual energy."

Mark proceeded to give her a summary of the investigation. Through the green haze of night-vision camera footage, she followed herself and the team on the recordings. He pointed out the noises and light anomalies he'd debunked, and highlighted the ones he considered "real."

"And after he said your name, we captured even more EVPs," Mark said, his breathing rapid with excitement. "Listen to this one—"

Mark pressed play, and through the static, Sage clearly heard a male voice say, "Die... Sage... Leave... Us... Mark..."

Bile rose in her throat, and her heart skipped in her chest. Mark reached over and covered her hand with his.

"Don't look so scared." He gave her a reassuring smile, but it didn't work.

"Are you serious? An evil entity says, 'Die, Sage,' and you want me to relax?" She pulled her hand out from underneath Mark's. Her eyes darted around the room; that eerie voice had been captured in this very house.

"I thought this was over. I let you in, you got your evidence. You're supposed to be here giving me my report and telling me what's going on. That's it. We're not doing another investigation," Sage said, shaking her head. "We should have enough with what we've got. There's no way I'm going to provoke it further."

Last night had been bad enough. Sage didn't know exactly what the demonic entity was, but she knew what it wanted. *Die Sage.* If it could knock Pia out, someone who was familiar enough with spirits that she could put some type of protection around herself, what would it do to an unprotected, unknowing Sage? Would it follow through with its threat? And what happened in the afterlife if a demon killed your human body? Would you be destined to spend the rest of time at the mercy of evil?

"We're better prepared now," Mark said.

Sage sat up straight and crossed her arms over her chest. "It's too dangerous." The entity was growing stronger by the day; it certainly had increased its power in the week she'd been here. What would it be capable of next time? Especially if Mark set up that EM pump again.

"Sage," Pia said gently. "We have to come back."

"No you don't. Nobody has to do anything they don't want to do." Sage shook her head. "Uh-uh. No fucking way." Nothing short of a nuclear holocaust would bring Sage back for more of last night.

"We have to find out what the entity is and what it wants," Mark said.

"We already know what it wants," Sage said sharply, then lowered her voice. "Isn't that enough? Why not just be happy with what you got? You have your footage, and EVPs of whatever it is you just played me. Footage of Ryan's push on the shoulder and the demonic scratch. Can't we just leave it at that?"

"We captured those things you mentioned, yes," Mark said, "But I didn't capture the doors slamming by themselves, the bedroom door upstairs locking, the birds that flew into the window shattering it, what happened to Pia, or the glass that shattered. So far, we've only captured what others have captured before us. We have nothing new." He paused, his eyes locked with hers.

"Sage, if I walk away now, I waste a golden opportunity. What I've worked my whole life for."

Her head began to pound with the onset of a migraine. The tension in the room had changed too, and the back of her neck prickled, as though someone—or something—was watching them. She glanced around, then lowered her voice. "But what if things are worse next time? Pia, you were out cold on the floor. We had to call an ambulance. We were terrified that something serious had happened to you. And now we know it's trying to communicate with me."

Pia and Mark exchanged a meaningful glance that set her already frayed nerves jangling.

Finally Pia spoke. "The difference is we'll be prepared next time."

"So you've said. I'm sorry. There will be no further investigation." Sage rose from her chair. Her whole body was twitching in agitation. "I'm going to pack up the last few things and head back to Adelaide so that I can forget about this whole sordid mess. I've had enough."

Once again, Pia and Mark shared a look.

"Will you stop looking at each other like that!" Sage snapped. Her head was pounding now, and the edges of her vision had blurred. Digging into her handbag, she popped out a couple headache tablets, and took them with a little water.

"Oh, for God's sake, Mark, show her," Pia blurted.

"Show me what?" Sage lowered herself into the chair. "Stop trying to hide things from me," Sage said. "I want the truth. The *whole* truth. If I find out you've been hiding anything from me, I'm going to be pissed."

"Okay, then." Mark thrust some black and white photos across the table. "These are stills taken from the video footage we captured last night. I debated whether to show them to you, because I didn't want to scare you. But you want the truth, so here it is."

Sage stared at the grainy pictures, tinted with the green haze of night-vision equipment. She recognized the scenes from the footage Mark had just played her. The pictures had been taken early in the evening, as they were still in the very front part of the shop. Ryan was to one side, and Sage was holding Mark's hand.

"Look closely, do you see what's behind you?"

To the left of Sage was a woman wearing an old-fashioned dress buttoned to the neck and wrists, her dark hair peeking out from beneath a white bonnet.

The air sucked out of Sage's lungs and her heart stopped dead.

This was no Hollywood-movie image, no manufactured monster.

God help her. This was *real*.

Sage's heart raced as Mark placed another picture on the table, then another two. All three were the same. The woman was always in the background, just out of focus, but clear enough for Sage to be certain of what she was seeing. And always, in every shot, closest to Sage.

"And this." Mark placed another two pictures on the table. This time, there were two figures, the same woman and a young girl with long hair and a white, collared night-dress. They were both facing the camera, as though posing, their faces drawn, white and unearthly. There were no hands at the ends of the girl's sleeves.

"How did you do this?" Sage shook her head. This had to be some kind of trick.

"We enhanced the video footage from last night, then printed the stills," Mark said again. "Sage, brace yourself for the next one." His expression was grim.

She slammed her eyes shut. *No more.* She couldn't take it. She heard the picture land on the table. What could be worse than that woman, that little girl with the missing hands?

Damn it, she had to know what was in this house. She *had* to.

She took a deep breath, and then another. Slowly she opened her eyes.

In the final picture, they were walking up the stairs. Behind Sage was a tall, black figure, wearing a cloak, and it appeared to be reaching out to her. Or *for* her.

She let out a pained cry and acid rose in her throat. That dark shadowy figure had been following her around. *Unseen.*

With a swipe of her hand, she sent the pictures flying off the table to scatter on the floor.

Mark was holding two more pictures in his hand, but he didn't place them on the table. Instead, he slid them back in the envelope. "You've seen enough."

"Sage, we need to come back," Pia said. "We are your only chance at getting the entity to leave you alone, and to do that, we need to understand more. I want to see if I can communicate with Mary next time. She may be able to give us more information about who the demon is."

Mark bent down to pick up the scattered pictures. "Sorry," Sage murmured, hating that she was unable to help. She simply couldn't bring herself to look at the pictures again just yet. Perhaps never. It was one thing discovering an evil entity was in your house, even a satanic one. It was another thing entirely seeing it trying to touch her.

Her stomach roiled, and Sage reached for the bottle of wine. Mark handed her his water bottle instead. "You shouldn't drink alcohol on top of those tablets." Of course he was right, but damn it, she was freaking out.

"Tonight you'll stay with us at the hotel," Mark said. "Pia will put a white light of protection around you and your room. You should be safe enough.

Last night, we angered the entity. When we used the EM pump, we gave it an extra boost of energy, which we think it used to attack Pia. When we turned the pump off, it used the batteries from the phones and recording devices. Tonight, we'll keep quiet. Pia will attempt to communicate with Mary and her daughter to see if they're peaceful, or if they too wish you harm."

Oh, God.

"You are not alone, Sage. We're here to help you, the whole team. We'll not let anything happen to you. I promise."

"Sage," Mark said, reaching for her hand, "as well as helping you, this is the opportunity we've waited our whole lives for. There are so many questions we need answers to. Answers that are essential for the investigation and more importantly, for your safety." He circled his thumb across the top of her knuckles, and she pulled her hand out of his grip. He was only trying to comfort her, but it didn't feel right.

A low, animalistic growl from across the room startled her, and she looked up to find Ethan just inside the entrance, glowering at Mark. She'd been so deeply involved in the conversation she had no idea how long he'd been there or how much he'd heard.

Ethan moved toward the table, and Mark's hands fisted. Tension crackled in the air, and this time Nate wasn't around to step between them.

When he reached them, Ethan placed a hand on her shoulder. Though she was still annoyed with him from last night, the comfort and protection she felt with his touch was exactly what she needed. "Are you all right?" Ethan said, his voice soft. She nodded, greedily absorbing the strength he radiated.

"Everything is just great, Detective Skeptic, or shall I just call you DS?" Mark said. "What good fortune befalls us to be graced with your presence this evening?"

Sage frowned. From what she knew of Mark, "DS" could stand for something else entirely. Ethan seemed to know it too. Storm clouds swirled behind his dark and narrowed eyes. It would take but a single spark to ignite an explosion between the two men.

"Mark, don't be so impolite." He had to stop antagonizing Ethan. It was becoming impossible to be around both men at the same time.

"I need to have a word with Sage." Ethan said to Mark.

"Alone."

———◆———

If he wasn't a cop and murder wasn't illegal, Ethan would seriously consider offing Collins. How dare that pretty-boy ghost hunter put his paws all over Sage? He rubbed his jaw, which ached from reining in his temper.

"You only just got here, didn't you?" Sage asked, appearing slightly... *relieved?*

"Yes. Why do you ask?" His stomach burned with acid.

Her shoulders relaxed under his hand, which of course, made his do the exact opposite. *What were they talking about that she didn't want him to know?*

And was it something personal, or because he was a detective? He ground his teeth together, making his jaw protest all the more. The urge to say his piece to Collins was strong, and the risk of getting Sage even more upset with him was the only reason he held his silence.

Sage didn't answer. Instead, she turned to Collins. "Mark, Pia looks as though she needs to rest. Why don't you take her back to the hotel, and I'll meet you there later," Sage said, as though reading his thoughts. Or defusing a landmine.

Wait. Meet him there later? And why was Sage so tense? If Mark had made a move on Sage, Ethan would send him a one-way ticket to see his ghosts. Permanently.

Collins rose and started to pack away his laptop. "Will you be all right, Sage? I mean, alone. *With him.*"

Ethan's hands curled into tight fists. That arrogant show pony had no sense of self-preservation. And no idea how tenuous Ethan's hold on his control was.

"Sage is much safer with me, than you and your band of merry wackos." Ethan ground out the words through gritted teeth.

"*What* did you just call us?" Collins narrowed his eyes in challenge. Sage stood abruptly, her chair screeching on the floor, and placed herself between the two men.

"Stop it. *Both* of you," Sage demanded, then turned to Collins. "You know I'm perfectly safe with Ethan. There's enough tension around here already without you adding to it."

Collins let out a gust of air. "Yes, of course. Sorry," he said, softening his expression. "I'll see you later."

"Thanks, Mark. And you too, Pia. For everything." Sage escorted her guests out the front door.

Ethan watched her walk back to him, her soft skirt swirling around her ankles, giving him enticing glimpses of strappy heels and painted pink toes. He wanted to reach out for her, but kept his arms at his sides. *Was she still angry with him over last night?*

She drew to a stop in front of him and put her hands on her hips. He kept his eyes on hers, and not on the way her stance made her breasts strain against the buttons of her sheer embroidered shirt.

"What do you want, Ethan?" Her expression was strained, and she sounded tired. Something protective stirred inside him, urging him to take control so he could care for her.

"I came to apologize." He kept his voice soft. "For not giving you the chance to explain what happened last night."

"I did explain last night. You chose not to believe me."

Ethan inclined his head in acknowledgement. Despite the fact that neither Sage nor Pia Williams had filed a report, he'd still managed to convince Ryan Donovan and Joe Clarke to voluntarily give their statements. Not surprisingly, their stories matched, pointing to the cause of the commotion as something unexplainable. Something supernatural. They'd either willingly supported

Collins's story, or he'd coerced, or even fooled, them somehow.

Ethan and the team had examined every door, every window, and there was no sign of forced entry, actual or attempted. No scratched paint around any latches, and no signs that anyone had been hiding in the bushes around the house. All the evidence pointed to the perpetrator already being inside.

Not surprisingly, Collins was high on Ethan's list of suspects. Collins had both motive and opportunity. He wouldn't put it past Collins to use last night's police-attendance footage in the adverts for the show to boost ratings. Publicity advantages aside, Collins would also enjoy nothing more than to drive a wedge between Ethan and Sage to clear the pathway for himself. Ethan saw the way Collins looked at Sage, and the very thought made him nothing short of murderous.

It was only a matter of time before Collins slipped up. And Ethan was watching. Closely. So far Collins had refused to voluntarily come in for questioning. And short of arresting him, Ethan had nothing to compel him.

Yet.

Sage's eyes narrowed as she assessed him. "So is that it? Was that your apology?"

What more did she want? "Yes. No..." Her icy green eyes bored into him. "I'm sorry," he finally said, the words sounding a bit lame.

Her gaze didn't soften. Apparently, *that* wasn't what she wanted. "Okay, you've apologized. You can go now." She picked up the wine glasses from the table and carried them to the kitchen sink.

He didn't know what to do, what to say. She was upset, but it wasn't all about him. Something had really shaken her up. No doubt those foolish stories Collins had been spinning more than anything Ethan had done.

She rinsed the glasses under running water. Eyes slightly unfocused, she seemed a million miles away. How could he reach her?

A glass slipped from her shaking fingers, the stem snapping in half when it landed in the sink. She let out a curse, gingerly picked up the pieces, and threw them in the bin. She stared at the discarded broken glass so long, he was just about to ask if she was all right when a single tear slipped from the corner of her eye.

His chest constricted. What the hell? He didn't know much about women, but she damn well wasn't crying over a broken wine glass.

"Sage, honey. Don't cry," he said, moving to her. Wrapping an arm around her shoulders, he pulled her against him. She didn't fight; instead she clung to him, her tears dampening his T-shirt. He routinely dealt with heinous crimes, saw the dark, evil side of human nature. But nothing affected him like Sage's tears.

"Tell me what upset you." He kept his voice gentle, though he felt the opposite. *Tell me what, or more accurately,* who, *and give me the excuse I'm looking for to kill him.*

"You wouldn't believe me if I told you."

He breathed in deeply, then slowly exhaled. Damn. He'd really fucked up last night. "I'm sorry I didn't listen to what you had to say. If you talk to me now, I promise to keep my mouth shut, and listen."

"Can't. It's not something I can explain."

"What is it, then?"

"It's something you have to experience."

Ethan nodded slowly, not wanting to anger her, but not knowing how to gain her trust. Something was going on, and he needed her to open up, not shut him down again. He was going to have to tread carefully.

"Okay, I get that. But there's more. The two of them said something that upset you just now, didn't they?" The edges of his vision blurred as he clamped down on his fury. His patience with the ghost hunter had run dry. She trembled, and he held her tighter. With his other hand, he lightly trailed his fingers down the satiny skin of her arm. He'd never felt anything so soft, and he wished his hands were smoother for her.

"You're trembling. Tell me what he said that scared you."

She didn't reply, just drew in a deep, wobbly breath and shook her head. How could he help her if she kept him shut out?

"Don't believe anything that comes out of that wacko's mouth," he couldn't resist saying. How could she feel more comfortable talking to *him*, when Ethan was the one who'd been there for her, twice now? He'd even stayed all night the second time to make sure she was safe. And then ghost boy just waltzes in from nowhere, with his bloody smiles, and now *he* was the one she confided in?

Sage pulled away and looked up at him. "Ethan, everything that Mark and Pia told me makes perfect sense."

Makes perfect sense? Jesus, Collins had brainwashed her. *Stay calm.* "He's just trying to add more sensationalism to his TV show. He's using you."

She closed her eyes and shook her head. "Mark is not inventing this. *I'm* the one who heard the footsteps when there was nobody there. Many times. And don't tell me you didn't hear the doors slamming. If you don't even believe the things you've experienced yourself, I'm wasting my time telling you anything else."

He stepped close to her and ran the back of his finger down her cheek, then under her chin. He tilted her face so that he was looking directly into her glistening emerald eyes. "Sage. Pushing everything aside, I need you to think rationally and ask yourself how something that doesn't have a body could make the sound of footsteps."

Her lips compressed into a tight line. "I don't know."

"You think a ghost has been slamming doors?" Ethan ran a gentle finger along the crease that had gathered between her eyes. "How could a nebulous mist, something without body mass, move something?"

She pushed his hand away and pursed her lips. He could have smiled at how gorgeous her expression was right now. If he wasn't so angry over how needlessly upset she was.

"I don't know." She bit out the words. "I don't have the answers to your questions, but—"

"I do. Sage, think about it. Even if—and it is a big if—even if there are such things as ghosts, and you happen to have one floating around in here... A ghost didn't kill your grandmother."

She took a step backward. "Then who did, Ethan?" Her voice cracked with emotion. "Who would want to harm a defenseless woman who never had a mean word to say about anyone in her whole life?"

"I made you a promise that I intend to keep. I *will* find out who murdered your nan; you can take that to the bank. It's just a matter of time." Ethan reached out for her but she stepped farther away, folding her arms across her chest.

"Discovering who murdered Nan is one thing, but it has nothing to do with what happened last night. I wish I'd kept those photos," she said, frowning.

"What photos?"

"When I get them from Mark, I'll show you. You'll have no choice but to believe me then."

He bit back a groan. Collins must have doctored some footage. What better way to control someone than to use fear? "Someone, for some reason, is going to great lengths to scare you." He fought to keep his voice even. "I'll find out who. You can count on it."

"I keep telling you who, or what, and you don't believe me." She paced away.

"A ghost?"

She threw her hands up in the air, muttered something impolite, and stalked over to the kitchen windows, slamming them shut. The sun was only just setting, but she yanked the curtains closed.

"What are you doing?" he asked.

"Leaving."

"Leaving," he repeated slowly. "To where?"

"I'm not staying here. And stop looking at me like I'm overreacting and being emotional."

She walked to the front of the shop, shutting the windows and closing the blinds.

"Look, can you stop for a minute? If you'll just sit down, you can explain to me what you think is going on."

She whipped around to face him, her face flushed and her chest heaving. "You and I, Ethan, may as well be on two different planets. You have your worldview and I have mine. The two don't blend."

He stepped toward her. "Like hell they don't. You've just had your head filled with—"

"Stop!" Frustration swirled behind her eyes, turning them a vivid green as she stepped forward and pushed him hard in the chest. He instinctively caught her wrists and held them. Her breathing was labored, and he was painfully aware of how close they were. His jeans tightened inconveniently.

"Don't you dare talk down to me, Ethan. I haven't had anything put in my head. That is a condescending, arrogant comment, and totally uncalled for." She made a half-hearted attempt to yank her hands away. His grip on her wrists wasn't that tight, but he was much stronger than she was. Her chest rose and fell deeply, and her eyes darkened as they scanned his face. Their bodies were almost touching.

She sounded a little breathless. "You don't know, Ethan. You can't know, because you weren't there. I was there. Mark, Pia, Ryan, and Joe were there. Let me tell you uncategorically, that everything that I have seen, and everything I have experienced, I did with my own eyes, my own ears, and my own mind. I don't doubt it because four other people will corroborate what happened too. That is not to mention Nan and Ada. If you refute that evidence, then it is you who is the fool. Not me."

He may have been angry enough to take a cheap shot at the credibility of Mark's team, but he wouldn't insult her grandmother.

"I know you're not a fool," he said instead. She was smart but tough, a little too feisty, but intriguing. Soft, feminine, stimulating, sexy... It was hard to keep his thoughts focused when her soft, warm body was so temptingly close.

"Mark said—"

"Stay away from Collins." His voice was a low rumble. In his heightened state of arousal, the mention of that crackpot's name sparked an intense rush of jealousy. *Mark said.* He didn't give a flying fuck about what Collins said. And he didn't want her thinking about *him* when it was Ethan's hands that were on her.

"Why?" Her tone was a challenge, her heavy-lidded eyes a silent plea. A contradiction that made him desperate to kiss her and put a stop to this frustrating conversation.

"Because I don't like the way he looks at you." He hadn't meant to be so honest.

"Oh, come on," she scoffed. She licked her lips and he felt her pulse racing beneath his fingertips. "Let me go," she whispered.

He didn't believe she wanted that. "No. Not until we've talked about this."

"I won't talk until you let me go."

Ooh, a challenge. He held onto her for a moment too long, then released his grip, his lips twitching with the urge to smile. "Talk."

Her eyes were shining, her cheeks stained pink. A tiny vein on the side of her neck pulsed. How he'd love to flick his tongue along it.

"Okay, then. Tell me why you don't like Mark. And don't give me any crap about how he looks at me."

"I don't trust him," he answered easily. "Next question?"

"Oh no you don't." She stabbed a finger into his chest. "Why don't you trust Mark?"

"Why?" What the fuck? People didn't ask him "why." When he spoke, people took him at his word. "I just don't."

"What have you based that expert opinion on? Where's your evidence?" she pressed.

"My evidence? I don't need any. I've got gut instinct."

"Ooh." Her eyes sparkled as she went in for the kill. "And why are *you* allowed to make a judgment not based on fact, and nobody else is, hmm?"

"You've got to be kidding. The difference is I'm not talking about a fucking ghost, that's what." Heat filled his body. He wanted to touch her so badly, to grab her by the shoulders and kiss her senseless. His hands opened and closed at his sides.

"You don't believe in ghosts because you can't see them."

"That's right."

"Well, I can't see your gut instinct, so I don't believe in it." She raised her chin and waved a hand in dismissal. Every time she inhaled, he could make out the hard peaks of her nipples through the sheer fabric. She placed her hands on her hips, making those two points of temptation even more prominent. He groaned.

"Mark is coming back tomorrow and—"

Gripping her shoulders, he pulled her hard against his body and crushed his lips to hers. She made a soft mewling noise before opening her mouth. The instant his tongue touched hers, it was like pulling the pin on a hand grenade. He dove into her sweet mouth, tasting her, learning her. The heated scent of desire swirled between them, and they breathed each other in.

She kissed him back with an intensity that matched his own. Her hands locked tight around his neck, fingers tangling in his hair. She smelled fresh, like the crisp air after a summer storm, and as she melded her soft, lush curves into him, she rubbed against his hard cock. It was painful pleasure, exquisite torture.

That rubbing sent him into a frenzy of need, which he then ruthlessly leashed. He didn't want to scare her. His desire sure as hell scared him. He attempted to slow the pace, but her hands that had been clawing at his back were now on his chest, and heading south.

She reached between his legs and cupped him through his jeans. He palmed her breast, discovering it to be heavier than he had remembered. Round, firm, and more than a handful. Her nipple was a hard pebble underneath his thumb.

She broke the kiss, his name falling from her lips in a ragged sigh. Her skin was flushed, her green eyes sparkling.

"I want you," she said, squeezing him through his jeans and shattering his control. "Now."

"Oh, sweet Jesus, Sage."

Bending his head, he flicked his tongue along the long column of her neck, and she cried out, desperately panting. He was going to find each and every one of her erogenous zones and tease and explore them mercilessly.

He took her mouth again, hard and urgent, and walked her forward, until her back was flush against the wall near the stairs. Eying the rise and fall of her chest, he ripped that teasing, flimsy shirt apart, buttons skittering across the floor. Her pretty bra, so sheer that he could see her rose-colored nipples clearly, looked so damned sweet and sexy that he left it on. For now.

Lids heavy, pink lips parted, she held his gaze as he ran a hand up her leg and lifted her thigh. She wrapped that endless limb around his hip, as he traced his fingers along her silky skin to the thin material that covered her pussy. He ran his finger underneath the elastic, exploring her. Fascinated, he studied the expressions that flitted across her face, learning how and where she liked to be touched.

With a flick of his wrist, he ripped away her panties, the scrap of lace falling to the floor. He ran a finger along her cleft and groaned in satisfaction at how ready she was for him.

"Ethan," she gasped, panting as his finger dipped into her wet heat, then circled her clit. Her desperate plea made him hunger for her even more, eager to hear how his name would sound when she screamed it.

Her upper body leaning against the wall, he supported her as he lowered himself onto his knees and hooked her leg over his shoulder. The buckle of her shoe's strap dug into his shoulder, and the scent of her desire flooded his senses.

He took a moment to appreciate how sexy she looked with her skirt hitched up and her legs spread wide for him. She had a beautiful pink pussy with a sweet rosebud shaped clit. Perfect, just the way he knew it would be. He leaned forward, breathed her in, and tasted her for the first time.

"Ethan! Oh, God!" she gasped. He glanced up long enough to see that her head was back, her breasts pushed forward, and her lips parted. Holy fuck, that was sexy. He wanted to watch her face, but it was what he was doing that was causing that reaction, so he continued to trace his tongue along her delicious folds, licking until she was writhing and moaning above him.

"That feels... oh, fuck, Ethan... that feels incredible." At least that was what it sounded like she was saying, her words thick and incoherent, spoken between gasps. One thing was for certain, the sound of his name mixed with the word "fuck" sent him to a new level of madness.

Sliding one finger, then two into her slippery heat, he sucked and nibbled on her clit.

She cried out, and her knee buckled. He carefully adjusted his position, rebalancing her in her weakened state. Chin thrust forward, her golden hair cascading down her back, she stood with her palms flat against the wall.

She tightened around his fingers, and he increased his pace, driving them deeper inside her, nipping her clit with his teeth.

She screamed and exploded above him. Her knee completely gave way, but he managed to hold her as tremor after tremor raked her body. He kept up his relentless rhythm, until her cries reduced to pleasured sobs. Moisture had rushed over his fingers as she came, and when he pulled them out of her body, he caught every drop with his tongue.

Completely boneless, she sagged forward, and he scooped her into his arms. She ran a hand over his hair. Through heavy lids, her glistening green eyes locked with his. His heart slammed against his ribcage, then stuttered in his chest.

Spellbound, captivated, he could do nothing more than stare at the limp woman in his arms.

Neither of them spoke when he carried her upstairs.

Chapter Twenty-Two

Sage trembled in Ethan's arms, the rhythmic sound of his heart beating against her cheek. "Which room?" he asked.

"The door on the left," she said, indicating the bedroom she'd used as a child. She turned the handle, and he kicked the door open with his boot. He didn't mention the girly décor as he laid her on top of the floral covers of her bed. She didn't know what he thought about the single bed, but it didn't feel right to take him into Nan's bedroom. She would have preferred this to happen in her apartment, or better still, his. You learned so much about someone by being in their personal space.

"You look so sexy lying there with your shirt ripped open and your hair scattered across the pillow." His voice was deep, his focus intense. Her pulse tripped, skittering along in a new rhythm.

"Don't move," he ordered. He removed his gun and utility belt and placed them on the chair. Grabbing the neckline of his fitted gray T-shirt with one hand, he tugged it up and off in one swift movement. Sage knew she was staring. She couldn't help it; his body was even more perfect than she had imagined. Well-toned, but not bulky, his muscles rippling with his movements. A thin and sexy trail of hair started at his bellybutton and disappeared suggestively into the top of his jeans. She struggled to swallow, her mouth suddenly dry.

Not taking his eyes off her, he undid the top button of his jeans and positioned his body over hers, resting his weight on his arms. His mouth captured hers, the deep kiss reigniting the fire that had barely banked between them.

She ran her hands over the taught contours of his abdomen, marveling at the way the individual muscles contracted beneath her fingertips. She played with that neat line of hair, and he sucked in a breath, catching her wrists as she tried to tug the denim down. Capturing both hands, he placed them above her head.

"Thought I told you not to move." His voice was barely recognizable, little more than a sexy rasp. He motioned to the chair where his utility belt lay. "Do I have to use my cuffs, or will you stay still?"

Cuffs? Oh hell, yes! An image of herself, restrained on the bed while Ethan teased and pleasured her needy flesh, flashed into her mind. The tender place between her legs throbbed its approval. But not here. And not now. He was too sexy not to touch, and she hadn't explored his body nearly enough yet.

"Next time," she said. His eyes darkened at the promise.

"I want you naked." He tugged at her skirt, the elastic waist making it easy for him to pull it down and off in one fluid movement. The heat in his gaze scorched a path across her skin. "Your body is beautiful," he said with what sounded like awe, his voice low and husky. "Your skin is so soft. Perfect."

Undoing the remaining buttons, he stepped out of his jeans and stood before her completely and stunningly naked. She felt as though she'd been hit with a sledgehammer. His was the most exquisite male form she had ever seen outside a magazine.

He was nothing short of magnificent. He ran a hand through his sexy mess of dark hair, biceps flexing impressively, and heat pooled between her thighs. His chest was broad and his waist tapered to slender hips that led to long legs with muscular thighs. She knew from her explorations during their kiss that his ass was just as glorious as the rest of him.

Her gaze moved to and lingered on what was nothing short of a very impressive erection. Large and straight, it stood tall and proud against his belly. She'd never been one to really appreciate a man's cock before, but this one was truly beautiful.

Not caring whether he wanted her to move or not, she pulled herself onto her knees and took his cock in her hands. He growled low and deep in the back of his throat as she ran her hands along his steely length. Lowering her head, she took him into her mouth, wanting to give him a taste of the pleasure he had given her. He hissed in a breath and with both hands on her head, pulled her away.

"Not now. I won't last to pleasure you as you deserve." His words were thick and gravelly, filled with need. She looked up at him and teasingly flicked her tongue along his length.

He pounced on her, a mountain of sexy muscle restraining her hands once again above her head. "I thought I told you not to move. You really are a naughty girl, aren't you?" he asked with a sexy twitch to his lips before his mouth melded with hers.

After long, pleasure-filled moments, his lips left her mouth and she drew in a ragged breath as he trailed kisses across her face and down her neck. Her skin prickled, every nerve becoming more sensitive than it had ever been before. Alive, so alive, every feeling magnified to an intense degree. He licked along her left collarbone, then over the swell of her breast before closing his warm mouth around her hard nipple. Streaks of white hot pleasure tore through her.

"Ethan!" she gasped. She couldn't drag enough air into her compressed lungs as he drew the nipple farther into his mouth, suckling deeply.

Lord help her, this man was a sexual god. Cupping her breast in his palm, he thumbed the nipple, still moist from his mouth, and then tongued the other, paying it the same attention. The fiery heat between her thighs intensified, until she was writhing in exquisite agony.

She shifted to ease her suffering, but her movements only served to make it worse. She needed him. Now.

"Ethan, please—" Her voice, barely recognizable even to herself, came out a breathless choked plea.

"Please what?"

"Please fuck me," she managed.

His eyes bored into hers. "That is so sexy. Say it again."

She held his gaze. "Ethan. You'd better fuck me now, or I'll find those cuffs and use them on you."

He groaned before snatching his jeans from the floor and swiftly locating a condom. He expertly smoothed it down his considerable length.

Her need for him escalating, she spread her legs wider in invitation. He positioned his cock at her entrance and growled low in his throat. When he looked at her again, his eyes were smoldering. Holding her gaze, he slid slowly inside her. He kept going and going, until she was filled more completely than she'd ever been before. It was pleasure, it was pain, then it was more pleasure. The combination consumed her.

"You feel so fucking amazing," Ethan panted as he began to move inside her.

Overwhelmed by him, unable to catch her breath, she was incapable of responding. From her position beneath him, he seemed even larger, even stronger, making her feel small and delicate. With the heated way he was looking at her, she'd never felt more sexy and desirable.

He set the pace, his hips rolling with each entry. Each thrust applied perfect pressure to her sweet spots. His style was unique; she'd had no idea how much pleasure this basic position could bring. She could just imagine what he'd be like when they began to experiment together.

He increased his intensity, driving into her harder and deeper. She gasped, calling out his name.

"Don't come just yet," he said. A lock of hair had fallen across one of his eyes, and it was moving in time with each thrust. It was so sexy she could come by looking at that alone. She bit down hard on her lip and struggled to hold back her imminent orgasm.

He shifted, changing the angle of penetration, sweat beading into a sheen on his forehead as he built her pleasure to an impossible height.

"Are you ready?" he rasped, his breathing hard and fast. "You ready to come for me baby?"

Oh lord and heavens above have mercy, I am beyond ready. "Yes!" she cried.

"Come with me... *now.*" The explosion tore through her body, wave after wave of pleasure ripping her apart. He didn't stop; he kept driving hard into her until he set off another intense orgasm.

Eventually, he stopped and rolled off her with a final groan. She opened her eyes to find Ethan leaning on his elbow, watching her lazily.

"You are exquisite," he murmured. The hard planes of his face were softened by a five o'clock shadow, and she traced her fingertips across the prickly-soft hair. A lump formed in her throat, and she couldn't speak. Couldn't breathe.

God help her. She was falling fast.

Chapter Twenty-Three

Many hours of lovemaking later, and still totally captivated by the golden goddess beside him, Ethan watched as Sage's breathing settled into a regular rhythm. Her sleeping body was limp in his arms, and he kissed the top of her head, breathing in the summery fragrance of her hair.

His heart swelled inside a chest cavity that felt too small to contain it. There was very little he wouldn't do for this woman. She'd brought to life a primal, masculine instinct that he hadn't known dwelled deep inside him. The protectiveness he felt toward her was powerful, overwhelming.

Sage was his.

He brushed a silky strand of hair off her face and tucked it behind her ear. He'd well and truly crossed a line tonight, but turning back was not an option. The door he'd walked through had closed and locked behind him, leaving him in a strange new world, one he would need to learn from scratch how to navigate.

A world where Sage was the guiding star. And follow her he would. Because if he didn't, the hole she'd leave in his heart would never heal.

Relaxed and totally satiated, content for the first time in as long as he could remember, he snuggled Sage closer and relaxed into the pillow. His heavy lids had almost closed when a door slammed downstairs.

Instantly alert, he glanced at the clock on the bedside table. Two thirty-three a.m.

They had an intruder. Was this his chance to catch the serial killer? Adrenaline pumped into his system as he eased out of Sage's embrace and, grabbing his gun and phone, stealthily made his way out the door.

The hallway was cold, middle-of-winter cold. Odd. A foul odor wafted along it, the stench of a dead animal or decaying corpse turning his stomach.

The hairs on the back of his neck stood on end, and every sense he possessed was on high alert.

He performed a quick but thorough search of the top floor to make sure he was not leaving Sage alone and vulnerable to the intruder. When he was satisfied the floor was secure, he made his way downstairs.

Halfway down, he heard another door slam, the noise echoing in the still, evening air. He tightened his grip on the pistol as he reached the ground floor. *Finally.* He was going to get his chance to catch the person who'd been terrorizing Sage.

Through the darkness, senses sharpened, he scanned the area.

"Whoever is here, step out with your hands up." His voice, steady and even, sounded loud and clear in the room. No response. The room was silent, almost unnaturally so. No sounds of outside nightlife penetrated the walls of the shop.

Every muscle was tensed, his heart in overdrive. He needed to remain calm, to enter that space that kept him clear-headed and neutral in his assessment and response.

"I know you're in here," he called. "Come out where I can see you."

He could see the shadowy outline of packing boxes neatly stacked, and edged closer, allowing his other senses to overtake his lack of vision. A prickle ran down his spine, and he felt a heavy sense of foreboding, but there was no sign of an intruder.

Thud. Something moved on the shelf on his left, and he swung around, pistol poised. Silence. Was someone there or not? He edged to the wall and felt for the light switch.

Fluorescent light flooded the room, momentarily blinding him. He crossed back to where he'd heard the noise and saw an ugly figurine lying on the floor underneath the shelving. Ethan bent down and picked it up, turning it over in his palm. It was some type of… gargoyle? Was this the same one he'd seen in Sage's hands that day she'd nearly fallen off the ladder? Sage had stared at it as though something about it deeply disturbed her. He remembered wrapping it up and packing it into a box.

Why would she have pulled it out again? Unless it was another one. He placed it back on the shelf.

He thoroughly searched the room, every square inch. No evidence of a break-in; nothing appeared damaged or disturbed. The windows and doors were all locked and secured. He peered outside and confirmed that the night was still, eerily so, with not even a breath of wind. The moon loomed high above, illuminating the trees like early dawn. Not a single leaf was moving.

Something shoved him hard on the shoulder, and he whipped around, heart pounding, as he braced himself for an attack. His gun followed his line of sight as he searched the room. He saw no one. How could that be?

He couldn't remember ever feeling this uneasy. Not on any of his undercover assignments, no matter how nerve-wracking, had he ever felt this impending sense of… doom, of dread.

No matter how hard he tried, he couldn't shake the uncomfortable feeling that he was being watched. But that was impossible. No one was there but him.

Come to think of it, he hadn't heard anyone approach him or move away after that shove. In his heightened state of awareness, sneaking up on him should have been near impossible.

What door had slammed? All the doors, external and internal, were firmly shut and locked. Even if one door had been open and then slammed shut due to a draught, how could it have happened more than once?

Sage had reported slamming doors, and he'd heard them himself before. He'd been so quick to dismiss them as a quirk of the wind, or the work of an intruder. At the time, he hadn't been certain that she'd locked the doors properly. But this time, the doors were definitely closed and secured.

The touch on his shoulder had left a residual cold, prickly sensation that made his entire arm tingle, and he rubbed at it.

What did any of this mean? Was it possible that something not of this world was at play here?

He shook his head. What the hell would he write in his report? If he so much as mentioned anything supernatural, Ian would have him pulled off the case and hooked up with a shrink before he had a chance to blink.

Thump… thump… thump… Footsteps came from upstairs. Somehow the intruder must have managed to get past him. Or he'd been up there all along.

Sage!

Ethan flew up the stairs, his feet barely touching a single step. Never had he moved so fast in his life. The door to Sage's bedroom was ajar, exactly as he'd left it, and he entered with his heart in his mouth. If anything had happened to her…

But all was quiet, and she was fast asleep in the same position she'd been in when he'd left her. He watched for the rhythmic rise and fall of her chest, and satisfied himself she was safe.

He performed a more thorough search of the upstairs floor, then he searched the entire house, leaving no space unexamined and no piece of furniture or box unchecked. The rotting-meat smell had thankfully disappeared, and the house was once again silent. Eventually he had to concede that no one was there.

Re-engaging the safety on his gun, he placed it within easy reach on the bedside table and slid back under the covers with Sage.

He didn't sleep the rest of the night, his mind grappling with what he'd experienced and the subsequent implications. For the first time in his life, he was forced to consider a possibility that his mind had been closed to.

If he could not see it, feel it, and touch it, it wasn't real. But after what he'd experienced tonight, he had some serious questions to ask himself.

He'd have to get Nate and go over every inch of the house again in daylight. There was still the possibility that the house was rigged somehow. If Collins was coming back to investigate, Ethan was going to be there. Inside, not outside, this time. He wanted to see with his own eyes what Collins did and how he operated.

Ethan needed answers, and he needed them fast.

Smothering a yawn, he checked his watch. He should get some sleep, but wouldn't. He wouldn't leave Sage unprotected for a single second.

Chapter Twenty-Four

Good morning, lovely." Sage opened her eyes to find Ethan smiling down at her, and her heart skipped. "Sleep well?"

The early morning sunlight, filtering in from the gaps around the roller blinds, highlighted sections of his defined torso and cast others in shade so perfectly it could have been an artist's deliberate intention. She couldn't help appreciating the way his muscles bunched and rippled as he used his fingers to comb back his hair. She sighed.

How could he look so impossibly handsome first thing in the morning? It took a couple coffees and a shower for her to amount to presentable.

She stretched in his arms and he released his hold. "I slept like a baby," she murmured, then realized how true that was. Sleep was never a problem when Ethan was with her.

She'd awoken refreshed, her mind cleared of fogginess. Whether it was the good sleep or the amazing night of hot sex she'd had before it, she couldn't say. Either way, the way she felt was due to Ethan.

She snuggled back into him. She couldn't imagine ever wanting to get out of bed.

"Did you hear anything last night?" she asked. His shoulders tensed, and she looked up at him.

"Can I get you a tea or coffee?" he asked, without answering her question. *Hmm.*

"Coffee would be wonderful. Do you know where it is?" Coffee in bed too. Was this man real?

"I'm fairly certain I can navigate a kitchen, unless you've hidden the coffee elsewhere?"

She laughed. "No, you'll find everything you need in the kitchen. Extra strong, a dash of milk, and one sugar. Thank you."

He slid out of bed and a warm thrill washed over her as he slid his pants up and over his high, firm ass. The sexy, confident way he moved around the room brought back flashes of how he'd looked last night as he'd driven powerfully and skillfully into her. The way his hips had rolled with each masterful stroke. The way his tanned skin had glistened with a sheen of sweat. Her fingers twitched as she remembered touching him.

He was the perfect example of a powerful male in peak physical condition. Strength and confidence radiated from his every pore. Simply watching him was a heady sensation, and she couldn't imagine ever getting her fill.

"I'll be right back." He left the room, and she sank into the pillows and allowed herself to absorb the warm, floating feeling of peace. She'd sorely needed last night's reprieve from the nightmare she'd been living. Until she'd woken so rested, she hadn't realized how sleep deprived she'd become. Her mind felt clear and alert for the first time in days.

And Ethan… Just a single thought of him gave her a full-body rush. She closed her eyes, unable to stop smiling, until the man himself pushed the door open with his bare foot and placed a steaming cup of coffee on the bedside table.

Seating himself in the chair beside the bed, he gripped his cup with both hands. How amazing he looked in her childhood bedroom with all its girly decorations, sitting there so strong, so large and masculine, with his bare chest and sexily mussed hair.

"Will you tell me about your nan?" he asked. The question caught her off guard, and she searched his expression, deciding he really wanted to know and wasn't just asking a polite question. He wasn't exactly in detective mode, but she knew he'd listen to her response fully.

"There was no one else like her. Never will be." Sage arranged the pillows so that she was sitting up in bed, then pulled the sheet around her and reached for her coffee.

"She was my mum," Sage said. "The only family I had since the accident." She fingered the angel around her neck and swallowed the keen sense of loss that arose every time she thought about Nan.

Ethan leaned in and took the angel from her fingers. "She gave you this? It's beautiful." His voice was soft and tender, his breath a caress on her cheek.

"No, it was my mother's. She gave it to me for my third birthday. I've worn it every day since." Sage paused, swallowing past the constriction in her throat, then continued. "She always called me her angel, but a week later she became mine."

Sage caught the shine in his eye before he bent down and pressed his lips to the angel. Turning the pendant over in his palm, he frowned.

"What is it?" she whispered.

"It's nothing," he said, his frown deepening. "It's just, the symbol on the back… I'd almost swear it's the same one on the metal charm I found on my father's bedside table. I remembered thinking it strange at the time. Dad wasn't the jewelry-wearing type, so I figured it was some sort of talisman he'd come across at work. Yes, it's definitely the same symbol. I remember being strangely fascinated by it."

His face cleared and he let the pendant fall from his fingers.

"Your mother was right. You are an angel." He kissed her nose, and she felt it right down to her toes. For such an outwardly hard and tough guy, he could make her melt with a simple gesture and few words. Just like the way heavy rock bands performed the best ballads.

"Before I tell you anything about Nan, it's important for you to understand that my nan was not a kook."

"I never thought she was," he said, appearing offended.

"I know how you talk about Mark, that's all. I'm going to explain some things to you, and to understand, you'll need to listen."

"I'm a detective; it's my job to listen."

"Listen with an open mind," she added.

He inclined his head. "I guess I deserve that. I'm sorry. For a lot of things."

Sage sucked in a deep breath and realized just how much she wanted, *needed,* him to understand. "Nan was a highly intelligent woman who just happened to be sensitive to the spirit world."

She scrutinized his reaction, prepared to stop right there, but found him completely unreadable. He had on his detective face, the one she imagined he used frequently in his line of work: expression relaxed, calm and neutral, giving nothing away. His eyes, however, almost burned her with an intensity and intelligence that missed nothing. They let her know that every word she said would be analyzed and catalogued. Ethan casually took a sip of his coffee and stretched, rearranging his large frame for comfort.

"I know you don't believe in spirits and the supernatural," Sage continued, "but I do. At least I do now."

Sage sipped her coffee in an attempt to shake the familiar childhood flashback of sounding like she was weird, a freak. She determined to finish regardless of what he thought at the end of it. It was her experience. Her truth. And she would not deny a single part of herself any longer.

"Nan often spoke of an angelic realm, and she had the ability to connect with souls that had crossed over. She used to pass messages through from beyond the grave—that's how the shop got its name." She'd need to take down the sign; she couldn't put it off any longer. It just seemed so... final.

"Before a reading, Nan would go quiet. She'd retreat into herself and somehow connect to a higher source, where she would then receive guidance and sometimes messages for whomever had come to see her."

Sage closed her eyes for a moment and allowed the memory of her nan to give her the peace and solace it always did. Nan could calm her with a single touch of her warm, loving hand. Soothe any hurt from the hateful words of the mean girls at school with a gentle smile and a few well-chosen words.

"I could never do readings, and it was not something she encouraged. Not something I wanted. She explained once that she was simply born with a gift, and it was her choice, if and how she used it. She told me that I had my own gifts, and when the time was right, and when I was willing, I would discover what they were."

Ethan didn't say anything, his eyes still focused on her, in that way he had of making her feel as though what she was saying was the most important thing in the world.

"People sought Nan out for the way she made them feel. I watched them walk into the shop angry, upset, or consumed with grief, and every single one of them left a little lighter. Their burdens eased in some way."

"But it made your school years hard." It wasn't a question, and she wasn't surprised. You couldn't talk to the people in the town without hearing about Sage the freak. Not that a nasty word would be said about her from anyone her nan's age. Only the kids she'd gone to school with, who were now grown women and men.

"The kids at school didn't understand," she confirmed but didn't explain further. Would the pain from their torment ever fully leave her, or was she scarred beyond repair?

The mattress dipped as Ethan joined her on the bed. "You know, you make me feel a lot like she used to," Sage said, smiling at him.

"How so?" A brow raised, he appeared surprised and pleased by her comment.

"Safe, warm, secure. As if all really is right in the world."

He wrapped his arms around her and kissed her. He tasted like coffee and powerfully sexy male.

Eventually, she broke the kiss and sat back against the pillows. There was more to the story, and she didn't want to get distracted before she got it out. She needed him to hear it, even if he could never understand.

"At some point, something changed. I don't know exactly when, and I had no idea that it had, until after Nan passed and I was back in this house."

"Define 'something changed.'"

Sage thought back to the Ouija board in the storm, the first incident after she'd come back, and shuddered. Nan had owned that ancient board, collected during one of her journeys to the Eastern part of the world, for years. Sage had believed it to be nothing other than an ornament, no different than the numerous other objects scattered around the house, cluttering shelves and cupboards. Never once had she seen her Nan use it. "I don't play with frivolous spirits," Nan had said. She didn't use her gift that way.

"After I came back, strange things began happening in the house," Sage continued. "Unexplained footsteps, objects moving, temperature fluctuations, doors slamming. You even experienced some of them yourself."

"And I thought they were from an intruder, at the time." She looked up at him then, trying to read his face. That was an interesting thing for him to say. As though he hadn't believed her before, but now did. Hope surged within her, and she forged on.

"What you don't know was that I found Nan's diaries, and she'd recorded the same things as I was experiencing. She mentioned discussing it with Ada, who apparently was quite concerned. Nan's entries became more harried, her tone urgent, and she believed she was running out of time. For what though, she never said. She was the one who encouraged me to leave and relocate to the city. I didn't know it at the time, but her entries mentioned that she wanted to keep me safe." Her voice cracked slightly, and she took a breath before she continued. "I had no idea Nan was in danger, or I never would have left." She'd probably never be free of that guilt.

"But you were gone for years, right?"

"Yes, five. From what I can tell so far, the strange occurrences were random but consistent over the years, not escalating until a few months ago. Something happened at the beginning of July that changed everything. It was about that time that Nan recorded genuine concern about her own safety."

"So you think the things that have been going on in the house have a direct link to your nan's murder?"

"According to Nan's diary, Ada believed there was. Ada seemed certain there was a direct link between what was going on in the house and the murders of that boy and the hitchhiker."

He nodded thoughtfully, as his fingers traced lightly across her arm. His touch was at once both comforting and exciting, her body instinctively responding to him in a primal way.

"I'd like to read the diaries if you don't mind."

Sage's lips curved. "I knew you'd want to."

"And that's why you didn't mention them earlier?"

"I didn't trust you as much earlier." As she said the words, she recognized the depth of truth in them. Something had shifted between them. Not just on a physical level. The strange pull she'd felt the moment he'd showed up on her doorstep had somehow solidified into something real. In some way she felt as though he was *meant* to be here. She ignored the fanciful thought. That type of thing belonged in romance novels.

"Sage, those diaries are evidence," he said, and she was reminded that the detective was never far from the man. "There may be important clues in them that could help solve the case. Lord knows I need every lead I can get," he added. "You really shouldn't have kept them from me." He kept his tone mild, steady, but he couldn't disguise the frustration, hurt, even anger, that laced his words.

"I would have told you if I'd read anything I thought would help. Like if she'd mentioned a name. But she didn't, and everything she wrote I knew you wouldn't take seriously anyway. You would have dismissed the entries as those of an old woman losing her mind."

"You can't know that." But he shifted uncomfortably.

"I do know just that, and so do you. But mostly I didn't tell you because..." She sucked in a breath. "I didn't want you to take them, and I know you would have. Evidence, like you said. Bagged and tagged. In those diaries are Nan's words, her thoughts. They still carry her energy. I can feel her with me, hear her voice in my mind as I read them. It would feel as though you were taking all I have left of her. "

Her throat constricted and he took her into his arms. "I understand. I won't take them away," Ethan promised. "I'll read them here. With you. Did she say anything else in the diaries that I should know about right now?"

Sage pulled back and pondered for a moment.

"Yes. She mentioned another diary. It belonged to a woman who lived in this house many years ago. A woman named Mary." Sage paused, unable to suppress a shudder as the photos Mark had shown her flashed through her mind.

"Are you all right?" Ethan asked. "You're cold." He rubbed his palm along her goose-fleshed arms. "Can I get you a robe?"

"No, I'm fine. Thank you. Apparently Mary's diary is also tied up in this. When I find this diary, I'll hopefully have some more answers." Sage almost mentioned the pictures, but at the last minute decided against it. They were the closest they'd ever been to having a conversation where Ethan was not shutting down any possibility of the supernatural. Telling him about the photos wouldn't help the case, and she risked turning the conversation toward a debate over the validity of Mark's work.

"You'll show me Mary's diary when you find it, right?" Ethan said. "There may be clues in there, vital pieces of information, that given you're not privy to the details of the investigation, you wouldn't know to pick up."

"Of course," Sage said. "Mary's diary won't be as hard to let go of as Nan's." Where on earth could it be? She had mostly finished packing the whole house now. The only rooms she had yet to tackle, aside from the kitchen, were this one and the attic. She didn't know what, if anything, was in the attic, because from what she could remember, Nan never had used that space and had warned Sage against ever going up there. But maybe the diary wasn't in the house at all.

"I haven't found Mary's diary yet, even though I've packed almost the entire house. Maybe Nan gave it to Ada. I tried to visit her two days ago, but she wasn't home. I left a note on her door with my mobile number. She hasn't got back to me yet." Her fingernails dug into the soft flesh of her palm as frustration clawed at her. Like Mary's diary, Ada could also answer some of the questions multiplying by the minute. Ada was the next best thing to asking Nan herself, only she seemed to have disappeared like a puff of smoke.

Ethan frowned. "Is that unusual? Nate and I also tried to speak to her in a routine follow-up interview yesterday, and she wasn't home then either."

Sage felt the first stirrings of concern. "I don't know Ada's daily routine enough to know if it's unusual or not, but I find it strange that she hasn't returned my call or made an attempt to visit me since I got back. Except that one time, she hasn't spoken to me at all."

"What time was that?"

"At the funeral. She warned me that I needed to leave before it was too late."

Ethan's spine stiffened, and she felt his detective mode kicking in. "You won't go see her again. I'll follow this up from here."

Sage sighed. "Just in case you haven't realized it yet, I don't follow orders." She didn't need to look up at him; she felt his smile.

"Yeah, I've pretty much worked that out for myself." She could hear the amusement in his tone. "And if you spoke to my boss, you'd discover that much to his frustration, neither do I," he added. "But I am serious when I say I don't want you to go anywhere alone. Until the murderer is behind bars, I'd prefer you weren't alone at all. I can't rule out the possibility that you are the killer's next target. If I can't be with you, I'll arrange for someone else to be. And where possible, we'll make visits to your nan's friends like Ada together. Is that better?"

"Much." She enjoyed the idea of spending more time with him.

"While I admit to finding the things that have been going on a little strange, I still can't rule out an intruder, or an elaborate hoax. Someone might have been going to great lengths to scare your grandmother and now you."

"Maybe. But it doesn't explain everything, does it? Nothing we've considered yet does. There are too many questions and not enough answers."

Hand on her cheek, he turned her head so that she could see he was earnest. "I know I don't yet have a good explanation. But that doesn't mean I won't find one."

"I believe you." Ethan wouldn't rest until he'd solved this.

"Sage, I'm not saying there's nothing going on that's out of the ordinary, but I can tell you one thing for sure."

"What's that?"

"A ghost did not kill your grandmother. And I'm going to find the person who did."

Chapter Twenty-Five

The steam from the shower filled the small room and fogged the mirrors. As Sage washed her hair, she considered Ethan's comment that a ghost had not killed Nan.

He was right. No doubt something evil was in the house, even without the proof Mark and his team obtained. But Nan had been murdered, and Sage didn't believe it was by a ghostly or demonic hand.

Two separate things were going on here. Which in itself was an almost inconceivable coincidence. Cryton was a small town. To have one extraordinary event occur in such a place was amazing. But two? And simultaneously?

The odds pointed to the events being linked in some way. But how? A demon couldn't stab someone. Or could it? Like Ethan said, they didn't have a body. But if they could slam doors, move ornaments, lower the temperature, make noise, push and even scratch someone, like Ryan claimed to have been scratched… Was it also possible a demon could pick up a knife and stab someone? Five times?

And then that story Pia had told, about the nursing home… A shiver rolled through Sage, from head to toe. She hoped with every fiber of her being that they were not dealing with the same entity here. Because if they were dealing with a master demon, Sage was in real trouble. The EVPs indicated that the demon was targeting her specifically, and in the photos, Mary's ghost and that of her daughter, even the terrifying dark shape in the black robe, were around Sage. Reaching for her. But why would they be after *her*? Simply because she was in the house? Could the house be a portal, a doorway to the other side, as Nan had wondered?

So much didn't make sense. A vein throbbed at her temple, and she rolled her shoulders a few times, trying to relax.

The only positive in this craziness was that she had met Ethan. He was her logic, her peace, in a world turning stranger by the minute.

She rinsed off the soap suds and stepped out of the shower, drying herself with her favorite fluffy pink towel. Sage was just coming out of the bathroom, hair still damp and nothing but a towel wrapped around her, when she heard Ethan's phone ring. He glanced at the screen and cursed before answering. His back was to her and he didn't appear to realize she'd returned.

"Jen." His voice was lowered, his shoulders tensed. A lump rose and lodged in Sage's throat.

"No." He ran his hand through his hair as he listened to whatever it was this *Jen* had to say.

Blood whooshing past her ears, Sage reached into her closet and pulled out the first dress her fingers landed on.

"Can't talk now. I'm in the middle of an investigation… I already said I don't know when I'll be finished." He spoke the next words through clenched teeth. "I can't do this now… No… I said *not now*… I'll call you later."

He pressed the disconnect button at the same time as he turned and saw her. She had dropped the towel and was stepping into her dress, not having the presence of mind to even put on underwear.

His initial look of appreciation faded as he took in the expression on her face.

Sage forced a smile, but was sure it was more of a grimace as she brushed passed him to grab her mobile phone and handbag from the bedside table.

"Judging by your reaction, I assume you heard that." Ethan touched her arm.

"You have a girlfriend." It wasn't a question. She shrugged off his hand and walked back to the closet to look for some shoes.

"No. Yes… Shit!" He rolled his shoulders, his neck cracking as he stretched it from side to side. "Not anymore. Not that I ever considered her one anyway."

"But *she* does." Sage was barely able to quell the overwhelming surge of nausea that had come over her. It had never even crossed her mind that he was in a relationship. She couldn't believe it hadn't occurred to her to ask. But how dare he not volunteer that information?

He said nothing, didn't try to deny it again.

Her heart splintered into a gazillion tiny pieces. Oh dear God, it physically hurt. She *had* been falling in love with him.

She rubbed at her chest to alleviate the crushing pressure there. *Damn him. Damn him to hell.*

Not that he probably even realized what he had done. He'd never made her any promises after all. It was she who had done all the assuming. Last night… how could he make love to her the way he had last night if he had a girlfriend?

Aside from her pathetically naïve heart getting her involved in something it had no business doing, he'd forced her to do something she never would have done. Because no matter how attracted she was to him, she would *never* have slept with him had she known.

Never.

She knew firsthand how it felt to be cheated on. And that wound was still fresh.

"You bastard." She threw her sandal because her shaking fingers couldn't do up the buckle. It bounced off the oval mirror in the corner, knocking it backward against the wall.

"It's not what you think," Ethan said, righting the mirror. If only it was that easy to set a life straight.

"Sage, honey. You haven't even given me an opportunity to explain. You have the wrong idea. The situation with Jen, it's… it's complicated."

Complicated. Great. Fantastic. Wonderful. And how did them sleeping together make it any less complicated?

"Don't bother trying to explain. It's not any of my business anyway." Sage slipped her feet into a pair of dressy thongs instead. No buckles.

"Not your business? Now wait a goddamn minute," Ethan growled, taking a step toward her. He stopped when she raised her hands in front of her. If the expression on his face was anything to go by, he was angry now too. Good. She wanted him to hurt.

He stood in the middle of the room, as she darted around, not really thinking about what she was doing. Not even looking at what she was throwing in her handbag. She didn't know where she was going. All she knew was that she couldn't stand still. She needed to leave this room. This house. Maybe if she kept moving, she could keep one step ahead of the crushing reality just waiting to bowl her over. And she wouldn't give him the satisfaction of seeing her crack.

A girlfriend! He had a goddamned girlfriend.

It was bad enough that her whole life was one huge nightmare. Now Ethan had just ripped away her only life raft.

God! He was *still* watching her, looking so calm, so *unaffected*. How much trouble did you get in if you threw something at a cop?

"Sage, honey—"

"Don't you dare 'Sage, honey' me!" Her hands had risen in front of her face as though to protect her from the endearment. It wasn't enough. Tears pricked at her eyes, and she turned her back to him.

"Get out!" she screamed, her voice cracking in the most humiliating way.

"Sage. You're upset." *Ya think? Nice work, Sherlock.*

"But you have no reason to be." He swore as his phone rang again. "I'm sorry, Sage, I have to take this call."

She spun around to face him. "I'll leave to give you and your *girlfriend* some privacy." She almost choked on the word.

"Nate." He answered the call, giving her a pointed look.

"What? *When.*" His face hardened. "I'll be right there. No, don't. Wait for me." He disconnected and slipped the phone into his pocket, strapped on his belt and gun, and grabbed his jacket.

He reached for her, but she backed away. A pained look crossed his face, and he released a long, slow breath. "I'm sorry to have to leave you like this, but something's come up that needs my immediate attention. You need to give me a chance to explain. I'll swing by as soon as I can."

He ran his fingers through his hair in frustration. As she watched, she remembered only too well how those strands felt. How they tumbled sexily around his face while he made love to her. How they smelled when his head was lowered, lapping at her nipples. Never again. Pain, razor sharp, raked her body, and she turned away.

"Baby, please don't do this." When she didn't look at him, he cursed under his breath. "I really have to go. I'll be back when I'm finished, and we'll straighten this whole thing out."

She didn't answer. "Don't judge me until I've had a chance to explain," he said. She couldn't see his face, but she heard the way his voice broke. She didn't move. Didn't breathe, and the silence stretched on. Eventually, he let out a slow pained sigh. "I'll be back as soon as I can."

And then he left.

She waited until she heard the front door close and lock before she deflated like a punctured balloon.

Sitting on the edge of her bed, she wrapped her arms around herself and hung her head between her knees, soft, anguished noises falling from her to the floor.

The devastation was so... *absolute*. She'd gone from euphoria to grief in a space of moments. She lifted her head just enough to drag a lungful of air into her constricted chest. She was crushed, but dammit, she wasn't going to cry.

Not over him.

She wasn't even going to think about him one second longer. She focused on her painted pink toes.

Why was she sitting here on the very bed she had just had the best sex of her life in, thinking her world had come to an end?

And about that sex part. What the hell had she been thinking? At what point had she thought *that* would be a good idea? He was the cop investigating her nan's murder, for heaven's sake.

If her life was a jigsaw puzzle, to use the analogy psychologists were so fond of, then someone had stood at the top of Ayers Rock and scattered the pieces into a cyclone. After this little trip back to her home town, nothing in her life would be the way it had been before. She'd have to create another life, with as many pieces of herself as remained at the end.

And maybe that was the whole point. Wasn't that what life was all about? Picking up the pieces, and putting yourself back together in a rearranged and hopefully improved version of your former self? And if so, where did the detective fit into the puzzle pieces of her life?

Nowhere, that's where. He was on one of the tiny pieces now blowing somewhere across the Murray River, far, far away. A memory. A beautiful memory, but a memory just the same. He didn't matter. The sex didn't matter. The fact that he had a girlfriend didn't matter. Because he didn't matter. He *shouldn't* matter.

Then why did it hurt so much? Her middle squeezed like someone was wringing out a wet rag, and she hugged herself even tighter as a strangled sob escaped her lips.

Stop being so pathetic. She didn't get emotional over men like this. Especially ones she'd just met and quite obviously didn't know very well. She hadn't been crushed even when she'd caught her ex—the *other* lying arsehole in her life—cheating on her.

Oh, that had hurt for sure. Her ego maybe, her pride definitely. She'd yelled, she'd thrown things. She'd left a message on his answering machine that would've peeled the paint from his walls. But she hadn't fallen apart. Mostly, she'd berated herself for being such a poor judge of character and had vowed to learn from it.

But she hadn't learned a damned thing. She used to think she was slightly less trusting and a whole lot stronger. But now she was just a whole lot less trusting.

Another cramp seized her stomach. Her breathing continued to hitch and her eyes stung. She blinked her eyes furiously.

She was *not* going to cry over him, dammit.

She wiggled her toes. The nail polish was chipped on the left big toe. Had she packed her pedicure kit?

She needed to do something. Anything to keep her mind off *him*.

It was in Nan's room, she remembered, shuddering as she thought of the last time she'd used the kit. She'd needed the tweezers to remove the shards of glass from the shattered pointer of the Ouija board.

Reality came crashing back. So what if the only time she'd felt peace during this whole terrifying episode was when she'd been in Ethan's presence? His arms. His innate sense of inner calm and strength washed over her whenever he was in close proximity. It was natural that she would be attracted to that at such a chaotic period in her life. But that inconvenient attraction to him would surely fade as her life returned to normal. Wouldn't it?

He had quickly become an addictive, soothing balm for the turmoil in her life. And he cared about her, she was sure of it. At least she'd been sure. He had showed her in so many ways. The way he'd stayed all night and watched her sleep. The way he'd worried about her. The way he'd acted all *possessive* over her when it came to Mark.

How could she have been so wrong about him? How could she have made such a fundamental error in judgment?

She'd allowed herself to believe he cared, and she'd let him in. Somehow he'd managed to get under her skin and into her bloodstream, and now she had no idea how to get him out.

She wriggled her pink toes again.

A tear escaped her eye and rolled down her cheek. She fought hard not to cry even as another tear followed the first. And then another, which was soon followed by another.

Damn him.

Chapter Twenty-Six

Ethan turned his Land Rover into the hotel complex to find Nate waiting for him, a look of grim determination on his face. Nate climbed in, then updated him as they headed to the local park.

"A jogger found the body of an elderly resident early this morning, hidden in the bushes. Same signature as the others. Stabbed five times, eyes removed and covered with black circular patches of cloth, symbol branded into the palm of her right hand."

Ethan thumped a fist on the steering wheel and let out a string of curses. Four victims, and he was still no closer to finding the killer.

On top of it, this latest murder was the reason he'd had to leave Sage so abruptly. It had almost killed him having to leave before he'd had a chance to clear things up. Sage was furious.

Jenny's timing couldn't have been any worse. She'd phoned to find out whether he was going to be back for her parents' wedding anniversary party later this month. As he just so happened to be with her when the invitation had arrived, she had taken it upon herself to assume he'd be accompanying her. He shouldn't have taken the call this morning, but she had an annoying way of continuing to call. He'd intended to get rid of her as briefly and efficiently as possible.

But he'd managed to fuck that one up because now Sage believed he had a girlfriend. He sucked at women. What a mess. He had to set Sage straight, and soon, but it was going to take time to explain about Jen.

He didn't know how he was going to find the words to fix this; he only knew that every fiber of his being depended on him doing so.

Ignoring the car park, Ethan drove over the curb and cut across the grass, coming to a stop alongside the crime scene. A small crowd of townspeople had gathered underneath the trees near the playground and were being held back by the local cops.

Ethan was aware of the curious gazes of both the officers and the crowd as he lifted the yellow and black strip of crime-scene tape so that he and Nate could step through.

The air was filled with the discordant squawks of police radios and urgent murmurs of discontent from the crowd as they began to speculate about the latest murder's connection to that of Celeste Matthews. Someone called out, asking if there was a "granny killer" on the loose. Just great. All they needed was for that rumor to get started and send a ripple of panic throughout the community.

So far, the townspeople weren't aware of the connection between the murders of Celeste Matthews and the two other victims, but there'd be no way to stop a flurry of media interest now, and once the reporters were on the story, they'd soon unearth the link.

As if on cue, a group of reporters stepped out of a large white van emblazoned with the local station's logo and began hauling out equipment. Ethan cursed under his breath. Nate would have to handle them with his usual finesse; Ethan's patience with journalists' questions was tenuous at the best of times.

"Detectives Blade, Ryder." Sergeant Robert Brady greeted them tersely, a pained expression on his sun-weathered face. His neatly trimmed hair, streaked with silver, would no doubt be fully gray by the end of this investigation. The sleepy town of Cryton was not prepared to handle crimes as heinous as this. The local police dealt mostly with small-time crime: wayward teenagers, drunken assaults, and speeding, along with the occasional traffic fatality. They were ill-equipped to delve into the psychology of a serial killer. Especially when the victims were so well-known to everyone in this close-knit community.

Without having to ask, Ethan knew what the sergeant needed most. Stepping forward, he placed a hand firmly on Bob's shoulder in an unspoken confirmation that he'd take over. Bob had such a look of gratitude in his watery, pale blue eyes that Ethan would bet that Bob had not only known the victim, but had been very fond of her.

Ethan turned away from Bob and crouched down, lifting the white sheet, careful not to disturb any evidence. His stomach tightened. Even through the black cloth circles that covered her eyes, he recognized her.

"Ada Slatterley."

"Yes," Bob confirmed, his notebook twisting in his tanned hands. "What a shame. Such a lovely woman. Just like Celeste."

Sage was going to be devastated. Ethan would have preferred to be tell her himself, but since the crowd was growing larger by the minute, he thought that was unlikely. With all the work ahead of him, it was going to be many hours before he could get back to Sage.

The police photographer was next to arrive, flashes lighting up the body as he began to document the crime scene and the areas where evidence was marked by small flags.

When the photographer had finished, Ethan bent down and studied the body, Nate on the other side. With a gloved hand, he carefully turned over her palm, knowing already he'd find the symbol burned into the skin. Just like he knew when he lifted the black eye patches, there would be empty sockets. There was irritation around her mouth. Forensics would no doubt discover the residue of duct tape there. Did he tape their mouths to keep things impersonal? To stop their screams? And why did he bother removing the tape before he returned their bodies to the scene of the abduction? Ada's body had been placed; it hadn't fallen. She was on her back, her legs together, arms out to the sides. As though she'd been placed on an invisible cross.

"We think she was murdered here around six this morning," Bob said.

"No. That's not correct," Ethan murmured, running a critical eye over the scene.

"What makes you say that?" the sergeant asked.

"The blood that should have pooled underneath the body is absent. She was placed here." Ethan pointed to the damaged blades of grass and other evidence of a body being dragged. Ethan motioned to Bob, and they followed the minute clues to the car park on the other side of the bushes. Unfortunately, he didn't see any trace evidence for the team to collect.

They walked back to the crime scene. "Who discovered the body?" Ethan asked. Bob indicated to his left, where a young woman, approximately mid-twenties, was sitting on the grass, huddled under a blanket.

A bystander broke through the tape. "Back off." Ethan's voice, raised in command, sliced through the air. The cocky teenager, low-slung denims hanging beneath his arse, froze in place. Eyes wide, he quickly retreated, despite the cajoling from his mates. The kid wasn't as dumb as he looked. There were very few adults brave enough to disobey Ethan's direction. Especially when his patience was already stretched thin.

He wouldn't leave until everything had been done to his satisfaction. Not that he didn't trust the local guys; he just couldn't risk any mistakes compromising their only lead.

His thoughts turned once again to Sage, who was alone and unprotected. The killer had struck the two people closest to her. His gut twisted and knotted.

"Bob, I need you to arrange something for me," Ethan said.

"Name it."

"I need a uniform or two to sit surveillance on Sage Matthews's shop until I can take over myself."

"Surveillance on Beyond the Grave? Detective Blade, surely resources would be better placed—"

Ethan cut him off. "I don't have time to argue."

"Detective," Bob said, standing up straighter. "You must know how highly I respect you, and Taipan, but I simply don't have the resources to spare. Crime is up thirty percent just these last four weeks. Three murders aside, I've got an increase in drug-related crime, and the high school has been broken into and vandalized, with pig's blood sprayed on the walls. I'm starting to think the whole damn town has gone crazy." Bob's round face was flushed red and a vein pulsed on the side of his neck.

Ethan sympathized with the sergeant. Resources were stretched thin at the best of times. "I'm well aware of the high school, and the other reports. I've requested resources be brought in from surrounding areas. Celeste Matthews' body was discovered in Beyond the Grave, and Pia Williams was attacked in the same location two nights ago. Until I rule out any connection between the murder and the attack on Ms. Williams, I need the location under constant surveillance." Ethan kept his voice even, his frustration and fear for Sage's safety out of his tone.

Bob nodded. "Of course. Anything I can do to help. I appreciate your calling in additional resources. Better arrange a bigger holding facility at the station while you're at it. Before long, I'll have the whole damn town behind bars."

Ethan waited while the sergeant spoke into his handset, before approaching the girl who'd found Ada's body. Ethan couldn't disagree with the sergeant's observation. Something very strange was happening in this town. The sudden spike in crime—burglaries, assaults, vandalism, and car thefts—had occurred in perfect timing with the actions of the serial killer. Although he couldn't prove a direct link, Ethan didn't believe in coincidences.

And just as Sage had told him of what her nan had written in the diary, Ethan too, had the sensation that time was running out. Someone had pulled the pin on a grenade, and it was only a matter of time before all hell broke loose in Cryton.

———— ✦ ————

Later that afternoon, Ethan was back inside his small and stuffy hotel room. Skin still damp from a recent shower, he sat down, sans shirt, at his computer and hit the icon to check his emails. He opened the one from Zach. It was the background check on Collins and his team. It had come through hours ago, but this was his first opportunity to read it. He scrolled through the comprehensive report and found nothing of concern. Work histories, scanned copies of business references, character references, two speeding fines paid on time. Taxes up to date. Dammit.

He leaned back in his chair and rubbed his temples. He'd hoped to find evidence of the team being involved, even remotely, in a previous scam. Reports of false representation, anything. But there was nothing. The reputations of Mark Collins and his team were exemplary. All four members had degrees and appeared to have met at the same university. That could explain their bond, and the apparent willingness to back each other's stories.

He read through copies of reports their company had given to previous clients. About seventy percent of the time, they had debunked the claims of paranormal activity and had provided logical, scientific explanations for the situation. For the remaining thirty percent where they did verify a supernatural presence, they'd assured their clients the presence was nothing harmful.

166

So if the members of Collins's team were legit, how did that change things, if at all? If they were to be believed, a whole lot of supernatural stuff had occurred during the night they'd spent in Sage's shop, events verified by everyone there. Including Sage. So how did that connect with the serial killer? And the sharp increase of crime in the town?

He stood up and began to pace. After his own taste of the unexplained last night, Ethan was forced to consider… what? That the supernatural was somehow responsible? Even if he were to secretly consider that angle, he'd never admit it to anybody else. He'd take that thought to the grave.

Ethan could protect Sage from predators in human form. He'd think nothing of taking whatever action was necessary to ensure her safety, including killing someone. Hell, it wouldn't be the first time he'd done so.

But if what Sage and Collins suspected was true? The idea of paranormal activity was so outside Ethan's comfort zone he didn't even know where to begin. How did he protect Sage from something like that? He couldn't arrest it, threaten it—hell, he couldn't even shoot it.

Ghosts, spirits, demons—*things*—haunting Sage, trying to attack her? That just couldn't be a valid possibility. It couldn't.

Ethan had this life thing all worked out. He'd seen evil in human form on many occasions. He knew how dark a human being could become. How cold and callous. That kind of thing he could deal with. It was his job. And the numerous commendations in a drawer at home proved he was good at it.

He needed to be able to protect Sage. Anything else was just too frightening to even contemplate.

And even if the unexplained and seemingly mysterious happenings at the house were somehow supernatural in nature, they had at most only a tenuous connection to the dead bodies. He was sure his attention was still best focused on a flesh-and-blood serial killer. Yet how could he focus on that, when Sage was planning on being in the house tonight with Collins, doing who knew what? Ethan rolled his tight shoulders. Fuck.

He had to talk to Sage before nightfall. He couldn't allow her to go into the investigation tonight with Collins, still mad at him. Ethan had left a couple messages on her phone, but she hadn't returned his calls, and the waiting was shredding his control. The sooner he straightened out this whole misunderstanding, the better.

Dragging his thoughts back to the case, he drummed his fingers on the desk. At Ethan's insistence, Ian had dispatched them twelve more officers from the surrounding area, far fewer than Ethan had requested. For some reason, Ian wanted as little attention on this case as possible. Why? Something didn't sit right. Ian should be throwing manpower at this case, if he wanted it solved fast. But he seemed more concerned about the media… After this afternoon, the horse had bolted on that one.

Ethan tapped his pen on the page. Twelve additional uniformed officers would help Bob keep on top of the current influx of crime and help Ethan expand the search for the serial killer farther into the surrounding areas. But they wouldn't be enough.

It was time for him to face the facts. The case had become personal. Ethan needed his own people. Men who took orders from him unquestioningly. And why not? He had the knowledge and the resources to direct and pay them.

Because of his inheritance, he'd been afforded the chance to participate in some high-risk, high-gain investments that had paid off handsomely. Money would never be an issue. He continued to work only because he believed in what he did. He had the opportunity to get pricks like this murderer off the street, and he took it. What he did saved lives.

A new email came in from Zach. *Now would you look at that.* It was the information Ethan had requested about the town's history. He tapped his pen on the desk as he scanned the details. When he finished, he leaned back in his chair and released the breath he'd been holding.

Zach had accessed sealed records in a government database that didn't officially exist. *Well, well, well.* Looks like he'd finally discovered the reason Taipan had been assigned to the case. Ethan rubbed the back of his neck. His boss had some major explaining to do.

In three rings, Ian answered the phone.

"Why were Nate and I assigned to this case?" Ethan demanded, getting straight to the point.

Ian sighed heavily, and Ethan heard the protest of his chair as he leaned back. "What makes you ask, Detective?"

There was a wariness in his tone. Ian rarely referred to Ethan so formally; it was a warning to remember his place. Fuck that.

"You assigned Nate and me to a case without the courtesy of supplying full facts or details. Why?"

"We wouldn't be having this conversation if you didn't already know the answer."

"Don't you dare try to brush me off. You bet your ass I know the details of the case now, but what I want to know is why I didn't hear them from *you.*"

"I'll call you back from a secure line." The line disconnected, and a few moments later his phone rang. Ethan answered it on the first ring.

"Why, Ian? Why did you feel you couldn't trust us? Sending us in without full disclosure can cost lives."

"I'm sorry. Really, I am, but in this instance, my hands are tied. The orders came from the very top. Absolute silence. Why do you think I sent in my best team? I was hoping you'd find the serial killer, lock him up, and that would be the end of it. At least that's what the powers almighty wanted."

"Jesus. Couldn't you have said something to me off the record?"

"I told you more than once to dig deeper, didn't I? I knew you'd come up with it on your own."

Ethan cursed. Ian knew, unofficially of course, of Ethan's contacts and sources, but relying on him to use them at his own expense when the information was already at hand was unacceptable.

"Goddamn it, Ian, I don't operate this way." Ethan tapped his pen loudly on the desk.

"I said I'm sorry. What else do you want me to say?"

"I want you, in your own words, to tell me what the hell happened in Cryton a hundred years ago."

Ian released a long slow breath. "My grandfather worked the case, your great-grandfather too, Blade. It was September 1915 when the department was called in to investigate a string of serial killings in the town. When the team arrived on scene, the whole town seemed to have succumbed to some type of madness. No one was themselves. They were rioting, running around naked, and committing depraved acts in the streets. Rituals were being performed that were deemed satanic in nature, but the final straw was when the team discovered young children, even babies, killed as some sort of offering. The situation was uncontrollable, total anarchy. My dad told me some horrific stories. And after what I've seen in my time on the force, you know I don't use that word lightly.

"Considering that the whole town appeared to be affected within a short space of time, they determined it was a contagious disease. Something that affected the brain. They couldn't let the outbreak spread into surrounding areas, so they took the only action they knew at the time to prevent such an occurrence. Remember this was during World War I; resources were strained, and there was a tendency to solve problems as swiftly and efficiently as possible."

Ethan cut him off. "Officers in full protective gear converged on the town, herded every man, woman, and child into the church, and burned it to the ground."

"The church was the only place large enough to put them all," Ian said weakly. "They had to be contained, like wild animals. The virus had turned them into savages. It was a tragic, yet necessary, operation. But one that, if discovered in this day and age, would cause untold problems for the department."

Ethan pushed his chair back and began to pace. "So that's why you didn't want the media involved."

"Those hounds have a way of sniffing out things they shouldn't. One word said in the wrong ear, and this would be headline news around the world." He adjusted the tone of his voice to one of official seriousness. "I trust that you will continue on as normal, and bring this case to a close as a matter of the highest urgency."

"What else haven't you told me?"

"Dammit, Blade, don't be like that. When you've calmed down, you'll see I had no choice but to handle it the way I did."

Ethan bit back a sharp retort. His gut still hadn't unknotted, and he hesitated for a second to make sure the hurt wouldn't show in his voice. "You did have a choice, sir."

Ian made a strangled noise in the back of his throat at the use of the formal title. "Ethan, please be reasonable."

"You want me to be reasonable?" Ethan exploded. "You send me out to the middle of fucking nowhere, blind. To a place where governmental officials once killed a whole goddamned town because they feared there was a contagious mad-cow type fucking disease. Without protection or protective gear. You risked my life, Nate's, and the lives of countless others." Heart pounding, blood pressure rising, Ethan had to pause to take a series of deep breaths. Nate was going to be just as furious as he was.

"Blade." Ian's voice whipped down the line, and Ethan heard his boss's hand slam onto his desk. "I didn't endanger your life, or Nate's, or anyone's. You know me better than that. Your father and I were close; you're like a son to me. There was no goddamned communicable disease."

Ethan sank back down into his chair. "Give it to me straight, then. No bullshit. What the fuck did happen?" He rubbed at his throbbing temple.

"I told you my grandfather worked this case. He told me things you'll never find in any official reports. He said the whole town appeared to have been taken over by something... demonic in nature. Some force had turned their eyes black and had given them forked tongues. They didn't get sick and die; they became infected with an unspeakable evil that made them capable of heinous crimes and unthinkable atrocities. My father knew some of the people who were killed that day. Knew them before they were infected. They were good people, like you and me. It broke his heart. He didn't agree with the course of action that was taken, but he had to admit it did solve the problem for many years. Until recently."

Ian paused for a moment before continuing. "Ethan, I've seen the recent reports. The increase in crime, the arrival of the serial killer. I can't afford to have history repeat. Bob Brady is so overwhelmed he's close to having a breakdown. You have to understand that of anyone in this department, only you would dig deep enough to solve this case once and for all. That's why I assigned you to it."

Ethan's head was aching. After all this information, he still had no fucking idea what was going on in Cryton. So it wasn't a disease. But how could it possibly be some kind of otherworldly force?

Think logically. There was one thing he knew without a doubt: a madman was stalking the streets of this town. A serial killer selecting people by an undefined set of criteria, removing their eyes, and branding "666" into their palms. Sure, that could be considered demonic in nature, but at the core of the crime, the perpetrator was still a vicious son of a bitch in human form.

"What can I do?" Ian asked in place of Ethan's silence.

"I want you to tell me if they would do something like that again," Ethan asked through gritted teeth. "Tell me if they're planning to quarantine the town, do something similar again."

Ian's pained sigh came down the line. "The case is time-sensitive, yes. It goes without saying, they'd handle things differently these days, but I'd be lying if I didn't tell you they're considering all their options. They've already drafted a press release about a new deadly and highly contagious disease, a weapon of war. Depending on what happens in the next weeks, they plan to begin taking people suspected to be infected to a hospital and handle the outbreak that way."

"You mean kill them in hospital instead of burning them in a church. Oh, that is *much* more civilized."

"It doesn't have to come to that," Ian said. "Do what you need to take out the perpetrators, catch the serial killer before this thing spreads. I'm sorry, but if anyone can do this, it's you, Blade." There was a quiet plea for understanding and forgiveness in his tone. "Whatever resources I have available are at your disposal. Tell me what you need."

"I want my team. Taipan. Every single one of them. Pull them off whatever they're on and get them here." Ethan disconnected the call.

Reaching for his mobile, he placed an additional series of calls. Some of the best undercover agents money could buy would begin to arrive over the next day or two. Screw unwittingly assisting in a government cover-up.

He was getting to the bottom of this, no matter what it cost him, whether that was blood, sweat, or money. Even if it meant taking on the whole damned government.

He'd do anything to protect Sage. Anything.

CHAPTER TWENTY-SEVEN

Sage forced all thoughts of Ethan, no, *the detective*, out of her mind.

She should be grateful that she'd discovered his girlfriend now and not later. That she'd received the reality-check before she'd fallen even deeper. It was still possible to harden herself against him. In any case, it was time she stopped allowing her heart to rule her head. She had far more pressing issues to deal with.

So what if she'd enjoyed a night of hot and heavy sex with him, if it gave her a moment's peace in the nightmare she was currently living? It had been a short respite that helped her remember that she was human. That there was a normal life out there that had nothing to do with ghosts or demons or whatever the hell was going on around here.

Now she had to get back to working out what was happening, making sure Nan's killer was found and punished. Then, she would worry about what she was going to do with her life.

First things first. Find answers to the questions that were mounting by the minute. She needed to find Mary's diary. Since her Nan had begun to discover what was really going on here, all Sage needed to do was find where Nan left off and continue from there. If Sage could retrace Nan's steps over the last few months, she'd learn what Nan had discovered; perhaps something important that someone wanted to stay buried? Had someone killed to ensure it?

Sage headed to the secret attic door at the back of the closet in the spare room. She turned the handle. It was stuck. She stepped more fully into the closet and bumped the old wooden door with her upper body. It didn't budge.

She let go of the handle and was looking around for something she could use to jimmy the lock when the door clicked open by itself.

She blinked in surprise, and her pulse quickened. She must have loosened it. Sometimes doors jammed in old houses like this when the dampness set in and swelled the wood.

The logic did little to relieve her anxiety. There was something very eerie about the doors in this house.

She shivered in the cool breeze that rushed over her from the stairwell. She'd never been allowed to play in the attic as a child, and in a strange way, she felt even now as though Nan was watching and frowning at her in disapproval. She attempted a laugh at herself, but it came out weak.

Sage took the first step on the staircase, and the creak of protest from the old wood echoed in the cramped space. She took a deep, fortifying breath and steeled her nerves. The passageway was dark, narrow, and covered in a lifetime of dust.

A spider's paradise.

A shudder rattled her teeth, and she clamped them shut. She began the steep ascent. The temperature plummeted, instead of rising, with each gingerly step she took. The icy dread that had settled over her was greater than was warranted by her fear of spiders, but she couldn't come up with another reason for it. She wasn't afraid of heights.

Near the top, she risked a glance at the webs. She didn't know how many beady eyes were watching her, but they were numerous. She bolted up the last few steps, bursting into the space.

The attic was larger than she'd imagined and full of what looked like unused furniture covered by aged, dusty sheets. Perhaps the items belonged to the people who'd lived in the house prior to Nan.

Sage scanned the room and froze, her heart skipping. Near the window stood a woman in a long flowing dress, her dark hair pulled back in a bun. The woman was not looking at her; instead, she was staring, unmoving, out the window. Sage blinked to clear her vision, but the woman remained blurry and slightly out of focus, perhaps because of the thick dust blanketing the air. For a single, glorious moment Sage thought she was an intruder. Prayed she was an intruder. A woman who'd somehow managed to get into the house and it was she who was making all the noises. How wonderful it would be to find some logical reason for everything that had happened.

But even as her mind rushed to come up with rationales for the woman's presence, the sensations in her body, the ice-cold terror, didn't abate.

"Who are you?" Sage's voice was barely more than a whisper.

Slowly the figure turned, somehow still appearing shadowed despite moving more fully into the light. It was enough though, for Sage to recognize who it was.

A strangled cry tore from her throat and she instinctively took a step backward, her leg knocking against something and sending it crashing to the ground.

She didn't turn to see what she'd knocked over. Couldn't. Wouldn't take her eyes off the... what was before her.

It was the woman from the photos Mark had shown her.

"What do you want?" A heavy weight pressed against her chest and squeezed her lungs, making it hard to speak. She struggled to breathe.

"You are looking for my diary."

"Mary," Sage said. "You are Mary." Sage's mind was racing. It was as though she were watching a movie in slow motion yet the sound was on fast forward. "Nan found your diary," Sage said dumbly, struggling to catch up with her thoughts.

"It's yours now." The words didn't come toward Sage in the normal way; they hung in the air. Floated around the room like ideas she struggled to grasp.

"Why?"

"You have picked up where Celeste left off." Sage had to concede that events had certainly conspired to ensure it happened that way.

"I want to bring my grandmother's murderer to justice," Sage said, her voice barely audible. At least that's what she'd initially intended when she'd stepped back into a town she barely recognized beneath the surface.

"You will need two things," Mary said. "My diary, and the grimoire. In my diary, you'll find everything I discovered about how to stop the demonic entities from breaking through."

"I don't understand."

"Not yet, but you will. Read my diary first. It will help you see the picture of what you need to do."

"I don't have your diary."

"It's in the drawer of the altar. Next to the Bible." Mary slowly raised her arm and pointed to Sage's left, the cloth draping from a limb that appeared to be all bone, no flesh. Sage shuddered.

Sage peered through the dim lighting. Her eyes had adjusted somewhat, making it easier to see the shapes of the items covered with white sheets. Pushed in the far corner were pews. There were pillars, candelabras, and to her left was an altar.

Although beautiful, the altar was disturbing, in that it was the only thing not covered in layers of dust. The ornately carved wood appeared almost lovingly polished. Had Nan done that? Why?

Sage opened the drawer and pulled out an old diary. She traced her fingers across the worn fabric cover and carefully opened to the first page. What secrets lurked in these pages? Why had Nan found it necessary to hide diary again after reading it?

"What is in it?" Sage asked, looking at Mary.

"My journey is now yours."

"How can that be? I'm not even meant to be here. I left this town."

"Your grandmother sent you away in an act of desperation and love. To spare you from this. Tried to fight him on your behalf, as it were. But you were always destined to be here, make no mistake," Mary said. "You are the seer's daughter."

Sage opened her mouth but no words came out. She clasped the angel around her neck, and finally found her voice.

"What are you talking about?" Sage knew precious little about her mother, just the few stories Nan had shared. They were stored in Sage's memory like brilliant, untouchable diamonds.

"We have much in common. More than you can know. Like me, you are the seer's daughter."

"You think my mother was a seer? You mean a psychic, like Nan?"

"Yes, but your mother's power was far greater. She was the master demon's first victim twenty years ago when he re-entered this realm."

Oh God! Sage's legs wobbled, and she reached out to the altar for support.

"Did Nan know this?"

"Not at first. The demon's influence has been rather limited, affecting only those who are easily swayed toward the darkness. He had a hand in your difficult childhood, the cruelty you suffered at the hands of those girls you went to school with. He has been watching you for twenty years, waiting for your return. He knew the death of your grandmother would bring that about."

"He killed Nan to get me back here?"

"Yes."

Anger surged through Sage's veins. She'd had enough. "What can I do? Tell me how I defeat this…" Sage raised her hands in a helpless gesture. She was unable to put a voice to the situation she found herself in. "Tell me the way to make this all stop."

"There is a way," Mary said. "The grimoire. It's a book of spells, but in this case, it is a specific set of spells, powerful phrases, and Bible passages that need to be followed. I used it to defeat him last time. If done correctly, the rite will force the demon back to the other side. But you have to do it before the portal closes. I know it works. I did it. But I was too late to save the town. To save my family."

Sage blinked back tears. "I can't imagine what you went through. How that must have felt. I'm so sorry." She wiped at her eyes. "You said I have to do it before the portal closes. How long do I have?"

"You have until the blood moon. At midnight, on the night of the blood moon, the portal opens. If you have not banished the demon before it closes, he will fully manifest and the demonic entities will remain on earth for the next hundred years. Life as you know it will be over. Evil, and suffering beyond your wildest imagination, will occur. Hell will reign supreme on earth."

Sage wrapped her fingers around Mary's diary. Images, like the paintings of Hell you'd find hanging in an old church, flashed through her mind. Agony etched on the faces of the naked and tortured.

"Yes, something like that," Mary said as though she could see Sage's thoughts. "What do you think inspired those paintings in the first place? Attempted demonic possession of human souls has been ongoing since the dawning of time."

"Where is the grimoire?"

"Celeste, knowing her time was up, gave it to Ada. It is beneath the floorboards in Ada's kitchen. You must get it, before *he* does."

Sage would ask Ada for it, as soon as she found her.

"You won't find Ada," Mary said, again seemingly able to read her mind.

"You'll need to get the grimoire yourself."

"Why?"

"Ada is dead."

Shock held Sage perfectly still for a moment before her eyes filled with tears. "Don't. Don't say that."

"It's true. He is taking more souls. Removing the obstacles that are in his way to get to you."

Ada is dead?

"The demon killed her?" The attic was spinning.

Sage didn't want to believe it. Any of it. He'd stolen Nan, and now he'd stolen Ada. They'd both tried to protect her, and they were the last people she could call family. Tears blurred her vision, stung the backs of her lids, rolled down her cheeks.

The air turned dark and choking, filled with a malevolent sensation that was foul, hateful. The sudden struggle to breathe shocked Sage out of her grief and back to the attic. Gasping for air, she blinked to clear her eyes.

Mary was no longer there.

Something like a shadow, something awful, something that hated her, was in the corner of the room. She screamed and the diary thudded onto the timber floor. She couldn't see the presence in the corner; she *felt* it. Felt its loathing for her rolling off it in vile waves and *knew* it was the figure in the dark cape in Mark's photo.

She didn't dare take her eyes off the shadow. She had the sense that if she glanced away, even for a second, he'd come to her. She lowered herself to a crouch. Blindly, she groped around on the floor, her fingers landing not on the rectangular shape of the diary, but something fist-sized, smooth yet sharp.

Ouch! Sage automatically looked at what had pricked her finger.

The gargoyle. Her stomach lurched.

A heaviness pressed her downward, pinning her to the floor. The ceiling was falling on her, and she looked up, horrified to find the presence hovering above her head, a dark mass of loathing and hostility. A guttural noise tore from deep inside her. It lodged in her throat, silencing her. She couldn't scream. Couldn't *breathe*.

This was the end. It was over. She'd failed before she'd even begun. She was going to take her last breath on the dirty attic floor.

She closed her eyes, clutched the angel around her neck, and braced herself for certain death.

The pounding in her head keeping time, a moment passed, then another.

She forced herself to look. The entity was still there, but it hadn't moved forward. Then somehow she *knew* it couldn't. An invisible cocoon of energy surrounded her, extending outward from the pendant enclosed in her hand. She couldn't see it, but she could sense it.

"Sage? Where are you? The door is open, are you up there?" Mark's voice travelled up the stairs from the door behind her.

She heard his steps as he ascended the staircase and rushed over to her. "Sage! Are you hurt? Did you fall?" Mark tested her arms and legs, poked and prodded, and seemingly satisfied he could, lifted her and held her crushed against him.

She should be dead. But somehow the pendant had saved her.

"Jesus, Sage. Why aren't you saying anything? You're scaring the shit out of me."

Mark's own heart was pounding against hers. Sage's gaze darted around the room, but it was now nothing but an unused, dusty attic.

No one was there. Mary had gone. The demonic entity had gone. The air in the room was once again normal. Dust particles danced in the block of light from the window as though nothing happened.

But it had. Because even though she'd dropped the gargoyle and its glowing red eyes were staring up at her from the floor, she could still feel it in her palm. A lingering sensation of an icy cold glove she could not remove.

Heart pounding out of her chest, her mind racing, Sage tried to make sense of what had just happened. And how could the gargoyle have gotten up there? It was packed in the box downstairs. She had sealed the carton herself.

Unable to move, she grappled to make sense of it. Any of it. And then the gargoyle's red eyes blinked once, twice, and even through the dim light, she could see the beginnings of a smile manifesting on its ugly face.

And then she heard a sound. A low, cruel sound that floated in the space between them, and she knew it was laughing.

Chapter Twenty-Eight

"Did you hear that?" Sage asked. Had the gargoyle's laughter been just in her head, or was it real? She looked at Mark for the first time, searching his face.

"Hear what?" Mark said, his brow wrinkled.

How come he hadn't heard it? Was *this* her gift? Could she communicate with those who'd crossed over now? Or was this some kind of exception? And what had just happened with the pendant? It had activated somehow, formed a shield around her, protecting her from that menacing shadow. Her mother had warned her to never take the pendant off. And Ada had told her at the funeral it was more than jewelry.

Had her mother somehow known about the dark entity and given Sage something to protect her when she no longer could?

"Are you all right?" Mark asked. "What happened?"

Sage stepped out of his reach, grabbed the diary, and tucked it into the waistband of her skirt. She didn't want to tell anyone about it until she'd had a chance to see what information it contained.

"I'm fine." With quick flicks of her hand, she swatted at the thick gray dust that covered her clothes. "I thought a spider was on me. It scared me, and I... uh, tripped. Fell." She took a deep steadying breath. "Over that... thing down there."

Mark picked up the gargoyle. It was still ugly, but its eyes no longer glowed. Once again, it looked like an inanimate object.

"Don't worry about me," Sage said. "This house is just giving me the creeps, that's all."

He studied her for a moment. "With everything that's been happening, that's no surprise. However, I was surprised that you didn't join us at the hotel last night. You weren't answering your phone this morning, and I got a little worried, so I thought I'd come by and check on you."

"Thanks Mark, that's sweet. I'm fine though. I'm just finishing the packing and wanted to see what was left to pack up here in the attic. My phone is downstairs in my purse, and I didn't hear it."

"Did you stay here last night?" Mark asked, looking a little impressed.

"Yeah. But not alone. I'd rather not talk about last night, if you don't mind."

"Okay then, have you eaten? How about I take you out to lunch?" Mark offered as they made their way downstairs.

"That would be great, thanks. But I have something I need to do first. How about I meet you at the bakery in the main street at say—" Sage peered down at her watch. "Two-thirty." She forced a smile. That gave her three hours. Plenty of time.

"If you're sure you'll be all right. What do you want me to do with this?"

Sage looked at the gargoyle in Mark's hand, and ice ran down her spine.

"Smash it into a gazillion pieces, then burn it, then bury the ashes underneath a concrete slab in South Africa. I never want to see that hideous thing again."

Mark laughed. "It is pretty hideous, but that's a bit drastic, isn't it?"

"No."

Mark frowned then, appearing almost reluctant to leave her.

She touched his arm, giving him her best reassuring smile. 'Really, Mark. Thank you for your concern, but I'm fine. Late for an appointment, but fine. I'll see you at two-thirty."

———◆———

Where was she?

Ethan couldn't shake off a feeling of unease. He was standing outside Beyond the Grave with Nate, but Sage wasn't there. The whole place was locked up and empty. He'd called Sage's mobile several times, and every time it had gone straight to voicemail.

The patrol that he'd requested to sit surveillance was nowhere to be seen, and he let out a string of curses. At least he'd have his own men here soon, and the other members of Taipan here within days, depending on where they were stationed. This type of lapse wouldn't happen then.

It was early afternoon, and they had finished interviewing the witnesses and filed all the reports. Ethan had taken Nate for a counter lunch at the local pub and filled him in on the conversation he'd had with Ian. Justifiably, and as he'd expected, Nate had been beyond furious. After allowing Nate sufficient time to calm down, they'd discussed it at length.

Neither appreciated the way that Ian had handled the case, but they were both professional enough to realize they had to push their personal opinions aside and focus. The background information they hadn't had before didn't add much clarification, but it did escalate the urgency.

"You don't think they'd really come in and do what they did a hundred years ago, do you?" Nate had asked, biting a chip in half.

"I don't see why not. They've done it before," Ethan replied grimly. "I've been thinking about it, and now I know why Ian demanded a media blackout, when using the media would be standard in situations like this. Calling for public involvement could provide the leads we're sorely lacking."

"So you think they're holding off in case they need the media to begin reporting on an outbreak?"

"The few media reports Zach could dig up from 1915 had reported an outbreak of a deadly mutating virus, possibly the result of biological warfare. No one questioned the way they'd handled it; the public was only too grateful to have it gone. The influenza pandemic in 1889 killed over a million people worldwide. The fear of disease back then was very real."

"But today? They can't get away with something like that these days."

"Who would question it? Picture this. The town is quarantined, big media report with the words 'deadly mutating virus,' 'fear of biological warfare testing.' They pan to a camera shot of doctors in full protective equipment hovering around someone strapped to a hospital bed. Add a few needles, and voila, you have public support for the government to step in and handle it in whatever way they deem 'necessary.'"

"Jesus. How long do you think we've got?"

"Two weeks. Give or take."

Nate had let out a string of uncharacteristic curse words.

And now with Sage missing, frustration was burning a hole in Ethan's stomach lining, and he caught himself frequently reaching for his phantom pack of cigarettes.

Instead of radioing in to the station, he dialed Brady's mobile number directly.

"Detective Blade," Sergeant Brady said. "How can I help you?"

"Where's the surveillance I requested?" Ethan demanded.

"The surveillance?"

"The patrol I asked to be stationed outside Sage Matthews's shop," Ethan said, annoyance peppering his tone.

"Well, Ben and Graham sat there all morning, and nothing happened. Nobody went in or out, and everything appeared fine. Then at about eleven, bit after, Mark Collins, you know, the ghost investigator movie star? He turned up. When he left with Sage a little while later, I let the guys go. Figured she would be all right if she was with him, and we need all the uniforms we can get working this case."

Ethan ground his teeth and resisted pointing out that Sage was part of the damned case. Getting the sergeant upset would not help. *If you wanted a job done properly, you had to do it yourself.*

Except Sage was far more than a job. And he still needed to clear up the Jen problem. The longer he left Sage with the wrong impression, the harder it would be to make her understand. And with the situation around her escalating, he needed her cooperation to ensure her safety.

Ethan gripped his phone so hard it was in danger of breaking, so he swapped hands. Sage had this number.

"Is everything all right?" Brady asked.

Ethan breathed out slowly through his nose before answering. "I would have expected you let me know before you called off a surveillance I had arranged."

"You were in the middle of an interview…" The sergeant cleared his throat uncomfortably on the other end, and Nate briefly touched Ethan's shoulder. A warning to let it go.

"Never mind." He disconnected the call and kicked the front door of Sage's shop. The door rattled in its frame.

"Steady on, mate. She'll be fine."

Back in the Land Rover, Ethan couldn't loosen the knot that had formed in his gut. No matter how hard he tried, he couldn't shake a strange foreboding.

Every instinct he possessed was screaming that something was wrong. Very wrong.

———◆———

Leaves crunched loudly underneath her sandshoes as Sage made her way across the front lawn of Ada's house. Her breaths came in short puffs, the blood racing past her ears as she ducked underneath the police crime tape and dashed across the stairs to the entrance.

So it was true. Ada was dead. Ruthlessly, she pushed back the onslaught of grief. She couldn't allow herself to think about that now. She had to focus on finding the grimoire and getting out again without being seen.

Meters of crime scene tape blowing in the breeze told her the police had been there earlier, but there was no sign of them now. She didn't know whether they'd be back.

Pausing in the shadow of the veranda by the front door, Sage held her breath. Silence. She slowly exhaled and tried to will her heart rate to slow.

Her back against the wall, she sidled along the front porch and down the left side where the large, leafy trees that towered over the house had cast it in shade. Sage moved past the potted geranium positioned underneath the kitchen window and to the side entrance.

Heart pounding wildly, she assessed the small wooden window to the left of the door.

A dog barked a few houses away. She'd better hurry.

Reaching into her handbag, she withdrew a large screwdriver. She forced it underneath the edge of the window and tried to jimmy it open. Wood splintered, chunks flicking off and landing near her feet.

Damn, this looked so much easier in the movies.

She kept digging with the screwdriver, and eventually the metal catch gave with a loud crack and the glass shattered. She groaned. So much for a stealthy entrance. No hiding her break-in attempt now. Which meant the cops would be back, the forensics unit dusting for prints. Sage had spent many hours of her childhood here, so her fingerprints would be all over the house. She had to hope that would be enough to cast reasonable doubt should she be questioned.

Damn it. Why hadn't she thought to wear gloves? A rush of heat washed over her face as she imagined Ethan's response when he found out she'd been arrested.

It would have been a far saner idea to ask him for access in the first place. And perhaps she would have. And he just might have let her. Had she still been willing to talk to his lying ass. Which of course she wasn't.

She was on her own. So maybe the life of a criminal wasn't in her skill set, but she was here now. And determination to find that book overshadowed her fear of being arrested.

She slid the wooden frame of the window upwards in short jerks, and soon there was enough space for her to crawl through. Glass crunched beneath her shoes, and outside, the wind picked up, howling through the trees. A cold breeze blew across her face, and she pulled her bag to her chest.

A noise to her right startled her, and she gasped. The front door opened by itself.

Huh, now would you look at that. Why hadn't she thought to try the front door? She shook her head in disbelief. She'd assumed it would be locked. Surely the cops didn't think a strip of police tape would suffice to secure a building.

An uneasy sensation came over her. She recognized it immediately. It was the same feeling she'd had when she was at Nan's shop, during the investigation, and the same feeling she'd had earlier in the attic after Mary had disappeared. However not as strong. *He* was following her, watching her. She knew it with every fiber of her being. But he was keeping his distance. Had the strange energy from the pendant made him more cautious? Her mother's words came rushing back. *Never take this off. Whatever you do, leave this on always.*

Did the angel provide some type of protection? If so, why had her mother not kept the pendant for herself? She'd died less than a week after handing it down to Sage. Had she somehow foreseen her own death? Tears stung Sage's lids and she blinked them away.

Mary had said her mother was a seer. And she was the seer's daughter. That all these events were somehow preordained. Part of some ancient prophecy. Dear God, what if Sage had something that could've saved Nan's life all along, and not known? More tears threatened to fall, and she blinked them away.

Picking up the pace, she dashed to the kitchen and examined the faded white and green linoleum, but nothing stood out. *What was I expecting, a painted X to mark the spot?*

The kitchen was as she remembered: old, but immaculately clean, with green doors on white cupboards and speckled laminate countertops. A large woodstove sat in the corner, and above the window hung the same carving of a witch on a broomstick that was in Nan's kitchen.

A large wooden table positioned in the middle of the space served as both a dining and meals preparation area.

Sage contemplated the floor. Mary had simply said it was in the kitchen, under the floor. She'd better make a start. She wished she had… what did one use to rip up linoleum? Wait. Was she really going to ruin Ada's floor? She couldn't see that she had any other choice.

A loud slam from a car door caused her to jump, her heart hammering in her chest. Was it the cops? Had they returned? Perhaps someone had seen her enter. She had to hurry. There was no time for second-guessing. She had committed the moment she'd broken the window. Starting at the closest corner, she prized her screwdriver underneath the edge of the old, worn linoleum and working toward the kitchen sink, began ripping it off.

Twenty minutes later, half of the linoleum on the kitchen floor had been torn to brittle shreds. Sage contemplated the floorboards. Where was it? Was she really going to continue ripping it all off? So far, she hadn't noticed any obvious signs of a hiding space under the floor. Sage began to tap the wooden boards, listening to any difference in sound as she crawled around. The relentless ticking of the old grandfather clock echoed from the sitting room, making her aware of how long this was taking.

The grimoire was not here. Did it even exist? Fire heated her cheeks. What if the whole conversation with Mary had been in her head? After all, Mary had been dead a hundred years. Did she fancy herself having a gift like Nan after all? Or her mother?

No, of course not. Except… how had she known Ada was dead? How had she known where to find the diary? There was no denying she knew things she shouldn't have known. Therefore… Mary was real. Which meant she *had* just communicated with someone who had crossed over. Nan had said Sage would discover her gift when the time was right, and she was willing. Was she *willing* now? She was certainly desperate enough to be open to anything to avenge the murder of three people she loved, and to prevent the deaths of others.

So where, then, was the grimoire? Sage surveyed the mess she'd made of the kitchen. There was no way she could repair the damage. She had to hope the police thought it was kids.

Perhaps Joyce, Pat, or Mona had already taken the grimoire? She'd have to go and ask them. It was time to leave. Getting arrested would only complicate things, and draw unnecessary attention her way.

Taking one last look around, Sage became aware of how much she'd really hoped to find the grimoire. She needed *something* that would help. Even a book of spells was more than she had at the moment. Having only herself seemed grossly insufficient.

Swallowing her disappointment, Sage went to the front door and found it had blown shut. She tried the handle, but the door didn't open.

Someone had turned the deadbolt.

With a gasp, she whirled around but saw no one. How was that possible? The door had swung open when she'd entered. She had seen it herself.

Or had she? She didn't know what to believe anymore. Her breath hitched in her chest, and she forced herself to breathe in and out. It didn't matter. She didn't need a creepily defective door anyway. She'd just crawl back out through the broken window.

A strange, fluttery noise came from the direction of the kitchen, followed by a clatter. What was that? She wanted to get out as fast as possible, yet she found herself walking in the direction of the noise.

Sage surveyed the space. Everything appeared to be the same big mess she'd left it in. Except for the witch on the floor by the large chest freezer on the far wall. It must have fallen from the ceiling. But it hadn't just fallen; it was quite a distance from where it had been hanging above the kitchen window. A chill skittered across her skin. It looked almost as if it had… flown?

Sage shook head to clear the crazy thought and walked to the witch, picking it up and placing it on the table. Turning to leave, she looked again at the square mat the witch had landed on. Lifting up the corner, she saw what she'd been looking for. A trapdoor. She found a small handle cleverly inset into the door and lifted.

There, on a bed of dirt, was an old-looking book. *Yes!*

Not wasting any time, Sage carefully retrieved what must be the grimoire and shut the trapdoor, setting the mat back the way it was.

A sheet of paper slid out and Sage only just managed to catch it before it fluttered to the floor. She carefully unfolded the delicate letter.

It was signed "Mary, September, 1915."

Dear God, Know my husband is a good man, your devoted servant.

He has no knowledge of what I intend to do. Cannot. He would not approve. Magic and sorcery are the Devil's work, he'd say. Yet how does one defeat Satan but on his terms?

God forgive me, but I can see no other choice. If there is one, you have not spoken loud enough for me to hear it. I'm trading my very soul, my everlasting life, to save my husband.

And my baby. My precious, precious little boy. My sole remaining child. I am not a martyr.

I'm a mother…

I'd pray for my soul, but after what I'm about to do, I doubt You'll hear my prayers. For fear they'll fall to the Beast, I'd best keep them to myself.

Forgive me, dear Raymond. I know not what else to do.

Although the result will be darkness, I do it out of the purest of love.

Mary x

To the seer's daughter,

If I succeed, when I'm finished, I'll secure the grimoire in the tomb in the graveyard behind the house. The markings will be clear only to those who know what they are looking for.

I cannot know if I will succeed, but if you are reading this, it means I did.

Take comfort in that. For it means there is hope for you too.

Nan must have discovered the grimoire in the cemetery behind the house.

Ada had known about the grimoire's existence and hidden it here, supposedly for Sage to find.

Sage secured the precious book in her bag, and stepped gingerly over the needlessly damaged chunks of linoleum with more than a little guilt. "Sorry, Ada," Sage murmured with a glance upward. The grimoire in her hands at last, she couldn't help grinning despite the mess she'd made of Ada's house.

For the first time in this whole waking nightmare, Sage felt as though she had a plan.

Sage sat at the small kitchen table with a cup of tea, Mary's diary and the grimoire in front of her. She now had both items she'd been searching for. Items, it seemed, that were intended for her.

Sipping her tea, Sage tried to calm the anxiety that fluttered like small winged insects in her stomach. Just twenty-four hours ago, she'd sat at this very table while Mark and Pia had given her the report on their investigation. Sage had known they'd find evidence of paranormal activity in the house; she'd seen enough by then to convince her of that. What she hadn't been prepared for, or even allowed herself to contemplate, was *why*.

It had simply never occurred to her that spirits—good, bad, or otherwise—would have their own agenda.

She picked up the grimoire first, and ran her fingers across the old, but well-preserved, leather cover. Embossed on the front was a series of three circles filled with symbols and fancy lettering. In the middle of the circles was a pentagram with intricate symbols at each of the five points. She recognized the design. It was the very same engraving as on the back of her angel pendant.

Mary had said this grimoire contained a specific set of instructions for how to cast the demon back to wherever it came from—the other side—before the portal closed. How long did she have?

Mary said the portal closed on the blood moon. Sage powered up her phone, and ignoring the sixteen missed calls from Ethan, did a quick Internet search.

Blood Moon: September 28.

She had only twelve days.

Sage was just about to close the browser when something caught her eye. She followed the link to the site and scanned the pages. There was something very significant and rare about the next full moon. Not only was it a "blood moon," a total lunar eclipse, it was the fourth eclipse in a lunar tetrad. There were sites proclaiming the upcoming eclipse had religious significance, as the timing of the fourth blood moon would coincide with a series of significant religious festivals. Sage scrolled further and found numerous sites predicting a biblical prophecy of the end of days.

How was this the first she'd heard about any of this? She took a sip of her tea. In the city, she'd gone to work, studied, and thought about Friday night drinks. She'd had no reason to look up moon cycles, much less worry about a blood moon. She had a lot to learn in very little time.

Mary had said if Sage had not done whatever was necessary before September 28, the demon and his legion of demonic entities would fully manifest and remain on earth for the next hundred years. *"The world as we know it will be over. Evil, and suffering beyond your wildest imagination, will occur. Hell will reign supreme."*

Sage took a deep breath, steeled her spine, and opened the cover.

She couldn't immediately read the words on the brittle, yellowed pages. The writing was in another language. Latin, maybe? The pages also contained sketches, diagrams, and numerous symbols. How was she supposed to use this, if she couldn't read it? Feeling overwhelmed, she flicked through more pages until she found some written in English.

The phrases appeared to have been taken directly from the Bible, which made sense if they were dealing with a demon as Mary believed. Toward the back, there was a page titled, "Rite of Exorcism." Some of the sketches were more than a little disturbing, and Sage closed her eyes. How had it fallen upon her to make sense of all of this? She felt vastly underqualified, and wondered if there hadn't been some kind of huge mistake.

She sifted through more pages, then something caught her eye.

A diagram depicting four crystals. *Crystals of protection from Satan.*

She recognized the four crystals immediately. The picture was not in color, but the descriptions were clear. Acting on a short burst of excitement, she picked up the books and raced upstairs.

In Nan's room, she used the diagram to place the crystals back into the corners. She then proceeded to read out the accompanying phrases the best she could, considering they were in Latin.

When she was finished, she silently assessed the room.

Nothing felt different, so she repeated the verses again and again, stumbling over the words less each time until they became a fluid chant.

This time, when she stopped, the room blurred, her head spun, and knees buckling, she fell on the bed, grasping her pendant. She took a deep breath, the air mountain fresh. Or so it seemed. She sat up. Did the room feel different? She couldn't be certain, but it seemed to sparkle. Did it feel calmer? More peaceful? *She* certainly felt more peaceful, so that was a good start.

If nothing else, she desperately needed a place where she could feel safe. Even if it was only a placebo.

After performing her first ritual, Sage felt in some way closer to Nan. As though she were watching and was proud.

A single tear slipped from Sage's eye and rolled down her cheek. "I won't let you down, Nan," Sage vowed and turned to the diary. Time to fill in more of this picture.

———◆———

An hour, maybe two, passed before Sage looked up from the diary. Several times, her blood had run cold. Her hand had been shaking so hard at one point she'd unintentionally ripped a page while turning it.

Sage felt she now knew Mary, as though she shared an affinity with the kind and gentle pastor's wife. The altar and other religious items in the attic now made sense. She even felt a certain kinship with Mary, as she read Mary's experience with the journey that Sage was about to embark on. She'd cried when Mary had cried. Shared her anger and sense of helplessness on the night they'd come, with their black hoods and crazed eyes, and had taken her two-year-old baby girl for sacrifice. The horror this town had endured a hundred years ago was unspeakable. Sweet Mary, who alluded to more than she wrote, as though unable to commit the words to paper, had a backbone of steel. Sage, at once awed and petrified, hoped she had half of Mary's inner strength.

Sage reread the section near the end. Intended for the person who held the diary a hundred years later.

> To the future seer's daughter,
> At the beginning of the first eclipse of the tetrad, the lead-up to the blood red moon, the veil between the dimensions will rapidly begin to thin. The master demon will have found a soul to possess. A disturbed soul, fashioned to the darkness, like a wood carving, through living a tortured life.
> I don't believe babies are born evil. I can't. I'm a pastor's wife. I have to believe that life is a series of events and choices. That sometimes circumstances of life can be so cruel, way too much for a gentle soul, and that soul becomes hardened. Bitter and resentful. The hurts and injustices suffered so great that they manifest as powerful anger and violence. From there, it is only a gentle slide into pure evil.
> The soul, once pure and white, is now bitter and black. It becomes vulnerable to the negative energies of another world. A world of dark entities spending eternity tortured by watching us play in the sunshine.
> Hell is watching happiness that can never be yours.
> They sit behind the veil, restless. Watching and waiting for that chance, that brief opportunity that arises every hundred years when the veil is thin enough to slip through.
> At first the entities come through and begin attempting possession of humans. They enter through the portal in Cryton, growing in number in the lead-up to the blood moon. Although they may seem to be through, they are still not fully in our dimension. They are still only spirits at this time. Their evil is persuasive and can affect the mind and actions of the host, but they are not fully manifest.
> They won't be until after the door to the portal closes on the fourth blood moon of the tetrad.
> This is where you play an integral role, future seer's daughter. The master demon must be identified, captured, and brought into the circle, and the rite of exorcism followed precisely before the portal closes. If done correctly, the demonic entities will be sent back to their world.

The timing is critical. You will encounter many obstacles. For evil can manifest in a multitude of ways.

This occurrence is not as rare as one would think. Similar happenings have been documented throughout history, but are usually written off as natural disasters, or the atrocities of a depraved human. No one makes the connection to the portal, or if they do, they don't make it publicly.

But there are those who know. Those who are aware and work quietly and independently to do what they can to keep these entities in their own world. Their work must remain secret so as not to cause mass panic of the general population.

The master demon enters exactly twenty years before the portal opens and chooses a host to possess. 1815 is the earliest record I can find of the demon in Australia, but more may be part of Aboriginal legends.

But know that there have been portals in other parts of the world; many have been closed permanently, but not all. Pray forgive my selfishness, but the sacrifice required to close the portal permanently is too great. You will suffer for my weakness, for the choice I have made has sealed your destiny.

I have documented as much of my journey as I can with the hope it may help you in yours.

Though my journey is ending, I pray for you and yours.

Sage slowly shut the cover of the diary, the quiet closing in loud around her. The house had fallen strangely silent. The room, even more so.

Now that she'd read Mary's diary, so many pieces of the puzzle fell into place. She finally understood how the disturbances in the house were tied to Nan's murder. Mary had succeeded in banishing the demon, but not in time to save her husband, her children, or herself. Such a brave woman, such a terrible tragedy. But what sacrifice had been too great for Mary to make? It must have been big, if she hadn't closed the portal permanently. Mary had no reason to ask for Sage's forgiveness; all Sage saw was a courageous woman who'd succeeded in an extraordinary situation against all odds.

But what Sage could take away from Mary's tragic story was that in the end, she had done it. She'd defeated the demon. With the processes and rituals as outlined in the grimoire. It had worked.

Sage squeezed her eyes shut and touched the pendant. Things were going to get a whole lot worse before they got better.

But she had the solution. She had the grimoire.

She prayed she had the strength to do what was needed.

CHAPTER TWENTY-NINE

Already ten minutes late, Sage hurried into the bakery where she'd arranged to meet Mark. The small shop was a hive of activity, and the smell of freshly baked pastries made her mouth water.

Sage held her bag close against her body. She'd put the diary and grimoire in there, not knowing what else to do with them. She'd thought of hiding them. But where? Initially, she'd put them in the spare-wheel cavity in her car, but she'd quickly changed her mind. She couldn't bear to part from them, so for now, she was keeping them with her.

"Sorry I'm late," Sage said, sliding into a chair across from Mark. The bakery had a seated section to the left, where diners had the option to eat their lunch on tables covered in red-and-white checked tablecloths. The bakery was crowded, and she was glad Mark had managed to secure them a table.

He looked up from his paper and gave her a smile. "No worries. I took the liberty of ordering you a coffee. It should arrive any moment."

"Thank you."

"How are you, Sage? Really." He folded the paper in half and set it aside. "I heard about Ada. I'm sorry."

Sage took a deep breath and blinked hard, trying to clear the sudden welling of tears. "Thank you." He placed a hand over hers. Her throat constricted, and she had to wait before she could speak again. "She helped raise me."

"I didn't realize you were that close." He gave her fingers a gentle squeeze.

The waitress arrived with their coffee, and Sage withdrew her hand. Wiping at her eyes, she pasted on a smile. "Ooh, cappuccino. Just what I need." She tore open a sugar packet and sprinkled it on top of the foam. Using her teaspoon, she began eating the sweetened topping. Mark watched her, his expression thoughtful, but he let her pretend she was okay.

"How's Pia?" Sage asked.

"She's much better today." He leaned forward. "Are you really all right?"

She looked away. Should she tell him about her encounter with Mary and finding the grimoire? Something told her not to, to keep that information close, at least for now. Turning back to him, she nodded. "I'm okay. Truly." She needed to switch the subject. "What did you do with the gargoyle?"

"I took care of it. You don't need to worry about it anymore."

Sage thought about pressing him for details, but she really didn't need to know. At least it couldn't turn up and scare the hell out of her again. "You're such a nice guy, Mark."

"Nice, huh?" Mark frowned. "Would have preferred handsome, or even better, irresistibly hot, but I'll take 'nice' for now, on the proviso that it is revised in the not-too-distant future."

Sage allowed herself a small smile, absorbing his easy, relaxed humor like a much-needed balm.

"I'm really looking forward to going back in tonight. Pia seems to know a bit more about what's going on, and we think with additional planning, we'll have a better chance of catching something worthwhile on film. We've decided to change the location and placement of two of the cameras, and I have a few ideas about what we can do to bring it on a little earlier."

Sage swallowed hard. Given all she'd discovered since her talk with Mark and Pia about tonight's investigation, she no longer thought continuing it was a good idea. In fact it was probably the worst idea she'd ever heard. And she now had a lot of the answers the investigation was supposed to provide in her hands already. She needed to spend some time going through Mary's diary and attempt to translate what she could of the grimoire. So many questions. So little time. And who could she trust?

It was so tempting to just blurt out everything.

She liked Mark, she really did. But something niggled at her. Even without the Ouija board's warning, which might not relate to him at all.

If she'd thought that warning Mark against going through with tonight's investigation would work, she'd have given it a go. But if she wasn't going to share what she'd found, it was pointless, and she might as well see what additional light Pia might be able to shed. She was a psychic medium after all. Perhaps there'd be more messages for Sage. From a good source this time. The demon could stick *his* messages where the sun didn't shine.

"Don't worry," Mark said, misinterpreting her discomfort. "Just leave everything to me."

"Why? I mean, why do you do this?" Sage asked. For better or worse, and through no choice of her own, Sage was part of this. But Mark chose to be here. To make a career of it. "I can't wait until it's all over and I can move on."

"Proof. I want to get irrefutable proof that things like this exist."

"You've told me that before, but why do you care what anyone else thinks?"

He looked at her seriously, a light frown marring his perfect features. "To show the world that people like Pia are not crazy. That I am not crazy. That you are not crazy."

"Is that all? Ghost hunting is such an unusual line of work, I suspect that something more than just proving there's an afterlife must have led you onto that path."

Mark leaned back in his chair and sipped at his coffee. "I don't call it ghost hunting. I prefer to think of it as exploring the paranormal. The words 'supernatural' and 'paranormal' have become tag lines for numerous shows and horror movies and are more clichés than serious subjects. But if you analyze the word parts 'para' and 'normal,' they simply mean above or beyond the normal or natural view of reality."

"But what made you get into that line of work? I mean originally. Most people hope they never see the supernatural except in movies. Even if they do believe there's 'something else' out there, they're usually quite content to leave it at that."

"I always remember feeling there was something more to the world than what you can see with your eyes, touch with your fingers," Mark said, playing with a sachet of sugar from the caddy. "As a child, I was fascinated by ghosts and what happened after we died, and I read everything I could get my hands on. There was so much material available. Because some of the most famous cases turned out to be hoaxes, it was hard to determine what was real, and what wasn't.

"There have been many documented cases of supernatural occurrences, but the evidence is usually flimsy. Easily debunked as trick photography or a play of the light. The technology back in the day was not as advanced, or the wrong sort of camera was used by the investigator. But it was the stories that fascinated me. The interviews. Something about people's stories just rang true."

"Did you have any of your own experiences growing up?"

He looked at her keenly. "Yes. Yes, I did. I felt things, and I had a few scary experiences, things I couldn't explain. But when I told my dad, he laughed at me. Told me I was reading too much garbage and it was warping my mind. I began to wonder if my father was right. Maybe it was a trick of a child's overactive imagination, just like he said. Like believing in Santa and fairy tales. He was so sure of himself. He was my father, and I looked up to him. So I put the books away and concentrated on my studies. But still things kept happening..." His voice trailed off, and then he laughed.

"I was supposed to be an accountant. Me? Can you imagine?" He raised his eyebrows questioningly at Sage and she laughed in agreement. She had a hard time seeing such a handsome, charismatic man sitting behind a desk in some dull office.

"Dad runs a successful accounting firm, and being the only son, I was expected to follow in his footsteps. Take over one day."

The paper on the sachet of sugar broke open, and Mark absently brushed the crystals to the side. "I met Pia while I was halfway through my degree. We hit it off right away. It was as though we were destined to meet. I had questions, and she had the answers. She explained so much of what I had seen and was experiencing myself and also some of what happens after we die." He took a sip of water and leaned back on his plastic chair, stretching his long legs.

"Pia spoke to my deceased uncle. I knew it was real because she mentioned things she couldn't have found out from anyone else. Things that were only between myself and my grandfather. It was his way of proving his identity. From that moment on, all my searching and questions regarding the validity of my curiosity were confirmed. Much to my father's disappointment, I dropped out of university and started a quest to prove the existence of life after death."

"To prove to your father."

"In part." He shrugged. "I may have understated it slightly when I said he was disappointed. He was downright furious. We argued, and he threw me out of the house. We haven't spoken since that day."

"I'm sorry."

"No need to feel bad for me." Mark's familiar, easy grin was back. "Someone has to do this type of work. It is real, and wonderful people like you need help. And you know I'd never miss an opportunity to help a beautiful damsel in distress. Ready to order?"

Sage's stomach rumbled in answer.

They lined up to peruse the selection in the display counter. There was so much to choose from among the array of pastries, a mix of traditional English and Cornish cuisine, and a little German influence from the nearby Barossa Valley. Pies, pasties, sausage rolls. She decided on a Cornish pastie, and a Kitchener bun, while Mark chose a traditional meat pie and chips.

The door opened, and the girls Sage had gone to school with walked in. Keeping a deliberate distance, they huddled up in the far corner of the shop talking in loud whispers. "The mean girls," Sage had labeled them. The ringleaders and the instigators of her worst pain before Nan's death. Of the seven girls Sage's age at school, only one had been brave enough to be her friend. And she had left Cryton years ago, like Sage.

Their words carried easily to Sage's ears, which meant Mark could hear their conversation too.

"Who's that guy she's with? He's hot!" Charmaine whispered loudly. In school, she was the girl all the guys had wanted to go out with. The one who'd worn the shortest skirts and tiniest tops and who'd made constant snide remarks about everyone's appearance. She had one hand on a stroller. The little girl inside it, dressed like a doll, looked at Sage and smiled. Sage smiled back at her and hoped she didn't someday end up as nasty as her mother.

"I've never seen anyone as good-looking as him—even in the movies," Charmaine continued in a loud whisper.

Her friend Wendy rolled her eyes. "Where have you been? He *is* a movie star, or close enough. Haven't you ever watched *Debunking Reality*? That's Mark Collins."

Charmaine whipped her head around to get a better look. Sage glanced at Mark, hoping he wouldn't encourage a conversation with them. That would be awkward. But to her immense relief, if Mark heard them, he gave no sign, instead he was focused on doing something on his mobile phone.

"What's he doing with Sage?" Charmaine continued, saying her name as if it tasted bad. "You don't think he's her boyfriend?"

"Sage the freak?" Wendy laughed. "Absolutely not."

"You have to admit, she looks good, especially since she's been in the city." That comment came from Anastasia. That was probably the nicest thing she'd ever said about Sage.

"That may be so, but inside she's a freak. That will never change. Did you forget how she brought that baby bird back to life right there in front of us on that excursion? I'm telling you, at night she turns into a gorgon with snakes for hair. She's a godless hag. A freak," Charmaine repeated. "Someone as hot as that guy would never give her a second glance."

"Will you two get with the program?" Wendy said with exaggerated patience. "What do you think a *paranormal investigator* is doing with Sage?" She paused for effect. "He's investigating freaks."

Sage's face heated as their giggles reached her ears.

"Shh," Charmaine said. "You don't want her to hear. She'll put a curse on you."

"Like she did her grandmother?" Wendy asked.

"She didn't curse her grandmother," Anastasia said.

"Maybe. Maybe not. Either way she's bad luck. Just like a black cat, don't let her cross your path."

Despite Sage's resolution to the contrary, their words still stung. She took a deep breath. She was not that little girl anymore.

Grinding her teeth, she felt the anger swirl inside her. All the things she hadn't said when she was that little girl were not buried after all; they were simmering just beneath the surface.

Scathing retorts and cutting insults banked up on her tongue as she mentally selected the ones that would do the most damage, inflict the most pain. The way they'd hurt Sage all those years ago. Body tense and fully prepared for the fight, Sage filled her lungs with air and turned to give them what was long overdue.

A dark haze hovering in the far corner of the room caught her attention and she stilled. Her heart was racing, her cheeks flaming painfully. A thousand words poised on the tip of her tongue, ready to leap off and inflict maximum damage. But she ruthlessly reined in her rage and stemmed the outpouring before it could start.

He was watching. Anger and hatred were what he wanted from her. He *wanted* her weakened, dragged down to their level, to be filled with bitterness and revenge. Mary had told her he'd been using these girls to torment her for the last twenty years.

Her fingers found the angel around her neck, and she felt a rush of calm. The red tinge that had blurred her vision cleared. Attacking those girls would only serve the demon's purpose.

She turned away and gave the demon the mental finger.

"Bitches," Sage muttered instead. Rather than feeling weak, she realized there was power in not allowing herself to be drawn in. Now that she knew she *could* fight, she no longer wanted to. Some things just weren't worth it.

Wendy looked in Sage's direction. The expression on Sage's face must not have been pleasant, because Wendy put up her hands in front of her mockingly. "Oooh! A freak glare. Let's go before she puts a hex on us or something."

"Can't wait to see what show about the freak *Debunking Reality* are doing," Charmaine said.

"And to think you thought someone as hot as him would be with *her*," Wendy said to Charmaine and actually snorted. "If only I wasn't married—" Wendy looked Mark up and down slowly and tossed her hair in a move that Sage remembered from high school.

At that precise moment when they all were turned to face her, Mark casually slipped his phone into his top pocket and turned so they could see him clearly. He reached out to Sage and pulled her flush against his body. Looking directly into her eyes, he lowered his mouth and kissed her passionately.

As surprised as she was, she clearly heard the collective gasps of the girls. Out the corner of her eye, she saw each one open-mouthed in astonishment.

Going along with the performance, Sage kissed him back. Mark's kiss was practiced. Pleasant. But it didn't make her pulse skip like Ethan's did.

"Come on, girls. Let's get out of here," Wendy said. The door jangled open.

Sage abruptly broke the kiss, her face heating with a mixture of amusement and embarrassment. She watched the women traipse toward the door. A man was standing just inside the entrance, and Sage met his eyes. *Ethan.*

Her heart stopped dead in her chest as her dazed gaze connected with Ethan's furious one.

CHAPTER THIRTY

It was a little after three p.m. when Ethan spotted Sage's car in front of the local bakery. Though there was barely a whisper of wind, the smell of fresh-baked pastries reminded him that he'd missed lunch. Several squealing children burst out of the shop and pushed past him and Nate, their harried mothers apologizing and calling out their names as they gave chase.

"I hope that's chocolate ice cream," Nate muttered as he wiped at the sticky brown residue left on his jeans by a child who'd grabbed his leg as he raced past.

Ethan was too distracted to reply, walking a straight line toward the shop. His stomach still hadn't unclenched from the knot that had formed when he'd been told she'd left with Collins. He didn't like the way the ghost buster looked at her—or the proprietary way he acted around her.

That pansy show pony wasn't capable enough to keep Sage safe, and with the murder of Ada, it meant the killer was close.

Ethan opened the door and stopped as though he'd slammed into a brick wall.

That bastard Collins was kissing Sage.

A wave of fury disabled all rational thought and he advanced on Collins, shoving him in the chest. Hard. Collins fell backward, landing on the table and knocking over the chairs.

Nate pulled him back from giving Collins the beating he deserved. "Blade, calm the fuck down. There are kids here, and you're scaring them."

Ethan shrugged his partner off. He relaxed his fists and flexed his fingers.

Picking himself off the floor, Collins brushed at his coffee-stained clothes. "I'm charging you for assault, arsehole."

What the fuck had he been thinking? He didn't go around assaulting civilians.

He'd received the highest-ever score of anyone in the department in a specially tailored program for Taipan, similar to the US training program SERE, Survival, Evasion, Resistance, and Escape. He hadn't been broken through sleep- and sensory-deprivation, electric shock, isolation, drugs, or torture.

So his impulse to act instinctively and without thought when seeing Mark kissing Sage was beyond disconcerting. For the first time in his life, Ethan fully understood just how powerfully jealousy hijacked the brain. He'd worked many cases where perpetrators had sat in the interrogation room, holding their heads in their hands in disbelief, unable to see themselves capable of doing what they'd been accused of. They'd appeared as shocked as anyone over what they'd done. And now Ethan knew why.

Instinct had taken over years of training. Something dangerous stirred inside him, something that howled to be set free. Sage locked her green eyes with his. His heart lurched and stuttered. The pain in her gaze almost brought him to his knees.

"Are you with *him* now?" he asked. Damn his voice for breaking on the words.

"What? No." She took a step to the side as if to prove her point. "Why would that bother you anyway?" She raised her chin and looked past him.

Shrugging off Nate's restraining hand, he took a step forward. "Why would it bother me?" How could she ask such a question? His hands twitched at his sides as he desperately sought some semblance of self-control.

Despite finding her locked in a kiss with Collins, he still wanted to take Sage in his arms, feel her body soften and curve against his. Erase everything that had happened between them these last few hours.

Collins attempted to put an arm around Sage. She glared at him and stepped away. The gesture gave Ethan a surge of hope. He wasn't going to lose her without a fight. Especially to *him*. "Sage, can I have a moment of your time?"

"I'm not sure that's a good idea."

Every muscle in his body tensed. "I need to explain about Jenny."

"I don't care."

"I don't believe you," he said, and her eyes glistened with unshed tears. "Sage, we have to talk. There are things you need to understand that I can't talk about here. I need to talk to you, alone."

She hesitated, and fidgeted with the angel around her neck.

"Please?" He poured as much emotion as he could manage into that one word. "If last night meant anything to you at all, then please give me the opportunity to at least explain…"

A tear slid down her cheek, and it was as if someone took a machete to his stomach.

"Come on, Sage. Let's go," Collins said, taking her hand and tugging on it.

She resisted, and for a heart-stopping moment Ethan held his breath. He held out his hand, hoping she would take it this time.

He shot Collins a warning glance. If that ghost buster said anything to make him lose this chance with her, Ethan would pummel him unrecognizable.

Sage looked at his hand, then up to him. "Why are you doing this?" she asked, voice cracking. "What do you want from me?"

"I want a chance to explain."

"Sage, let's go," Collins said, pulling her away.

"I'm sorry, Ethan, but I have bigger things to worry about than you and your girlfriend."

There was so much left unsaid between them. He wanted to run after her, grab her by the shoulders, and demand that she listen. He wanted to crush his mouth to hers and remind her what it was like between them.

But he did none of those things, and watched her walk out the door.

Chapter Thirty-One

Sage brought her white Holden Astra to a stop in the gravel driveway of Joyce Booth's house. Originally intending to go back to the shop with Mark and help with preparations for tonight's investigation, she instead found herself battling a sense of restlessness.

To take her mind off Ethan and what had happened at the bakery, she'd decided to check in on Joyce. Sage needed to know she was doing okay after the murders of two of her closest friends. That had to be hard for anyone to go through, let alone someone in her eighties.

The scene at the bakery had strained Sage's already fraught nerves. To her mortification, Ethan had seen her locked in that kiss with Mark. Ethan's extreme reaction, the way he'd attacked Mark, could only have been caused by one thing. Jealousy.

She hadn't been wrong. He *did* care for her. And damn her traitorous heart for still caring about him.

But it still didn't change the fact he had a girlfriend. Ethan had wanted to talk, but right then, with their emotions dangerously high, it was not the time nor the place. The wound was too deep, too fresh. And she'd told the truth when she'd said she had bigger things to worry about.

She had intended to find out from Ada what she and Nan had been doing in preparation for the blood moon. Ada had warned her at the funeral to leave. Told the other ladies that she'd handle it. Out of love, both Ada and Nan had tried to spare her. And they'd lost their lives in doing so. With Ada no longer here to ask, she now had to hope that Joyce, Patricia, or Mona knew something that would help her.

Sage stood on the front porch of the hundred-plus-year-old stone house, and knocked.

"Joyce, are you home?" Sage called through the rusty wire screen.

Sage heard the sound of someone moving around, and then Joyce appeared and opened the door, her face drawn.

"Oh, Joyce. How are you?"

Joyce shook her head as she let Sage in. "Come in, dear, we've been waiting for you." *Waiting for me?* Well, that was a change of tune.

"Lock the door behind you," she said, turning her back and heading to the rear of the house. Sage locked the door, which consisted of sliding a thin bolt into a hole drilled into the aging wooden door frame. She could imagine what Ethan would say about this "why bother" lock and lack of security. Ignoring a sharp stab of pain in the pit of her stomach, she forced thoughts of him away.

Sage followed Joyce as she shuffled along the linoleum hallway. The room to the right at the front was the lounge, which held a two-seater couch covered with one of Nan's multi-colored crocheted blankets. A faded plastic plant sat atop the television in the corner, not a flat screen, but one of the old box-type models. They passed a couple bedrooms off to either side of the hallway, and as they reached the kitchen, Sage's eyes went to the black witch hanging above Joyce's kitchen sink. Identical to the one that she'd just seen seemingly fly by itself in Ada's house, and a replica of the one that had always hung in Nan's kitchen window.

They exited out the rear door, its wooden frame, once painted green, now chipped and peeling. Another flimsy lock. Sage made a mental note to get some better security for Joyce. Especially considering what had happened to Ada today. She couldn't rule out the idea that the demon could be targeting Nan's friends. Joyce might be next.

At the rear of the house, she found Pat sipping tea from a dainty rose-decorated china cup. A gold-edged plate with homemade biscuits sat in the center, beside a teapot with a colorful crocheted cover.

"Have a seat, dear," Pat said.

Their warm welcome put Sage on guard. She'd been expecting a cool reception like the one she'd received at the funeral, perhaps even a hostile one. Instead, they both seemed almost *pleased* to see her.

"I'm sorry about Ada," Sage said, and lowered herself into the chair Pat had indicated. A pile of scrunched tissues sat alongside their box on the table, and Patricia dabbed at the corner of her eye with a lace handkerchief.

"So devastating. Raylene. Celeste. Now Ada..." Patricia paused to delicately blow her nose, then pulled a fresh handkerchief, ironed into a neat square, from her handbag. It had slipped Sage's mind that Raylene had also passed away. She couldn't remember how now, either. Sage hadn't been as close to Raylene as she was to Ada and the others, and Raylene's death had occurred after Sage had left Cryton to live in Adelaide.

"I just came by to see how you were. Where's Mona?"

"She left not long ago," Patricia said. "Her son will be calling, you see, but she'll be back later. She left some cookies. Would you like one?"

"Thank you, no. Is there anything I can do? Anything you need?" Sage's heart broke anew over the visual signs of their grief. Both had puffy eyes and red noses, and appeared to have aged ten years since she'd seen them last. They were probably scared to be alone in their houses now.

"Oh, we need something all right," Joyce said, anger lacing her words.

"You do?" Sage replied. "I'll do whatever is in my power to make it happen."

"Catch that demon and hurl his sorry ass through the portal and back to the fiery depths of Hell." Joyce's china teacup crashed loudly against its delicate saucer.

Well then. Sage leaned back in her seat. At least that answered the question of whether they knew what was going on. So why, if that was the case, hadn't they spoken to her about it at the funeral? Had that strange crow really scared them off? They'd said, *he* was watching. That comment had made no sense to Sage back then. But now… How could they know about the demon and not warn Sage about it?

"You said you'd been expecting me. Why?"

"The prophecy," Joyce replied. "Ada had it in her head that because of the promise she'd made to Celeste she'd try to spare you. She'd foolishly thought she could take your place in the prophecy. She had hoped that with what she'd learned from Celeste, and having the grimoire and all, it would be enough. She was crazy enough to think she could fight the demon on her own. Without protection."

Joyce's gaze lowered to the angel pendant around Sage's neck.

"My mother gave this to me." Sage automatically touched the precious crystal. "It *is* protection, isn't it?" Sage asked, remembering what had happened in the attic.

"It's a very powerful amulet, yes."

"If that's so, why didn't my mother keep it?" Sage asked. "Why did she give it to me? Had she kept it, would she have been protected from the demon all those years ago?"

"Fretting over an unchangeable past is a terrible waste of energy," Patricia said. "Oh, Sage I don't mean to be so impolite. You really ought to try some of Mona's cookies. They're the best she's made yet." As though to prove her point, she took a bite of one, then flicked off the tiny crumbs that landed on her immaculately pressed cream shirt.

Sage cleared her throat. "I can't eat right now. What can you tell me about the amulet?"

"No more than what you'll discover yourself," Joyce said. "But make no mistake, it was always meant to be yours."

Joyce's was wearing a pale blue dress with a collar. Her hair appeared freshly washed, her curls newly set but her hand was unsteady, rattling the cup in the saucer as she picked it up and sipped her tea.

Taking the grimoire from her handbag, she set it in the middle of the table. Neither woman appeared surprised to see it there.

"I found this beneath the floorboards in Ada's kitchen. What can you tell me about it?" Sage asked, watching their reactions carefully.

"The only thing we know for sure is that it's meant for you," Patricia said. "It's the prophecy. There is a letter in there, to the seer's daughter. That's you."

"By that, do you mean my mother was a seer? I know Nan was a psychic. Tell me what you know about my mother." Sage clasped the angel around her neck.

"Your mother, Maeve, was a white witch. A seer. *The* seer. But of course we don't use the term 'witch' or 'seer' any more. We use more new-age terms: clairvoyants, psychics, mediums. Whatever label you wish to assign her, your mother, like Celeste, was gifted. As are you."

Sage's eyes welled. Nan had never spoken much about her mother, and sensing the pain it inflicted on Nan, Sage had never pressed her for details.

"Sage, the crash that took your mother's life twenty years ago was no accident," Pat said gently.

"I found that out today," Sage said, remembering the conversation she'd had with Mary in the attic. "Twenty years ago, when the demon first slipped through."

"Celeste was ever so distraught," Joyce said, picking up the story. "Being a witch herself, sorry, a *psychic*, she'd had visions of your mother's death for many years. It's why she'd travelled so extensively, sought out wise counsel in places like Peru. She consulted Tibetan monks, did everything she could to understand what the negative energy was, and how to be rid of it. Turns out what she was looking for was here all along. But of course, she discovered it too late to save your mother."

"My mother must have known," Sage said. "When she gave me the pendant, she made me promise not to take it off. That tells me she had some idea of what would happen. And the symbol on the back is the same as the one on the grimoire."

Joyce shrugged. "Who's to know? Perhaps she never got a chance to tell Celeste. Perhaps she chose not to. Perhaps she didn't know all the details, but just enough to know she needed to keep you safe. She loved you so very much, you know."

"Celeste, too," Pat added, fidgeting with a serviette. "She refused to lose you to the evil, the way she lost her only daughter. She made us all promise as well. Promise to keep you as far away from *him*, the demon, as possible."

"Why did Ada think she could take this on? Was Ada… gifted too?" Sage asked, not liking the term "witch."

"No," Pat said, "but she was Celeste's protégé, for want of a better term. Ada was spiritually open, a willing student, and eager to learn. She put everything she had into taking this on. She didn't want to let Celeste, or you, down."

Sage blinked back tears and tried to breathe through the tightness in her chest. She felt somehow undeserving of such unconditional love. All this had been happening, while she'd been away somewhere else. Oblivious. Had she not left in the first place, had she been here, things might have turned out differently. She might have been able to save them.

Or… did they think she wasn't *capable*?

She'd never even been given the chance to prove herself. No one had thought to tell her. Anger flared inside her, cutting through her grief like a flame to cotton wool.

"You said there is a prophecy. If I'm the seer's daughter, why didn't Nan speak to me about it?"

"Celeste didn't know about the prophecy until recently. Until she'd found Mary's diary actually. Of course Celeste being Celeste, she knew of the negative energy, the 'darkness' as she called it. It played with her for years. But for a long time she didn't understand what it was. What it wanted. Who it was. And she had no idea of the power, or the depravity, of what she was dealing with."

Nan hadn't told her because she'd wanted to protect Sage. Not because she didn't think she was capable. Anything Nan had done was out of pure love.

That demon was going to pay. How had Joyce put it? *Hurl that demon's sorry ass back through the portal and back into the fiery depths of Hell.* Now *that's* a plan.

"So what do you suggest I do from here? I'm trying to pick up from where Nan left off." Sage turned to Joyce. "I noticed on the way through, that you have the same witch hanging in your kitchen as Ada and Nan had in theirs. Do they have any significance other than decoration?"

"The witches. Yes. They're very special. We've had them for many years, but just recently Celeste imbued them with power, protection. They're a symbolic reminder that together we are more. United, we will succeed. We can and will defeat the Beast."

Sage resisted pointing out that the little witch hadn't protected Ada. Spell-enhanced witch or not, Sage was still putting bigger locks on all their houses.

"Okay, so moving forward. You've obviously been working with Nan on this, as a team it seems. Nan would have had a good understanding of what was going on by the end. Do you know the last thing she discovered before—" Sage broke off. It was still so terribly hard to say the words.

"She was on the verge of finding out who the serial killer was. She'd been reaching out to the spirit of that little boy, Toby. *He* didn't like it. The Beast, I mean. That was what we were doing the night before Celeste was taken from us. Find out who the serial killer is, and you have your master demon. You'll then follow the ritual as outlined in the grimoire—"

Sage released a long breath and regretted that she could no longer comfortably ask Ethan about the details of the case.

"Now, you cannot mention any of this to that handsome detective of yours," Pat said, as though reading her thoughts.

"Oh, he is handsome, isn't he?" Joyce fanned herself with her napkin. "If I were a few years younger...."

"He'd never look twice at you," Pat said. "A few years younger indeed. Not even thirty years younger. And anyway, he's *meant* for Sage."

Sage was just about to ask what she meant by that when Joyce raised her chin. "Excuse me! I was quite a prize in my heyday. What I would do if I had him to myself for an hour or—"

"Why can't I tell him?" Sage interrupted, not wanting to know what Joyce thought she would do with Ethan.

"Because a hundred years ago, the pastor's wife, Mary, had succeeded in exorcising the demon. But, unaware of what was really happening in the town, of what Mary had managed to do, the government moved in and killed everyone. Men, women, and children. They, in my opinion acted no better than the demon himself. If the government gets wind that this situation is happening again, they'll act quickly. They can't afford for the cover-up to be exposed. They'll step in swiftly, and you, indeed all of us, will be in grave danger."

"How do you know all this?" Sage asked.

"Celeste had a few dreams in which Mary spoke to her. That poor woman and what she went through. Tragic. Just tragic."

"I don't think the government would come in and kill a whole town these days," Sage said.

"Wouldn't they? A great atrocity occurred. At best, if we spoke out about this, we'd be removed, locked up for the rest of our lives in a mental institution. Can you imagine what will happen if you don't manage to banish the demon before the portal closes? What life will be like for future generations? It will be hell on earth. Everything we do must be kept completely secret. You cannot trust anyone."

That expression again, *hell on earth.* The images in the grimoire and the stories of horror from Mary's diary flashed through Sage's mind. A chill seeped into her bones.

"Well, you certainly know quite a bit of what is going on. What I don't understand is, with time so short, so valuable, I could have started working on this earlier. Perhaps even done enough to save Ada. Why didn't you tell me any of this at the funeral?"

"Oh, believe me, I wanted to," Joyce said, sniffing. "At the funeral, we were so angry with Ada. We'd been arguing for two days straight over whether to come to you and tell you everything. But no, Ada wanted to hold fast to the promise she'd made to Celeste. The day before she…" She paused and took a shaky breath. "The day before Celeste died, we'd been sitting right here enjoying a cup of tea and Mona's blueberry scones, when Celeste suddenly sprang up out of her chair. Her eyes were glazed, and she grabbed Ada's arm. 'It's Sage that he wants. She's not simply the one who can stop him, she is the one he *wants*.'"

"We all became a little worried about her at that point," Patricia said. "She was in a near panic. Whatever she'd seen in the vision had disturbed her greatly."

"Whatever it was, tortured her more than the vision of her own death." Joyce added. "It took a full twenty minutes for us to get her calm enough to sit back down in the chair. 'Don't let him take her,' she'd cried over and over. 'Promise me. Promise me you'll keep her away from here. I've seen. He doesn't have the power to go to her, he needs her here. I've seen what he has planned…'"

"He can't move far from the portal," Patricia explained.

"Which is here. In Cryton, right?" Sage asked for clarification.

"Yes. Over the circle. Or the house, we think."

"What is the circle? When I'd originally heard that term, I thought *you* were the circle. Nan's circle of friends. But it is something else, isn't it?"

"Yes. A sacred circle that will be used to harness the energy of the earth when the time is right. Celeste had a vision of the circle, near the old graveyard behind the house. The girls and I had been helping her clear the area around the graves, in preparation. We've been practicing what is to be done. We'll show you where the circle is."

"No need. If it's in the graveyard behind the house, I'll find it. I don't want any of you to go anywhere near the circle for now. You never know who's watching, and the last thing I want is unnecessary attention to any of this. I'll check it out tomorrow, then come back here to make a plan for the ritual," Sage said. "Do you know what Nan saw in her vision about me?"

"No. Not exactly, other than it upset her greatly, and when she was murdered the very next day, we tried to convince Ada to go to you. Begged her to tell you everything. But she held fast to her promise. She'd have done anything to protect you. And she did."

"I don't want to die like that," Patricia said. Her hand shook so badly, she could barely hold the tissue to her nose.

Sage leaned in, took both their hands and covered them with hers on the table. Tried to convey a confidence she didn't feel.

"All right. I might have arrived late at the party, so to speak, but I want you to know if I am meant to be doing something about all this, I'll do whatever I can to make sure it happens. I'll need you both though, Mona too, to think about every detail of every conversation you had with Nan or Ada about this. Write it down. Any detail, no matter how small, may help. I don't have a gift like Nan—"

"Oh, but you do, dear," Joyce interrupted, sitting up straight.

"I do?"

"Yes. Celeste spoke of it. You have a very great gift, more powerful even than her own."

"But..." Sage broke off, her head spinning. "If that were so, how come I haven't known about it? I don't have visions like Nan did. Surely if I had a gift after all these years, I'd have some sort of clue."

"You have had clues all your life," she countered. "You chose to deny them. Do you remember that potted fern in your classroom, how you brought it back from the dead?"

Sage remembered clearly. It was her first year at school, the year her mother had died, the year the tormenting had started. She'd come back from the first school holidays to find the fern dead. It was the very first thing she'd seen when she'd walked through the door. She'd *felt* its pain. It had been dry and shriveled up, but its *essence* remained.

"Nobody had watered it during the holidays. I just gave it a little water."

"Sage, it was *dead*," Joyce said. "It caused such a commotion, the principal called Celeste in. It was your touch that brought it back to life, not the water.

The whole class saw it."

And that's the first time anyone had called her a freak. But Nan had told her it wasn't true, that she was normal. That her classmates were just imagining things.

Had Nan lied to her? Sage cast her mind back. Nan had held her, made her feel better. She'd told Sage it was a good thing to care about plants. The environment. Sage had always been able to know what plants needed. You just had to know how to be silent and listen. That's all.

"Nan said I was born with a green thumb," Sage said weakly.

"That you were," Joyce said. "And a whole lot more. Remember what happened at school with the bird not long after that. Then there was the time Pat's puppy, Rolo, got stuck in that barbed wire fence, the rabbit that fell from the eagle's talons—"

"Okay, that's enough. I'm catching on." Sage frowned, her hand finding the angel pendant. It was true that she somehow *knew* what plants wanted. Animals too. She'd "rescued" more animals than she could possibly remember. They'd always been drawn to her. They too "told" her what they needed. She'd always known what was broken or in need of attention from the first touch. To her it was natural. No one had told her it wasn't. But would she have wanted to hear it even if they had?

"Why didn't Nan tell me the truth?"

"Because of the teasing at school, you tried even harder to be 'normal.' It was what you wanted more than anything else. Celeste cried a river of tears for you. She remembered her own painful childhood, your mother's too. Kids can be cruel. And of course, we didn't know anything about the prophecy back then. You'd simply inherited certain genes."

"Celeste would have plucked a star out of the very sky and given it to you if that is what you wanted," Pat added.

"You are of the earth. Sage of Earth," Joyce said.

Sage leaned back in her chair and covered her hand with her mouth. *Sage of Earth?*

"Celeste had an envelope for you. We don't know what was in it, but it could have been about this. Your gift. We were talking about it at the time she gave it to us. Joyce put the letter somewhere safe, but we can't find it," Patricia said, casting her an accusing glance.

"It wasn't me," Joyce argued. "Ada took it when she hid the grimoire."

"No—"

"Stop," Sage interrupted, her head beginning to pound. "Please, if everyone would look for it, I'd greatly appreciate it. Obviously, I need to know as much as I can about this gift. I'd like everybody to search everywhere for the letter. Don't go into Ada's house though. I'll do that."

Sage would need to leave it a day or two, considering the police would have found the mess she'd made by now and probably upped surveillance on the house. She might have to sneak in at night.

Sage stood. "If you're scared, or remember anything important, I want you to call me. Day or night. Especially if you find that letter from Nan. Here's my mobile." Sage pulled out some business cards from her work and, quickly scribbling out the office number to avoid any possibility of confusion, placed the cards in the center of the table. "Please put the number somewhere safe, and give it to Mona too. I'll come back tomorrow after I've seen the circle. In the meantime, write down everything you can remember about your conversations with Nan and Ada. Is there anything I can do for you before I go?"

Joyce and Patricia both stood and embraced her. Sage, an arm around each, hugged them back.

"We're glad you're home, Sage," Joyce said her voice muffled against her shoulder. "We know you'll be the one who can set things right."

Sage choked, unable to reply. She could only hug the women back and pray they were right.

CHAPTER THIRTY-TWO

Alone, Sage sat on the edge of the River Murray behind the shop and tried to clear her mind. She attempted to slow her erratic thoughts and make some sense of how her life had been turned upside down since she'd returned to Cryton. She fingered the angel around her neck, watching the colors from the setting sun bleed into the sky.

Century-old gum trees lined the river, their roots and branches tangling along the shoreline. As darkness descended, they appeared to emerge from the water like eerie bone-figures. The last of the sun's light faded from golden, to orange, to dark red.

Blood red. *In less than two weeks, the next full moon will be the fourth eclipse of the tetrad.* Everything she'd discovered these last twenty-four hours ran through Sage's mind, and she rubbed her arms. The evening air felt cool against her skin, but she resisted the impulse to put on her jacket, enjoying the freshness on her heated face.

She took a deep breath and released it. She needed to take a moment or two for herself before heading back to help Mark with the investigation.

A heavy sense of foreboding had settled over her. Would Mark's paranormal investigation attract the master demon-slash-possessed serial killer tonight? She hoped she didn't run into him until she was ready. Although, it would be handy to know who he was.

She wished she could talk this over with Ethan and wondered if he had any leads on the case. But even if she had still been talking to Ethan, Joyce had warned her not to tell him about any of this. If it got back to the authorities, what action would they take? And if Ethan was anything to go by, they couldn't be trusted. His darkly serious, ruggedly handsome image hovered behind her lids.

How could I be so stupid?

What was it about men and their need to have their cake and eat it too? The way he'd looked at her and said *please* in that tone of voice... She'd known she was going to forgive him. Fall for his lies a *second* time.

How long would he have made a fool of her? Did he sleep with women on every case, like a sailor with a girl at home and different ones in every port?

She sighed, and as tears rose to sting her lids, she blinked them back furiously. She refused to shed one more tear over him. But how did she go about severing her overwhelming attraction to him?

She couldn't solve that problem. And it was time to stop thinking about it.

Carefully, she pulled the grimoire out of her bag and ran her hands across the cover. It soothed her somehow. The leather felt cool and comforting beneath her fingertips. A peaceful, calming energy came from it, but she didn't know how that could be so. Inanimate objects weren't alive. They didn't have energy. Not like plants and animals. Perhaps it was just because she knew the importance of the grimoire's contents that she felt drawn to protect it. If everything she'd been told was true, it was her *only* chance. Except... of course there was that part about her gift. Sage of Earth, Joyce had called her. There was a letter, but Sage really wished beyond measure her Nan could have been here to speak to her about it in person.

Pia could communicate with those who'd crossed over... Perhaps she could contact Nan? Sage pushed the thought aside. One step at a time.

She would have loved to talk to Pia about all this, get a second opinion, but Pia would tell Mark, and Sage couldn't risk that. Not yet. Given what it contained, the grimoire would be extremely dangerous in the wrong hands. *Were Mark's the wrong hands?*

Beware. Lucky. Mark. Though she didn't choose to dwell on them, those words were never far from her mind. She couldn't be sure that the message from the Ouija board was a warning about Mark or even a warning she was supposed to heed at all. Perhaps Mark wasn't a name, but a marking of some sort? Maybe the branding that had reportedly been found on Ada's hand. Or maybe it meant that she had to beware, and that Mark was lucky? Would he be the one to *help* her?

But the most prominent questions on her mind were: Who had tried to send her a message, and what was their motive? Was it Nan, or the spirit of someone else? Perhaps Mary, or one of the people who'd lived in the house and been murdered? Could the message have been from the demon? Perhaps the entity feared Mark and his team and had tried to warn her against him? Confuse her?

She still had so many questions that had yet to be answered. She'd do as Mary had suggested and pick up Nan's journey. Uncover what she could, *then* decide who else she could trust with the information she discovered.

An inch-long black ant crawled over her bare foot. "Hello," she said softly. The creature paused only briefly before continuing on its way. Nothing out of the ordinary about that, Sage thought.

The setting sun reminded her it was soon time to get back to the shop.

Mark had kissed her cheek before he'd left her this afternoon, but she was careful to keep her distance. She didn't want to give him the wrong signals and lead him on. That afternoon in the bakery had been bad enough. Mark had looked at her differently before he left. A little more tenderly. He was nice, but he wasn't Ethan.

Ethan. No matter what she did, her thoughts always returned to him. What had he thought when he'd seen her kissing Mark? The expression on his face had been tortured. There was no way he would have been so hurt if he didn't feel something for her. He had wanted the chance to talk, and she hadn't given him one.

She needed to. After what they'd shared together, after how deeply she had begun to care for him, she owed him—them—at least that much. Even if it was only to hear him out before breaking things off. She wasn't going to be the other woman. Ever. No matter the excuse.

She threw a rock, and it bounced across the water before disappearing.

"There you are." A male voice startled her. She glanced over her shoulder to see Nate walking toward her. "We've been looking for you for hours."

Turning away, she gazed back across the river, and felt his warmth as he took a seat next to her. For a long moment he said nothing as they sat together, watching the moonlight gleam off the gently moving ripples of water.

"It's so beautiful here," he said, his voice soft. "Is this your private place?"

"It was," she said, then immediately regretted her tone. "I'm sorry. That was bitchy."

"I apologize for dropping in on you uninvited, but Ethan has been frantic with worry. You shouldn't be on your own at the moment."

Sage shrugged and swallowed a stab of hurt. Was Ethan's concern only for her safety? "I don't give a toss what Ethan thinks."

Nate slowly released a breath. "You do know that Jenny is not his girlfriend, don't you?"

"Do I have 'idiot' written across my forehead?" she snapped. "He admitted she was. You must think I'm as stupid as Ethan does."

"Ethan doesn't think anything of the sort."

"You disappoint me, Nate. I wouldn't have thought you'd be part of the boys' club."

"The what?"

"You know, the boys' club. What happens in Vegas, stays in Vegas."

"Whatever are you talking about?"

She turned to face him. "I know men all stick together. Corroborate each other's stories. Watch each other's back and all that. If Ethan is concerned that his girlfriend will find out about our fling, tell him not to worry. I deeply regret what happened. My lips are sealed."

Nate appeared genuinely surprised at her summation. "You really think Ethan thought of you as some cheap thrill? A fling? You truly believe that's what he wants from you?"

Sage looked back across the water and sighed deeply. "I have no idea what he wants. I only know that I don't want any part of it."

"You have Ethan all wrong." Sage snorted, and Nate stiffened beside her. "Listen, I'm the first to admit that my partner has his faults, but I will not stand by and have him convicted for something he hasn't done."

"Of course you're going to defend him."

"Believe me, I'd be the first person to throw him under the bus if I thought he deserved it. But he doesn't. Look, Sage, I've told you the truth. What you do with it from here is up to you."

She glanced at Nate and saw nothing but honesty on his face.

So he wasn't just defending his buddy. She felt around for another stone. "Why are you here, Nate?" Sage asked, suddenly tired of it all. "And more to the point, why do you care?"

She threw the stone and it skipped across the water, bouncing four times. She was getting better.

"Because my partner and my best friend had his heart ripped out today."

A lump lodged in her throat. Why did he have to say that?

"All he wanted was a chance to talk with you, to explain. Jenny's call wasn't what you thought it was, and it killed him that you wouldn't let him put it right. You should have given him the opportunity to explain," he added, accusation creeping into his tone.

"You... you're *blaming* me?" Sage asked. Ethan was the one cheating on his girlfriend. Wasn't he?

"You're both at fault," Nate said, his voice flat. She inwardly cringed as she remembered the incident in the bakery.

"That was not what it appeared to be," she said, but the words sounded weak. And she was saying them to the wrong person.

"Ethan is good at his job. Damn good. The best damned detective the department's got. Besides me, that is." Nate winked to lighten the mood, but she refused to be drawn in.

"Good for him." She didn't care if he was Captain America. And where was Nate going with this?

"Ethan didn't get to be the best by being emotional. Total chaos can be raining down around him, and he can keep a level head. That detachment has kept him alive in some very dangerous situations. Kept me alive too. I trust him with my life. Hell, he's saved my ass more than once."

"That's all very nice. But what's it got to do with me?" Sage rubbed her arms as a breeze brushed across her skin. Nate flicked the sand off his jacket and placed it around her shoulders.

"Thank you," she said and glanced his way. She didn't need his jacket; she'd brought her own. But it would have been rude to take it straight off and give it back. He was only trying to be kind. He really was a nice guy. Good-looking too.

She was surrounded by handsome men at the moment, but only one had the power to make her heart race.

Instead of answering her, Nate was focused on something to their left. "What's over there?" he asked. Sage tensed. He was indicating the area in the trees and bushes behind the shop. The graves that Nan and her friends had begun to clear, where the circle was supposedly located. Sage had wondered whether the headstones visible were the graves of Mary and her family, but it had been too dark for Sage to read them this evening.

She fully intended to investigate them first thing in the morning when she came back to locate the circle. She wasn't too worried about anyone else interfering with the area, since this part of the riverbank was not a thoroughfare. The only access was via a pathway from the back garden of the shop.

"Is that some type of cemetery?" Nate asked, pointing to where the moonlight reflected off a headstone.

"I don't know." She didn't want the cops anywhere near there. The last thing she needed was to draw any attention to the graves, or the circle.

"Weird that they weren't buried in the town, with everyone else," Nate said. Sage shrugged, a deliberate, careless action, and Nate turned back to the river. Sage slowly released the breath she'd been holding.

The glow of the moon illuminated parts of his face, highlighting features she hadn't noticed before. She couldn't take her anger out on him any longer.

"Nate, why are you here instead of Ethan?"

He shifted to face her. "Because you wouldn't listen to him, but maybe you'll listen to me. No matter how much Jenny deluded herself, she never was, and never will be, Ethan's girlfriend. He's been trying to get that through to her for a long while now. He sucks at communication at the best of times, but even more so with women." Nate turned to her, his cop's eyes assessing her. "And what about you and Collins?"

Sage didn't turn away, letting him see the truth in her response. "I don't think of Mark that way. That kiss was not what it appeared to be."

Nate nodded, obviously satisfied that something in her response rang true for him.

"Good. I didn't think you had a romantic interest in Collins. I'd hoped I wasn't wrong. I don't want to see Ethan hurt. He's a good man. I've never seen him like he is about you," Nate continued. "I've watched him try—and fail—to switch off his feelings for you, or at least tone them down, so that he can work the case. You've shaken him up. He's never let anything interfere with an investigation before. Hell, I never thought I'd see the day. But then he met you."

Nate looked back across the river, which was now almost completely in shadow as a cloud passed over the moon. "For the very first time, I thought that maybe, just maybe, my partner was human." Peering at her out the corner of his eye, he grinned.

"Seriously though, he's never fallen hard for someone. After what happened to him, I'm more than a little relieved to see it. I'd hate for this misunderstanding with you to ruin him."

"What happened to him?"

"I'm speaking way out of place now, so I won't say anything more than that. He'll tell you everything in his own time, when he's ready." Nate reached out and squeezed her hand. "If you think half as much of him as he does of you, then please give him a chance to tell you all this himself. He's bloody hopeless, but to once again defend his sorry ass, he hasn't been in this situation before."

"Get your hand off my girl." Ethan's deep voice sent a wave of mixed emotions through her body. How could he affect her so much?

Nate slid closer, and with a soft chuckle, wrapped an arm around her shoulder.

Ethan's low growl resounded in the still night air as he walked briskly toward them. "Get your hands off her, or I'll be meeting you at dawn."

Nate tightened his embrace. "Go easy on him," Nate whispered in her ear, as he rested his head on her shoulder, pretending to snuggle up to her.

With each step Ethan took toward her, her heart pounded, and then her throat closed over. He had hurt her so badly, yet she still wanted him with every fiber of her being.

Ethan drew to a stop, and Nate let her go. He rose and approached Ethan, then leaned in and spoke words low in his ear, but she heard every one. "You have one last chance. Don't fuck it up this time." Nate thumped him hard on the shoulder and walked away.

CHAPTER THIRTY-THREE

E than looked down at the beautiful woman sitting on the bank of the river, knees tucked underneath her chin and wisps of long blonde hair moving softly in the gentle evening breeze. She was not looking at him, and for a moment he floundered, not knowing how to repair the distance between them. More than anything, he wished he could erase the last few hours and go back to that point in time when he'd had her naked body wrapped in his arms, her soft cheek resting against his chest. Had that really been only that morning?

"I'm sorry." The words were inadequate, but they were all he could think of. He was very sorry. Sorry that he'd had to leave without explaining about Jenny. Sorry that they couldn't have had the chance to talk earlier on. Even though he'd seen Collins kissing her, he couldn't believe she was romantically involved with him. Her actions afterwards didn't ring true to that theory. And when he'd asked her directly at the time, she had denied it. He didn't know what the kiss was about, but he was hoping she had a reason he could live with.

"I'm sorry I didn't give you a chance to explain," she said.

"It's okay. You were still mad. Can I sit down?"

He waited for what seemed like an eternity for her response. Eventually, she patted the ground next to her and he nearly sagged with relief.

He took a seat beside her and felt Nate's warmth still trapped in the sand. He didn't know what his partner had been telling her, but he hoped it was in his favor.

"I'm sorry too, about Ada," he said gently. "I know how close she was to your grandmother. How close she was to you. How are you holding up?"

She drew in a shaky breath and released it slowly. "Just catch the son of a bitch before he hurts anyone else. Do you have any idea who it is?"

Ethan stared out over the river, now in darkness as a cloud passed across the moon. "No. But I won't give up until I do." A muscle twitched along his jaw. "Jenny is not my girlfriend," he blurted.

"I know. Nate explained."

"You and Collins…?"

"No."

The silence stretched. "Damn it, Sage. Why were you kissing him?"

She flicked her eyes in his direction, and he saw a glint of amusement in them. "We were just annoying some girls I went to school with."

"I knew there'd be a good reason," he said, stretching his fingers in an attempt to relax his clenched hands. "Find another way to annoy them next time."

She let out a soft laugh, and some of the tension between them lifted.

"Tell Jenny she can't pretend to be your girlfriend."

"Deal." He twisted so that he was facing her and took both her hands in his. "Sage, I don't know how to explain how I feel about you, except to say that I've never met anyone like you before."

He wasn't sure how to say things in the way she needed to hear them. The smooth way someone like Nate might. But he reached inside and did his best to describe how she made him feel. "You're more than just visually beautiful. You are a feeling. The difference between admiring a beautiful painting or being moved by it."

She was playing with the edge of her skirt, listening, but still didn't speak.

"You mess me up inside, because part of me wants to capture you so that I can protect you, and part of me wants to stand back and watch you take on the world."

He brushed his thumb across her knuckle. "In my line of work, I see so much evil. The worst of human nature. You cannot even imagine. And then, out of the blue, I meet you, and somehow… somehow you manage to sneak in and light me up on the inside. You make me smile, more than I have in a long time."

Unshed tears glistened in her eyes. They mirrored his own.

He twisted a strand of her silken hair through his fingers. As though he'd opened a floodgate, he couldn't stop talking. "You taste of sunshine, especially when I kiss you here." He traced his finger along her slender neck and she trembled. "Did you know you have a freckle that lies just beneath your angel?"

She shook her head, and he tenderly placed his lips on the spot. Her pulse fluttered beneath his lips. He paused and savored her reaction. "If I'm reading you correctly, your body responds to me as strongly as mine does to you." His throat had constricted, making his voice deeper and rougher.

He reached for her hand and turned it over, exposing her wrist. Slowly, he brought his head down and traced his tongue along the veins pulsing under the delicate skin until she trembled.

He placed her hand back in her lap and looked out into the vast, dark sky, now thick with stars. There was no longer a breath of wind, and the night had turned almost eerily still.

"I'm not sure how to make you understand how I feel. There are probably better ways to say all of this, but I don't know what they are. All I can do is try to explain what effect you have on me. You're different, Sage. Special. The way you make me feel... well, to be honest, it scares the fuck out of me."

"Shut up." Her voice sounded thick, and a single tear rolled down her cheek. What did that mean? If she told him to leave, now that he'd sliced his heart open and handed it to her, he didn't know how he'd survive it.

"Sage?" His voice cracked. "What are you thinking? You're killing me here."

She didn't answer. Instead, she touched her mouth to his. The moment their lips connected, his mind blanked to everything but the taste of summer on his tongue. Summer sunshine in the moonlight. *Jesus, was he a poet now too?*

She pulled back, then climbed onto her knees and straddled him, her skirt hitching up around her thighs.

Her bracelets jangled as she tilted his chin so that he was looking up at her. Her gorgeous hair cascaded around her head and shoulders like a halo, and her sweet fragrance and the lacy blanket of her skirt enveloped him. Her expression was serious, and he waited, intrigued and totally captivated, for her to speak.

"Firstly, Detective Blade, in relation to all the strange things going on, you will never tell me that I am overwrought or imagining things again. I have considered all angles, and I believe there is something other than ordinary, everyday reality at work. And further, I won't stop searching until I have sorted it out. You will not stand in my way nor will you attempt to stop me. Are we clear?"

He swallowed past the lump in his throat, and his pants tightened painfully. Goddam, he would agree to anything when she was like this. He forced his lips to clamp together, but couldn't stop them from twitching at the corners. "Clear, Ms. Matthews."

"Secondly," she continued, all serious and sexy. "I want you to know that if you find it hard to believe in said otherworldly goings-on, you are to keep those opinions to yourself. Your belief issues are yours to deal with, not mine."

His cock was straining and his mouth was dry. He fought the urge to toss her over onto her back, tear her panties off, and fuck her until the sun rose. But he was smart enough to let her believe she was in control. For now. She'd been hurt. Hell, *he* had hurt her. He'd made her feel small, and used, and even though that hadn't been his intention, it was what had happened. She felt the need to draw clear lines in the sand of what she would and wouldn't accept from him. He didn't understand women, but even an idiot could tell she was reopening her heart to him, while warning him not to break it again.

"Yes, ma'am," he said, but not mockingly. He'd do anything, say anything, and agree to anything as long as she forgave him.

"Good. Because I won't accept anything less," she said, and he believed her. There was a certain standard she expected him to meet, to be with her, and God help him, he'd do anything within his power to live up to it.

She pushed his jacket off his shoulders and tugged at the bottom of his shirt. He sucked in, so that she could easily pull it out of his jeans. He took off his holster and utility belt and placed them under his jacket, off to one side, but still within easy reach.

She had wriggled down and was tugging at his jeans, and he suppressed a grin at her impatience. She was as hot for him as he was for her. He lifted up on his arms and she removed the remainder of his clothes. Naked in the gentle light of the full moon, he lay back on the riverbank, and waited to see what she'd do next.

Sage stood, her bare feet sinking into the soft cool sand as the moonlight bathed Ethan's perfectly sculpted body. He was nothing short of an Adonis. Lying prone and naked did nothing to detract from his virility and power. With his arms resting casually behind his head, and a lazy half-smile on his face, he looked every inch the confident alpha male he was.

She wanted to be every bit a match for him, and more. "Don't move, Detective," she ordered, echoing his words from last night.

A raised eyebrow and a twitch of his lip were the only outward signs that he'd heard her. She took them as his assent. She was wearing a sheer cheesecloth top that tied at the neckline, and she tugged at the bow, letting the fabric fall apart in the middle, exposing her lacy white bra. His cock twitched against his stomach, and she smiled. For all her bravado, this was the first time she'd ever stripped for a man, and it was nice to know he was enjoying it.

Deliberately slow, she removed her top, her bra, and then unzipped her skirt, letting it fall to her feet. She tugged at her lacy thong with her thumbs on her hips before she let it drop. They were now both completely naked. A cool breeze sprung up and blew across her heated skin and teased her hard nipples. Moisture pooled between her thighs as her body prepared itself for him.

Parting her legs, she slowly straddled his thighs. His eyes darkened and he swallowed hard. He moved his hands to touch her, but she gave him a stern look and shook her head.

"I didn't say you could move." He put his hands back behind his head, his biceps flexing. His eyes flicked a heated trail down her body, and back again. The gleam in his eye let her know that she had control only because he allowed it. Even still, she was onto a good thing and was determined to make the most of it.

Leaning forward, she spread her hands and ran her fingertips tantalizingly across his chest, down his abdomen, to brush ever so lightly across his erection. It leapt at her touch, and he watched her intently with narrow, heavy-lidded eyes. She traced the underside of his sac, fascinated by the way it pulled up and tightened. Increasing the pressure of her fingers, she teased, then gently stroked and circled his full length.

Gripping him with one hand, she lowered her head and flicked her tongue across the tip of his cock and was rewarded with the sexiest growl she'd ever heard. Wanting to elicit more of the same, she took him deep into her mouth, and his whole body trembled. She took her time, savoring the feel of his cock on her tongue.

She alternated between sucking and tracing her tongue along his length, marveling at how the soft, warm skin moved easily over the steel underneath. His body jerked, and his hands formed fists at his sides.

Opening wide, she took him in as far as she could, her tongue flicking along the sensitive underside as she withdrew. She explored every inch of him until she had every groove committed to memory. He didn't taste of anything at all really, perhaps slightly salty, but mostly just clean and masculine. She blew cool air across the tip of his cock before sucking it back into her mouth, and he groaned.

When she glanced up, she found him watching her, his eyes dark and intense, the connection like a powerful jolt of electricity. Eyes locked with his, she continued to pleasure his cock until his breathing became labored and his chest heaved. Increasing the pressure, she took him in deep and hummed.

He cursed and gripped her head, staying her. "Stop," he choked out. "I'm too close." His voice was low and gravelly and the sound of it made her tingle all over.

She gave him a mock glare, and he hesitated before placing his hands back behind his head.

But she heeded his warning and respected his desire to not finish yet. She'd planned on tasting his cum on her tongue, but swiftly changed course instead.

"Condom?" she asked.

"Front pocket of my jeans."

He didn't move to get them, and she took that as permission to help herself. Digging through his clothing, she found one surprisingly easily, and caught him eyeing her rear in rapt appreciation as she sat back up.

"Like what you see?" she teased, hoping he wouldn't notice the flush on her cheeks. She rolled the condom down his shaft.

"Very much," he rasped, sounding as though his control teetered on a very fine edge. She positioned his cock at her heated entrance and slowly, slowly sank down.

His groan, low and deep, mixed with hers. He felt so damn good inside her, filling her completely. She waited until her body had adjusted to his size before she began to move on top of him.

She set the pace, gradually building the intensity. "You are so damned sexy," he said, his dark eyes fixed on her every move; they flittered across her face, to her bouncing breasts, to where their bodies joined. His obvious appreciation inflamed her even more.

As the momentum built, he grabbed her by the hips, and she let him. He held her firmly and took over the thrusting, his movements deeper and more powerful than hers, altering the energy and urgency of their passion. She let go and surrendered control, and the sensation was heady.

The rhythmic slapping of their bodies carried across the water and far into the still, night air. He thrust into her as though he'd never satisfy his hunger for her, his hips moving powerfully, grinding inside her, so that she was powerless to do anything but hold still and let him pleasure her. She gasped his name, cried it. She was so close now. Her orgasm built to an intensity that erased all conscious thought.

"You're killing me." Ethan's voice was throaty, deep and husky. That was all it took. She exploded, the orgasm ripping through her with an intensity that was all-consuming. She knew she cried out, possibly screamed, but she couldn't find it within her to care who heard. He jerked inside her, his orgasm blending with hers, as wave after wave of pleasure rolled through her. She surrendered to its power and let it carry her away.

Eventually, she came to, finding herself boneless and satiated on top of him. He had her wrapped so tightly in his arms she could barely breathe. His heart was still beating too fast, and she decided she'd rather not breathe than move from him.

Gradually, the heat from their passion subsided and she shivered. Ethan immediately stirred, wrapping his jacket around her shoulders. He pulled her back to him, and she snuggled into his chest. It was the nicest feeling being held by him like this, the scent of their lovemaking adding to her sense of euphoria.

As she lay in his arms and her awareness of where she was came back, she began to realize that it wasn't only the cool evening that was giving her a chill. The hairs on the back of her neck were standing on end. The sensation of being watched washed over her, making her feel vulnerable and exposed, despite being in the safety of Ethan's arms.

She sat up, scanning the shadows that she no longer looked at as privacy, but that now appeared… menacing somehow.

Her gaze was drawn to the gravestones. There was someone there. Watching her. Someone, or something.

A shooting star streaked across the night sky with its long tail before dissolving into nothingness. She normally would have enjoyed the sight, perhaps even made a wish.

But not tonight.

Ethan sat up, fully alert. "What is it?"

"I've got a bad feeling." She didn't know how else to describe it in words he would relate to. He was standing and dressed in record time. She turned away and fumbled with her own clothes. As he strapped on his belt and checked the gun in his holster, she felt something behind her.

She wanted to look, but was too afraid. "Ethan?" Her voice came out a choked whisper.

"Yes?"

"Are we still alone out here?"

He scanned the surrounding area, eyes narrowed, jaw set in full detective mode again. Tall, handsome, and formidable. Full of strength and power. And yet, his presence did nothing to quell the sickening premonition that something bad was about to happen.

"Some arsehole vandalized Ada's house this afternoon," he commented offhandedly, eyes searching the darkness.

Her throat closed over and a wave of guilt washed over her. "Really? That's odd."

"It's more than odd. It's damned disrespectful. What the hell is wrong with people these days?"

"Perhaps they had a good reason."

He pulled back slightly and glanced down at her. "Tell me you don't know anything about that."

She couldn't look him in the eye.

"Sage?" Placing a finger underneath her chin, he tilted her face up.

"I was told she had a book. A very valuable book. A book that could be dangerous in the wrong hands. I just went in to get it, but couldn't find it. Then one thing happened, then another, and before I knew it, the floor was a little damaged." She managed a weak smile. "The good part is, I got the book."

Ethan cursed. "Breaking and entering at a crime scene. What the hell were you thinking? Why didn't you call me?"

"I wasn't talking to you, remember?" If everything she'd discovered turned out to be true, a B&E charge was the least of her worries. "And I'm pretty sure I'll need to go back in too," Sage added, remembering the letter.

He cursed again and crushed her to his chest. "Don't tell anyone else about this. *Anyone*. I'll see what I can do to handle things on my end. I've set Nate on the case, and he's damned good at his job. Just… just don't do anything like that again. I'll arrange your entry, legally."

"I don't make a habit of breaking into places," she said indignantly.

"What was in the book?"

She hesitated. The answer to that question was not something she was prepared to get into here and now. "I don't know."

"Why?"

"It's in another language." That was mostly true.

She felt the low vibration of his laugh rumble through his chest and she pulled back, slapping him playfully on the arm. "It's not funny," she said, but couldn't help the smile on her face. "Let's go. I promised Mark I'd help with the investigation tonight."

A cool gust of air blew over them, and something shoved her on the shoulder. She screamed and fell forward, landing on her knees. In one swift move, Ethan pulled her to her feet and wrapped her protectively in his arms.

"What is it?" he asked, eyes searching. She didn't need to look behind her to know that nothing was there. It would have been in plain sight of Ethan if there was.

The push had not been overly rough, although it had startled her enough to make her fall. It was more of a… reminder. That even though Sage had managed to distract herself for a small amount of time, the demon was still there. Watching. Waiting. "Something bad is about to happen," Sage said. "I can *feel* it."

Despite her conversation with him earlier, she still half-expected him to say something along the lines of it being all in her imagination. But he didn't. He held her tighter.

"I won't let anything happen to you," he vowed, his eyes continually scanning.

She knew he meant those words. Only now they didn't make her feel safe. Ethan couldn't protect her from this. He couldn't arrest a demon, drag him in for questioning.

This was *her* journey. Her fight. There was not a place on this earth she could hide to protect herself.

A tremor raked down her spine, and on some level of her subconscious, she knew her fear made "it" smile.

And then she realized. The demon fed off fear, just like he fed off those poor trapped souls he tortured and made angry. He was intelligent, his actions deliberate. Calculating.

Well, she wouldn't give her energy to him.

She filled her lungs with air and pushed her shoulders back. She didn't know what exactly she was meant to do, but she had the grimoire now. She would continue the journey Nan had embarked on. Died for.

Picking up her bag, she clutched it to her chest. She wasn't going down without a fight.

Chapter Thirty-Four

From his vantage point in his van parked across the road from Beyond the Grave, Lucky inhaled deeply on his cigarette, holding the acrid smoke in his lungs until it burned.

And waited.

She was not here yet. But she would be. Anticipation fired through his loins. Ash from the end of his cigarette fell onto his jeans and he wiped it off with a sweaty palm.

A shooting star, brilliant white, streaked across the sky.

A sign from Virgil.

The engine started with a spluttering protest and a cloud of smoke before he drove away.

He'd be back soon. When it was time to play.

CHAPTER THIRTY-FIVE

Ethan pulled up across from Beyond the Grave and killed the engine. After their lovemaking, he'd walked back to his Land Rover with Sage, and then they'd gone for a quick bite at the local diner. He'd texted Nate to let him know things had worked out with Sage and outlined his plans to join the ghost hunters on tonight's vigil. Nate had texted back a thumbs up, and a comment about sticking to the "living room."

A dirty white van drove by. It looked like the one Ethan had seen driving past the ambulance the night before last. He'd glimpsed it for only the merest second that night, but it was enough. Reaching for his phone, he texted its plate number to Zach.

"What are you doing?" Sage asked, twisting in her seat.

"Finding out who owns that van that just passed by."

"Looked a bit like Lucky's," Sage said, then appeared to look thoughtful.

"What?"

"Nothing. I was just thinking of something that happened when I first arrived, that's all."

"We'll find out soon enough." Zach would get back to him in a few moments. Placing his phone in his jacket pocket, Ethan reached over and grabbed Sage's hand. "Ready to go in and find out what's happening?"

"Not really," Sage said, but she smiled easily.

"Don't you wonder what he's up to in there?" Ethan asked, narrowing his eyes on the shop.

"I thought I did." Her earlier confidence appeared to have waned now that they were here. He too, had a prickling sense of foreboding he couldn't shake. And when Sage had voiced those same thoughts earlier... He hoped Nate could manage on his own tonight. There was no way in hell he was letting

Sage out of his sight.

She released a long slow breath. "No time will ever be a good time. Let's do it."

He gave her hand a reassuring squeeze and the dashboard lights turned off, sending the interior of the vehicle into darkness.

"What happened?" Sage gasped.

"Must be a faulty battery," Ethan said. It couldn't be flat, the vehicle was brand new. He frowned. He wouldn't be able to arrange a new vehicle from the city until the morning.

"Look!" The fear in Sage's tone had him instantly alert. She was pointing across the road to a strange glow around the roof of the shop.

Ethan frowned, looking for the source of the strange light. A plane, or helicopter search lights. He couldn't hear or see anything.

He'd head over to get a better look. He tried the door handle, but it wouldn't open. Holding the lever in the open position, he nudged the door with his shoulder. Odd. It was stuck, as though the central locking mechanism had come on, trapping them inside the vehicle. Except even with a faulty battery, it shouldn't behave that way.

The screen door at the front of the shop opened and then slammed shut, but no one came out. Sage's fingernails were digging into his leg.

"Just the wind," Ethan said. Looking out the windscreen, he could see the branches of the trees moving. "I wouldn't be at all surprised to learn that Collins didn't lock the front door."

"He always locks everything up tight when he does an investigation," Sage said, her voice wavering slightly.

"He probably left it open for you." He leaned forward to peer through the windscreen at the cloudless sky. Thunder, a low and angry growl, rumbled above them. With a metallic clanging, an empty can rolled down the street, propelled by a sudden gust.

"It's just the wind," he repeated. "Sometimes happens." But not like this. Storms were usually accompanied by clouds, not a bright moonlit, starry night.

"Ethan?" Sage's voice was little more than a squeak. Eyes wide, she stared at the dash. The lights on the large center digital panel were flickering, forming numbers, then letters. And then they formed a word...

Sage.

Letting out a small cry, she released his leg and pulled her bag to her chest. "I'm not ready," she said, though to herself and not to him.

Ethan could no longer deny something very strange was going on, and the fear on Sage's face made him nothing short of murderous. His hands tightened into fists as anger burned like an out-of-control wildfire through his gut. When he found the son of a bitch who was terrorizing her, he'd kill him with his bare hands.

He tried his door again. Still wouldn't budge. Maybe if he could get the engine to turn over, it would release the central locking system and the doors would open.

He turned the key, but the engine wouldn't start, just making a sick *rar-rar* noise, then nothing but a click, as if the battery had been completely drained. And yet the goddamn dash was blazing bright, with her name. *Sage.*

He eyed his Maglite torch, hoping it wouldn't be necessary to smash the window to get out. Filing a vehicle accident report was a lot of paperwork. And he'd have to think up a lie, because he sure as hell couldn't put the truth in it.

A loud bang on the Land Rover's roof startled them. A branch must have broken off from the gum tree overhead. *That's it. We're getting out of here.*

Sage scrambled over the center console, landing in his lap, her hands wrapping around his neck, her breasts pushed hard against his chest as she snuggled close. He eased the seat back so she could fit better and held her tightly. He could break out of the car a little later.

Ethan fingered silky strands of her hair and carefully considered the strange happenings. His car had been left alone and unattended while he was at the river with Sage. He couldn't rule out the possibility that someone had messed with his vehicle's central computer. He'd get his men to examine it in the morning. In the meantime, he'd run another search through Zach, this time listing any residents with advanced technical knowledge or experience. Someone like Joe Clarke, from Collins's crew. He had means, motive, and possibly the opportunity as well. Ethan certainly couldn't discount him.

"We're stuck in here, aren't we?" she asked, seemingly unable to take her eyes off the green glow of her name on the dashboard. Despite the side of his brain that searched for a rational explanation, a small part of him felt uneasy. It wasn't his logic; it was his *instincts* that were in overdrive. A man with a gun, hell, even a group with machine guns, he could handle easier than the uncertainty of who or what they were dealing with. Because if, *if,* it *wasn't* a flesh-and-blood person, as Sage kept suggesting, where did he direct his fury? What he now knew about the town's history came to mind, and he quickly squashed the images. He had to keep his mind clear and analytical and think of the facts as he knew them to be right now, not what someone supposed them to be a hundred years ago.

He took a deep, calming breath. "Let's think logically," he said, more to himself than to her. "There has to be a rational explanation for all this."

"Oh, Ethan, when are you going to realize there is no rational explanation?" She groaned, pulling her bag closer before she continued.

"There is some freaky shit going on here that not even you can explain away. I've witnessed it myself. So has Mark. And Pia. The rest of the team, Ryan and Joe. Ada and Nan. The list goes on. The only one who refuses to believe it is you. One day you're going to have to learn to open your mind and think outside the box."

Ethan was momentarily taken aback. No one had ever said anything like that to him before. His mind and his sharp thinking were what people had always commended him for in his line of work. If he ignored the stab to his ego, he had to admit that what Sage was saying couldn't be overlooked. She was right. There was evidence that backed up what she was saying. Witnesses.

Maybe he should try to set aside his preconceived beliefs and treat this like any other investigation.

"Okay. I admit that you're bringing up some good points. Even though the things you're telling me are..." He wanted to say "unbelievable," but rethought his word choice. "Out of the ordinary." He ran his fingers through her hair. "I admit I'm skeptical about the whole paranormal angle, but I'm willing to go with my gut and help you find the evidence you're after in order to prove or disprove what's occurring. Even if that means not just observing, but actually working side by side with the... uh, Collins." He felt an internal shudder at the thought. But if that's what it took, for her, he would do it. In fact, there was very little he wouldn't do for her. He'd work through noise by noise until he'd debunked every single sound. Such work might very well lead directly to the killer.

"Gut instinct," she said, straightening.

"What?"

"You always talk about your gut instinct."

"Yes, I rely on it." It'd saved his life on many occasions.

"That's intuition," she said with satisfaction.

Ethan frowned. "No, it's not." Intuition was something women had. Men had gut feeling.

"What is it, then?"

He was going to say something along those lines, then thought better of it. "Okay." He had promised to hear her out. "Although I'd prefer you call it 'gut feeling,' I'm willing to admit it could be similar to intuition."

"Then you do believe in something other than what you know as cold hard fact. You believe in something you can't see, hear, or touch."

"I suppose..." He could see where this was going, and didn't like it.

"And what about anger, can you touch that?"

"No."

"Fear, grief, sadness?"

"No, but you're now talking about feelings."

"Yes, but if you can trust your feelings, if those are real, even though you cannot see or touch them, it's not too much of a stretch to say that we can feel other things too. Use the same senses we use unconsciously every day to become aware of more than we're used to."

"I suppose so." He frowned, considering. "But since it's never happened to me, it's difficult for me to believe, that's all."

"But it *does* happen to you, Ethan. All the time. You say you rely on your senses for work. You sense when someone is watching you even when you can't see them. You sense when something is 'off.' You somehow just *know* when someone is lying to you or not telling you the whole truth."

He opened his mouth to refute what she was saying, then closed it again. Could she be right? Was he not the man of hard evidence he'd always believed himself to be? What she said was true. He did rely on those very senses more than the other guys on the force did. That's why he was so good at his job. Perhaps he had more in common with the ghost buster than he'd thought. His stomach roiled.

"I still think there's a rational explanation for all of this." How did something without a body cut out black circles of material and place them over empty eye sockets?

She slumped against him. "I almost thought you were going to understand. Tell me, Mr. Detective Extraordinaire. Give me the oh-so-rational explanation for all of this. And don't forget to explain how it is that we're trapped in this car with a dashboard flashing 'Sage,' my *name*, Ethan, when I would bet my last dollar that that word was never programmed into its computer. And while you're at it, you might explain why the streetlights are going out one by one."

He glanced out the window. Sure enough, the whole street was now in a blackout. The sky was clear, the moon bright, and he could still see clearly without the streetlight. He peered out the windscreen; the wind had dropped off again, not a single leaf stirred on the nearby trees. A black and white magpie, wings outstretched, hovered nearby. He blinked. Magpies didn't hover. They sometimes flew against the wind, making it appear that they weren't moving, but there was no wind.

And magpies didn't hover.

Loud clanging noises, like furniture being overturned, came from the shop.

"What was that?" Sage asked, staring at the store. "I hope everything is okay in there."

"We need to go over and have a look," Ethan said, easing her back into her seat.

"I've changed my mind. I'm not going in there." Eyes wide, she held her bag tight to her chest, like a shield. She was petrified. And that pissed him off to no end. He needed to find an outlet for his anger. Now.

"I have to go and have a look. They might need assistance. Someone might be hurt," he said.

"I can't go in there. That's… that's what it wants me to do." Her breath was coming in short bursts. "I haven't read the book yet. I'm not ready."

"Who wants you to? What book? And what do you mean, you're not ready?"

Sage's eyes glistened as she stared with sheer terror across the road. "It is getting stronger. I can feel it. There are still twelve days to go, but it is already drawing on increased power. The push on my shoulder at the river, my name on the dash—it wants me to know this is personal. It is watching. It wants me scared, to use my fear. And I *am* scared, dammit. I need more time to prepare, to school my emotions. I need to read the grimoire. Need time to prepare. To understand. I'm not ready." Fear was making her ramble.

"Sage—"

"I can't go in there," Sage said, her tone resolute. "Not tonight. I'm not ready to face it yet," she repeated.

Ethan gripped the steering wheel. He was torn. Although he didn't understand what she was talking about, she was adamant about not going in there. He didn't want to let her out of his sight for one second, but if she didn't want to go with him, he wasn't going to force her.

He couldn't waste any more time. He had to go. He was a cop, and the killer could be in there right at this very moment. This might be his one and only opportunity to solve the case and ensure Sage's future safety.

That was the thought that sprung him into action. She would probably be safer in the car than in there anyway. He wished Nate was here to watch over her, but he couldn't wait for Nate to get here. He'd just have to be quick.

Ethan grabbed the handle of his Maglite torch, but the split second before he used it to shatter the window, the car sprang to life. The door locks popped, the dashboard blinked the time, and the radio turned back on.

He didn't have time to worry about his sudden good fortune. "I'll be as fast as I can. Lock the door behind me."

He paused for a split second as their eyes met. The fear shining in hers tugged at something deep inside him. If anything happened to her... He touched her face, letting his thumb graze her cheek, then gave her a quick, hard, possessive kiss, and locked her safely inside. He crossed the street in a few short strides.

A vehicle of some sort had turned onto the street, its engine giving a sick cough, but he didn't turn to look. He was getting to the bottom of this, tonight.

Chapter Thirty-Six

The front door of the shop opened before Ethan even touched the handle. Okay, that was starting to get old. If something like a ghost or demon was doing this, maybe it had a sense of humor—or perhaps just really good manners?

"Thank you," he mumbled irreverently as he walked through the door, deliberately leaving it open in case it decided to do the locking trick that had happened in the car. He would prefer not to have to smash any of the shop's windows, if he could help it.

He was surprised to find the whole place in darkness, despite the light glow that surrounded the outside of the shop. He turned on his Maglite torch, and shined it around the room. One of the team, Joe Clarke, was sitting in front of some monitors set up on a desk in the rear. Ryan Donovan was behind the hand-held camera being pointed at Collins. Collins took the camera from Ryan and pointed it at Ethan.

"And now, ladies and gentlemen, I'd like to introduce to you Detective Skeptic, who'd better have a damn good reason for bursting in here and ruining our investigation. Detective, your constant interference is grounds for harassment."

Collins peered at him through the viewfinder, the red light indicating that it was recording.

"Cut it out, Collins. What's going on in here? What were the loud noises?" *Just cut the shit, so I can get back to Sage.*

"Everything is fine, and we have permission to be here. We're not doing anything illegal, so unless you're here for anything that requires me to need a lawyer, I ask you to leave."

He couldn't see Collins's face behind the camera, and it irritated him.

Ethan relied on more than just words to ascertain if somebody was telling the truth. He'd never consciously realized how much he relied on his "other" senses before Sage had pointed that out.

"Can you put the camera down? Quit the theatrics for one goddamned second? The sooner you talk to me, the sooner I'll get out of your hair." *Gladly.*

Collins let out a long, put-out sigh and set the camera down.

Pia was sitting in the chair across from Joe, her expression sullen.

"Where is Sage?" she asked abruptly.

"In the car. Why?"

"By herself?"

"Yes."

"Manage to upset her again, did you?" Collins jeered. "I can always go over and console her. Wouldn't mind kissing those sweet lips again."

Ethan refused to be drawn in. He didn't have the time or energy to waste on Collins. Instead, he walked up to Pia. "What is it, Pia? What do you know?"

"Nothing," she said, glancing nervously at Collins.

Ethan's phone signaled an incoming email. Must be Zach. That had taken longer than usual. He briefly scanned the information. The vehicle was registered to Luke Graham Keyton.

A familiar prickle crawled up the back of his neck. He remembered the way that Lucky had stood back from the crowd at the funeral and the way he'd watched Sage. The subsequent interview had turned up nothing concrete, but Keyton had triggered his instincts in a way that nothing else had so far on this case. He'd also not yet been able to locate and validate Keyton's alibi. No one that he'd asked had heard of a Virgil in the area.

Zach's email said he was running further searches on Keyton and would get back to him shortly. Whether Zach turned anything else up didn't matter. Ethan *knew* Luke Keyton was his man.

"I don't have time to hang around here, I have to go. Pia, if there's something you want to tell me, you'd better make it fast."

"It's too late," Pia said, her eyes wide and slightly unfocused.

"What's too late?" he asked, wondering if she was on drugs. He'd give her five more seconds.

"The demon already has her," she said, tears rolling silently down her cheeks.

Something gripped his chest, squeezing it tight.

"What are you talking about?" He kept his voice calm and even. "There's no demon. I just found out who the killer is."

He had to go. He was wasting time. Wheeling about, he walked briskly to the door. He dialed Nate's number to bring his partner up to speed. Zach was Ethan's private contact, and therefore any information gleaned from him would not be on the central database. He wanted Nate to issue an APB on Lucky's van. It had driven past less than ten minutes ago. He couldn't be too far away.

"Luke Keyton," Pia said, the name stopping him dead in his tracks.

He whipped around to face her. "What did you just say?" Ethan narrowed his eyes at her. How the hell did she know that? There was no way she could have seen the screen on his phone.

"Detective," Pia said, her face ashen. "Lucky and the demon are one and the same."

His heart stopped dead in his chest.

"You're insane." Ethan's nails dug into his palms and fought to control his fury. His patience with this bunch of paranormal psychos had run out.

"Stay away from Sage," he said, his voice deep and chilling. "Your talk of ghosts and demons has her terrified. She's alone, shaking in the car, too damn scared to even walk in the door of her own home. It's cruel, and I won't stand for it any longer. From now on you'll stay away from her. You'll *all* stay away from her," he said raising his voice to encompass the whole room.

"You finish your freak-show investigation tonight and leave town in the morning. You'll have no further contact with Sage. No emails or phone calls with stories of whatever paranormal hallucinations you believe you found. Your reign of terror over her ends now. You got that? Not one more fucking word to her."

The lights turned on and Ethan found himself face to face with Collins. "I don't like your attitude," Collins said.

"I don't give a rat's arse what you like." Ethan's tone was pure ice. "Think very carefully, Collins. Choose your battles wisely. If you decide to fight me on this, it is a fight you *will* lose." Collins flinched, something in Ethan's words, or perhaps the absolute conviction behind them, finally getting through.

"I've never been more serious about anything in my life. Stay the hell away from her, Collins." Ethan made his way to the door, letting it slam behind him.

He felt a heavy smack on the back of his head, followed by blinding pain. His vision darkened and his knees gave way, cracking against the hard, cold cement. Sage's image danced in his mind. She was crying, she was screaming, she was calling for him. Pleading. But he couldn't get to her.

He'd let her down. He'd failed.

He reached out for her, a thousand apologies spilling off his tongue. He'd told her to trust him, but he was too late.

Her image faded and his world turned black.

———◆———

Sage woke to the metallic stench of blood and stale cigarette smoke so strong she dry-heaved. The dirt floor was cold underneath her legs, and as her eyes adjusted to the lack of light, she peered at her body, almost fearing what she would see. She searched her skin, but couldn't find any evidence of serious bleeding. She felt sore. Bruised. Her mouth was dry and tasted bitter, and she had a splitting headache. Some of her ribs felt tender; perhaps one or more were broken. But other than that she was unharmed.

The grimoire! She felt around on the cold, dirty floor for her bag, but couldn't locate it. Where was it? She'd been holding it when she'd been pulled from the car, but she must have dropped it on the footpath. Or did Lucky have it? Had she failed to keep it safe for even one day?

Her hand automatically felt for the angel, and she let out a strangled cry. It was gone.

On hands and knees, she blindly scrambled around in the dirt, in the remote hope that it had fallen off in here. Frantic, she searched every square inch of floor she could reach. *Whatever you do, leave this on always.*

What would happen now that she didn't have it? Had she just become easy prey to the demon? She felt as vulnerable as a lame rabbit to an eagle. Without the amulet and the grimoire, she'd lost all hope of being able to defeat the demon and save the innocent people of the town. Joyce, Pat, Mona… Ethan. She'd failed them all. She'd be lucky if she made it out of this cabin alive.

She rose, eying the room cautiously. Was she truly alone, or was Lucky hiding in the shadows, watching her?

She might have only herself now, but she wasn't going down easy.

Mercifully, Lucky didn't appear to be in here with her.

"Hello?" she called out.

She seemed to be in a wooden cabin, something rustic, and judging by the rough, uneven, splintery finish of the wood that made up the nearest wall, more than likely handmade. She continued to search for her bag, checking along the timber workbench in the center of the room. Various tools cluttered its surface. An assortment of surgical knives, a hammer, a saw. Dark-colored fabric, scissors, a Bunsen burner, a spatula, a lighter, and a metal symbol on the end of a long wooden handle.

Sage grabbed the lighter and tucked it inside her bra, then picked up the strange implement with the metal symbol at the end and turned it over. In the dim lighting, the symbol appeared to be a flower of some sort. A circle with three curved lines coming from the center. Was the metal heated with the Bunsen burner and used to… brand something? She remembered it mentioned at some stage that the killer had left a brand of sorts on his victims.

Images flashed through her mind, like stills advertising a horror movie. Dear God, could this be what he used?

Senses on high alert, she silently and carefully moved around the room. Lucky had brought her here, but where was he now? Why had he left? She'd been in Ethan's car impatiently awaiting his return when the door had unlocked itself. She remembered thinking for a brief moment that Ethan was back. Then she'd seen Lucky open the door. Startled, she'd greeted him. Hell, she'd even smiled at him before he reached in, gripped her firmly around her mouth, and ripped her out of the car.

She'd been surprised at his strength; for such a slender man, he'd had no trouble dragging her kicking and struggling along the pavement. She must have dropped her bag around then. She remembered biting his arm, hard. She gagged when she realized it was his blood she could still taste on her tongue. He'd let out a cry, then picked her up as if she weighed nothing at all, and had thrown her into the back of his van. She must have passed out from whatever was on that bitter-tasting rag he'd then pressed over her mouth and face because she didn't remember anything else until now.

What did Lucky want with her? Was Lucky the serial killer they were all looking for, or was he at least involved somehow? It didn't make sense though. Lucky was a little slow, not some clever killer who could elude the police like this.

But… A chill ran down her spine. If he *was* the actual serial killer, and not just an accomplice, then Lucky was the one possessed by the master demon. The one Sage needed to lure into the circle before she performed the ritual as outlined in the grimoire. A lead weight settled in the pit of her stomach. How could she do whatever was needed now that she'd lost the book? The amulet? Mary's diary?

If Lucky had the grimoire, would he destroy it, sealing the fate of every single person in town, and more? Who knew how far the evil would spread?

But if Lucky intended to kill her, why hadn't he already done it? That single thought gave her a spark of hope.

Not sure how much time she had before he came back, she made her way around the room, surprised at how much she could see in the moonlight streaming through the planks of wood haphazardly nailed across the windows. Despite the storm that seemed to be brewing earlier, the moon was so bright the night must still be cloudless.

She found the door and tried the handle, not surprised to find it locked. She slammed into it as hard as she could with her shoulder, but the door was solid.

Rickety wooden shelves lined the walls, littered with rusty old tins, building tools, pieces of wood, another hammer or two, and containers of nails. But one shelf stood out because of its neatness. As though someone had placed those items with loving care.

She inched closer. Ten, maybe fifteen, jars of various sizes and shapes sat at eye level in a perfect line. She reached for one and held it up in front of her. Round objects bobbed and floated in some type of fluid. What were they? She withdrew the lighter from her bra and flicked it on. Dozens of sightless eyes stared out at her from behind the glass. Sage screamed, and the jar fell from her hands and smashed on the hard-packed dirt floor. Heart pounding wildly in her chest, she kept her fist in her mouth to keep from crying out again and bit down firmly.

She backed away from the little round objects that had rolled to a stop on the floor.

Lord help her, they were eyes. *Please don't let them be human.* Although animal eyes wouldn't make it much better. *Who keeps eyes in a jar?* Oh dear God, were Nan's eyes in there too?

She turned to the side and heaved.

Moving to the corner farthest from the door, she sank to the floor and huddled into a crouch. She couldn't bring herself to look in any of the other jars just now. Something was on the floor to her right, and she instinctively cringed away, thinking it was a rat. She stared at it for a moment, but when it didn't move, she reached out, hoping not to find something warm and furry under her fingertips. But it was cold and round. She picked it up, and held it to the light. Duct tape. She tucked it into the corner.

Where was Lucky? She didn't know how long she had been there, but doubtless he would be back for her soon. The duct tape, the tools on the bench, the Bunsen burner and the metal brand. The eyes in the jars. *Is this what he has planned for me?*

There was no doubt in her mind now. Lucky was the serial killer. Luke Keyton, the touched son of God-fearing church-going model citizen Raylene. Her son, her baby boy, now a serial killer most likely possessed by something dark and evil and not of this world.

And Sage was locked in his sadistic playroom.

Instinctively her fingers reached for her angel pendant, but found only skin. Fear held her paralyzed for long, timeless seconds, while her mind raced to come up with a way to get out of there alive. The timber cabin creaked in protest as a sudden gust of wind pressed against it with large unseen hands. Branches scraped across the roof, scratching like clawing crow's feet.

That's it! Sage jumped up and rifled through the contents on the table until she found the hammer. The cabin was made out of timber, not brick.

She'd bust her way out.

The splintering of wood as the hammer buried into the crudely fashioned boards securing the window was deafening in the silence.

She was taking too long. Making far too much noise. If anyone was anywhere in the vicinity of the cabin, they'd hear her for sure. Perhaps Lucky thought she was still passed out and was waiting for her to come to before he started with whatever he had planned.

She stopped, listened.

She was no longer alone. Her eyes searched the shadows, peering through the thickening air. Someone was in there with her. Fear closed her throat as she continued to scan the space. Someone, or *something*, was close. Too close. She could feel the malice, the pure unadulterated evil like a claw to her skin.

But the room was empty. And yet it wasn't.

The air was heavy now. Almost tangible, thick, like syrup. She tried to suck oxygen into her lungs. She felt as though she was being dragged beneath the water, surfacing only for the briefest moment to gasp in air.

She cried out, but terror stole her voice.

There was a knock on the door and she froze.

The only sound now was the deafening pound of her heart, and the blood roaring in her ears.

Who was it? Was it Lucky? Oh God, she *had* been too loud. He'd heard her, and now he was back. Her hand tightened around the handle of the hammer.

But... why would Lucky knock? Presumably, it was he who had locked the door. Unless he had an accomplice. Or was Lucky the accomplice? Was there more than one?

Another knock.

She retreated until her back was flush against the far wall. She brought the hammer up in front of her chest, her fingers digging into the wooden handle. A splinter speared under her nail and into the bed.

There was no pain. Just an icy, numbing fear.

Chapter Thirty-Seven

Ethan sat in his vehicle, holding Sage's bag, his gut churning as painfully as if he'd swallowed a bucket of live piranhas. Pounding his hand on the steering wheel, he took a deep breath and almost choked on it.

He cursed violently. The car still smelled like her. Sage's delicate summery fragrance hung in the air, and the image of her clinging to him in fright was clear in his mind. He never should have left her. What he wouldn't give to turn back the clock.

Earlier, he'd woken to find himself flat on his back on the cold pavement outside Beyond the Grave. Nate had hovered anxiously over him, the radio crackling as he called in "officer down." Those words brought him to his feet, faster than any others could. He couldn't afford to be taken in to hospital. He couldn't waste one single second.

Sage was gone. Lucky had her.

He knew that even before he'd bolted to his vehicle, only to find it empty. No signs of a break-in. The door had been left open as though Sage had simply walked out, vanishing into the night. But he knew that wasn't the case, even without Pia telling him she'd been taken by Luke Keyton. He'd found Sage's bag on the pavement a few meters behind the car, her angel pendant nearby. With the way she'd been clinging to her bag earlier, she wouldn't have parted with it willingly, and he knew how precious the angel was to her.

The pendant's clasp had been bent, as though it had been caught on something, or ripped off. His fingers felt big and awkward, but he managed to bend the tiny piece of metal back into place so that the catch would close. It would need to be fixed professionally, but it would do for now. He slid the angel into the inside top pocket of his leather jacket. Close to his heart.

An agonizing stab of pain in his head focused his attention back to the fact he'd been hit from behind. Jesus Christ, how could he have allowed that to happen? He'd been so focused, so *consumed* over getting back to Sage, he'd all but tuned out the rest of the world. He should have *known* someone was outside the door. His gut should have warned him. But in his concern over Sage, he hadn't been listening.

A mistake. An almost fatal one. He couldn't afford any more. The palm-sized egg on his skull and blinding headache would serve as a reminder to stay on his game. Stay sharp. He wouldn't be surprised if he had a mild concussion, but as long as he could still function, he'd do whatever it took to get Sage back. Alive.

She was in the hands of the serial killer. How long did she have?

He needed to think, damn it. *Think.* And to do that, he needed to take a step back, distance himself from his feelings for Sage. There'd be plenty of time to berate himself later. After he found her. He tuned into that headspace that made him such a successful detective. If this was a case like any other, what would he do?

He'd been hit on the head after Lucky had taken Sage. That meant someone other than Lucky was involved. Virgil? One of the PRI crew? It was not improbable that one of them could have snuck outside.

He turned to his partner, who was no longer arranging an ambulance for an officer down, but firing off APBs for Lucky's van and feeding information through to every cop in the vicinity. Road blocks were in place. The townsfolk were being warned through local media outlets to stay indoors and lock their doors and windows. The whole town was in lockdown.

"Ready to get this bastard?" Ethan asked, as he started up the Land Rover.

"More than."

Ethan had received responses from most of the agents he'd requested urgent assistance from, and the first was due to arrive just before ten tomorrow morning. Tomorrow was too late. He had to make do with his current resources.

First things first. They had to get to Lucky's house this very minute. God only knew what he was doing to Sage.

———◆———

Ethan wanted to punch something. No, he wanted to punch Lucky. To pulverize him.

But he couldn't find the son of a bitch. All he seemed able to do was chase his own tail, while Lucky was off somewhere with Sage. Hurting her, maybe even...

He slammed his fist against the Land Rover's steering wheel and brought it to a halt outside the police station. Now what?

They had just finished searching Lucky's dilapidated stone house on the outskirts of town from top to bottom. They'd found several reference books on demonic possession, which fit in with Pia's theory that Keyton imagined himself doing the Devil's work. They'd also bagged into evidence a dog-eared book about the Truro murders and various other novels about infamous serial killers. They'd bagged and tagged plenty of dark stuff, but nothing they could link directly to the murders. No murder weapon, no remnants of black cloth, no brand... He and Nate had left the cataloguing of evidence to the local guys.

Sage was Ethan's only concern, and she wasn't there. Ethan and Nate had searched the property for a trapdoor to a cellar, a secret room, or another place a person could be hidden, only to come up empty-handed. Was Sage still alive? If so, how long did she have left? They had no way of knowing how long Lucky kept his victims alive before killing them.

She'd been gone for two hours and sixteen minutes.

Sitting in front of the station wasn't going to help. Ethan cursed and revved the Land Rover impatiently. He pulled out and began to drive. He wasn't heading in any particular direction, but he had to do something.

"Take it easy, mate. We'll find her. Let's think calmly. What's your gut telling you?"

He glanced at Nate, who of course had no idea of the conversation Ethan had just had with Sage. It was funny how Nate and the other cops accepted Ethan's ability to use his gut, but if he called it intuition like Sage had, he'd be laughed out of the force.

He took a deep breath and concentrated, deliberately putting himself in a cop's headspace. "There's a place he frequents that we haven't found yet. He needs space to perform the killings. He has a specific routine. A ritual he performs. He has a place only he knows about. A room, or perhaps a small house. Somewhere secluded, maybe underground. Somewhere quiet where no one would hear a scream or report strange noises. He selects his victims, the criteria of which is unclear. He places tape across their mouths, to keep them quiet. He takes them to his secret room, his work room, acts out his ritual, and prepares the body. When he's satisfied, he returns the victim's lifeless body to the scene of the abduction, covering their eye sockets with black circles of cloth. The cloth he brings with him has been pre-cut, because no fiber traces have been found at any of the crime scenes. He wears gloves, a mask, and maybe even a protective coverall of some type, as no trace of clothing fiber or hair has been left at any of the scenes."

He met Nate's gaze. "We need to find his workroom. Sage is there right now." Frustration and desperation swirled with alarming ferocity inside him.

"Every uniform in the area is out patrolling all the places Keyton has ever been known to frequent," Nate said "It's a small town; everyone knows everyone's business."

"Not in this case." A police car, lights flashing, flew past in the opposite direction. Ethan's anger and frustration had escalated to dangerous heights.

Where was that police car going in such a hurry? He'd heard no new developments on the scanner running constantly in the background.

Ethan instinctively turned the car around, heading in the same direction as the marked car that had just blazed past.

"Cryton had no idea what Luke Keyton was up to," Ethan continued. "These people had a serial killer living amongst them and they had no fucking idea. The local cops are going to be driving around chasing their tails looking in all the usual spots. Keyton's workroom is somewhere else. Someplace only he knows about."

His mobile rang, the screen showing it was Sergeant Brady. He answered it hands-free so that Nate could listen in.

"What've you got for me, Bob?"

"We've got him."

Ethan's heart stuttered in his chest. "Keyton?"

"Yep," Bob said, sounding smug.

"Where is he?"

"In the interrogation room."

Ethan was already headed in the direction of the station, and he gunned the motor.

"Is Sage all right?" His whole body was rigid with tension while he prepared for the answer.

"She wasn't with him." The wind left Ethan's chest like he'd been sucker punched.

"What do you mean, she wasn't with him?" His voice was pure ice.

"A uniform pulled his van over on the main highway. He'd been to the hardware store, can you believe it? We think he's got multiple personality disorder, because he was having an imaginary conversation with someone called Virgil about running out of supplies. It appears that he misplaced his duct tape, and had to buy some more."

"He misplaced the fucking duct tape…" Nate repeated, incredulous.

"Told us that he had a full roll somewhere back at his house, but couldn't find it. He wanted to use something else, but this Virgil was specific as to how it was to be done, so he had to go out and buy some more."

"I didn't know the hardware store was open this late at night," Nate said.

"It's not. Smashed the rear window in. Didn't take anything else, didn't even open the cash register. Just took a single roll of duct tape."

"Find out who the fuck this Virgil is," Ethan demanded. "That was who he used as his alibi for the time of the murders. Looks like there's more than one perp involved. Bet he's the son of a bitch who hit me on the back of the head. Whoever Virgil is, he must have Sage. Find him, and we'll find her."

"At first we thought someone else was involved too, but when you listen to him, you'll hear he's clearly talking to himself."

That was a first. He'd never had someone use a multiple personality as an alibi before.

"He hasn't told us what he's done with Sage yet," Bob said. "Do you want us to increase the pressure?"

"No. Leave him. We're just pulling in now. Let us handle it."

———•◆•———

Ethan and Nate walked into the station, and the noise level fell silent. Ethan was used to that kind of reaction from not only uniformed officers, but people in general. It happened whether they walked into a room full of bikies, a pub, or a coffee shop, and had more to do with their size and the way they carried themselves than their rank within the police force.

They'd just been informed that Luke Keyton had been transferred to a holding cell after having an apparent psychotic episode. He'd turned violent, screaming that Virgil needed him, upending desks and attacking an officer with a chair.

Keyton was lying on the cold concrete floor, hugging his legs in the fetal position, mumbling. The steel door screeched as it opened and hit the wall with force as Ethan entered.

"On your feet, Keyton," Ethan ordered.

Lucky didn't respond, just kept up an incessant rambling. He appeared to be catatonic.

Ethan dragged him up off the floor, lifting him underneath the arms. He tried to stand Lucky on his feet, but his knees were like jelly. It was like trying to hold up a marionette.

"I'll hold him for you," Nate said, walking behind them and slipping his arms underneath Lucky's shoulders. Keyton appeared drunk, but Ethan couldn't detect any alcohol on his breath.

"Where is she?" Ethan spoke directly into his face.

More incoherent mumbling. Ethan snapped his fingers near Lucky's nose to get his attention. His head wobbled on his neck and his mouth formed a sick-looking smile. Finally his eyes cleared somewhat and he found his feet. Nate let go of him. Keyton stood, hands on hips, grinning.

"She's sweet. Pretty. Never could get me a sheila like that." He licked his lips in a suggestive manner. Ethan exploded. In a split second, Ethan had him by the collar and up against the wall. It took all the willpower he possessed to not take that first punch. If he did, God help him, he wouldn't be able to stop. He needed Keyton conscious and talking. He needed to know where he'd taken Sage.

Ethan forced his hands to open. Keyton stepped to the side and smoothed down the material bunched around the neckline of his blood-stained polo shirt. Was that Sage's blood? The tenuous grip Ethan had on his control slipped a little more.

"Luke, I need you to tell us where you took Sage," Nate said in a cool, reasonable tone. "You can save yourself a whole lot of trouble if you tell us now."

"Couldn't look at her without sunglasses. Her light... It's too bright... hurts my eyes...Virgil needs me to make it go away... Said she's the daughter of the first one. The chosen one."

"What the fuck is he on about?" Ethan asked.

"What light, Luke? Did you take her somewhere where there's a lot of light?" Nate asked. He turned to a local uniform watching from the door. "Anything around here resemble what he's talking about?"

The uniform shook his head. "No."

Nate turned back to Luke. "I'm going to ask you one more time. This time, you *will* tell me what I want to know. Where. Is. Sage?"

"Her light hurts my head… Got to put it out…Virgil is mad. I made mistakes. I lost the book. I lost the tape."

"That's it, I've had enough," Ethan growled. Nate put a hand up, staying him.

"What did you say?" Nate asked. Luke was mumbling incoherently. "Speak a little louder."

The silence in the tiny cell was absolute, as three sets of ears were trained on the ramblings of a madman, hoping to get a break.

"Virgil, get me out of here… I was the one who got her for you… I want to be the one… no… I can't get back, they won't let me… No!… Why won't you wait for me?… Use me… use *me* to do it…"

Luke Keyton went limp, collapsing to the floor, a dead weight.

He lay on the floor, his mouth slack. His eyes had rolled back in his head, leaving two eerie white globes. His body twitched in tiny convulsions. He was having some type of seizure.

The uniformed officer was already calling for an ambulance. Nate immediately moved forward, rolling Lucky onto his side in the coma position, leg bent, airway open, so that he didn't choke or injure himself before the ambulance could arrive.

"Fuck. Fuck. Fuck!" Ethan pounded his fist on the cell wall and walked out in disgust. "How the fuck are we supposed to find out where that arsehole has her?"

Despite the incoherent ramblings of the psychopath in the cell, there was still a very real possibility that Virgil was in fact a real person, and that person might actually be the serial killer. Lucky, clearly not the full bottle, could be the killer's sidekick. If that was the case, then Sage was still in imminent danger. She'd been in the serial killer's hands for just over three hours. It might already be too late.

His stomach spasmed violently, feeling shredded, as though he'd swallowed razor blades. His eyes stung, and he walked toward the exit before anyone noticed.

"Blade!" Nate called out, "You need to calm down. You can't think clearly while you're this angry."

Ethan stormed out of the station and back to the Land Rover, Nate following, but saying nothing further.

The night was clear, a million stars twinkling in the sky. It was warm and still. Too still. And silent. He leaned against his 4WD and heard himself take deep breaths. After a while he realized that was all he could hear. He could hear Nate's breathing too, and faint voices coming from inside the station, but no night creatures. Not a single cricket made its high-pitched racket.

Ethan stood up straight, and a strange sense of calm washed over him. Why weren't there any of the normal night sounds? The station was situated on a hill, and as he looked over the town, lights were going out in patches. Not only house lights, but streetlights as well.

Perhaps there was some kind of electromagnetic disturbance in the location of Cryton. He'd read once about a connection between supernatural phenomena, such as seeing ghosts, and areas where there was a very high level of electromagnetic activity. He'd run it past Zach later.

Something troubled him, niggling him in the back of his mind.

Everything led back to the supernatural, which in turn led to Collins. And the PRI team.

Damn it, he was an idiot. Why hadn't he thought of it sooner?

"Pia wanted to tell me something earlier," Ethan said, rubbing the back of his neck. "Something about Sage, but I cut her off. It was at the same time the report about Lucky came through from Zach. I want to go back and talk to her. How the fuck did Pia know it was Lucky the same moment, perhaps even before, I did? What if they're all involved in Sage's abduction somehow? Collins and his crew were all acting weird. Almost as weird as our friend Lucky in there."

"Get in," Nate said, climbing behind the wheel. "All exits out of town are blocked. No one's getting in or out. Officers are combing Keyton's house. We'll talk on the way."

Ethan didn't bother arguing over who was driving; they'd waste precious seconds. He got in and slammed the door, and Nate took off, tires squealing. "Lord help me, I'm actually starting to believe there is something out of the ordinary going on in this damn town. But for this interview, let's forget she's a psychic and look at it like another lead we need to follow. She told me the killer was Keyton; she told me he had Sage. If they aren't involved somehow, how the fuck did she know that?"

"Good point." Nate nodded grimly. "At the very least, she's a lead. The only one we've got. And you never know what will fall out of a tree until you shake it."

Chapter Thirty-Eight

Ethan and Nate pulled up outside Beyond the Grave. The front door was wide open, and the detectives walked straight in, flicking on their Maglite torches as they entered.

Collins was moving around the shop, commenting, with the cameraman, Ryan Donovan, following his every move. When they stepped inside, Collins looked over at them. "We'll pause this recording while we're graced with the presence of not one but two detectives this time. Earlier this evening, one of these upstanding pillars of the community threatened us. I'll leave the camera running for my own protection."

Mark placed the camera on a nearby table, facing in their direction. Ethan's hands had turned into fists. "How can you continue your bloody dog-and-pony show while Sage is missing?"

"I thought you told me to stay out of police business," Collins said. Ethan wanted to wipe the cocky expression off his face and into next week. He raised the torchlight closer to his face. Collins's eyes appeared to be glazed and out of focus. Perhaps they were all on drugs?

Collins hissed in a breath, cursed violently, raised his hands and turned away as though the light pained him. The torches were bright, but Ethan hadn't directed his into Collins's eyes. But Collins was an actor. He was probably just playing it up for the cameras.

"For someone who's spent so much time flirting with her, you can at least appear to look a little concerned," Ethan said, pushing past him. "Nate, keep this arsehole away from me. He's one comment away from becoming the next victim."

Joe Clarke appeared not to have shifted from his chair in front of the monitors since Ethan had been there last.

"Where's Pia?" Ethan asked, drawing to a stop at the other side of the desk.

"Fuck off," Clarke said without looking up from the computer screens. Friendly guy.

Ethan couldn't see any sign of Pia Williams.

"Pia?" Ethan called out from the bottom of the stairs.

The air in the room felt as though it was thicker than normal, making it hard to breathe. They really needed to open some windows and let in some fresh air. Ethan scanned the room. Something was off. The tiny hairs on the back of his neck were standing on end. Nate stretched his neck from side to side and Ethan knew he could feel it too.

Collins was acting strangely—walking in an exaggerated way, making the occasional comment into the camera he'd picked up again, his behavior off-kilter. The whole scene was surreal. Comical almost, if Sage's situation wasn't so deadly serious.

"Where is she?" Ethan demanded, turning to Collins. Collins shrugged and made a zipping motion over his mouth. "I'm too scared to make a comment," Collins said, despite the irony.

Ethan took a menacing step toward him, and to his immense satisfaction, saw him flinch and his eyes widen. Damn right he should be scared. If he wasn't a cop...

"Donovan, is Pia here?" Nate asked as the cameraman walked down the stairs into the room.

"Yes. Out the back. She couldn't be in here anymore," he said, eying Collins cautiously.

Interesting. What had Donovan meant by that? Ethan and Nate found Pia sitting on a chair in the far corner of the backyard. She looked up as they approached, and Ethan took in her hunched demeanor. As they got closer, the moonlight allowed him to see pure terror in her eyes. If she was involved in the abduction, was she having second thoughts? Did she actually give a damn about Sage?

They needed Pia to talk, and it needed to happen fast. And maybe accusing her wouldn't be the best way to make that happen.

He gave Nate a look and shook his head slightly, giving his partner the signal that he was switching his approach. Ethan crouched next to Pia, while Nate remained standing, but a little to the side so as not to appear intimidating. *Stay cool, Blade.*

"Pia, do you know where Sage is?" He kept his tone neutral, his voice soft.

"So *now* you want my help?" Pia asked.

Interesting again. She certainly wasn't reacting like someone with a guilty conscience. No, she was acting like he'd ignored her earlier efforts to help, as if they were genuine... and maybe they were. What was his gut telling him?

He looked into her eyes, and saw nothing but hurt. And worry.

He hoped like hell she'd accept his apology. "I'm sorry about earlier. I was out of line. I... I just wanted to protect Sage. I didn't want to believe what you were saying. To be honest, I still can't say that I do. Please help me, Pia. Do you know where Lucky has hidden her?"

"You care deeply for her. Love her, although you haven't admitted it to yourself yet."

"Pia—"

"Don't. I already understand why you behaved the way you did. You are terribly worried about her. Tortured. I can feel your pain and grief so strongly." Tears filled her eyes and rolled down her cheeks and she wrapped her arms around herself. "Poor Sage."

Christ, he could never have imagined how much two words could shatter his world. *No.* He refused to be drawn down that path. He regained his focus.

"Pia," he began again in a calm, clear voice. "If you have any idea where Sage is, this is the time to tell me."

"Poor Sage," Pia repeated, and Ethan ground his teeth so hard, his jaw ached.

"What do you mean, 'poor Sage'?" Nate asked. "Tell us what you know."

Pia glanced up at Nate. "Lucky took her."

"Lucky is at the station. We've arrested him. He must have hidden Sage somewhere. Do you know where that could be?" Ethan asked.

Pia didn't answer, just chewed on what was left of the black nail polish on her tattered nails.

"Do you know who Virgil is? You knew about Lucky. Is there someone else? Someone named Virgil. Do you know where he is?"

"No."

This was getting them nowhere. "Pia, you wanted to tell me something earlier. What was it? We don't have time to waste playing games. If you know where Sage is, you must tell me now."

"I don't know. Exactly."

He wanted to pound his fists into something. The menacing sound he made in the back of his throat was almost inhuman. Damn it, he needed to rein himself in.

"Anything you can tell us, no matter how small, might be able to help," Nate said, kneeling in front of her, his tone soft and cajoling.

One precious minute ticked by, then another, while Pia held her head in her hands.

"We're wasting our time," Ethan groaned. "Every second could mean the difference between life and death for Sage." He couldn't believe he'd wasted precious time on a goddamned psychic. Fuck, he may as well start wishing on fairies.

"Let's go,' Ethan said, turning and heading back toward the shop.

"Wishing on fairies won't help," Pia said, sitting up straight.

What the hell? He hadn't said that aloud.

"You are a disbeliever."

"Damn straight. It's my job to question the validity and authenticity of every spoken word, every action. It's what I do to cut through the crap and isolate the facts. I have to reject things that have no hard evidence to substantiate them. Hard evidence is what gets convictions."

"Then I feel sorry for you." His eyes narrowed, but Pia held his gaze.

"Pia," Nate said, "Ethan doesn't mean to offend you or denigrate your ability. This case has been extremely frustrating, and we're running out of time to find Sage before she's hurt, or worse."

Pia looked at Ethan. Then through him. She released a long slow sigh.

"I normally wouldn't do this. I make it my business not to attempt to alter someone's beliefs. But you are the one. It is no accident you are here. You are already going to discover that on your own, so it won't matter if I give destiny a little helping hand right now. Plus, I know what you feel for Sage. And I know how she feels about you. But to be clear, I am doing this for her, not you."

"Doing what for her?"

"Making you believe," she said. "You used to smoke."

Ethan returned the few steps to stand in front of her. He'd give her sixty seconds. "Yes." It wasn't exactly a ground-breaking revelation. He still had faint nicotine staining on his fingers.

"You stole your first pack of cigarettes from your father. He knew you took them, but you held fast to your denial the whole way through the beating he gave you. It set the precedent for the power struggle between you and him. Despite attempting many times over the years, he was never able to break you through physical domination."

That gave him pause. How could she have known that? He sure as hell never spoke to anyone about his childhood.

"You didn't smoke the cigarettes you stole from your father. You kept them hidden in a brown teddy bear you called Gruff that you unzipped and removed the stuffing from."

What the fuck? There was no way she could have known that. He'd never breathed a word of it to another living soul. Not even Nate. A year later, he'd thrown Gruff, complete with its hidden cigarettes, into the fire and watched until it had cindered to nothing but black ash.

"You kissed your first girl at the age of fourteen behind the toilet block at school. She fancied herself in love with someone else. She didn't tell you, and when you found her kissing your best mate at the school disco, it broke your heart."

He swallowed hard. Nate was watching him intently, brows raised in question. Unable to speak, Ethan gave a slight nod. Still, it wouldn't be hard to take a stab at high-school heartbreak and get it right.

"You were closer to your grandfather than your father. Like your father, your grandfather has crossed over. He called you... instead of calling you a kid, he called you a 'skid' because of how you used to leave skid marks all over the driveway with your BMX bike. He is often around you and is with you on investigations—"

"Enough!" Ethan snapped and she flinched. He lowered his voice. "All right. You've made your point. Somehow you know stuff you shouldn't be able to know. Just don't... don't say anything more. That's more than enough for me right now."

If she somehow knew all that, was it possible she could tell him where Sage was?

"Use your gift, Pia. Tell us what you see. Sage is your friend, and she needs you," Nate urged her.

"Poor Sage," Pia began again, and if Ethan never heard those words again it would be too soon. Pia closed her eyes. "Lucky has her."

And just like that, any hope he had drained away.

"Lucky has been arrested," Ethan said.

"He took her. Hid her. Was coming back. Went to get something he forgot. She's in a dark room. Dusty. Dirty. Eyes. There are jars of eyes floating... There's fire..."

"The place is on fire?" Ethan's stomach twisted.

"No. A camp fire. It's how he talks to the demon." She wasn't making sense. Ethan flicked a glance at Nate. Was he buying any of this?

"What else do you see? Can you see Sage?" Nate asked when she'd been silent for a moment.

"Yes. She's scared. Trying to break out. Bashing at the walls. He's in there with her. She can sense him. He frightens her. She is worried about a book. And she needs her angel. Her amulet. It's important. Imperative she finds it."

The book, if it was the one Sage was telling him about earlier, was in her bag, safely in his car, her pendant secure in his pocket.

"Who is in there with her, Pia?" Nate pressed.

"The demon," she answered. "In spirit, not person. Lucky cannot help, so he's sending someone else."

"What does Lucky, this killer, want with her?" Nate asked.

"She's the one who has the power to stop him. Her, and what she can do to them with the book."

"How does she have the power to stop him?" Ethan rubbed at the back of his neck. Christ, it was like trying to assemble a million-piece jigsaw puzzle.

"Sage is special. Something about an angel. There's some type of connection. Something to do with her grandmother. No, her mother. And now she knows about the book of spells. She has the power to stop this. But she needs to do it before... something about blood and the moon. The demon will kill her though. Make no mistake. He wants her. Wants her badly. He will use someone to do it. Possess them, like he did with Lucky to kill the others."

"What others?" Ethan asked, watching for her response carefully.

"The other victims. The extremely clever boy with extrasensory perception. The hitchhiker. Celeste. Ada. Long before that, Lucky's own mother Raylene. Now he wants Sage."

Ethan straightened his spine, and his head spun as he and Nate locked gazes.

He didn't know how Raylene Keyton fit into this, but Pia couldn't have possibly known that the fifteen-year-old boy was gifted with an unnaturally high IQ. That was something Ethan had only just found out in a secondary report that came back from Zach after accessing the boy's school and psychology records. He hadn't filed that report yet.

"Why did this… *entity* kill them? What's their connection?" Ethan asked, not because he believed an entity was responsible, but to see what else she knew about the case. He'd worry about *how* she knew later.

"The light. The seer's gift is often seen to others as a light. To demons it is painfully bright. But compellingly attractive at the same time. It draws them, like moths to a flame. The brighter the light, the more powerful the energy. He's building up the energy he needs to use when he brings himself through from the other side before the doorway closes."

"Sage has this light?" Ethan asked, remembering how Lucky was going on about light. "Her grandmother and the other victims too?" Was this the connection between the victims?

"Yes. The boy was what we call a sensitive; he was gifted, like Celeste. The hitchhiker was a millionaire whose life had become meaningless, so he sold his business empire and spent his time travelling from place to place helping people by redistributing his money. His light was brilliant too. But there will be others. As his power grows he'll become more indiscriminate…"

Pia began to rock back and forth. "We're running out of time. You have to get to Sage. You have to go *now.*"

"Where? Tell us where she is so we can help her."

"Behind Lucky's house. In the bushland behind it. You'll see the trail. It's faint, but look for it and you will find it. Follow it. It'll lead to a clearing. She's there… can't move… there's feathers… she's scared. All those eyes are looking at her. You must hurry. There isn't much time."

Ethan and Nate thanked Pia and turned to leave.

"Lucky is behind bars, at least we won't have to worry about him hurting her before we get there," Nate said, briefly placing a hand reassuringly on Ethan's back.

"But the demon is not behind bars," Pia said, sounding exasperated.

Nate stopped. "What?"

"You don't understand what you're dealing with. The entity is a very powerful, dark demon. A master demon linked to Satan himself."

"What are you talking about?" Nate said, looking confused. "I don't understand all that stuff about demons and light, or even what's so special about some book, but the crux of the story you just gave us is that Lucky took Sage and hid her in a cabin behind his house. Tell me straight, Pia. Did Luke Keyton take Sage and hide her or not?" Nate's tone had taken on an uncharacteristic sharpness. It was obvious he thought he was being made a fool of. "You can get in serious trouble for hindering a police investigation. Especially one as serious and time-sensitive as this."

"He did take her," Pia told him. "The demon and Lucky are one and the same."

Nate's mouth dropped open. Ethan remembered having a similar response when she'd said that to him earlier.

"You must hurry. Sage is in danger."

"You can relax now, Pia," Ethan said. "We've arrested Lucky, so if the demon and Lucky are one and the same, they are both safely behind bars. So if there is no one else involved, all we have to do now is find Sage."

Pia rose, all five foot three inches of her. She placed her hands on her hips and glared at them. "You still don't understand." Her eyes flashed with anger. "A demonic entity uses bodies like they're appliances. Electricity will flow through a kettle, but it doesn't *become* the kettle."

"What are you saying?"

"The demon is using Lucky, but it hasn't become him. The entity will use him up and move on. You cannot destroy energy, only transmute it." Suddenly Pia closed her eyes and grabbed her head. "Oh God, no!"

"What?" Ethan asked, unable to mask his rising panic. What if she'd seen something bad happen to Sage?

"It… it has already found someone else to use."

"Who?"

"I… I can't quite see…"

"Pia!" Donovan called from the shop's back door. "Is Mark out here?"

"No," Ethan and Nate replied in unison.

Donovan let out a string of curses.

"What's the problem?" Nate asked.

"We were filming in the upstairs bedroom, and Mark went downstairs for something. He was acting very strange. We were becoming concerned. He didn't come back, and when we came down to look for him, he was gone."

———— ✦ ————

The drive to Lucky's property was the longest of Ethan's life. At normal speeds, it would take about twenty minutes; at their current speed, they'd be there in ten. But each of those minutes felt like an hour. He patted the top pocket that held Sage's angel pendant and clutched her bag as though it were Sage herself. They were the only tangible links he had to her, and he was protecting them with his life.

Nate was silent as he drove, so Ethan let his mind replay the conversation with Pia.

Although he still wasn't ready to believe in beings that weren't human—he couldn't deny she knew things about him that she shouldn't have known. In that respect, she had to be the real deal. That was as far as he was prepared to go at this point. And he would never have believed even that had he not experienced it himself. There was still a stretch between acknowledging someone's psychic ability and the existence of evil spirits that walk amongst us. Wasn't there?

It was Pia's alleged psychic ability that had him travelling at impossible speeds to check out her insights. Her visions. Whatever you called them. He just hoped to hell she wasn't going to make him look like a fool.

If this turned out to be a farce, he could just imagine how the report would read. "Had run out of leads. Consulted psychic. Brief lesson on demons and evil entities. Followed psychic vision to location…" He shook his head, halting that particular train of thought. It wouldn't serve him now. He'd made the decision to trust Pia, and he would run with it.

He wasn't sure what to make of the demon stuff, but in a strange way, it kind of made sense. It fit in perfectly with the things that were going on. If Keyton had really somehow summoned a demon or evil entity, lots of things would fall in place. The theory would fit even if he *believed* he'd summoned one. If Keyton was convinced he was working with an evil spirit, it would explain how a human being could commit such acts of brutality. But could a demon—supposing such a thing existed—actually possess someone and use them to do evil things? Or was that just an excuse for the sick and depraved behavior of a psychopath? The fact that Ethan was even asking disturbed him. What he'd learned about the town's sordid history had no doubt implanted itself into his subconscious. He'd need to be careful not to let it color his handling of this case.

This case challenged his fundamental beliefs, the foundation on which he dealt with the world. Meeting Sage had changed his life in a way he couldn't even begin to explain. It was easy to see Sage as a beautiful sparkling light, just the way Pia described her. He just had to hope that no one dimmed that light because heaven help him, he would kill that person with his bare hands.

The Land Rover skidded to a stop in a cloud of dirt in front of Lucky's stone house. The cool comfort of his pistol in hand, Ethan alighted from the vehicle, Nate following, and moved to the rear of the property.

With their Maglites, they searched for the trail, and it wasn't long before they found a disruption of the natural bush landscape. Broken branches lined a faint, but definite, path. Silently, with Ethan leading the way, they followed the trail, bending and weaving through the dry scrub.

After a while, the trail opened to a clearing, just the way Pia had described. In the center of the space was a crude wooden cabin. Although appearing reasonably structurally sound, it in no way looked to have been built by an accredited builder.

To one side of the structure was a fire; so far, everything was exactly as Pia had described. Surrounding the fire were rocks placed neatly into a ring.

They'd found the right place. But had they arrived in time?

Chapter Thirty-Nine

Lucky struggled against his restraints in the too-white room, the handcuffs clanging loudly against the metal frame of the hospital bed.

He shouldn't be here. Sage was waiting for him in his special room. And he'd made plans.

Light bounced off the walls and the smell of disinfectant offended him. Too bright, too clean, it made his stomach heave.

Lifting his head, Lucky assessed the officer they'd left to watch over him and scoffed. He reached out with his mind. Young, bright, and had only recently celebrated a full year on the force. Still was eager to please, full of ambition and youthful exuberance. Pitiful. *Disgusting.*

And insulting too, leaving a boy to watch over a man like him. Well, they'll be sorry. He'd show them what he was capable of. What *Virgil* was capable of.

His top lip curled, and a low noise bubbled up from deep within, erupting outward into a sinister laugh.

The cop flicked the briefest glance his way, before focusing his attention back on his phone.

Adrenaline surged through Lucky's body, the careless dismissal triggering a ferocious rage.

Do you know who I am?

Blood pounded through his veins, the bass beat of a heavy-metal rock band. The young punk had underestimated him. They'd *all* underestimated him.

Say goodbye to your career, arsehole.

"Oi! Coppa," Lucky called out.

This time, when the young constable looked up, their gazes met.

Held.

Slowly the constable rose from his chair and walked toward Lucky. They exchanged not a single word as the officer released the handcuffs and removed the restraints. Lucky sat up in bed and stretched his arms above his head, admiring the way his muscles flexed. *Such a handsome bastard.* He rubbed at the red welts across his wrists where the pigs had fastened the cuffs overly tight.

He thought of the sprinklers in the ceiling on the other side of the hospital and triggered them to start spraying. The fire alarm screeched and wailed, causing panicked feet to scuttle and scurry like frightened mice.

That should keep the minions busy.

Lucky helped himself to the sunglasses from the cop's top pocket, then leaving him as dazed as a deer in headlights, strolled right out the door.

Chapter Forty

Is anyone in there?" Sage recognized the voice coming through the door. Mark!

What was *Mark* doing here?

Relief that it wasn't Lucky must have clouded her reasoning because she called out to him before she'd had a chance to think.

"Sage? I'm going to come in now. Don't be scared."

She took three steps toward the door. Hesitated. Her logical mind, her judgment returned. *Why* was Mark here? How did he know where to find her? Perhaps they were all out looking for her, and he had somehow stumbled across her first.

This was not *Lucky*, she reminded herself.

This was Mark. Her friend.

"Mark, thank God you're here." Sage heard the sound of a key in a lock and a rush of fresh evening air washed over her as he opened the door. Mark stepped inside and she moved forward, intending to throw her arms around him, when she noticed his eyes were glassy, vacant, and unfocused. His pupils were dilated, as though he were high on drugs. But that didn't seem like the Mark she knew.

Instinctively she took a step back, but kept her attention on the now open door that Mark was still blocking.

A door he had the key to.

"Mark, how come you have a key?" She wanted so desperately to get outside, but what if Lucky was out there? She couldn't decide if it was safer to stay in here with Mark, or if it was Mark she needed protection *from*.

His gaze swept the room, before focusing on her. His eyes widened in surprise, as though seeing her for the first time. "Sage! What are you doing here? Your detective has been looking for you."

"Me? What are *you* doing here?"

He blinked a moment. "I, uh…" He frowned, considering. "I don't really know. I remember getting into my car, and just driving. Then I was following this walking trail and came across this cabin. I stumbled across a key on the way, underneath a half-decayed pig's skull. I was here, the key fit, so I opened the door. And, well, here I am." He shook his head as though to clear it. Then he looked at her.

"What are *you* doing here and what happened to your face?" he asked, taking a step toward her. She brought her hands to her face and flinched. The skin felt swollen and hot, and when she brought her fingers away, they were coated in blood. Her face was stinging, but she had no idea what had happened. Who knew what Lucky had done to her while she was out cold? The idea chilled her.

"How did you get here?" he asked again, squinting through the moonlight. He opened the top cupboard right near the door, took down a lantern and placed it on the bench. He fumbled a little then struck a match from the nearby packet. The flame flared, then faded so that the lantern cast a gentle, even glow across the room.

Mark wiped his hands on his pants and turned to her. "There. That's better. Now let's take a look at your face." He took a step in her direction and Sage took a step backward.

"Mark, how did you know there was a lantern in that cupboard?"

"Just did." He took another step toward her and a squishing sound filled the space between them. Lifting up his foot, he assessed the stickiness on the sole of his shoe, his face wrinkling in distaste. Then fascination. Sage watched in horror as his face contorted into a malevolent grin, turning him almost unrecognizable.

"Eyes are the mirror of the soul," Mark said in awe. Mark, but not Mark. He noticed the other eyeballs on the floor and bent down to pick one up. Sage barely contained a wave of nausea as he rolled it between his thumb and forefinger.

Blood pounded past her ears, and her heart skittered in her chest. The look in his eyes was cold. Distant. With none of the flirting warmth that was normally there.

Beware… Lucky… Mark.

The Ouija board's message slammed into her with the force of a freight train. It was a warning. Beware of Lucky. Beware of Mark. Had the demon possessed both of them? Which one was the master demon? He was still blocking the open door. She'd placed the hammer on the bench and it was now out of reach, but there was a knife on the side of the primitive-looking kitchen sink. Could she reach it before Mark?

"Mark, let's get out of here," Sage said, relieved her voice sounded calm. Almost normal. "Lucky will be back any minute. He's the serial killer. He killed Nan."

"Wasn't Lucky," Mark said, the words sounding thick on his tongue. It was Mark's voice, yet it wasn't.

"Okay—" Sage edged backward, putting the bench between them. "Mark, please, let's get out of here. I don't know what makes you so sure Lucky is not the serial killer, but I do know he knocked me out and locked me in here. We've got to go, Mark. Get out of here before Lucky gets back."

"Lucky can't help him anymore. Needs me." Mark squinted as he looked at her, his eyes wrinkling at the corners. He put one hand up as though looking into the sun. "You're so bright, it hurts to look at you. *He'll* be here soon. Where's the book? He wants it. Come closer. I want to see your eyes."

Sage's gaze flicked to the knife on the sink. Two steps away, maybe one if she lunged for it. "Mark, what's wrong with you? Stop talking like that, you're scaring me."

He stared at her, his gaze vacant, as if he'd been lobotomized. His features looked strange, distorted. Definitely not the Mark she knew.

"I... I like you," he said in that same strange voice. "I don't want it to be more painful than it needs to be. Nice, quick, and easy. Lucky wasn't going to be quick." For a moment, he seemed to almost come back to himself. He blinked, and his expression found some of its normal contours. "Wow, I can read thoughts, just like Pia."

Something had come over Mark. He wasn't himself. And then he was. It was almost as though something was trying to possess him but had not fully succeeded. Yet.

Mark's eyes went blank again, his face twisting.

"Mark. Stay back." Sage's heart was pounding in her chest. She took a deliberate step backward, hoping he would follow. She needed him one more step away from the open door, so that she could make a run for it. Whether Lucky was out there or not, she'd take her chances.

Keep him talking. "Does Pia know you're here?" she asked.

"Pia?" He blinked, his eyes momentarily clearing, then glazing over again. "The fear is rolling off you. It tastes so good."

Sage inched closer to the door.

He reached into his pocket and withdrew something. As he held it in his hand, his lips curved. "Do it again. Give me the fear." Slowly, he placed the object on the table.

There, its eyes glowing red, its mouth open in a sick, twisted grin, was the gargoyle.

The blood drained from her head, leaving her dizzy, her stomach heaving. The damn thing looked almost... *alive.*

Mark smiled, eyes gleaming, and he licked his lips. "Yes. Damn it, yes!" He was breathless, as though her reaction excited him. *Sexually.*

Sage's stomach spasmed, and she ruthlessly reined in her emotions. He wanted her scared, and she wasn't going to give it to him any longer.

"Why have you got that?" She glared at the gargoyle, anger pushing out the fear.

She eyed the door. Four steps away. The knife on the sink was still closer.

She leapt toward the sink and grabbed the knife. "Keep away from me."

Sage raised the weapon threateningly and tried not to notice the dried blood that darkened the long, stainless steel blade.

Mark raised his hands. "Sage, what are you doing?" he asked, his eyes on the knife. "I would never hurt you." His eyes had cleared and he appeared almost… offended?

Confusion stayed her hand. Mark's face looked familiar again. His voice was no longer thick and raspy.

"Don't come any closer," Sage said. "Something is going on here, and it's scaring me. You're not yourself. Why did you ask about the book? Who told you about it and why do you want it?"

"What book?" he asked, brow wrinkling in confusion.

"You asked about a book. Why?" Sage asked, carefully watching his reaction.

"I didn't ask about a book, Sage. I don't know what you are talking about." Mark slowly raised a hand and scratched his head. "I feel as though I've had a blackout. My head is pounding. But Sage—" His voice choked and his eyes glistened as he focused on her. "I swear to you, I would never hurt you."

Sage lowered the knife, but didn't let it go. His expression relaxed.

"Let's get back to Pia," Mark said, breath releasing from him in a rush. "I don't know what's going on, but she will. One minute I was filming in the shop, and it was like any other investigation. Then the temperature plummeted and a foul odor filled the room. A dark shadow appeared and moved toward me. I was frozen to the spot, couldn't move. It kept coming, and then it felt as though the devil himself passed through me. I've never felt such a… volatile hatred before. It is an entity like no other. It is vile, malicious, and it wants to destroy everything." He paused, and his eyes widened. "Oh, God! *Pia*. We have to get back. We have to go to her."

Should she go with him? Could she trust him? He seemed normal enough right now, but what if he turned again?

"Put your hands in the air!" Ethan's voice boomed through the cabin. Six foot two inches of solid muscle stood in the doorway, gun drawn. Icy fury hardened Ethan's features, but Sage had never been so relieved to see him.

Sage dashed toward Ethan, but Mark lunged forward, his fingers raking down her back, before he got hold of her shirt and jerked her backward. She landed hard against his chest.

She screamed, and Mark wrapped an arm tightly around her, holding her in place. Instinctively, she struggled, kicking his shins and twisting her body. He roared, startling her, the sound almost deafening her right ear, then he wrested the knife from her hand. It was then she felt the coolness of the blade at her throat.

A tremor ran the length of her spine, and she stopped breathing. Mark's voice was a whispered undertone in her ear. "Relax, Sage. I'd never hurt you, but if I don't protect myself, that detective boyfriend of yours will kill me."

"Collins! Drop the knife," Ethan demanded, gun steady and trained on his target.

"And spoil all my fun?" Mark taunted him. "You and I both know that if I let Sage go, you'll shoot."

"Cut the theatrics, Collins. We're not on your show now. We have you surrounded. Let Sage go, and step outside the cabin."

Sage involuntarily shuddered at the power and authority in Ethan's command. He was furious, but in complete control. She couldn't imagine anyone willingly disobeying him when he was like this.

Except Mark. Mark didn't appear concerned in the slightest. Just a bit put out.

She felt his body tense, and when he spoke next, his voice was low and husky and slightly slurred. "Looks like we'll have to wait just a little bit longer, Sage. Detective Skeptic wants to play."

His voice no longer sounded like Mark's.

———◆———

"Drop the knife and let her go," Ethan repeated. Never could he have imagined how powerfully he'd be affected by seeing a knife at Sage's throat. His whole body tensed, all senses keenly alert and trained on Collins. His reaction to keeping her safe was on a level that was deep and primal. A basic instinct to kill to protect.

Moonlight glistened off the six-inch blade that hovered against Sage's tender neck, the sight sending a chill down his spine.

Or was it the weather? He could have sworn the temperature just plummeted ten degrees.

"I said, drop the fucking knife." Ethan kept his pistol trained on Collins, but Collins had positioned Sage in such a way that Ethan couldn't risk taking the shot. Fury threatened the tenuous grip he had on his control as he took in Sage's swollen, red face. Had the bastard *hit* her? If Ethan found out he'd done anything else... *Breathe. In. Out.* Sage's life depended on his ability to remain calm and think clearly.

Collins's eyes were glazed and unfocused, like a junkie coming down off heroin. Was Collins into drugs? That would certainly account for his erratic behavior in the shop earlier.

"Back off!" Collins shouted. He shifted his weight from side to side, as though searching for a way out. Ethan couldn't risk Collins panicking and lashing out with Sage in such a precarious position. Collins was highly emotional, crazed. Possibly even insane.

Ethan wished he'd had time to assemble his team. Hell, if he'd known in the beginning what he now knew, he'd have insisted that Ian send each and every member of Taipan in the first instance. If his team were here now, in position, ace marksmen in place, they'd storm the cabin hot, like a well-oiled machine. Collins wouldn't stand a chance, and Sage would be safe and back in his arms.

Fuck Ian for not being upfront. He and Nate would have to do the best they could on their own. His priority was Sage and he'd do whatever was necessary to keep her alive. To hell with procedure.

"You can come outside," Ethan said, taking a step backward. Just one. Enough to encourage him. Not enough to lose the advantage.

Collins pushed forward, and keeping Sage in front of him, moved into the open.

"Collins," Ethan said in even, measured words. A tone that left no question that he was in full control of the situation. "Lower the knife and let Sage go. You have an opportunity to end this here and now. Be smart and take it."

Ethan took a slow step toward them, recovering his ground. He kept his movements even and deliberate. He sensed Nate's presence behind him to his right, and knew his partner had him covered.

Ethan took another step and Collins growled. Not a normal sound of discontent, but an atavistic snarl that sounded more animal than human.

The ghost hunter's eyes became even more wild and glassy, his breathing intermittent and labored. The knife wavered at her neck, but Ethan remained focused and calm. He couldn't afford to get emotional. Never before had anything so crucial been riding on his behavior.

The pure terror in Sage's eyes would haunt him until the day he died.

A shriek rang out, and out the corner of his eye, he saw Pia running into the clearing. He inwardly cursed. He'd told her to stay at the shop, but she must have followed them here in her own car. He couldn't allow her to distract him. He trusted Nate to keep her back and out of harm's way.

He inched forward, slipping easily into his hostage-negotiation mindset. "Collins. You don't want to do this. Drop the knife and let's talk about this." *Keep him calm. Keep him talking. Get close enough to disarm him.*

"Bring the knife away and let it fall at your feet." Another inch closer.

"Stand back!" Collins shouted.

"Mark! Stop. What are you doing?" Pia attempted to rush forward, but Nate restrained her.

"Stay back, or I'll... I'll..." The knife trembled at Sage's neck. Despite the confidence Collins had shown only moments ago, he seemed to abruptly falter.

"Mark!" Pia screamed, thrashing against Nate as he held her firmly by the arms. "Fight him. Don't let him take over."

"Pia," Collins said. "You're here! I can see what you see. I can see into people's *minds.*"

She choked out a pained sob. "Mark, it's not the same. You can only see the darkness. The evil. Only the dark thoughts."

"I see the darkness everywhere. In the minds of people in their cars on the way here. Thoughts like big black blobs hovering around their heads."

"You're seeing emotions. Fear, anger, and powerlessness are the lowest-vibration emotions. That's why you can see them. It's what the demon is made up of."

"But Sage," Collins continued, "and to a lesser degree, you... It hurts to look at. There's a blinking light around her head, like a high-wattage torch shining directly into my eyes." He glanced down at Sage and his face contorted into a wince.

"Remember how you tried to describe the auras you see?" he asked. "I can see them now. Except it's not quite the same. I don't see colors. I see dark splotches, and the God-awful light. It pierces my skull, makes it throb."

The wind buffeted the trees, rushing in Ethan's ears with an eerie howl. Pairs of yellow eyes peered at him a few inches from the ground at the edge of the clearing. Some type of animal. Foxes?

Gun still trained on Collins, Ethan kept an eye on Pia to his right. Her eyes were closed, and she appeared to fall into some type of trance-like state. A white glow extended from around her body, rising up into the air above her head. What the fuck? He'd seen some seriously weird shit tonight.

It was time to bring this to a close. "This is your final chance to end this peacefully." A step closer; he was less than two meters away. Keeping the tone of his voice low and soft, almost soothing, he said, "Drop the knife. Let her go, mate."

Collins hesitated before stirring back into action. The knife hovered over Sage's neck, his eyes taking on a wild, erratic look. This was it, the moment when things could swing either way. Ethan barely breathed while he watched for Collin's next move.

Ethan's trigger finger twitched. He was going to have to take action. One slice of that knife and Sage's life would be over.

Collins blinked rapidly, appearing to be caught in a moment of confusion. Was he backing down?

A gust of wind swirled up out of nowhere, a mini-cyclone stirring the dust on the ground, the tiny grains of sand whipping against Ethan's face. The knife was no longer glistening; the sky had turned pitch black, neither the moon nor a single star in sight. He'd never seen a storm brew so swiftly.

The yellow-eyed foxes howled into the night. That was impossible; foxes didn't howl like... *wolves.*

There was a flash of light, a small golden flame, and Collins let out a pained cry.

He jumped, and his knife wavered in his hand as he patted the flames on the shoulder of his t-shirt. "Bitch just burned me!"

Ethan took advantage of the split second of temporary confusion. Using his whole body as his weapon, he lunged at Collins, sending him sprawling to the ground. In one smooth movement, Ethan had rolled him onto his stomach, crushed his face in the dirt, and secured the cuffs over his wrists behind his back.

"Stay down," he ordered roughly. Ethan pulled himself up and immediately sought out Sage. She was standing nearby, eyes wide, lower jaw trembling slightly, her cheek swollen and bruised, but otherwise she appeared unharmed.

Grabbing her roughly, he crushed her soft body against his. She pawed at his back, her nails digging into his skin. The sensation was heady. Dear God, he could have lost her.

Pia had said earlier tonight that he loved Sage but hadn't realized it yet. Pia was right about a lot of things, and she was right about that too. The realization slammed into him with great force. His throat closed over, and not trusting himself to talk just yet, he kept the revelation to himself. Helpless, he could only stroke his trembling hand down her hair. Now that she was finally in his arms, he was powerless to let her go. It was as though she was the missing piece needed to make him whole.

"Are you okay?" Ethan whispered urgently.

"Yes."

He pulled back far enough to allow his gaze to travel over her body, assuring himself she was indeed all right. "Your cheek—"

"It's fine. Mark didn't do it. Lucky did." Ethan kept a tight leash on his anger. He'd have his moment with Keyton. Alone. He'd make sure of it.

"Oh, I nearly forgot." Ethan pulled away, reached into the inside pocket of his leather jacket, and withdrew her mother's pendant.

Sage visibly sagged with relief. "Oh God, Ethan! I thought I lost it. Thank you." She threw herself at him, almost bowling him completely over. She wrapped her arms around his neck and kissed him furiously.

"Wow," he said, when she pulled back enough that he could breathe. "Think I'm going to make your pendant go missing more often.

"Don't you dare," she said, mock-punching him, her smile lighting up her whole face. "Oh, Ethan. You have no idea what this means to me." He pressed his lips to her forehead as he fastened it around her neck.

A strange sensation came over him. He felt a brief vibration, a crackle in the air. As though placing the chain around her neck had reconnected some type of power source. But that didn't make sense.

"My bag?" Sage asked. "Did you find that too?"

"It's in the car. Safe."

She released a breath. "Thank God. I can't lose that book."

"You haven't."

Nate swore, and Ethan whipped his head around to see Pia's teeth firmly embedded in Nate's arm. She kicked him in the shin, broke free, and threw herself over Collins.

Reluctantly, Ethan released his hold on Sage to assist Nate in removing the wild little hell-cat from Collins. "Stop it, or I'll cuff you," Nate growled. It took both of them to restrain her without hurting her. What the hell was wrong with the ghost hunters? They were acting like they'd taken drugs. Powerful ones.

They had to cuff Pia as well for her own safety. With both Pia and Mark back on their feet, Ethan radioed in the arrests and requested assistance. Ethan would let the local guys take them in; he wanted to stay here and check out the cabin. He hadn't seen much of the details, but the glimpses he'd gotten confirmed that it was the killer's playroom.

The air thickened, became heavy, and a crack of lightning lit the sky.

A movement to the left of the cabin caught his attention. A dark, shadowed figure stepped out from behind the tree. Ethan couldn't make out who it was, but the space between them became as charged as the electrical storm forming in the sky. A sword of ice raked his spine, the race of his heart more befitting being faced with imminent death, rather than the appearance of a single person.

With a swipe of his arm, Ethan pulled Sage behind him. He drew his weapon, his body falling instinctively into a fighting stance. "Come out and put your hands above your head where I can see them." His voice boomed across the clearing.

Pia froze, turned toward the shadowy figure, and let out a blood-curdling scream.

Holding the whole situation in his awareness at once, Nate with Pia and Collins on one side, Sage at his back, Ethan fixed his gaze on the man through the sight on his pistol.

"It's him," Pia shrieked. "It's the demon." She ran forward and tripped, falling to her knees. Nate helped her up, and she thrashed, shrieking like a banshee. "Let me go!"

"Get her out of here," Ethan said to his partner. Pia was irrational, and if she kept going, she was going to seriously harm herself. She was also a distraction he didn't need. He knew with every fiber of his being that the person in front of him was the serial killer. This was the Virgil Lucky was talking about. And there was no way he was letting him out of his sight.

"I'm not leaving you," Nate argued.

"I've got this. Just get her out of here," Ethan repeated, not taking his eyes off his target. "She's likely to get herself killed. Or us. Lock them both in the car. Backup will be here any moment, and then you can rejoin me."

"What about Sage?" Nate asked.

"She stays with me."

Nate hesitated the barest of seconds before following the directive of his partner, his superior, and hurried Pia and Mark down the bush track.

A silence descended upon them, so complete in its totality, it was louder than any rock band. The man stepped forward, and just like in the movies, the clouds parted, allowing moonlight to fall on his face.

It wasn't Virgil; the shadowy figure was Lucky. *How the fuck did Luke Keyton get free?*

A low, sinister laugh floated in the air and rustled the leaves of the trees. "Surprise!"

"Put your hands up where I can see them." Ethan's finger tensed on the trigger, and despite his training, he seriously debated not taking him in. After all, he'd already escaped once. Ethan had the chance to end this here and now. Should he?

The image in the gun's sight blurred, and suddenly he wasn't looking at Keyton.

He was looking at Sage.

CHAPTER FORTY-ONE

Ethan was going to kill Lucky. Sage knew it with chilling certainty. She could feel *him* watching. Could feel his attention, with the sickness that comes with a physical brush with death.

When Lucky laughed a second time, a deep, eerie, seemingly disembodied sound that rose into the sky and carried far into the night, Sage no longer had any doubt. That he was the serial killer possessed by the master demon was chillingly clear. She didn't understand what had been happening with Mark, but it was Lucky who mattered.

Luke Keyton was the one who Sage had to perform the ritual in the grimoire on. And she couldn't do that if he was behind bars, or dead from Ethan's bullet. There was much she still had to learn, but one thing she did know was that killing Lucky with a single bullet from a gun wouldn't destroy the demonic entity. Anyone who'd watched movies or read a book knew that. So what would happen if Ethan killed Lucky? Would the demon find another body to infest? How then would she know who it was? She'd be back to square one. And she was running out of time.

She had no choice. She couldn't allow Ethan to kill Lucky.

Swallowing the bile that rose in her throat, Sage steeled herself and stepped in front of Ethan's gun.

"Sage, for God's sake, what are you doing? Get out of the way." She braced herself against Ethan's rage. His features set in cold fury, he side-stepped her and she repositioned herself in front of his gun.

"Ethan, you can't kill him."

"What? For fuck's sake, get out of the way." Ethan lunged to the side and again, Sage mirrored his movement.

Ethan's mood was as black as the swirling sky above them, his anger rolling off in tangible waves. "Have you lost your goddamned mind? Get. Out. Of. The. Fucking. Way."

"Sorry, Ethan. I can't." Briefly she closed her eyes in silent prayer that he would forgive her this. She was likely ending the relationship they'd only just begun, and the realization was a knife to her gut. But what choice did she have?

The storm raged overhead, the lightning illuminating them, giving the situation a surreal air. Foxes, with glowing yellow eyes, howled like wolves and pawed at the ground. Watching. As though waiting for a signal to attack.

Behind her back, she sensed the instant the shadow began to move forward.

"Sage, he's coming. Get down!"

She could feel its approach, its evil creeping toward her, its contempt enveloping her like a rotting coat. Hatred rolled off it, reaching out to her. She shivered as something she could only describe as satanic, touched her back, an ungodly claw of ice so vile, so depraved and unspeakable, it chilled her to the very core. A nasty stench permeated the air, filled her with stomach-turning revulsion.

"Freeze!" Ethan's voice, the command full of fury, was clear even above the violence of the storm.

Sage was paralyzed, frozen to the spot in the grip of true fear.

And still, it came closer.

Perhaps she *should* let Ethan kill him?

The demon inside Lucky was laughing, a chilling, disembodied sound she heard with her mind, not her ears. He was playing with her, a cat toying with a mouse. All this was a twisted game to him. No, the prelude to the game. The real game was yet to come. She wondered how she'd ever believed herself capable of stopping him. She doubted she'd even survive the night.

She gripped the pendant around her neck. It wasn't simply a keepsake from her mother. It was an amulet. A powerful amulet. Time for her to see what it could do.

Sage turned and faced Lucky.

He was three meters away, no more. A scrawny, scraggly-haired man with a physique more reminiscent of a teenager's than a serial killer's. But with eyes so black, and so, so cold. The color of death.

"Don't move any closer." Ethan had retrained his gun on Lucky.

Keyton laughed. A deep, eerie, seemingly disembodied sound that rose into the sky and carried far into the night.

His eyes not leaving Sage, he raised his hand, pointed toward Ethan. The gun dropped, slipping from Ethan's hand as though his fingers had turned to water.

"What the fuck?" Ethan shouted, before his body lifted off the ground and he was held suspended, powerless. His body shook and his feet dangled limply.

"No!" Sage screamed. "Put him down, you bastard." She ran toward Ethan, one hand outstretched, hoping that if she touched him, she could extend the amulet's power to him. Heat suddenly seared her fingertips, sparks flying from them, her body coming to an abrupt halt a foot away from Ethan. She tried to press forward, but flames seemed to lick over her skin, as if a wall of burning energy surrounded him. A wall she couldn't penetrate. Ethan was trapped, and she didn't know how to help him.

Lucky, hand still raised, holding Ethan writhing in the air, did not move closer. But he watched her. Coldly. Intently. Expectantly. He was waiting for her next move.

Anger coursed through her veins. She needed to think. She'd lost her mother, Nan, and Ada to the demon. She refused to let him take the man she loved.

Sage thought of the attic, how she'd seemingly been surrounded by a circular field of energy, protecting her as the demon's black mist-like shadow hovered menacingly above her. It had held him back then. Could she do it again now?

Gripping the angel, she willed it to work its magic again. Surround both her and Ethan with a cocoon of protection. When nothing happened, she shut her eyes and squeezed the pendant as hard as she could.

Still, nothing happened. No glow, no field of protection. Nothing. The amulet remained still. Placid. A pretty pendant between her breasts.

The Beast inside Lucky roared with laughter. "You're pathetic. Is that all you've got?"

The foxes circling the edge of the clearing moved closer. Their pointy, beak-like mouths opened in sinister smiles, revealing red gums and long sharp, hungry fangs.

Why can't I do it?

Oh Nan, I'm so sorry. Seems I'm not special after all. Despite Nan trying to provide Sage the tools she'd need for this moment of confrontation, the demon had caught her before she was ready.

He'd been watching her. Of course he had known, using her lack of preparation to his advantage.

Angry tears stung her eyes and she blinked them back furiously. She scrunched her face hard in concentration, tugged on the amulet and silently screamed with intent and determination.

Still, nothing happened.

Lucky turned the wrist of his extended arm. As though showing off, he moved his fingers. Ethan made an anguished sound as the demon twisted his body, wringing it like a dishcloth.

"No!" Sage screamed. Something deep and primal inside her reacted. "God damn you, put him down!"

Suddenly the entity flung Ethan through the air, and he slammed into the rough timber wall of the cabin. The demon had discarded Ethan, as though it were a child, and Ethan nothing but a toy that no longer held its interest.

Ethan lay crumpled, still, beside the cabin. Was he dead? Tears pricked her eyes and anger surged through her, burning her up inside, corroding her veins like acid. She was going to kill the demon, rip it apart, piece by piece, shred it until nothing was left.

Hideous laughter floated across the clearing, and it smiled, the demon inside Lucky. Something suddenly clicked in her mind. She was feeding the demon, giving it the hateful energy it craved. It had used Ethan as a pawn to drag her down to its level.

Sage took a deep breath, mentally blocked the demon out, and quieted her mind. Her intense anger stemmed from the strength of *love* she felt for Ethan. A love that went deeper than she'd consciously understood. He *belonged* in this somehow. He was as tangled up in this prophecy as she was. They were in this *together*. An unusual warmth flooded her body and she felt stillness. A peaceful floating, like being in the eye of a storm.

The ground trembled. Trees shook and flocks of birds left the safety of their nests and flew panicked into the night. A wave of energy rose up from the earth and burst through the top of her head. Like a waterfall, sparkling light rained down on her. Sage saw the recognition on Lucky's face.

"Yes," he hissed through his teeth. Excitement gleamed in the black orbs that were his eyes.

A white light cocooned her, coming from the amulet on her chest, and radiated outward. Her ears popped, but she continued to push. Lucky smiled a sick smile, showing yellowed and decaying teeth. "Yes, you are the one. And you'll be mine."

"Never," Sage vowed.

Whatever force she'd unleashed continued to grow and spread upward and outward. When it reached the demon, he let out a screech, the ungodly shriek of a wounded animal. He hissed, bile bubbling, foaming out the corners of his mouth.

Two pillars of fire rose on either side of him. Two pointed wings of fire. They would have looked magnificent if they were white and on an angel. Instead, their fiery heat turned him into an angel of death.

She called to the wind, knew that she could. It whistled through the trees, obeying her summons, and rushed the demon. The twin flames bent and flexed in the hurricane force wind, but did not blow out. The wings spit and crackled, then joined together as one, and turned into a swirling vortex of fire. The fire-whirl expanded briefly, then with a *whoosh*, it disappeared as though sucked up into the sky.

And then there was nothing but a loud ringing in her ears.

Sage rushed to Ethan's side, pulling his limp body into her lap. Tears rushed down her cheeks and into his hair as she cradled his head against her chest.

"You bastard," Sage shouted, her voice an angry fist pounding against the empty night air. "If you've killed him—"

She lowered her arm and ran her fingers through Ethan's hair, the silky strands she wanted feel for the rest of her life.

"Ethan, don't you dare die on me. You hear me. Don't you dare die."

And then he began to move. He stretched his legs and struggled out of her arms and into a sitting position.

Heavy booted footsteps pounded in their direction. Loud shouts and short barks of police scanners. Sirens sounded in the distance.

Then Nate was by her side.

Ethan's eyes were open, but he was unmoving. Sage wrapped her arms around him and repeatedly said his name. "I'm fine," he said, struggling to stand.

Nate knelt down and held Ethan firm. "Hold still, mate," Nate said, then to Sage, "I have field medical training." Nate checked him over and just as he seemed satisfied that nothing was broken, Ethan shoved his hands away and stood of his own accord, slightly unsteady. "If anyone is going to put their goddamn hands all over me, it's going to be her. Not you," Ethan grumbled. Then took Sage in his arms, locking her into a crushing embrace.

"You're all right, mate?" Nate asked.

"Just dandy," Ethan replied.

Nate grinned and winked at Sage. He slapped Ethan on the back, then went to issue orders to the dozens of armed uniforms that had swarmed on the scene. Nate, who'd obviously called in reports that Lucky had been found, began coordinating a thorough search of the area.

"Are you going to tell them?" Sage asked, thinking of how the officers would be wasting their time.

"What am I going to say?"

Wrapped tight in Ethan's arms, Sage glanced up to see the sky filled with a million twinkling stars. The storm had disappeared as abruptly as it had come. The swirling wind, that had been as harsh as a mini-tornado, was now a gentle evening breeze. She could even hear regular night-life, the noisy screech of crickets, and she welcomed the sound with relief. Her bruises were the only reminder of the recent ordeal. There was a residual smell of smoke, but other than that, the night was once again normal.

It was as though everything that had just happened had been nothing but a vivid nightmare.

She looked across the clearing into the dark shadows of the woods. Although Lucky seemed to have disappeared, she knew *he'd* be watching. Enjoying the scene he'd created.

She also knew they wouldn't catch Lucky.

Not tonight.

Chapter Forty-Two

Ethan and Sage were parked high on a hill, a tourist spot overlooking Cryton. The Land Rover was warm and cozy. They'd been quiet for several long minutes as they stared out across the view, each lost in thought.

They'd spent hours at the station, giving statements. Ethan, after arranging for her to be checked thoroughly by the doctor, had left her in the care of Jane, a lovely senior constable with a wicked sense of humor, while he went back to the cabin with Nate. Sage had bruised ribs as well as numerous other cuts and abrasions to her body. They were all superficial however, and required no treatment other than standard first aid and some mild painkillers. She refused to be taken to hospital for any additional tests or monitoring. There was no need for further fuss.

Eventually, they'd all been free to leave, and for want of a better destination, Ethan and Sage had headed to the lookout for some much-needed alone time. Fingers entwined with hers, Ethan hadn't let her go, driving the whole way one-handed.

"Thanks for looking after my bag," Sage said. She'd been relieved to find the grimoire and diary safe inside and intact. "And of course, my pendant," Sage said, her fingers clasping the angel that had no doubt saved her life and Ethan's tonight.

"They were all I had of you," Ethan said, his voice rough.

The sun was rising in the east, as it did every day, streaking the sky in brilliant reds and oranges. A day like the billions that had come before it. She could almost imagine her life as it was a few weeks ago. Going to work, coming home to her apartment. Nothing more serious to worry about than where was the best place to go for drinks after work on a Friday afternoon.

Ethan walked around to her side, opened the door, and assisted her out. Kicking the door shut with his foot, he pulled her into his arms. "Am I hurting you?" he asked.

"No," she said. Her need for him overshadowed any discomfort from her bruising. Sage didn't need to ask about the injuries he'd sustained when the demon had flung him against the cabin wall. She'd felt them fade beneath the warmth of her fingers when she'd cradled him in her arms. After what she'd discovered about herself last night, about her gift, she understood that Ethan's healing, maybe his very life, had been assisted in some way by her. By something that flowed *through* her.

She thought of that little bird, barely alive, that she'd cupped in her hands, then watched fly away. It seemed incredible to think that she'd had a special gift all along, but because of teasing and bullying had deliberately kept herself unaware of it—or in denial—until it became imperative that she acknowledge its existence. Became willing, as Mary had suggested.

They clung to each other, both of them trembling with an excess of residual emotion. Eventually, Ethan loosened his hold and searched Sage's face. Looking deep into her eyes, he tucked a strand of hair behind her ear, his fingers trailing down the column of her neck. The caress sent a butterfly-shiver across her skin.

"Tonight scared the hell out of me," he said, his voice thick with emotion. "In all my years of working on the force, even during undercover operations when I'd infiltrated bikie gangs and thought I'd been made, nothing terrified me as much as seeing Collins holding that knife to your neck. And then," he cleared his throat, "seeing you in the sight of my gun. That image will haunt me the rest of my life. I was so close to pulling the trigger. Damn it, Sage, you have no idea how close I came. If I'd hurt you... it would have killed me too." His voice was hoarse, choked with emotion. "But then... Jesus, Sage, I can't even come to grips with what happened after that." His features turned to stone, and she felt each wave of anger as a rumbling vibration through her body.

"I wanted to kill him. I should have killed him," Ethan said. Sage swallowed, She could understand his anger. And in a way, she deserved to be a recipient of it too. She had helped a serial killer escape. The man who had killed her precious nan.

"I made many mistakes in this case," Ethan said, oblivious to her inner turmoil. "Mistakes I would never have made had it not been for my feelings for you. You, and what you mean to me, clouded everything. My lack of control could have even cost you your life. And that terrified me." Ethan had lowered his guard, allowing her a rare opportunity to glimpse inside him. To see the truth in his words.

She realized something then, and it hit her with a shocking force. He wanted her to understand that *she* was his vulnerability. Her chest squeezed, stealing her breath.

"Why'd you do it?" he asked, the hurt in his voice shredding her. The look in his eyes was a combination of tenderness, confusion, and... disappointment.

"I had him," Ethan continued. "I had an opportunity to end it tonight. Before it all got so badly out of control. Before he... before he did the impossible. Let me tell you, there's nothing more tormenting in the whole damn world than being forced to watch you confront whatever the fuck that was tonight, and not being able to do a goddamn thing about it. I was powerless. Held captive like a bird in a cage. I fought him with everything I had. All my training. All my experience. And I couldn't do a goddamned thing to help you." His voice broke and he took a minute. Cleared his voice and continued. "Goddammit, Sage, I just want you to tell me why. Why did you get in the way when I had the chance to end this?"

They'd given matching statements earlier on, omitting everything that came after Lucky's appearance, both stating that Lucky had simply backed into the shadows and Ethan hadn't been successful in going after him. She'd known what it had cost Ethan, signing the report. But he'd said it was better that way for now, better to modify the facts than deal with questions they couldn't answer.

"I'm sorry, Ethan. I hate that I needed to let him go. And I hated what happened after. What he did to you. And I admit to, at one point, having my own doubts over whether I'd done the right thing. But even if I'd let you kill him, it wouldn't have ended it." Sage touched his cheek. "If I'd let you arrest him, or even kill him, it only would have made the problem worse. Who knows where the demon would have gone then, who he would possess next? No one would be safe. And I don't have much time before the next full moon. The blood moon. It is imperative that I know who the master demon is. There is something I need to do, a ritual that involves Lucky—"

"No," Ethan said abruptly. "We'll find another way. You could have been killed tonight. On multiple occasions. Lucky is the serial killer, and he had you in his damned playroom. Who knows what would have happened had we not arrested him and delayed his return so that I was able to get there first. Let me, and my team, handle this. It's police business."

"Oh, and the police handled it so well a hundred years ago, didn't they?" Sage regretted the sharpness in her tone. What had happened back then wasn't Ethan's fault.

He narrowed his eyes. "How do you know about that?"

"I think you'll be surprised at just how much I do know about what's going on. How much I've discovered these last couple days."

"The government did what needed to be done," Ethan said. "Although I can't believe I'm defending them. They were wrong. Without doubt. But they acted in the only way they knew how at the time."

"And what if they think that's the only way again?" Sage asked. "I can't stand by and watch hundreds of innocent people murdered."

"You don't know me at all if you think I'd do nothing and allow that to happen." Hurt permeated his voice.

Sage sighed. "I'm sorry. I don't mean to imply that you would. I... I'm just overwhelmed about what is going on in this town. About how much worse it is still going to get. And the role I'm expected to play."

"What role? I sure as hell can't make any sense of what happened tonight. Explain it to me."

"I believe I have a chance to fix this, hopefully before anyone else gets killed." She swallowed. "I've a lot to learn, but I have more confidence, not less, that I can succeed after what happened tonight. I discovered something about what I'm up against. Knowledge is power. Whether I win or lose, I'm going to give it my best shot."

Storm clouds swirled in his dark eyes. Anger, frustration, and yes, even admiration and respect. "I don't know whether to be furious or scared witless about whatever you have planned. I have a mind to take you back to my hotel, and tie you to my bed until this is over."

"You wouldn't," Sage said, and in spite of her agitation over the heavy-handed way he was acting, couldn't stop her body's instinctive response to the image his words conjured.

"I would," he countered, his eyes narrowing. "Since I know I'd be wasting my breath trying to convince you otherwise, you might as well tell me what it is you think you're going to do."

"You really want to know?"

He closed his eyes briefly. "Yes."

"Well, I still have a bit of research on the exact steps I need to perform, but whatever they are, I know I need Lucky alive to do it." Ethan's whole body tensed, but he remained silent. Before she lost her nerve, she pulled out the grimoire and placed it in his hand.

The instant the old leather hit his skin, his whole demeanor changed. For long moments, he did nothing but hold it.

"That symbol," he said eventually, and with more than a little awe. "It's the one on the back of your pendant. The one on my father's talisman." He looked thoughtful a moment. "I wonder if they're connected. I'm going to arrange for it to be brought here, and I'll ask Ian, my boss, if he's seen the symbol before. My great-grandfather and his grandfather worked this case together a hundred years ago. It's a hell of a coincidence—and I don't believe in coincidences—that that symbol just so happens to be on Dad's talisman, this book, and on the woman I love."

He stopped abruptly, and she blinked up at him.

"Well, don't look so bloody surprised," he said gruffly.

Sage smiled and pulled back just far enough to look deep into his eyes. "I love you too, Ethan Blade." She let him see the truth in her words, know their depth, then touched her lips to his. He cupped his hand behind her neck and deepened the kiss. The sun caressed her cheek, warming her from outside while an outpouring of emotion heated her from the inside.

He made a low gravelly sound from the back of his throat, and broke off crushing her hard against his chest. The moment lingered and she felt the heat from his body, the pounding of his heart... and the grimoire digging into her ribs. She winced and pulled back.

"Sorry," he said, his attention moving once again to the book in his hands.

He opened the cover and began sifting through the pages, stopping on one just over halfway through. "The green dragon and white tiger firmly in place, summon the elements earth, metal, and water, and speak the following verse—"

"Ethan!" Sage interrupted. "You can read it."

Ethan's brow wrinkled. "Of course. It's in Latin."

"I didn't know you could read Latin."

Ethan shrugged. "Why would you?"

"I swear sometimes I think it was more than just luck that I met you. Do you believe in destiny?"

"I'm starting to." He closed the book.

"Ethan, I need to know what that book says," Sage said, trying to take it out of his hands.

"Looks like a whole lot of spells and witchcraft if you ask me."

"That's exactly what it is," Sage said, pleased despite his frown. "It's the grimoire. The specific set of rituals I need to perform to banish the demon. Can you read it to me?"

"Not now. I've reached my limit of supernatural for today."

"But you'll help me?" Sage pressed.

"Of course. You don't think I'd let you just take off and deal with this on your own, do you?"

"So you believe me, then?"

"Yes," he said simply.

Her body sagged. She'd had her persuasive argument ready, prepared like a lawyer about to embark on a high-profile case.

"It's a bit hard to deny once you've seen it with your own damn eyes," he grumbled.

"Which is what I've been saying the whole time."

"I'm sorry," he said, catching her gaze and holding it. "And I really mean that. I know it took a while, but I believe you. I saw the same thing you did tonight. I wasn't knocked out so much as paralyzed. Held by an invisible energy. I saw what he did. I saw what *you* did," he said. "You hurt him. And you scared him. And on an instinctive level I know that. I *felt* his fear. Of you. He said you are 'the one.' And after what I saw tonight, I know that's true. As much as I'd like to whisk you away, wrap you up in cotton wool, I also know that you are the key to solving this."

Ethan took a deep breath and continued. "So this is what we'll do. We'll go through the book, the grimoire, together. We'll make a plan that we both can agree on. One that keeps you as safe as I can possibly make you. I have the money, I have the resources, and I have the manpower. I'll help you do whatever it takes for this to be over."

"You will?" Sage asked. "Even if it means helping a felon escape?" What if Lucky was arrested again?

A muscle twitched in Ethan's jaw. "Let's cross that bridge if we come to it."

"You know I'm quite possibly a witch, right?" Sage said. Happiness was a golden glow in her belly. She and Ethan were finally on the same page. Not only did Ethan believe her, he was going to help her. The demon had no chance. She hoped.

The corners of his lips twitched. "Seems you might very well be. You certainly have me bewitched." She mock-punched him in the arm. "Ouch!" Ethan said, rubbing his arm in pretend pain. "That's it. Assaulting an officer. Twice in less than twenty-four hours. You'll have to be punished."

"I think I'll enjoy that, if you're the one doing the punishing." Sage grinned. Ethan moved closer as though about to ravage her mouth, a wickedly sexy gleam in his eye. She placed a finger across his lips.

"Wait. Something else while I'm thinking of it. How did you find me?"

Ethan sighed and looked at her lips with regret and longing. "Pia. She's one pretty remarkable woman. Aside from her apparent lapse of judgement over her friendship with Collins, she is rather impressive. She somehow *knows* stuff she shouldn't know. And considering everything else I've seen these last twenty-four hours, I find that idea far less strange than I did yesterday. Pia saved your life, Sage. Somehow she could see where you were and gave us directions on how to get there."

"Nan could see things too."

"It might be a good idea if we have a chat with Pia about all of this in the next day or two. I'd say she'll be a great source of information we could draw on. For instance, she knew where you were. She could be the one to tell us where Lucky is when you need him."

"You're right. I hadn't thought of that."

"I still think you should have pressed charges against Mark." Ethan all but growled the words.

"It wouldn't have been right. That wasn't Mark. Not the *real* Mark," Sage added when Ethan looked about to protest. "Pia explained it to me. Because Lucky had been arrested and was no longer of use to the demon, he was forced to use another. Mark had been fighting stage-one possession."

"And the demon conveniently chose Mark. Why?"

"Don't be like that," Sage said. "At heart, Mark really is a nice guy." Sage deliberately pictured how he'd been before last night. The way he'd held her hand during the paranormal investigation, the way he'd looked after her. Looked after all of them.

Ethan gave a disbelieving grunt, his jaw working back and forth like he wanted to say something but held back. It was going to be a hard sell to get Ethan to agree with her when it came to Mark. And after the events of last night, she could hardly blame him.

"Pia believes it's her fault she didn't do more to protect Mark. She said there were several contributing factors that led to Mark's attempted possession, including timing and environment. Mark was in the house—a place we know the demon can easily enter—and he was openly seeking out the entity. During the investigation I accompanied PRI on, I heard Mark invite the entity to use and draw on his energy. Mark was openly encouraging it and subsequently became the demon's most convenient target. It's powerful, and it knows how to use human weakness to his advantage. The demon entered Mark's body and affected his mind. Pia said mind games are a demon's tool, making the host easy to manipulate."

"Then surely it would be safer for everyone if Mark was behind bars," Ethan said. "If Mark has been possessed once, what's there to stop it from happening again?"

Ethan voiced the very same concern that lurked in the back of her own mind. It was still going to be a while before she'd be able to look at Mark and not see him in the cabin, all crazed eyes and murderous intentions. She didn't yet share Pia's confidence that it wouldn't happen again. Not for a long time. Maybe not ever.

Even so, it *had* broken her heart to see Mark so shattered when he'd come to earlier. Pia had taken him through what had happened, and he'd been physically sick over it. The last time Sage had seen Mark, he'd been a shell of the bright, charming man she'd met just days ago.

"Ethan, I was there. I was with him during the possession. I didn't understand at the time, but now that I look back, I know he fought it every step of the way." Again and again, Mark had bounced back and forth between his personality and the demon's. He'd also been worried when he'd realized that Pia was alone back at the shop. "Pia is going to make him some type of protection—"

She opened her mouth to say more, but Ethan stopped her.

"Sage. I'm tired, and I don't want to argue with you. We'll deal with Collins later. I've been flung around by a demon, and I haven't slept properly in days." He touched her cheek and gave her a knowing grin. "Talking is no longer what I intend to do with you."

She knew how he felt. In the light of the new day, everything that had happened last night felt like another lifetime, and it was impossible to concentrate on anything else while he was looking at her with such dark sensual intensity.

The world, their troubles with it, blurred then receded into the background until there was only the two of them, perched high on the hill overlooking the town.

"What do you want to do with me?" Her words were a breathless whisper. At the wicked gleam in his eye, her heart flipped.

He crushed his mouth to hers. Hard. Possessive.

Her body ignited, the energy between them becoming a charged electrical current. Wrapping her arms around his neck, she pressed herself into him, deepened the connection. She clung to him, hard, as though she could never be close enough. Her nails clawed through his shirt, digging into the soft skin on the back of his neck. He groaned into her mouth, and heat pooled between her thighs.

His arms completely enveloped her, her breasts pressing into the warmth of his chest. His low groan was a tangible vibration that rolled through her, stimulating her from the inside out. He licked deep inside her mouth, as she swallowed the outdoorsy masculine scent that was uniquely his.

Sage kissed him furiously. As passionately as if it were their last time. She needed him more than she needed her next breath. She poured everything she felt into their kiss. Let him feel every bit of love, fear, hope, and uncertainty.

His hands dropped to her waist, and he crushed her against him, his erection a hard ridge against the softness of her belly. Her body tingled with the charged crackle of unfulfilled desire, every cell craving the satisfaction only he could provide.

He lifted her top, caressed the naked curve of her back. His touch drove her wild, her need for him fierce. He ravaged her mouth with an intensity that promised he would not be gentle. She didn't want him to be.

Eventually, he broke the kiss and rested his forehead against hers, his breathing harsh and ragged. "I want you so badly," he said, his voice barely a rasp. The heat from his breath warmed her bruised lips. "If I don't stop now, I'll take you right here and now on the hard ground. Fortunately, I still have sense enough to realize the lookout probably gets busy during the day, and I don't want to rush. I want you. Every inch of you. Slowly. I won't stop until I get my fill." His dark eyes glittered in the gentle sunlight.

He gripped her hand tightly as he led her to his car, as if he'd never let her go. There were still so many questions that remained unanswered, still so many things to say. But that wasn't what they both needed.

Today was for them.

Tomorrow, she would worry about the demon and everything that needed to be done before the blood moon.

THE END

CHAPTER ONE

MONDAY
SIX DAYS BEFORE THE BLOOD MOON

CRYTON, SOUTH AUSTRALIA

"Stop!" Sage Matthews demanded, bounding down the narrow staircase at the back of Beyond the Grave, her late grandmother's shop. "What the hell do you think you're doing?"

Sage confronted two burly men hefting her grandmother's boxes into their arms. The front door had been propped open with a beer carton, and Sage could see through the shop-front windows that a large moving van was parked outside, ramp extended from an open rear door.

"You Sage Matthews?" Burly Guy One set down his box, wiped his palms down the front of his pants, and faced her. His heavily lined face said he was around fifty. Somehow, the toothpick stuck in the corner of his mouth managed to stay in place when he spoke.

"I am," Sage replied. "And you have to stop what you're doing right now." She pushed past Burly Guy One to stand directly in front of Burly Guy Two, who was still attempting to remove the box he was carrying. The carton that Sage had just unsealed this morning was full of Nan's diaries. Diaries Sage desperately needed.

Sage's grandmother, Celeste Matthews, had been killed in a brutally ritualistic manner, and Sage had been looking for a specific journal that Nan had been keeping before her murder. The notebook, Sage believed, contained detailed notes about her grandmother's discovery of an ancient prophecy, a prophecy that directly involved Sage.

"We were told everything would be packed up." Burly Guy One said from behind her, annoyance peppering his tone. "If we have to wait around for you to finish packing, it will be extra. *Bloody women*," he added beneath his breath.

As though oblivious to the conversation around him, or perhaps deliberately ignoring it, Burly Guy Two stepped around Sage and carried the box that contained the only written account of her grandmother's final days toward the door.

Furious, Sage placed herself between him and the door. "I told you to stop."

Burly Guy Two, with his flannel shirt stretched tight over his beer belly, was a country man, a man's man. He frowned, peering down at her from over the top of the box, clearly not pleased with what he no doubt considered an irrational woman who had not done the job she should have.

"Don't have time to stop," Burly Guy One said, stepping toward her. "Got exactly one hour to finish up here, so we can be at our next job on time. Because of what happened with Roger here last week," Burly Guy One said, indicating his partner, "we're both bloody well on probation. If I lose my job, my wife will shoot me. So out of the way, lady."

Ugh! "I cancelled the job." Sage ignored the uncomfortable twist in her stomach at the lie. "Look, uh, what's your name?"

"Bob."

"Look, Bob," Sage said in her best I'm-being-reasonable tone, "I'll phone through to your office and clear everything up right now. Just put the boxes down."

It was enough to make Bob hesitate. Roger, not so much. He shuffled his feet and glared at her.

With everything that had happened since Sage's return to her hometown for her grandmother's funeral, cancelling the movers she'd booked when she'd arrived had been the last thing on her mind.

Originally, Sage had intended to stay in town just long enough to attend the funeral and make sure Nan's belongings were safely in storage. Then she'd discovered Nan's murder had been part of a satanic ritual. Celeste's life, and quite literally her eyes, had been taken by Luke "Lucky" Keyton, a local lad who had turned serial killer when he'd become possessed by a malevolent spirit entity. A demon.

And as if that weren't disturbing enough, when Sage had delved into the final days of Nan's life, retracing her last steps, Sage had discovered a shocking truth about herself, and who she really was.

Sage Matthews was the seer's daughter, a white witch destined to fight a master demon and keep the forces of Hell from reaching the earthly realm.

Go figure!

According to an ancient prophecy, the fight was destined to happen in six days:

"Every hundred years, at midnight on the night of the blood moon, the veil between this world and a far darker one will be at its thinnest, unsealing a doorway that should never be opened, allowing the unspeakable to come through and unleash hell on earth."

This Sunday night, Sage would be coming face to face with the demon.

The idea should have terrified her—and it did—but when Sage had learned that the demon had been responsible for the deaths of her beloved grandmother and her mother years before that, her fear had quickly transmuted into anger.

Sage was livid.

And more determined than ever to learn everything about the prophecy and her role in it.

The answers lay in the pages of an ancient grimoire, a book of spells and rituals that Nan's best friend, Ada Slatterley, had given her very life trying to protect.

Sage was running out of time to prepare for Sunday night's battle with the demon, and a couple chauvinistic moving men were not going to stop her. She pulled her phone from her jeans pocket and dialed the number for the moving company.

At least the phone reception isn't an issue today. Lately, it had been becoming more and more unreliable, no doubt due to the strange disturbance in the electromagnetic field across the town. Unusual static electricity saturated the air and clung like a nefarious smog in the sky above Cryton, interfering with electrical devices and radio reception.

Along with the change in atmospheric conditions, Cryton itself seem infused with an unsettling energy, a sense of impending doom. The air tasted like anger, but the change was in fact something far more menacing.

It was pure unadulterated evil.

Demonic.

But this was just the beginning. According to the prophecy, the changes in town were about to become much worse as the countdown to Sunday's blood moon continued.

Sage prayed she'd be ready in time.

But there was still so much to do. She tapped her nails on the phone. *Come on!*

The line was a bit crackly, but the phone was finally ringing. It looked like her call would go through.

Roger bared his teeth in a silent snarl, stepped around Sage again, and continued to walk toward the door, oddly determined to remove the box of Nan's diaries. Out of nowhere, the hairs rose up on the back of Sage's neck and a thought planted itself in her mind: *Stay away from him.*

Except she couldn't let him walk out the door with those diaries. With the phone between her shoulder and ear, Sage ducked in front of Roger, placed her body in the door frame, and spread her arms, palms flat on either side of the opening.

The static finally cleared from the line and the call connected to the moving company. "Good morning," Sage began. "My name is—"

An odd sound, low and menacing, like something a wounded animal might make, rose up from Roger's chest. He raised his Blundstone boot and kicked Sage's thigh, knocking her leg clean out from under her. While she struggled for balance, Roger transferred the box to one hand, and with the other, pushed her out the door and into a large potted plant, which crashed down on top of her.

Momentarily stunned, and covered in soil, Sage opened her mouth to abuse him when she saw a six-foot-three pissed-off male charging at Roger.

Ethan.

Detective Sergeant Ethan Blade, Homicide Squad, South Australian Police Force, her lover and so much more, had left her sifting through boxes of Nan's things searching for the journal barely ten minutes ago, to walk down the main street to the bakery for much-needed takeaway coffee.

Ethan tossed the coffee onto the sidewalk and lunged at Roger. Before Sage had time to do more than blink, Ethan had Roger face down on the ground, his hands cuffed behind his back. The box of Nan's diaries had spilled, emptying across the concrete.

Anger surged through Sage's veins at how carelessly Nan's precious diaries had been treated, but then Sage caught sight of Ethan, and momentarily lost her train of thought. Ethan was something else when he was like this, all furious alpha male in full protective mode. His almost black hair was mussed and collar length, more through not having time for a cut, than by design or fashion. Either way, it worked. From his stormy dark eyes, all the way down his finely honed body, Ethan was the sexiest man she'd ever laid eyes on.

And he's all mine.

A concept that still blew her mind.

Ethan cast a speaking glance at Bob, who held up both hands in a *Do I look stupid? I'm not going to fuck with you* manner.

Seemingly assured that that was indeed the case, Ethan was at her side in a heartbeat, picking up bits of broken terracotta pot. The power, the sheer energy, that radiated off him was nothing short of intoxicating. Sage took a breath and inhaled a mixture of heated virile male in the prime of his life and the worn leather of the jacket Ethan wore to hide his gun. A heady and delicious combination.

"Angel, look at me."

Her pulse fluttered at the way his pet name for her rolled languidly off his tongue. He'd coined the endearment based on the angel she wore constantly around her neck, an amulet of protection given to her by her mother before her death when Sage was just three years old.

"I'm okay." Sage picked herself up and started shaking soil off her clothes.

"You fell quite hard." Ethan had been a bit... overprotective of her since last Wednesday night. But she supposed he had just cause. Having your girlfriend get abducted by a serial killer and then coming face to face with a malevolent spirit hell-bent on killing you was bound to bring out a man's more... dominant qualities.

Sage's thigh throbbed from the kick with the steel-capped boot, her shirt had been ripped in a couple of places, and she was covered in dirt, but aside from some scrapes and bruises, she'd be fine. Just as well; she didn't have time to be out of action. "Really, I'm okay."

Ethan's intense gaze raked over her body one final time, as though he were cataloguing her scratches in order to calculate just how severe his retribution would be.

"Care to tell me what the fuck is going on?" Ethan demanded, moving toward Bob and flashing his badge.

"Easy mate, uh, Detective Sergeant, sir," Bob said. "We're just doing our job."

"Angel?" Ethan turned to her. "Were they just doing their job?"

"Perhaps a little too well." Sage briefly explained the encounter to Ethan.

"So why the fuck didn't you leave when Sage asked you to?" Ethan demanded of Bob. "Seems to me it would have saved you a whole lot of trouble. And pain."

Bob raised his hands in surrender, then clapped them to his head and winced, as though in severe pain.

"No one lays a hand on Sage," Ethan said, glaring at first Bob, then at Roger, lying still on the ground. "But me."

Ethan clenched and unclenched his fists a few times before pulling out his radio and barking through a couple of codes. A 212 and a 415, and then he gave the address of the shop. Bob edged his way toward the door.

"Why didn't you leave?" Ethan asked again, his voice low, yet forceful. Bob had justified himself to Sage earlier by saying he was on probation and scared of losing his job, but now he appeared strangely dazed. And very eager to leave.

"The question is not that hard," Ethan said, clipping his radio back onto his belt. Bob froze, flinching. "Why the fuck didn't you leave when Sage asked you to?"

"I—" Bob's shoulders sagged and he released a breath. "Something... I don't know what came over me." Bob glanced at Roger, lying on his stomach with his hands cuffed behind his back. He hadn't moved since being cuffed. "And I've never seen Roger lose his temper. And especially not at a pretty sheila, no matter how frustrating she might be. I... I can't explain it."

A patrol car skidded to a stop in front of the shop. As the moving men were loaded into the squad car, Sage heard pieces of the conversation between the local police officers. *Another assault... six more arrests last night... people acting strangely... unprovoked violence... something not right in this town...*

Yes, Sage agreed. There was definitely something not right in this town. And it had been that way for quite a while.

Leaving Ethan to do his police thing, Sage packed Nan's spilled diaries back into the box, carefully straightening the pages that had been bent. She then crossed the pavement and picked up the empty takeaway cups, looking at their spilled contents with regret. The scent of coffee would have to be enough to recharge her.

As Sage reached the porch of the shop, she paused at the empty wooden chair where her cat, Liquorice, usually slept on top of a crocheted blanket her nan had made. With a stab of pain, Sage wondered for the umpteenth time since last Wednesday where her little friend was. More than a pet, Liquorice was her companion, and they had a certain... connection that had rekindled and deepened since her return to Cryton.

Where are you, little buddy? Sage called out with her mind, hoping he could hear her, as she'd recently discovered he often could.

Sage hadn't seen him since she'd been abducted by Lucky. She pictured Liquorice, with his silky charcoal black fur and the white tip on his tail, and felt a sharp tug in her stomach. She hoped that wherever he was, he was safe. And would come back soon.

Sage walked back inside the shop, threw the empty cups in the bin, and stilled. The temperature seemed to have dropped several degrees in a single second, and she caught a sudden movement out of the corner of her eye. She whipped her head around. Nothing. As usual. The tiny hairs on the back of her neck were standing on end, and her pulse was racing.

She couldn't see anything, but every fiber in her being told her that she was being watched. By *him*.

He was here. Unseen, but the sudden, unexplained rush of anxiety confirmed his presence. She'd learned to recognize what the demonic entity felt like. It was a heavy coat of darkness, of anger and hatred, that sent a chill running down her spine. A foul odor filled the air, making her gag. Planting her feet, she clasped the angel pendant around her neck and imagined it casting a protective cocoon around her.

She took a deep breath, then jumped when Ethan called out to her from the door. "You pressing charges, Angel?"

She let the amulet slide through her fingers and fall against her skin. "Uh, no."

How could she? She understood better than anyone that Roger wasn't himself just now. It was this town, this house. The dark energy that had moved into Cryton had seeped into the air. You inhaled it into your body, dragged it into your lungs, and it changed you into something you weren't.

Roger was no more responsible for what had happened just now than her friend Mark Collins had been on Wednesday night when he'd attacked Sage. Mark was a paranormal investigator and star of the TV series *Debunking Reality*. He'd been investigating the strange goings-on in the house and had helped her discover that a demon was stalking her.

She'd been shocked when her friend succumbed to the demon's influence and turned on her. But friendship was no match for a malevolent demonic entity who had the power to possess human bodies, if the conditions were right.

Suddenly the unsettling feeling in the room was gone. The temperature returned to normal, and she could *breathe* again. She rolled her shoulders.

Then she sensed something else. Sage whirled around, sure someone was in the room with her. Had come up from behind and was now standing right next to her. She wasn't scared, not like she was when *he* was around. But the feeling was so strong, it was unnerving. She looked around, but no one was with her.

Then she saw it. A notebook on the otherwise empty bottom shelf.

It hadn't been there before. She'd cleared all the shelves during her packing. Perhaps it had landed there when the box had fallen. And yet... it appeared to have been neatly placed on the shelf. Sage crossed the room and picked up the notebook. Opening the cover, she flicked through the pages. *This is it!*

Sage finally had Nan's journal.

She just hoped it contained the answers she needed. She had six days to prepare for the demon's attempt to breach the portal, and she was going to need every scrap of help she could find. If she failed, the world as she knew it would be no more.

ABOUT THE AUTHOR

Athena Daniels is the #1 International bestselling author of the award-winning Beyond the Grave paranormal romance series and romantic thrillers *The Scream Behind Her Smile* and *Desperate*. In 2016, Athena was nominated for Author of the Year and Best New Author in *AusRom Today*'s Reader's Choice Awards. Her latest novel, *The Scream Behind Her Smile*, won the Silver Medal in the 2019 Readers Favorite® International Book Awards.

Girl Unseen won the Silver Medal in the 2017 Readers' Favorite® International Book Awards and was awarded a Silver Medal in the 2017 Literary Titan Book Awards, and finalist in the TopShelf Book Awards 2018. *Girl Unseen* is a semi-finalist in The Kindle Book Review Awards, "Official Selection" in the New Apple Annual book Awards and nominated for 2017 Book of the Year in *AusRom Today*'s Reader's Choice Awards.

When Darkness Follows won the Bronze Medal in the 2018 Readers' Favorite® International Book Awards, Silver Medal in the 2018 Literary Titan Book Awards, and was nominated for the TopShelf Book Awards 2019 and nominated in the Australian Romance Readers Association (ARRA) 2018 awards for Favourite Paranormal Romance.

The Seer's Daughter was the solo Medalist Winner in the Suspense/Thriller category of the 2016 New Apple Annual Book Awards for Excellence in Independent Publishing.

The Seer's Daughter was also a finalist in the 11th Annual National Indie Excellence Awards in Suspense and in the 2016 Readers' Favorite® International Book Awards. Additionally, *The Seer's Daughter* was nominated for 2016 Book of the Year and 2016 Cover of the Year in *AusRom Today*'s Reader's Choice Awards.

Girl Unseen and *The Seer's Daughter* are both 5-star Top Picks at The Romance Reviews.

Athena holds several qualifications in metaphysics and natural therapies. She is a neuro-linguistic programming (NLP) practitioner, life coach, and feng shui specialist.

Athena lives on the northern beaches of sunny Western Australia. Follow her on Twitter @AthenaDaniels11 and on Facebook at /AthenaDaniels11.

athenadaniels.com